DAUGHTERS OF THE OCCUPATION

DAUGHTERS
OF THE
OCCUPATION

A Novel of WWII

SHELLY SANDERS

HARPER

NEW YORK · LONDON · TORONTO · SYDNEY

HARPER

Also published in Canada in 2022 by Patrick Crean Editions, an imprint of HarperCollins Publishers Ltd.

Map in PS Section reproduced courtesy of the U.S. Holocaust Memorial Museum.

FIRST U.S. EDITION

Library of Congress Cataloging-in-Publication Data has been applied for.

ISBN 978-0-06-322666-1 (pbk.)
ISBN 978-0-06-324789-5 (library edition)

22 23 24 25 26   LSC   10 9 8 7 6 5 4 3 2 1

To the Jews of Latvia murdered in the Holocaust

One is not truly dead until one's name is forgotten.
—Talmud

DAUGHTERS OF THE OCCUPATION

RIGA, JUNE 1940

THE DAY THE SOVIETS INVADED LATVIA, MIRIAM'S WATER broke. She'd just wedged her swollen feet into ivory sling-backs to meet Helena at the Riga's Opera Café for lunch when her abdomen strained and water gushed onto the vestibule floor. Miriam's hands went cold. What if this baby came as quickly as her first? Blood would never come out of her good rug, or her divan, for that matter.

Miriam lunged for the telephone, on a tall oak table, dialed Max's dental office and spoke brusquely to her husband: "You need to come at once or I won't make it to the hospital."

MAX TURNED HIS car right when he came to the forest at the end of their street, onto Meza Prospekts. He clumsily shifted his black Ford-Vairogs into fourth gear, jolting Miriam in her seat. The baby kicked her bladder, as if he or she were angry about the bumpy ride.

"If you're not more careful, I'm going to have this baby in the car."

Max's fretful eyes jumped from Miriam's face to her spherical midsection, underneath her linen trapeze blouse. "You can't," he said, his broad chest rising and falling with frantic breaths. "Just keep breathing slowly." He hunched his shoulders and gripped the steering wheel with knuckles as white as his jacket. He'd rushed from his dental office and smelled of the germ-killing soap he used on his hands so often; his skin was as dry as stone. "Try to think of something else to keep your mind off, you know, the hospital."

Miriam balled her fists. "Something else? Like what, dancing?"

He gave his wife a sheepish smile. "Sorry. Bad suggestion."

They passed the Vanšu Bridge, halfway between their Mežaparks home and the Jewish hospital, Bikur Holim, on the other side of Riga. Miriam looked out her window and saw a man riding a bicycle along the edge of the Daugava River, stretched out like a shimmering piece of turquoise silk. She loved the river. Just one week ago, Max, Ilana and Miriam had picnicked at a sandy point north of the bridge, with a feast of cheese on black bread, pickled beets, iced tea and chocolate pastries. Ilana played in the water with Max while Miriam baked like a potato on the sand. The bottom of the lake was too rocky. She might have slipped and fallen. She couldn't wait to give birth and have her body back to herself.

Max tugged his whiskers. "Just a few more hours and then we'll have a new baby and life will go back to normal."

Miriam gaped at her well-meaning, oblivious husband, who'd slept through Ilana's cries as a baby nine years earlier. His life would chug forward while Miriam's would stall, and though it was entirely unreasonable, she resented him for being able to have children and go on without missing a step. She thought about her friend Helena, who never complained about the sacrifices she made, as the mother of three children, and worried there was something wrong with her for not looking forward to a second baby.

Max veered left, away from the river. Miriam caught a glimpse of the Central Market hangars. About time. They were finally near the hospital. She dug her heels into the floor to steady herself for the next contraction, already whirling like a blizzard in her abdomen.

Max hit the brakes. Miriam's shoulders jerked forward. Her heart sprang to her throat when she saw an olive-green tank blocking the road about fifteen meters ahead of them. A red Soviet flag hung from the gun protruding from the tank and there were clumps of men in Soviet uniforms, instantly recognizable with their blood-red collars. Joseph Stalin's Red Army. Joseph Stalin, who deported people to Siberia if they spoke out against Communism or if they were wealthy. The dictator who had built and presided over a culture of mistrust and terror, one in which even children betrayed their parents. Ten months ago, Stalin had signed a non-aggression pact with Hitler, shocking for its blatant *mishegoss*, craziness. Why would two countries, known for their flagrant mutual hostility, suddenly agree to be friendly?

A contraction hit. Miriam folded and moaned as the pain shot through her tailbone. It waned as quickly as it had begun. She went limp in her seat. Could hardly catch her breath.

"Max." Miriam clutched his arm.

His muscles tensed beneath her grip. He peered over his shoulder, shifted the car into reverse and backed up until they came to Marijas Street. He turned sharply and nosed the car down the narrow road that led to Station Square, in the center of Riga. She heard the frenzied voices first, before she saw hundreds of people congregated in the main square, surrounding four huge Soviet tanks.

Shivers ran down Miriam's sternum at the sight of a man pounding the side of a tank with his fists.

"*Dievs Padomju*, goddamn Soviets!" a long-legged man bellowed at another tank, on Miriam's right, about six meters away.

Miriam raised her eyes to a unit of armed Red Army soldiers on top of the tank. They wore identical shiny helmets that gave off a menacing air. They seemed oblivious to the jeering below.

"*Sasodits*, dammit," another man yelled, before kicking the wheels of the same tank, almost as tall as he was.

She jumped in her seat when two Soviet tanks roared to life, their booming engines swallowing up the crowd's feverish voices as they advanced with a menacing rumble. Beads of sweat drizzled down her forehead as she saw children madly pedaling bicycles out of the square. A peddler, caught unawares, staggered to get his pushcart out of the way of a tank rolling toward him. A vendor's white-and-pink roses were splayed on the ground. Young boys in school uniforms darted across the square, glancing over their shoulders as if they were being chased.

Then a tram appeared, a jumble of arms and legs, with passengers clinging to every inch of its exterior, even the front, blocking the driver's view. The tram parted a cluster of people on the street as it rolled along curved tracks, directly toward an oncoming tank. Terror rose in Miriam's throat as the tank swerved left, headfirst into a knot of pedestrians, crushing them as if they were just stones on the road. Screams ricocheted through the air. Blood splattered across the pavement. The tank continued without stopping, leaving a trail of bloody, flattened bodies.

"My God." Max's face went gray.

Miriam's eyes burned from the ruthless glare of murder, an atrocity she wished she could unsee.

Max began to back out of the square, but only made it three meters before the crowd blocked the car. Guttural voices burst through Miriam's open window. Russian voices. She hugged her belly. She watched, puzzled, as a column of odd-looking Latvian men walked behind a moving tank with military-like precision.

Their out-of-place hip boots caught Miriam's eye. Hip boots were usually worn for fishing or heavy rain—not in a city during sunny, hot weather like today. And there was an unnerving camaraderie among the men as they raised their fists together and shouted, "Long live Stalin."

Max leaned over Miriam to see. "Those men are as Latvian as I am French," he scoffed. "Russians pretending to be Latvians to rouse support. Soviet infiltration and propaganda."

Miriam squinted and clenched her gut. Max was right—they were surrounded by Russians posing as Latvians. Handfuls of real Latvians looked on, baffled and frightened, but the majority were Soviets, dressed as civilians, hailing the murderous tanks as if they were heroes. Miriam clasped her abdomen as another contraction tore through her insides.

A loud cheer rang out as a Soviet soldier hoisted a fair-haired boy into the air like a prize. The soldier wore a peaked cap over his shaved head, and his chin jutted out almost as far as his nose. He grinned at the boy, who looked back at him warily. All of a sudden Miriam's heart swelled with love and dread for her unborn baby.

Suddenly, a mounted Latvian policeman placed himself in front of the crowd, one hand holding the reins of his horse, the other gesturing for people to calm down.

Max jumped out of the car.

"Where are you going?" Miriam's agitated voice melted in the crowd.

Max approached another Latvian policeman, standing about a meter from the car, and pointed at Miriam. Just then, the mounted policeman's horse cried out in pain, a deep bellow that rattled Miriam's bones. Soviet soldiers were striking the horse and officer with canes and stones. The horse reared back onto its hind legs. The Latvian officer gripped the saddle but fell sideways.

A shot ruptured the air and the fallen officer clutched his neck, blood gushing through his fingers.

A gasp ran through the mob, followed by indecipherable shouts. Men and women scattered in all directions. The sulfurous tang of gunpowder swamped the air. Miriam longed to be invisible. She wanted to look out the window for a way out, but was afraid of being noticed. Of being killed. Of her baby dying. A suffocating pressure crushed her insides and took her breath away.

Max hopped back in the car. The Latvian officer he had spoken to was clearing a path for them. In a strained voice, Max said the Soviets had captured the Latvian border. The Soviets controlled Latvia. Miriam couldn't speak. She didn't want to believe Max, but knew every word was true when another shot blasted in the square and people sprinted in all directions like the sun's rays. Miriam rolled up her window and crossed her legs as a contraction hit like a punch in the gut.

The baby shifted roughly within her womb, squashing her bladder. Miriam panted. Looked down. She felt as if her insides were about to drop, along with the baby. She heard the engine roar to a higher speed, for all of five seconds—until there was a ferocious clang of metal striking metal. Miriam was thrown forward. Her head smacked the dashboard.

Everything went dark.

2

CHICAGO, NOVEMBER 1975

CHICAGO WAS HIT BY THE EARLIEST SNOWFALL IN YEARS that Wednesday in November, the day twenty-four-year-old Sarah Byrne attended her mother's funeral. Snow glazed the front-yard birch and maple trees in a sugary white, a striking contrast to the ochre and burgundy leaves, clinging to almost bare branches like old dresses on hangers you can't give up though they no longer fit. Sarah sat rigid in the passenger seat of her father's car as he drove slowly to the funeral home, his wide forehead deeply creased with concentration. The windshield wipers swished the falling snow out of the way, but it kept coming down, smearing when it hit the window, like tears.

Sarah's heart lodged in her throat when she pictured her mother, Ilana, collapsing in the grocery store, surrounded by strangers. She dried her eyes with a tissue and held her chin up, determined to look strong on the outside, the way her mother would want her to be. *Keep your feelings to yourself*, she used to tell Sarah, when she was upset about a grade or a lost volleyball game or a boy who liked her one day and didn't the next. *Crying makes you look weak.*

At the corner where the creek narrowed and ran below a bridge, her father turned right and drove his Chevy into a parking lot, up to a space in front of the main door. Sarah stared at Green Meadows Funeral Home, which resembled a sprawling redbrick house, and thought, This is the last time I will see my mother.

Her father shut off the ignition. He heaved a long, heavy sigh and said: "I can't get my head around the fact she's gone. I keep expecting her to come waltzing into the house and tell me to put my boots in the closet, where they belong."

"We didn't even get to say goodbye." Sarah's throat closed with grief.

"It's how she would have wanted it, don't you think?"

Her father was right. Her mother avoided goodbyes, as if she were allergic to departures. She never came when Sarah's father had driven Sarah to the University of Chicago at the beginning of every semester, even when Sarah deliberately asked her to come. It was one of the many quirks Sarah had noticed about her mother over the years, including her unwavering demand for privacy, shutting the drapes on glorious sunny days, making the house feel like a crypt, and barring Sarah from the usual childhood pastimes such as sleepovers and trips to the mall without parents. By her senior year of high school, with her mother's oppressive rules dividing them like a fence, Sarah had been counting the days until she left for college.

As soon as Sarah was out of the house, their relationship improved, though she continued to wonder about her mother's habits and excessive anxiety. There was so much Sarah didn't know about her mother, with conversations skirting emotions and the past as if her life had only begun with Sarah's birth. Now she'd lost the possibility of discovering whatever her mother had been so determined to hide. She'd lost the chance to establish a deeper relationship.

Sarah's father opened his door, letting in a sliver of icy air, and looked at Sarah with swollen, bloodshot eyes. His grief was sobering. For the first time in her life, her father needed her the way she'd come to rely on him. It was just the two of them. Unless she lost her mind and decided to date again, after breaking up with Henry. About as likely as Jimmy Carter becoming president.

"Ready?" her father asked.

Sarah saw the droop in his shoulders, the chin hairs he'd missed shaving and the tremor in his pale, fleshy hands. She'd have to keep an eye on him, prone to lapsing into a trance since her mother's death, his ruddy face going blank and still. "Let's go," she said with forced brightness. She opened her door, walked around the car to her father, linked her arm in his and together they entered the funeral home, their heads dusted with snow.

WOODEN CHAIRS WITH beige seat cushions were arranged in tidy rows in the chapel, jammed together so there was no elbow room between mourners. The room was well-lit, with a tall window on one side, wall sconces and chandeliers at both ends. A golden-oak lectern, like professors used at college, stood in front of the casket, and burgundy roses sat atop pillars at both ends. It was surreal—the depressing classical music, her father's pinched face, her mother's body laid out in public—like watching someone else's life unfold. Sarah flattened her palm against her chest, rising in quick swells.

She scanned the chapel looking for Henry, though she didn't expect him to show. He certainly was not obligated, now that they were no longer a couple, and he had sent flowers to the house, with a thoughtful note. Still, his eternal optimism would have been a great comfort as she stood uneasily, like a three-legged chair. No sign of his wiry, six-foot-one-inch frame towering over the rest of the mourners, his dirty-blond crewcut that made him look more like a police officer than a stockbroker. He wasn't handsome in the traditional sense, with squinty eyes that were too small for his elongated face, and large canine teeth, but he had an extraordinary warmth that drew people to him. He made Sarah feel special, which no other man had been able to do. This flattered and frightened her. What if he changed his mind?

Sarah avoided looking at the open casket as she and her father made their way to the front row and took their seats. She blinked back tears and couldn't help but notice the absence of religious symbols, crosses and images of a crucified Jesus, which had given her nightmares as a kid. No elaborate stained-glass windows like the ones that garnished the church she'd attended as a child. Her heart pulsed in her ears. She never went to church anymore, like her mother; they'd both given up religion as easily as an old pair of shoes.

Now, sitting in front of her mother's lifeless body, unsure about heaven and terrified at the idea of hell, Sarah was afraid she'd made a mistake. Abandoning God seemed like a minor decision when her mother was alive, when death wasn't looming in front of her with a frightening ambiguity.

"It doesn't feel right, having Mom's funeral in a place she's never been, with some stranger talking about her as if he knew her," she said to her father. "Her service should have been at your church. You're a member. That should count for something."

"She didn't want it in a church." He rubbed his freckled hands over his thighs and loosened his tie. "To be honest, she didn't want a funeral at all."

Sarah was taken aback by his disclosure. She wanted to press her father on the point—it struck her as a strange final request, even for her mother—but was distracted by a soft tap on her shoulder and a whiff of bergamot and jasmine. Shalimar perfume. Sarah spun around and was drawn into her best friend Heather's long arms.

"You look tired," Heather said, her plucked brows arching in concern. "Have you gotten any sleep in the last few days?"

"A few hours, here and there."

Heather gathered her mane of ash-blond hair in her hands and lifted it out from under her coat. Her gaze drifted to the casket. Robotically, Sarah's eyes followed, resting on a waxy rendition of her mother's face. Her skin was an unnatural peach shade, and her short auburn hair had been molded into a helmet, nothing like the soft waves her mother achieved with a quick blow-dry. In a way it was a relief, not seeing her mother the way she'd actually been. It was easier to look at her without dissolving. Still, warm tears pooled in the corners of her eyes.

"I can't believe she had a heart attack," Heather murmured. "Your mom never sat still. She was always cooking or knitting or sewing."

"I know. It was like she had to fill every minute with something. She couldn't just sit and watch TV or read. She had to be moving all the time."

"She seemed so healthy."

"The doctor told us it's not uncommon, a heart beating normally until, one day, it stops."

Heather clasped the back of Sarah's chair with her left hand, the diamond in her engagement ring glittering as it caught the light streaming through the window. Sarah glimpsed her own bare ring finger and curled her hand into a fist. If she got married, her mother would never see her walk down the aisle, would never know her grandchildren.

"Heather, it's good to see you," Sarah's father said warmly.

"I'm so sorry about Mrs. Byrne."

"Thank you." Sarah's father tugged the cuff of his suit jacket. "She wasn't one to make a fuss, but I know she was really glad you and Sarah were such good friends."

Sarah and Heather exchanged sad glances. Heather dried the corners of her round eyes with a tissue and folded her hands together.

As Sarah turned to face the front of the chapel, she inhaled the fruity acetone smell of nail polish and the caustic whiff of cigarette smoke. An elderly woman took the seat beside her. She looked like a dated actress, afraid to let go of the limelight, with eyebrows drawn in thin swirls and red lipstick smeared along the rutted skin above her mouth. A form-fitting black dress clung to her thin, sturdy frame, and a black cardigan was draped casually over her shoulders.

The woman regarded Sarah with hauntingly familiar green eyes, underlined with mauve half-moon pouches.

Miriam.

Her grandmother's remarkable likeness to her mother made the hairs on the back of Sarah's neck bristle. Sarah stared at Miriam, flustered. Afraid to look away for fear she'd vanish. Everything around them receded to a dull hum. Sarah hadn't seen Miriam in years, because Miriam and her mother had been estranged, though Sarah had no idea why. Her mother would change the subject every time Miriam's name was mentioned, even when Sarah pushed hard, reminding her Miriam was her only living grandparent. *You don't need that woman in your life,* her mother had responded, in a barbed voice leaving no room for argument.

Miriam leaned in. She regarded Sarah with unblinking eyes, as if she were committing her to memory.

Something indescribable passed between them.

"I'm glad you're here," Sarah said.

Miriam lowered her gaze, but not before Sarah saw her eyes darken with sorrow.

Why didn't you call me? Sarah wanted to say. *I had nothing to do with the problems between you and Mom.*

"I've missed you," Sarah pushed on.

Miriam looked up, skeptical.

"Really," Sarah insisted.

Miriam nodded, though doubt crossed her eyes.

Sarah didn't know how to convince her. She hadn't seen her grandmother since she was around fourteen. It might have been a birthday. Miriam had always appeared for her birthdays, with generous checks and blatant warnings to save for a rainy day. The checks continued, even after her mother and Miriam stopped talking. Sarah always bought one book, a mystery, then diligently put the rest of the money in her savings account and wrote a formal thank-you letter, but she never heard from her grandmother between birthdays. Miriam took on a mythical air, unseen and unheard yet eternally present.

No, it wasn't a birthday. Sarah recalled being woken by an argument, notable for its particularly nasty tone and volume, in front of a tinsel-strewn Christmas tree. She had no memory of what ignited their anger, but was certain that was the last time Miriam had been inside her parents' house.

Sarah nudged her father.

"What?" He raised his brow then bolted upright. "Miriam."

"Hello, Paul." Her leathery face registered no emotion.

Miriam pinched her thin lips and patted her short hair, dyed the same unnatural, brassy red as Sarah's mother's hair. Sarah couldn't believe how much her mother resembled Miriam; if she had lived to be Miriam's age, their features would have been almost interchangeable. Images of the three of them flashed in her head—three generations, markedly similar. Sarah didn't like seeing her own future in Miriam's seasoned face. And she was struck by the injustice of a mother attending her daughter's funeral, of her mother's forty-four-year-old heart giving out while her grandmother's stubborn old heart kept beating.

Sarah recalled her mother's dour expression whenever Miriam was woven into a conversation. Mom would be livid if she knew Miriam was sitting beside me, at her funeral, Sarah thought. The last thing Sarah wanted to do was go against her mother's wishes. Still, like it or not, Miriam was her grandmother, the only blood she had left, besides her father. Whatever drove a wedge between the two women was their problem, not hers, Sarah reasoned.

"Welcome," the mousy funeral director announced from the lectern, in a baritone voice that contradicted his small physique. "We are here today to celebrate the life of Ilana Eve Byrne."

Sarah's father took her left hand and held on tight. On impulse, Sarah reached for Miriam's hand, cold and gnarled, and clasped it in hers.

"It's difficult, making sense of why such a good person, a nurse who cared graciously for her patients, was taken at this time. It is not for us to wonder . . ."

Sarah struggled to focus with her grandmother so close.

"Ilana was a private person . . ." The director's sonorous voice went on.

Miriam wrenched her hand from Sarah's and whispered: "This is not what Ilana wanted. You know that, Paul. This is what you wanted."

Sarah's ears perked up at the resentment in Miriam's voice. Her father's hand slipped from hers. He slouched in his chair.

Suddenly, Miriam rose from her seat and moved to the casket with a vigorous stride despite her frail build. She had an aura of stony resolve. The room was pin-drop quiet. Every pair of eyes in the chapel, including the funeral director's, was riveted on Miriam, who positioned herself behind the casket like a dark canopy. She grasped the rim of the head panel and strained to lift it, to shut it and thus conceal Ilana.

Sarah took in a sharp breath, realizing Miriam would never be able to move the head panel.

"For the love of God." Her father groaned.

An audible hush came over the room. The funeral director mopped his sweaty face with a handkerchief and frowned at Miriam. Sarah was offended by the director's manner. And she was overcome by an impulse to protect her grandmother, the bridge between Sarah and her mother. Sarah stood, back upright, and walked toward Miriam. She took the head panel with both hands and raised it over the casket, then lowered it until the rim closed, shrouding her mother.

Sarah turned to go back to her seat, but Miriam began chanting in an evocative language Sarah couldn't identify. Yet it was strangely familiar. It roused something in Sarah that lay dormant— an uneasiness about the Jewish blood she'd inherited from her mother, who'd rejected her faith before Sarah was born.

"May her memory be a blessing." Miriam bowed her head over the closed coffin.

"May her memory be a blessing," Sarah echoed reflexively.

"You remind me of your mother," Miriam said to Sarah as they made their way back to their seats.

"I do?" For as long as she could remember, she'd fought any comparison of herself to her mother, but now that she was gone, it felt good, being told she embodied some of her spirit.

Miriam's eyes flickered with grief. Or regret. Sarah wasn't sure. Miriam nodded briskly at Sarah's father, slung her purse over her shoulder and walked out of the funeral hall. Her shoulders were rigid. She looked unshakable, yet there was a trace of vulnerability in her brittle step. Sarah stared at the empty doorway, surprised by the loss she experienced at her grandmother's departure. A low whisper rose through the mourners like a flurry of wind, followed by silence.

The funeral director tilted his head and eyed Sarah as if he was waiting for permission to speak. She flushed. Nodded. Stared at her hands, so much like her grandmother's, with her long fingers. The director proceeded, his somber voice background noise, elevator music, the muted notes playing on the edge of her subconscious. She was touched and confused by Miriam's devotion to the language and culture her mother had renounced.

Her mother's Jewishness was as foreign to Sarah as Europe, unspoken, a rustle of wind, a broken thread. Yet there it was, exposed by Miriam, out in the open for everyone to see and acknowledge—the faith into which her mother had been born. The faith she had denied.

3

RIGA, JUNE 1940

MIRIAM WOKE FROM A DREAM SHE DIDN'T WANT TO leave, where she felt suspended between bliss and a cozy stupor. Her head began to thud. She opened her eyes. Pitch black. *Am I blind?* She tried to bring her hands to her eyes, but her arms wouldn't budge. Something was wrapped around them. Something warm and tight. *What happened?* She felt herself sinking into an unfamiliar bed that stank of carbolic soap, urine and feces. She wondered where she was. If she was alive.

Her mind retreated into shadows like dark rooms she could see but not touch, a void where time and memory evaporated.

A SOFT WHIMPER crawled into Miriam's ears. She floated on its rhythm like a wave in the Baltic Sea, rising and falling, rising and falling. Then it grew stronger, pitching her up and down with an urgent force.

"I think you need to try nursing him."

A woman's matter-of-fact voice banged into Miriam's consciousness like a wallop of sand.

"What?" Miriam barely recognized her own voice, hoarse and feeble. Her eyelids ripped apart. Her vision was blurry, distorted shapes, silhouettes in front of a gritty brightness.

"Here he is," the woman said. She looked ethereal in her white cap and smock, fair hair severely pulled back, following the contours of her scalp.

Something was pressed into Miriam's arms. She looked down. Her eyes converged on a small white bundle. Tiny hands fluttered. Wide eyes beheld her. A gummy mouth opened and bawled. Miriam looked at the woman, perplexed.

"Open your gown and guide his mouth to your nipple," the woman instructed.

"What?" Miriam said, her voice just above a whisper.

"This is your son," the woman continued. "He's hungry. It's your second child. You know what to do."

"My son?" Miriam gasped and extended a hand to her belly. The bulge was gone. "I didn't . . . I don't remember giving birth." She lay still with disbelief.

The woman heaved her buxom chest up and down. "You were in a bad state when your husband brought you in. Your car hit a truck. You received a nasty bump on your head."

"I did?" She couldn't recall being in a car. "My husband?" Miriam asked.

"He is fine. A little shaken, but no injuries."

Her baby cried. His lips made a sucking motion. Miriam watched him, stunned by his existence. "I remember every detail of my daughter's birth. How could I have this baby and not remember a thing?"

The nurse's eyes darted to the window. "We had no choice."

"What do you mean?"

The nurse folded her arms as if she were cold and gazed out the window. "When you came to, you were thrashing and screaming. We were afraid you were going to scratch your eyes out, or compromise your baby. We had to secure your arms with straps, and bandage your eyes."

"You didn't," Miriam said, appalled at the idea of being constrained. "My husband trusted you. I trusted you to take care of me, not treat me like a lunatic."

"It was for your own protection," the nurse continued flatly. "We injected you with morphine and scopolamine to stop the pain and get you into a twilight sleep."

"You mean I slept through my delivery?"

The nurse turned to look at Miriam, and cocked her head. "Do you remember the Soviet takeover?"

Miriam stilled. "What?"

"Yesterday. The Soviets arrived in Riga."

Miriam was flummoxed. Then she shifted from incredulity to dread, the way she might go from sunlight to shade.

"Amnesia." The nurse opened Miriam's gown. She brought the baby to Miriam's nipple. "It's really quite common in pregnancies such as yours."

The baby's hands grabbed Miriam's saggy breast. He planted his mouth over her nipple.

My son.

"Such as mine?" Miriam supported him with her hands.

"Difficult, with extenuating circumstances."

Miriam chafed at the nurse's words and at the sting of her son's mouth pulling at her tender skin. He let go and wailed. His face turned splotchy red.

Instinctively, Miriam rocked him back and forth.

"Hmm," said the nurse. "Your milk might not be in yet." She sighed. "It's common, in deliveries like yours, for the milk to take longer than usual." She regarded Miriam. "I can see if a wet nurse is available."

"No!" Something bloomed deep inside her. Love. Miriam was moved to tears. "I am his mother. I will nurse him."

The nurse straightened. "Very well." She turned, took a couple of steps. Stopped and glanced over her shoulder. "Your husband will be here soon."

"When?"

"I'm sure he will be relieved to know your son's birth went smoothly, without incident," she went on with an air of reproach.

"But you said—"

"You slept through the delivery. That's what I said," the nurse interrupted Miriam, in an insinuating tone that gave Miriam pause. She turned on her heel and vanished through the door.

It was for your own protection.

Miriam searched her baby for any sign of injury after what sounded like a tumultuous birth. His skin had a healthy pink tinge; the only imperfection she could find was a tiny red birthmark on his right eyelid. She ran her finger along the question-mark curve of his ears and breathed in his distinctively sweet newborn aroma. The scent of eternity. Babies kept family names and traditions from fading to oblivion. Miriam's name came from her father's grandmother, she and Max named Ilana after Max's mother, and they would name this baby after a dead relative.

She watched his chest rise and fall, and it came back to her, how she'd dreaded giving birth. How she wasn't looking forward to her life changing with a second baby. Then—nothing until she'd woken up in the hospital. She felt undeserving of the perfect baby asleep in her arms. She kissed his downy cheek and was overcome by panic, seeing his helplessness. If anything had happened during his delivery . . . if anything had gone wrong . . . She let out a sob.

He looked back at her, his big eyes clear and sympathetic, as if he forgave her for everything. Her heart filled. She wouldn't tell Max about her hospital experience. She didn't want him to think of her tied up like a madwoman. She didn't want her son to know how he'd arrived. The baby grew fidgety. He began to whine hungrily and grope for her breast, drooping and empty. Her milk still wasn't in. She worried it might never come. She felt useless as a mother, unable to feed her own child. She clasped him tight to her chest. Cradled his head with her left hand. And called out for a wet nurse.

I will never let you down again, she promised her son. *Never.*

MAX ARRIVED AN hour later, haggard in a wrinkled shirt, his hair a mass of unruly auburn curls, his eyes bloodshot. Miriam feigned a smile. She'd begun to feel the tear from delivery, the stitches where her son had emerged, and there was a relentless pounding in her head. The medication she'd been given must have worn off, she thought, annoyed and relieved.

Max saw the lump on Miriam's head and grimaced. "How do you feel?"

"Like I've been in a car accident and gave birth on the same day," she said drily.

"I should have paid more attention to the road." He took a deep breath. "When I think about what could have happened if the truck driver hadn't slowed down . . ."

"Don't," Miriam said sharply. "What's done is done. I'm fine, and your son"—she gestured with her chin at the gurgling baby in her arms—"is perfect."

His gaze fell to his son. "The nurse says you need to rest but won't let him go to the nursery."

"I don't want him out of my sight," she said with vehemence.

"You weren't like this with Ilana."

She met his bleary eyes and desperately wanted him to know how callously she'd been treated, yet at the same time realized all it would do was make him feel worse about the accident.

Keep your feelings to yourself, her mother would say. *You don't want people thinking you're helpless.*

"This is my last baby," Miriam explained. "I want to savor every moment I have with him before we go home and get busy with routines and schedules."

He nodded. He leaned over and brushed his lips over the baby's forehead. The baby shuddered and opened his eyes when Max's whiskers grazed his skin. Max lifted him from Miriam's arms and held him close, gazing at him with admiration. Miriam was overcome by the sight of her husband with his much-wanted son, as well as a terrible feeling of angst over the Soviets' unexpected invasion.

"What's going on out there, with the Soviets?" she asked Max.

"Shall we call him Moses, after my great-uncle?" he replied, ignoring her question.

"Tell me. I need to know. Even if it's bad news."

The baby started fussing. Max rocked him in his arms and said, "Shh. It's all right, baby Moses."

"Stop it, Max. I haven't agreed to the name and won't even discuss the subject until you let me know what's going on with the Soviets." Her breasts swelled uncomfortably. *My milk. Finally.*

The baby turned his little head in Miriam's direction and stared at her before opening his mouth wide and wailing at the top of his lungs. Max immediately returned him to Miriam's open arms. She felt a satisfying sense of triumph, guiding her baby's mouth to her nipple, able to do something Max, or any man, would never be able to accomplish, then flinched as the baby's sharp gums pierced her skin.

Max settled into the wooden chair beside the bed, drew the *Segodnia* from his suit jacket and read the speech President Ulmanis gave the previous evening, while Miriam had been in the throes of labor. "'Soviet troops entered Latvia with the knowledge and agreement of the government, which for its part continues the flow of friendly relations between Latvia and the Soviet Union. I wish that the inhabitants of our country will treat the occupying forces with friendship . . . I will remain at my place, if you will remain at yours.'" Max folded the paper and shook his head. "Ulmanis. What a coward. He should be ashamed of himself."

Miriam was struck by a pang of despair as she absorbed the news of the president standing idly by while the Soviets waltzed in and conquered Latvia.

"There's a curfew now," Max went on. "We can't be outside between ten at night and four in the morning, and public groups of more than four are banned."

Miriam looked at him in dismay. In the *Segodnia* newspaper, she'd read about the Soviet government confiscating its own citizens' property. How educated and wealthy classes, the bourgeoisie, would immediately be deported to Siberia. Soviet rule meant a constant fear of being arrested for saying the wrong words. It meant a terrifying future for her children.

"Moses is an awfully big name for such a little baby," Miriam said softly.

Max stood, clasped his hands behind his back and turned to the window, where the morning sun peeked through the curtains. "He could be Moses on his birth certificate, but we could call him

Monya." He spun around and smoothed his whiskers with his fingers. "When he is older, he can be Moses, if he chooses."

She nodded at his compromise and looked at her son. A drop of milk lay on his upper lip and his long eyelashes were damp from crying. She watched him sleep, afraid he and Ilana would never understand the meaning of freedom.

A WEEK LATER, when Miriam and Monya were back at home, Andrey Vyshinsky, the prosecutor who'd orchestrated the Soviets' Great Terror—the execution of 750,000 people and the exile of more than a million others to forced labor camps—addressed Latvians from the balcony of the Russian embassy. Speaking in Latvian, he proclaimed with vigor, "Long live free Latvia." People cheered as if they trusted him.

Two days after Vyshinsky's speech, thousands of Russians arrived in Latvia and immediately held protests demanding that Ulmanis be eliminated as president. A number of criminals doing time in Latvian prisons were released and awarded jobs as policemen. In July, elections to the Saeima, the parliament, were announced, but the Soviet list of pre-approved candidates was the only list allowed. The Soviet candidates were, of course, elected, and their first order of business was to unanimously affirm Latvia as a Soviet Socialist Republic, an illegal occupation as it didn't adhere to Latvia's constitution. Then Ulmanis was arrested and deported to Russia, and the *Segodnia* was taken over by the Soviet newspaper *Trudovaia Gazeta*.

Miriam grew increasingly disillusioned with the barrage of Soviet propaganda—photos of smiling factory workers, headlines claiming the Red Army lifted the burden of oppression from the Latvian people and, more unnerving, that Jews should be prepared for dangerous, anti-Semitic Latvians who, under the Soviet regime, would no longer tolerate capitalists, Zionists or believers in Moses as prophet. As if that wasn't bad enough, the newly installed Soviet government decreed that Jews now had to be called *ebrejs*, or Hebrews, in Russian.

"Why do the Soviets care what we're called?" she complained to Max. "Latvians have always called us Zids, Jews. That is who we are."

Max scratched his whiskers. "We are not in Latvia anymore. We are in the Soviet Union, and if the Soviet Union wants to make us Russian Hebrews, that is who we are."

"But why? What does it matter?"

He squeezed Miriam's hand. "Hopefully, it is nothing more than the Soviets flaunting their power."

"I don't know. It feels like we've lost part of who we are. It feels like an insult."

He gave her a thoughtful look. "For our children's sake, we must focus on what we have left, not on what we've lost."

Miriam yearned for the day another country's army would intervene and overpower the barbaric Soviets. She wanted to be optimistic, but was frightened by the capriciousness of hope. And she never imagined Latvians, the people they'd lived among for generations, turning on them like spies betraying their country.

4

CHICAGO, NOVEMBER 1975

HE GRINDING NOISE OF A CAR'S BROKEN MUFFLER WOKE
Sarah the day after the funeral. It was the same sound an old
boyfriend's beater used to make when he pulled up into her
driveway on long-ago Saturday nights. So similar, she woke dis-
oriented, and thought she was a teenager for a minute, in her old
bedroom with the candy-floss-pink walls she'd loved at ten and
despised at fourteen. Then the funeral sprang into her head and she
was disappointed not to be back in high school, when her relationship with her mother was tumultuous at best. Strange, how she was
nostalgic for an era she couldn't wait to escape at the time.

She glanced through her window. A cherry-red Mustang roared
down her street. Some teenaged boy showing off. The most exciting
thing that ever happened in her neighborhood. Growing up, snow
days were winter highlights. She'd played kick the can on the road
until the streetlights came on in the summer, and bought her first
bra at Crawford's Department Store during a mortifying excursion
with her red-faced mother, who never said "menstruation" out

loud, preferring the less specific "time of month." She avoided the topic of fornication altogether.

Sarah wandered into the kitchen. Her father sat at the breakfast table in front of a mug and a plate of toast, his reddish-blond hair tousled and his face droopy with sleep. It occurred to Sarah that she still didn't know why her father had planned a funeral for her mother, who'd explicitly said she didn't want one. She'd meant to ask him, but Miriam's haunting words and actions had turned the funeral upside down. It was all people talked about after the service, peppering Sarah and her father with questions about her grandmother's ancestry. By the time the last person walked out the door, Sarah was sick of saying, "I don't know." And she was annoyed with her mother for erasing her heritage, causing Sarah to be ignorant about where she came from and the people who came before her.

Sarah peered into the cereal cupboard, stocked with enough boxes of Shreddies and Life for months. Her mother collected cereal the way other people collected stamps, buying as many boxes as would fit in her cart when it was on sale, or if she had a coupon, then stacking them into the cupboard, careful to put the newest ones at the back so the oldest would be eaten first, before going stale. The neat rows of boxes brought a lump of grief to Sarah's throat. She closed the cupboard, poured herself some coffee and leaned against the counter.

"Why did you go against what Mom wanted and have a funeral?" she asked her father.

He rubbed his forearm. "She made that choice a long time ago, right after we had you. She said hard decisions didn't get easier over time, and that it was best to face them head-on." He planted his hands on his thighs and sat up tall. "I didn't like the idea of no funeral, but Mom was only nineteen and she'd just had a baby, and I thought we'd have plenty of time to go back and change things."

"But you didn't."

"No. We didn't." He paused. "So many nurses called to say they were sorry and asked about the funeral. They wanted to pay their respects, and frankly, so did I. And I remembered something my dad told me, when my mom died and I didn't want to go to the funeral. He said funerals were for the living, not the dead, and that I'd regret it forever if I didn't say goodbye."

"So you had the funeral to make yourself feel better?" Sarah took a sip of coffee and made a face. It was terribly bitter.

"Your mother used to make the coffee. Too strong?"

In answer, Sarah poured her coffee down the sink.

"You're right," her father continued. "I had the funeral for me and your mother's co-workers and everyone else who came." He broke a piece of toast in half, then dropped it back on his plate. "It seemed like the right thing to do, but now I'm not so sure. I never imagined Miriam showing up and causing a scene." He smacked his forehead with his palm. "What a mess."

"I'm going to call Grandma, maybe go for a visit," Sarah said.

Her father got to his feet, his belly hanging over the waist of his trousers. "I don't know if that's such a good idea."

"Why not?"

He looked at her. "Didn't you see how she was at the funeral?"

"At least she came. She cared about Mom."

"Maybe. I don't know," he said tightly. "What I do know is that the two of them argued whenever they were together." He paused. "Mom was her worst self when she was with Miriam."

Sarah shook her head. This wasn't what she wanted to hear. She felt as though she'd been backed into a corner. "Well, just because they fought doesn't mean I won't get along with Miriam," she pushed back at him.

"True. I just think it's a good idea to keep her at arm's length. And don't expect too much."

She recalled how good it felt, being near Miriam at the funeral, as if she still had part of her mother. She was certain there had been a connection between them, and that Miriam wanted to know her only grandchild. Sarah had lost the chance to mend her relationship with her mother; she wasn't about to give up the chance to get to know her grandmother.

Her father poured the entire pot of coffee down the sink. "I'll do a Dunkin' Donuts run. What do you want, besides coffee?"

Sarah opened the cereal cupboard again, groaned and slammed the door shut.

"How about one of those powdered donuts, with jam in the middle?" he asked.

Sarah's mouth watered at the thought of powdered sugar. Sweet things always managed to fill the empty spaces in her heart, if only for a moment. "All right."

He grabbed his car keys off the counter. "I'll be back in half an hour. I'm going to the paint store too. I'm off the next two weeks and can't sit around and do nothing the whole time. Your mother asked me to paint the house, new colors, freshen it up, but I kept putting her off because I was tired. Now . . ." He swept his hand across the kitchen. "Every room reminds me of her and my pathetic refusal to do what she asked."

"Mom wouldn't want you to feel guilty about not painting, Dad."

"I know, but I do. I would give anything to go back and paint, make her happy."

Her father went out the door and Sarah was left alone, with the unsettling realization she didn't know how much time Miriam had, or her father, or even herself. Her mother's premature death had opened her eyes to the worrisome vagueness of the future, to the stark realization that life is fragile, even if people seem unbreakable.

AFTER A SHOWER and a sugary donut breakfast, Sarah dialed her grandmother's number, listed in her mother's address book with a red line through Miriam's name. It rang five times before a click and a throaty, "Hello?"

"Grandma?"

Long pause.

"Who is this?"

How many people called Miriam Grandma? "It's me. Sarah."

"Sarah? What time is it?"

"Ten thirty. Sorry. I didn't mean to wake you."

"I wasn't asleep."

"Oh." *Yes, you were.*

Dead air.

"I didn't expect to hear from you, after your mother's funeral."

Sarah twirled the phone cord around her finger and carefully considered her words, to avoid antagonizing Miriam. "That's why I'm calling, actually. I wanted to ask you some questions about Mom."

"What kind of questions?"

Sarah pressed forward. "How about I come over? It would be much nicer to talk in person."

Silence.

"Are you there, Grandma?"

"I don't think it's a good idea."

"Why not?"

"Because I don't want to be ambushed."

"Ambushed? That's not my intention at all. At the funeral, when you were praying over the casket, it occurred to me I don't know as much about Mom as I should."

"Why stir the pot? Just leave well enough alone. If your mother wanted you to know, she would have told you."

"I really believe Mom would have told me more, eventually, but she didn't have the chance. You're the only person who can give me the answers I need. Can I come by today?"

"Today's not good."

"How about tomorrow? I'm off this week, staying with my dad, so I have a car."

"Even worse."

"I could bring dinner. I promise I won't stay too long. We can eat and then I'll go."

"You have no idea what I can and can't eat in my condition."

"What condition?"

"I have to go." Miriam hung up.

The dial tone jarred Sarah. She set the receiver down, mystified by her grandmother's responses. Deep down, Sarah had expected Miriam to put aside her differences with her mother and welcome her only grandchild with open arms. But Miriam sounded cagey over the phone, exactly like her mother when Sarah prodded her for information, as though she had something to hide. Most bothersome was the fact that this secret, whatever it was, took precedence over Miriam's interest in getting to know her.

Sarah shifted her eyes to the telephone and decided to go to Miriam's the next day and stand outside her door as long as it took to get inside. Her grandmother had no idea how stubborn she could be, no idea that when she was a child and her mother made liver and onions for dinner, she'd refused to eat, no matter how hungry she was, not even when her father said he'd take her out for ice cream if she'd eat her dinner. Not even when her mother said she didn't know how lucky she was, a plate full of iron in front of her, when other children were starving.

"Just let her have a bowl of cereal, Ilana," her father would say, to keep the peace.

And let her think she's in charge, that she can waltz in here like she's too good for my food and do whatever she wants? Absolutely not.

She and her mother would glare at each other like rivals, neither one backing down until her father demanded a truce so he could eat his dinner before it got cold. It was a drama that played out until Sarah left for college.

5

RIGA, AUGUST 1940

MIRIAM WAS REVIEWING THE MONTHLY ACCOUNTS FOR Max's practice at the kitchen table. The logic of numbers reassured her, the way equations were either right or wrong, with none of the ambiguity that came with emotions. Two-month-old Monya was asleep, gathering strength to keep her up all night, and Ilana was sulking in her room after another bad day at her new school. The Soviets had closed all Jewish schools, as well as synagogues and churches. Religion was banned. Ilana now attended a Latvian school, where European history had been replaced by a Soviet narrative as false as the election.

The front door opened and Max walked in, two hours earlier than usual, his pinstriped trousers wrinkled and a dark blob of something on his vest. Miriam looked up from a receipt for tooth powder to clean patients' teeth, and dropped her pencil when she saw his somber face.

He removed his fedora and regarded her for a long moment. "The Soviets have replaced lats with rubles." He exhaled. "We have only one hundred lats in our account."

"That's impossible," Miriam gasped. "We have thousands in the bank."

"Not anymore. Nobody does. The Soviets stole all of our money."

Miriam gave a violent shudder. "They can't do that."

He scrunched his hat. "Yes, they can. And more."

She looked at him blankly.

"We have to bring our safe to the bank. The Soviets are going to confiscate all of our jewelry and silver."

Rage and fear twisted up from her gut to her throat. Miriam nearly shrieked. She was frightened of her own helplessness, of her family's vulnerability. She was thirty-one years old, and the stability she relished was about to be snuffed out in an instant, like candlelight.

MIRIAM'S FAMILY LOST a substantial portion of their income a few months later, when Max's dental practice was seized by the Soviets. He was ordered to continue working, but only for Soviet officers and their families, with almost every ruble he earned confiscated by the government.

"Maybe we should leave," Max said one evening, after working ten hours straight for enough rubles to buy a loaf of bread and a few potatoes. He lit a cigarette.

"And go where, with what money?"

"I don't know. Anywhere would be better than this." He puffed on his cigarette and stirred the watery potato soup Gutte had made earlier.

With their drastically reduced income, Gutte came only three days a week, to help with the children and cook a few meals. Miriam paid her in boots, shoes and coats, items no longer available in stores, which Gutte needed for her growing family. She now had two grandchildren.

"I could never leave my parents," Miriam said. "They have nobody else here." Miriam's mother had given birth to three other children, a boy who died from pneumonia at one year of age and two stillborn babies.

"We should let them at least know what we're thinking," Max suggested.

"You mean what you're thinking," Miriam replied, defensive. "I'm not ready to surrender." She paused. "Besides, we'd have to sell our house so we could afford to go, but if people's bank accounts have been emptied, who would be able to buy it?"

Max squashed his cigarette in a glass ashtray. "I never said we'd be able to sell it." He looked at her with a quiet resignation that made her feel as if there were pins in her stomach.

ILANA AND MIRIAM were in Ilana's bedroom, quarreling about her hair.

"I brushed it yesterday." Ilana tossed her wavy auburn mane over her shoulders and fixed her defiant green eyes on her mother.

"You did not," Miriam replied, struggling to keep her voice calm. "You have a nasty tangle at the back."

"I missed that part." Ilana perched on the edge of her bed, her back as straight as the birch headboard, and pulled at the widow's peak in the center of her forehead.

"Let me brush it out."

"No." She scooted back against the sky-blue wall and covered her head with her hands. Her fingernails were gnawed to the skin.

Miriam stiffened at the sight of her daughter's chewed nails, a nervous habit she'd acquired after changing schools. Seeing Ilana's inflamed fingers, some crusted with dried blood, made her wonder how on earth Ilana would manage the family's looming crisis ahead if she couldn't adjust to a new school? Ilana needed to be stronger. Miriam grabbed a handful of Ilana's hair and pulled her from the wall.

"Stop, Mama, you're hurting me," Ilana cried.

Miriam ran the brush through her daughter's long hair, yanking it through the tangles. "If you brushed your hair like I told you, it wouldn't be such a mess."

Ilana's eyes welled with tears. "I'll do it now. I'll brush until every knot is gone."

"That's what you said yesterday."

"I meant to brush it. I forgot."

Miriam grasped Ilana's trembling chin. "You need to learn to do what you're told without arguing. You may think I'm being harsh, but I'm doing this for your own good." She let go of Ilana's chin and dragged the brush through her hair.

Ilana pinched her eyes shut and whimpered.

Miriam saw tears dribble down her daughter's face and knew she'd gone too far. "If you want to survive in this world, you need to know life isn't fair," she said grimly.

Ilana nodded slightly, her eyes still closed.

"Did you hear me?" Miriam prodded.

Ilana opened her eyes. She flashed a blistering glare that took Miriam aback. "I heard you," Ilana said, with an edge to her voice.

Despite her exasperation, Miriam felt a smug sense of approval. Her daughter's obstinate streak would pay dividends one day.

MIRIAM'S FATHER, IN his charcoal suit with a sage-green bow tie, stood in the vestibule, holding Monya up to the window beside the door to see the streetlights. Miriam, halfway down the stairs after getting Ilana to bed, studied their profiles, the contrast between Monya's silky hair and plump skin and her father's pockmarked cheeks, full head of gray hair and walrus whiskers. She hoped her son would inherit her father's hair but not his taste in clothing. She much preferred the subtle neckties most men, including Max, wore over her father's garish bow ties that drew attention to his fleshy jowls.

Monya noticed his mother and flashed a gummy smile. Miriam descended the stairs and tickled Monya's bare foot. He giggled, a laugh from his belly that could have put a smile on an ogre's face. He reached out to the windowpane, touched it with the tips of his fingers and snatched his hand back.

"Cold, isn't it?" Miriam's father smiled.

Monya regarded his own chunky fingers as if he'd never seen them before. This would be his first winter, thought Miriam. The first time he'd feel ice in his bones, the first time he'd see snow fall from the sky like sugar, Ilana's first verbal description of snow.

Where will we be in the winter?

"Alexander, Miriam," Max called impatiently from the sitting room, "are you going to join us?"

Miriam's father blew out his cheeks. Miriam gritted her teeth and led the way to the sitting room, where her mother, in a cap-sleeved navy dress that fell just past her knees, sat primly on the divan, legs crossed, exposing her black mules and beige stockings. A strand of pearls she'd inherited from her mother adorned her long neck, and her cinnamon-brown hair was arranged in a tidy chignon. Max stood at the hearth, puffing on a cigarette.

"Why isn't he asleep?" Miriam's mother asked, gesturing with her sharp chin to Monya, squirming in his grandfather's arms.

Miriam's shoulders tensed at her barbed voice. "He's on a bit of a backwards schedule. He sleeps all day and is wide awake at night."

"For goodness' sake, Miriam." Her mother sighed. "It's your responsibility to get him on a proper schedule."

"Monya is a happy baby, which is all that matters," Miriam's father chimed in.

Miriam wanted to expunge her father's words; once he took her side, her mother would never back down. They could be up all night arguing for the sake of arguing.

"Don't be ridiculous, Alexander," her mother snapped. "Children need to be on schedules as soon as possible or they'll take over your lives."

"Isn't that the point?" Miriam's father kissed Monya on the forehead.

"Important as this is," Max interjected, "we have something far more urgent to discuss." He scrunched his cigarette in the glass ashtray on the coffee table.

Alexander turned so Monya could look out the window at his reflection.

"He can't very well talk to your back, Alexander," Miriam's mother chastised him.

"My ears can hear just as well from the back as the front, Dora."

Miriam dropped heavily onto a chair. Their petty arguments made her feel as if she was five again, listening to them disagree about everything from the weather to the rabbi. For the life of her, she could never understand why they got married or how they'd lasted so long.

"I don't care if Alexander is standing on his head," Max said. "As long as he listens."

Dora gave a dramatic sigh and folded her red-manicured fingers on her lap. "Very well."

Max cleared his throat. "I really think we need to consider moving out of Latvia, before things get worse."

His words filled Miriam with an inky gloom.

Miriam's mother brought her hand to her throat and glanced

sideways at her husband. Alexander reeled around, clasping Monya tight.

"I must admit, the idea has crossed my mind, more than once," Miriam's father said, his voice muffled as though he were speaking from behind a closed door. "But we don't even have enough money for train fare across Latvia."

Monya began to cry. Miriam couldn't sit still. She extracted Monya from her father and walked the length of the room, rocking him in her arms.

"Even if we had the money," Dora added, "where would we go? Countries aren't exactly opening their borders to Jews right now."

Max's eyes shifted from Alexander to Dora. "I wish I had a fail-safe plan, but I don't. I just have a gut feeling that we need to get away from Riga."

"No, Papa, no!" Ilana's voice sprang into the room like a stiff breeze. She scurried to Max and threw herself against his legs. "I don't want to move."

Miriam stared at her daughter, aghast. Ilana had chopped her hair to her shoulders, her ears, her chin, depending on the angle. She was hardly recognizable without her long auburn waves. It looked like she had a mop on her head.

"My God, Ilana," Dora exclaimed. "What have you done to your hair?"

Ilana's hand sprang to her head. Her lips curled to a mischievous smile. "Cut it, so I won't get any more knots, Bubbe."

Guilt enveloped Miriam like a chill. "I told you to brush your hair, not lop it off like the gardener who trimmed our hedges. Do you have any idea how long it will take to grow back?"

"I don't care if it takes a year," Ilana replied in a huff. "I like it short." She looked at her grandfather. "What do you think, Zeyde?"

"Job lost everything except his faith and in the end he prospered," Alexander said, distracted, as if he hadn't heard Ilana.

"What?" Ilana said, confused.

"That's a nice story," Miriam acknowledged, "but faith isn't going to put a roof over our heads or food on our table."

Ilana looked at her mother for an explanation.

"Faith helps you turn your face to the future," Dora said, in support of Alexander.

"This is hardly the time to ponder religion," Max said sternly. "Ilana, this discussion is for adults. You need to go back to bed."

"But Papa—"

Monya cut his sister off with an ear-scratching wail.

"My God, Miriam," her mother scoffed, "are you raising children or farm animals?"

Miriam pulled Monya to her chest and rubbed his back to calm him.

"I believe the children should be here," Alexander said. "They will be just as affected by our decision as any of us, even more."

"For goodness' sake, Alexander."

"Come, Ilana," Miriam said firmly. "Back to bed."

Monya's cries grew more insistent.

"No." Ilana wrapped her arms around her grandfather's waist. "Zeyde says I can stay."

Alexander looked sheepishly at Miriam.

Monya flailed in Miriam's arms.

"Fine. You can drag her tired body out of bed tomorrow and get her off to school," Miriam said tersely.

"I can stay home if you like," Ilana quipped.

Alexander looked at Ilana. "Tell me, sweetheart," he said, "why do you want to stay in Riga?"

The grin slipped from Ilana's face. "Because my friends are

here." Her eyes slid from Miriam to Dora. "Because Mama and Bubbe always tell me not to run away from problems, to be strong even when I'm afraid."

A lump lodged in Miriam's throat. She caught her mother's astonished eyes, and was at a loss for words.

"Well." Alexander gave Ilana a thin smile of approval. "I think this discussion is over."

Max looked thoughtfully at Ilana and nodded.

Miriam could tell from Max's silence that he was not convinced they should stay. But she had a feeling he'd feel the same if they decided to go. There wasn't really a choice between good and bad, but rather between terrible and more terrible. She went upstairs to put Monya to bed. Outside, the wind howled. She gazed at Monya, nestled under the warm wool blanket her mother had knit for him, and was grateful for that moment.

6

CHICAGO, NOVEMBER 1975

SARAH PARKED HER MOTHER'S SKY-BLUE PLYMOUTH FURY in front of a three-story building across from a bank on Washington Street, in Skokie, about fifteen miles north of the Chicago Loop. Gigantic oak trees lined the street, their leafless branches stark against the overcast sky. With its old low-rise apartment buildings and stores, it was the kind of street that was stuck in the thirties, where modernity's ranch bungalows and side-splits hadn't yet arrived.

Sarah breathed in her mother's lingering scent of stale cigarettes and the familiar antiseptic soap from the hospital, and got out of the car, carrying a paper grocery bag with food she'd made for the inauspicious occasion. Her legs shook with nerves as she faced her grandmother's building. Her breath swirled in the cold air, damp with the threat of snow. A station wagon drove slowly down the street, tires crunching over the ice. Sarah debated whether she should follow through with her plan or abandon it altogether. It wasn't as if her grandmother was waiting for her; Miriam didn't know she was coming.

The squat rectangular building looked old but well-kept, with a neatly trimmed cedar hedge running around the perimeter and a pine tree towering over the salmon-brick facade. The potent aroma of meat loaf and banana bread, in Sarah's bag, made her stomach growl. She squared her shoulders and trod along the rutted stone walkway to the front door.

Eight metal mailboxes hung on the beige wall in the landing. Names were stamped in raised white letters on red adhesive labels. *Talan* appeared on the second box. Apartment 2. She started up the wood stairs, covered in a well-worn black runner, to the second floor. She set the bag down in front of Miriam's door, fiddled with her ponytail and knocked. No sound from the apartment.

Maybe Miriam wasn't home. Maybe she was asleep. She pressed her ear against the wood. She smelled nicotine, then heard voices on the other side of the door. A television or radio. Sarah knocked again, harder. Once, twice, three times. Footsteps clicked toward the door.

"Who's there?"

"Me. Sarah."

"Who?"

Really? "Sarah. Your granddaughter."

"What are you doing here?"

"I told you over the phone. I want to talk about Mom."

Silence.

"I brought dinner. My specialties. If you open the door, I'll show you."

"I have a finicky stomach. I can't eat your food."

"You don't even know what I brought."

"I can't eat it. Besides, I have work to do."

Sarah pictured Miriam on the other side of the door, arms crossed, eyelids hanging like broken window blinds. "I promise I won't stay long. Can you please just open the door?"

Nothing but her grandmother's raspy smoker's breathing that reminded Sarah of her mother.

"Please. Go. Leave things the way they are." Her grandmother's voice sounded muffled, as if her mouth was pressed against the door.

"I can't. I don't want to."

"What's the matter with you? Don't you understand the word 'no'?"

"I'm not leaving until you open the door and let me in, which might be embarrassing if your neighbors see me."

"I never talk to them."

Sarah gave a silent scream. She sat down, her back against the door. "Then I'm going to enjoy my meat loaf and potatoes out here." She took out the steaming food, peered into the bag and made a face. She knocked on the door.

"What now?"

"I don't have a fork or knife. Can you slide them under the door for me?"

The click of the lock. The door opened. "I'm only letting you in because of Mrs. Levi upstairs," Miriam said in a clipped voice. "She has a mouth like a hippopotamus and if she saw you eating outside my door, the whole building would know my business by tomorrow morning."

"Thank goodness for Mrs. Levi."

The smoky air and late afternoon light spilling through tea-colored sheers cast a sepia glow throughout the apartment, reminding Sarah of an old photo. Macramé planters hung in front of the sheers. Potted plants lined the teak coffee table and gathered dust on the ancient television set. The low-backed orange-and-green-floral sofa had a noticeable dent in one cushion, the spot, Sarah figured, where Miriam sat most of the time. Walter

44

Cronkite's grandfatherly face appeared on the television screen, his trusty voice filling the awkward gaps between them.

Miriam, in a maroon dress and black mule slingbacks, bustled past Sarah and switched off the avocado-colored stove where a kettle gurgled and spouted steam. Sarah followed her into the galley kitchen and set the food on the counter. An opening led to a small dining area that contained a round table adorned in a lace cloth, with three potted plants in the center, along with an amber glass ashtray overflowing with cigarette butts.

"Your plants are lovely," Sarah began. "You must have a green thumb."

Miriam poured the boiling water into a white teapot, stained with tea on the spout. "There is no great secret to plants."

"Mine always die."

"Too much water."

"What?"

"You are overwatering. This is often the reason plants die. Too much of a good thing brings trouble."

"You're right. I watered them almost every day, thinking they needed water like we do."

Miriam looked past Sarah with glazed-over eyes. "Plants require far less than people—less water, less time, less love—yet they can bloom for years."

Sarah twisted her watch around her wrist. A siren's peal came from somewhere outside. Miriam dunked the tea bag in the pot.

"Where can I find cutlery?" Sarah asked, opening and closing drawers. She glanced over her shoulder and shivered when she saw her grandmother's heavy-lidded eyes swollen with tears. "Are you all right?" Sarah asked delicately.

Miriam's face blanched. She drew back, opened the drawer across from the sink and took out two forks and two knives.

Sarah had the feeling Miriam had unintentionally tumbled into the past, and debated the pros and cons of pushing her further. In the end, she plunged onward, partly out of curiosity and partly because she felt entitled to the information withheld by her mother.

"I should have come years ago. I should have insisted. I wanted to spend time with you, but whenever I asked why the two of you weren't speaking, Mom got upset and told me I was going to give her an ulcer if I didn't stop bothering her about things that weren't my business."

Miriam's lips curled up ever so slightly, enough for Sarah to see her grandmother was amused by her mother's obstinacy.

"Do you think . . . Can you tell me what happened between you and Mom?"

"Shouldn't that be warmed up?" Miriam gestured with her head at the bag of food.

"Right. Three-fifty."

Miriam turned the oven dial and lit a Chesterfield cigarette in one fluid motion.

Sarah waved the smoke out of her face. "It'll only take a few minutes to heat up. Can you wait until after dinner?"

Miriam rolled her eyes like a teenager reprimanded for bad behavior and pressed her cigarette into the ashtray lightly, to keep it for later.

Sarah opened the oven door and set the meat loaf and potatoes on the top rack. "When was the last time you were at our house?" she asked casually, as if she were asking what Miriam wanted to drink.

Miriam opened a cupboard door above the sink and took out two white-and-green Pyrex plates. She told Sarah to bring the ashtray from the table in to the kitchen and empty it into the garbage beneath the sink.

"Mom smoked the same brand," Sarah offered, turning the ash-tray upside down over the garbage.

Miriam carried the teapot to the table.

"The doctor said smoking likely contributed to Mom's heart attack," Sarah continued.

"Is this your way of telling me I should stop smoking?"

"No . . . I mean, yes. My dad just stopped, cold turkey, years ago. He says he feels a lot better."

Miriam cocked her head and regarded Sarah as if she were seeing her for the first time. "You'll make a good Jewish mother."

"But I'm not Jewish."

"Is that what your mother told you?"

"She told me nothing. That's why I wanted to come here, to get to know you and to learn about Mom's past, your past."

"The past is over and done with," Miriam said with a finality that took Sarah aback.

Sarah's debate team experience came to mind. Miriam would have been a formidable opponent, the type who used to embolden Sarah, who didn't like losing. "Winston Churchill said, 'A nation that forgets its past has no future.'"

Miriam's low forehead creased into lines of surprise or awe, Sarah wasn't sure.

"Then there are many places without a future," Miriam said plainly.

"Where? What do you mean?"

Miriam reached for the yellow-and-red pot holders hanging on a hook on the wall and opened the oven door. A garlic-tomato fragrance scented the air. Miriam pulled out the loaf and tray of potatoes. "Probably hot enough by now."

"Where was Mom born? What city?"

"I'm not very hungry."

"It's my dad's favorite," Sarah explained, as she cut a generous piece and set it on a plate.

"Don't give me so much."

Sarah put a smaller portion on the second plate, then added potatoes to both plates. "I should've brought a salad or some green beans."

Her grandmother poured tea into two ribbed glasses with handles and set them on the table. "This is more food than I eat in a day."

"Really?" Sarah carried the plates to the table. Embarrassment flooded her chest when she saw Charlie the tuna, wearing a beret and coke-bottle glasses, in a television commercial for Star-Kist. She'd run the focus groups for this Charlie ad, where people went mad for the brash talking fish, rejected because he didn't taste good enough. Now, seeing Charlie on her grandmother's screen, she lamented her job, with its tedious end goal of selling cans of tuna. She turned the television off, ignoring Miriam's irritated frown.

Her grandmother dug through the meat loaf with her fork as if she were looking for buried treasure, or poison. She chewed like it was rubber.

"So, where did you say Mom was born?" Sarah asked in a nonchalant tone, to catch Miriam off guard.

"I didn't."

"Can't you tell me? What's the big secret? I'm sure I could find out if I go through Mom's things."

"Why don't you?"

"Because I'd rather hear it from you. A piece of paper won't tell me about the place, or what my grandfather was like."

"I've been here for years and you were never interested in me or your grandfather before." She dragged her fork across her plate, scooping up a pile of meat loaf and potatoes.

48

"That's because of you and Mom. I told you. She would've gotten mad at me for seeing you."

Miriam ate another forkful of food, hobbled to her feet, shuffled back to the kitchen, and returned a moment later with a second, generous helping of meat loaf and potatoes.

Sarah wanted to ask why Miriam had claimed she wasn't hungry, but changed her mind. If her grandmother was anything like her mother, it would only bring trouble, pointing out the disparity between her words and her actions. "So, what do you do?"

"What?"

"You said you had work to do."

"I still keep the books for the lawyers I used to work for, and for a couple of their clients."

"You're an accountant, like Dad?"

"No. A bookkeeper. I didn't go to college."

"Oh." Sarah glanced sideways at Miriam and tried to guess her age. Mid-sixties, possibly older. It was terrible, really, how little she knew about her own grandmother.

Miriam drew her fork over her plate to get every last morsel of meat loaf.

"I've been wondering," Sarah continued. "Since the funeral, what you said when you went up to Mom's casket."

"It's personal," Miriam replied flatly.

Sarah was irked by Miriam's quick refusal, the same reaction she'd gotten from her mother whenever she'd asked a question.

Miriam ate a forkful of potatoes and picked dead leaves from one of her plants.

For a second, Sarah wished she had a normal grandmother like Heather's, who'd lived with her family and baked pies and played Scrabble with Heather and her friends for hours on end. She'd died when Sarah was ten years old and she had mourned the loss as if they'd been related. Then she'd seen the long black car picking up Heather and her family for the funeral, and realized that as much as she'd loved her, she wasn't family. Too bad you couldn't adopt grandparents the way people adopted children.

Sarah watched Miriam run her finger over a plum-colored leaf with a wistful tenderness that bothered Sarah. She wanted Miriam to look at her that way, as though she cared about her. She wanted Miriam's approval. She wanted answers, but was beginning to see this would take time and sensitivity.

Her grandmother turned her fork between her fingers. She avoided eye contact with Sarah, focusing on her plate.

Sarah drank her tea and gagged. "This is really strong."

"It's brewed, how tea should be, not like the dishwater stuff people drink here."

Sarah ate a bite of meat loaf to get the bitterness out of her mouth. "Is this what tea was like in Russia?"

"Russia? Who said anything about Russia?"

"Mom. She said you and my grandfather were from Russia."

Miriam drank down her tea and poured herself another glass. "We spoke Russian, but we were born and raised in Riga. Latvia."

"Riga? Where's Riga?"

"Didn't you graduate from college?"

"Yes, but—"

"Then you should know your geography."

"I didn't major—"

"Latvia's on the Baltic Sea, between Estonia and Lithuania. Riga is the capital, the biggest city. Used to be called the Paris of the Baltics. Now it's the Latvian Soviet Socialist Republic. Part of the Soviet Union."

"So, technically, you are from the Soviet Union."

"No. Latvia. There's a big difference."

"Why was Riga called the Paris of the Baltics?"

Miriam got a wistful look in her eyes. "I didn't understand until Max and I traveled to Paris a year after we married. We stayed in a hotel overlooking the Seine River and I remember thinking how similar it was to Riga's Daugava River. There was just something about Paris—"

The telephone rang. Miriam blinked. It rang again.

"Aren't you going to answer it?"

"Why? I'm not expecting any calls."

Another ring.

"It could be important."

"Or it could be another pesky salesman. If you ask me, there should be a law against barging into people's lives over the telephone."

The phone went silent.

"Riga sounds beautiful. So does Paris. I've always wanted to go to Europe."

"Why? It's not the same as it was before the war. Europe is old and rundown."

"That's exactly what Mom said when I talked about going."

A muscle in Miriam's jaw pulsed. "Your mother had a lot of common sense. I hope you listened to her."

"I should've listened more." Sarah dragged her fork through her mashed potatoes, leaving a trail of four identical lines. She considered her mother and grandmother, how alike they were though they hadn't spoken in years. Did women become their mothers and grandmothers? Could she look at Miriam and see herself in forty years? A sobering thought. It made her question her future as a mother. Neither Miriam nor her mother were soft, nurturing women, and Sarah feared she'd inherited this questionable personality.

In junior high, she and Heather began babysitting every weekend, Sarah for the measly fifty cents an hour and Heather because she genuinely liked kids, even babies who cried nonstop and made disgusting messes in their diapers. By the time grade eight rolled around, Heather had a regular Friday night gig for a family with four noisy kids, and visions of herself as a wife and mother, while Sarah eschewed babysitting and began delivering the *Tribune*.

"How old was Mom when her dad died?" she asked Miriam now. "She never talked about him. It was as if he never existed."

Miriam rose and began clearing their plates. "I think it was for the best, your mother not telling you—"

"Telling me what?"

Miriam put both plates in the sink, squirted dish soap and ran the water. She turned and faced Sarah. "Things that would bring back enormous pain."

"I don't understand. Is this about my grandfather?"

Miriam's eyes hardened like black ice, casting a chill in the apartment. "You should go now."

"I'll help you clean up."

"I don't need your help. Just leave." She waved her hand dismissively.

"But we didn't have the banana bread . . ."

"Take it home. For your father."

"I made it for you." Sarah's shoulders dropped. She'd ruined everything by mentioning her grandfather.

"That's more than I eat in a month."

"Share it with your friends. I'll be back next week to get my pans."

"Take them now."

Sarah wiped beads of sweat above her lips with the back of her hand and collected the pans and uneaten banana bread, her jumpy nerves causing a cramp in her side.

"Guess I'll go," she said, opening the door, hoping Miriam would relent and tell her to stay.

"Call first next time," her grandmother said tersely, making it clear she'd had enough of Sarah for one day. "I'm not big on surprises."

Sarah scurried to the coffee table, left the banana bread on a *TV Guide* and headed for the door. She moved slowly down the stairs, her imagination running wild with reasons her grandfather was such a contentious subject. Maybe Miriam and her mother wrote him off because he was a criminal. Or he'd died of a painful disease that made it too hard for them to think about him. Or he'd abandoned his wife and child, and they'd erased his existence from their lives forever.

Outside, the frosty air steadied her racing mind. Sarah wanted the truth. She needed the truth, even if it was horrific. The unknown was beginning to nag at her like an itch she couldn't reach to scratch.

7

RIGA, APRIL 1941

On a crisp April morning that smelled like fresh grass, three imposing men appeared at Miriam's door. The shortest of the three introduced the group as representatives of the Soviet government, with orders to confiscate the Talan property and car, along with their household assets.

Miriam tightened her shaky grip on the doorknob. She'd been dreading this moment since the announcement, over a radio broadcast the previous day, that housing was going to be nationalized, but she had never imagined it would happen so quickly.

"My husband is working and my baby is asleep," Miriam managed. "Please, could you come back later, when my husband is home?" She sidled over to the telephone to call Max.

The man yanked her hand away from the telephone and said, in a voice with claws: "Either you follow orders now, or you will end up on a train to Siberia."

Miriam's blood went cold at his touch. She stepped aside.

"Here are the things you may keep." He handed her a piece of paper with a typewritten list:

1. One bed and two sheets
2. Two plates and spoons
3. Three pairs of shoes
4. Two coats
5. Two hats
6. Only those books associated with work
7. Your wedding ring

"There must be a mistake," Miriam said after a cursory glance at the list. "We are a family of four. We need at least two beds and a crib, and four plates, and we must have winter coats for our children." She held the list out to the group.

The tallest man, with a mustache like Stalin's, shoved the list back to Miriam. "There is no mistake."

"But—the books. Can't we take a few of our children's favorites?"

He moved closer. She could smell the briny scent of herring on his breath. "Do your children use their books for work?" he asked.

"Of course not."

"Books stay with the house."

She grew dizzy and faint. She watched the men take inventory of her family's cherished furniture, vases, paintings, books, porcelain, linens and draperies with a vile callousness. She felt small and powerless as they made their way through the first floor, her world shrinking one object at a time.

When two of the men moved to the second level, she set Monya down on the oriental carpet in the sitting room with a few wooden blocks. The man with the Stalin mustache stood guard in the corner of the room, eyes glued to her as if he was afraid she was going to steal her own property.

She sank onto her velvet divan and lit a cigarette, her twelfth or maybe thirteenth of the day. The late morning sun cast beams of light like bars on the sitting room's ivy-green walls. She listened to the menacing thump of feet above her and looked at Monya, creating a tower of blocks, blissfully unaware his secure world was about to fall apart.

Thank goodness he won't remember any of this, she thought. *Thank goodness he won't remember the day we lost everything.*

THE NEXT AFTERNOON, the Talan family moved to a flat assigned by the Soviet government, a constantly damp two-bedroom place that stank of rotten milk and cabbage and looked as if it hadn't been cleaned in decades. The building was on Avotu iela, a busy road north of the train station, lined with rundown shops and apartment buildings. Though it was just a fifteen-minute cab ride from their Mežaparks house, it felt like another world.

Miriam perfunctorily scrubbed the grimy kitchen and bathroom and told herself this was temporary. She told herself the Soviets were just living in her house for a short time, like tenants, and that she would be back in her own kitchen soon. Then she felt ill, picturing drunken soldiers lounging on her divan, eating at her dining table, their wives wearing her fur coats, their children reading her children's books.

Her parents received orders to give up their flat and belongings one week later. They moved into a dilapidated five-story building across the street from Miriam's family. When she went over to see her parents' "new" flat, Miriam wanted to weep at the sight of her formidable mother standing there, arms loose by her sides, with an unnatural vulnerability.

Miriam helped her father assemble the bed, then she washed the floor and cleaned mouse droppings from the kitchen cupboards. She needed to stay busy to keep her mind from thinking about where they could be if they'd left the country, and to keep from worrying about what was to come.

On her way back to her apartment, Miriam felt as if her world had been chipped down by the Soviets with each consecutive loss and restriction. Their empty bank account. Losing her jewelry. The Soviet takeover of Max's dental practice. Their home. There was nothing left to take. She'd been reduced to a cube of ice, small enough to drop into a glass of vodka, where she would melt and disappear.

8

CHICAGO, DECEMBER 1975

H ER MOTHER ILANA'S ENGLISH YARDLEY PERFUME LIN-
gered in the air like mist, sending a chill down Sarah's neck.
She turned the doorknob. It was the first time she'd entered
her parents' room since her mother's death. Her knees buckled.
Without her mother, the floors tipped sideways, falling out from
under her feet.

Sarah dropped onto her parents' bed, plucked the round blue
tin of Nivea cream from her mother's nightstand and unscrewed
the lid, releasing the familiar soapy rose aroma. Her mother had
diligently applied Nivea all over her face and neck, "to keep my
skin looking young," she'd explained when Sarah was little and
observed her mother's nightly routine with awe. Sarah dipped her
fingers into the white cream and rubbed a generous amount on her
cheek. She drew her knees to her chest and longed to continue the
last conversation she'd had with her mother, after Sunday dinner
two weeks earlier.

"I broke up with Henry," Sarah had announced casually, as she
dried the salad bowl.

Her mother, up to her elbows in soap suds, puffed out her chest. "What was it this time?"

We were getting too serious, she wanted to say. "He likes baseball. I like theater," she said.

"Your father reads sports magazines, I read *Time*. He likes steak, I like chicken. It is no problem for us."

Sarah sucked in her cheeks, regretting the way she'd started this conversation. She should have begun with something innocuous, like the price of milk, rather than open herself up to her mother's sharp tongue.

"Last time—I forget the name, there are so many," Ilana went on, stacking dishes on the rack to be dried, "—you said he made too many jokes, like Johnny Carson."

"True."

"You don't like Johnny Carson?"

"I do. I just don't want to date him."

"Johnny Carson?"

"No, Brad. The one before Henry." Sarah vigorously dried a plate, running the towel in circles over the floral pattern as if trying to erase it. "And there were only a couple before them."

"If you are looking for a man who likes all the same things, you will never get married, like that television woman you admire so much, the skinny one with three names, Mary something something."

"It's Mary Tyler Moore, and in real life she is married."

"Then why doesn't she have a husband in her television show?"

"Because she doesn't need one. Mary has a terrific career, a cute apartment, lots of friends, and she can do whatever she wants." Sarah paused. "She has a mind of her own."

"You think I lost my mind when I married your father?"

Sarah's lips twisted into a smile at her mother's unfortunate choice of words, an endearing consequence of speaking in a language that was not her native tongue. "That's not what I meant. Don't put words—"

"I just wish you had a nice man to settle down with, like Heather."

Sarah scrunched the dishtowel with both hands. Her parents got married a few months after her father graduated from college and her mother graduated from high school. A year later, Sarah was born, before her mother even finished her nurse's training, before they even had a decent income. It was as if they were afraid time was running out.

"I don't want to rush into anything," Sarah said, more decisively than she felt. She wanted the security of an intentional future (which she'd get with Henry), but she also craved the excitement of the unknown.

"Loneliness breaks the spirit," her mother mumbled as she washed a fork.

"I like the quiet, after talking to people all day at work. And I'm happy for Heather, but don't know if marriage is right for me."

"Never get married?" her mother said, appalled.

"I didn't say never. I said I'm not sure. I just want to focus on my career right now."

"You think you are so smart, but you are not so smart." Her mother regarded her with an owlish sharpness. "You don't know what it means to be alive."

"What?"

Her mother ran her hands through the soapy water and opened the drain. The water gurgled down the drain, leaving a foamy residue in the sink. She dried her hands, caught Sarah's eye and held it for a second before letting go. The noise in the kitchen receded to clock-ticking silence.

Sarah looked expectantly at her mother.

"I'll put the kettle on for tea," her mother said.

"I don't feel like tea, Mom."

She filled the kettle with water. "It's good for the digestion."

Sarah tilted her head and frowned.

"The tea will be ready in just a couple of minutes." Her mother set the kettle on the coiled electric burner and turned it on high.

"I told you, I don't want any tea." Sarah paused to collect her thoughts. "I want you to talk to me."

"What do you think I'm doing?" her mother said, indignant.

"Not like this."

"I don't understand."

"Neither do I. You say I don't know what it means to be alive, then make tea, as if we were discussing a new recipe."

Her mother looked at her. "Sometimes words are not enough."

The kettle made a hissing sound. Tendrils of steam began to gush from the spout. Her mother stood ramrod straight, a wall that nobody could scale, and poured boiling water into a teapot.

Now, in her mother's bedroom, her cryptic words, *You don't know what it means to be alive*, rang uncomfortably in Sarah's head. Wind drummed against the window, joggling Sarah's thoughts to the present. She picked up a nail polish called Aubergine Allure and smiled, recalling her mother sitting at the kitchen table painting her nails in this purple hue. Vibrant nail polish, as well as bright lipstick and eyeshadow, were some of the more obvious differences between Sarah and her mother; Sarah preferred muted shades, and rarely applied makeup on weekends, whereas her mother never forgot lipstick and mascara, even for a quick trip to the 7-Eleven or the grocery store.

Sarah opened the top drawer of the dresser. Bras and panties with a faint trace of lavender from an old sachet. The second drawer contained stockings and slips. Wool cardigans and shawls were folded neatly in the third drawer. She tried the bottom drawer, but it didn't budge. She sat on the floor, pulled harder and jiggled the drawer, then planted her feet against the bottom of the dresser and heaved. The drawer flew open. She fell onto her backside and the drawer landed with a thump on the floor.

She scrunched her forehead, bewildered at the dozen or so yellowed sepia photos of strangers dressed in old-fashioned clothes, on stiff cardboard. Words she couldn't decipher were written at the bottom. Latvian? Jewish? She recognized some of the letters, a backward *N*, an upside-down *M*, a backward *R*, while the rest were a mystery.

These had to be her mother's relatives, *her* relatives. Here was a photograph of an older couple and here, one of a family with two children, a girl and a baby, and more showing babies and young mothers. They couldn't be her mother's immediate family; she was an only child and the photo showed two children. Plus, the little girl's plump cheeks and impish eyes looked nothing like her stern mother. Yet the mother in the photo bore a striking resemblance to Miriam, with her thin lips, high brow and demure smile. Did Miriam have a sister?

There was a shoebox beside the loose photos. Sarah sank down onto the olive-green shag carpet and took off the Kinney Shoes lid. Two crinkly envelopes addressed in similar characters to those on the photos. There was a black imprint of a partial circle, with a blotchy star, on the corner of both stamps. One showed the year 1959 and the number 25, and had a teal background overlaid with the coffee-colored image of a female scuba diver. No date appeared on the second stamp, only the number 40, and it was printed in the same teal shade with a light-brown image of a man and woman.

A crisp one-page letter was in each envelope, frustratingly

indecipherable. Sarah set them aside for Miriam to translate when she caught her grandmother in a rare good mood, and reviewed the black-and-white photos she found beneath the letters. One that jumped out at Sarah showed her mother and grandmother standing in front of the Statue of Liberty. It had no date on the back. Odd—her mother had never mentioned a trip to New York City. She pinched the edge of the photo with her fingers. The shot must have been taken right after they'd arrived in America.

She held the photo closer and studied the image. They were both wearing bulky winter coats and sulky expressions, a not-so-subtle hint of their future estrangement. But the girl's eyes were almost too large for her narrow face, and the braid didn't fit the memory of her mother. She was about thirteen or fourteen, but that was all Sarah could discern. There were more questions in the photograph than answers.

She wiped her teary eyes with her sleeve and returned the photo of her mother and grandmother to the shoebox. She rummaged through more photos and had goose bumps when she came to a photo of her grandmother in a chair, holding Sarah as a baby. Miriam appeared to be captivated by her granddaughter. A heavy gloom settled over Sarah, thinking about what could have been if her mother hadn't expunged her past, and her relationship with her own mother.

Sarah speculated as to her mother's furtive life. Maybe she didn't want to leave the Soviet Union. No—who wouldn't want to leave such a dismal country? She found another photo, this one of her mother dressed for a high school graduation ceremony. Her smile didn't reach her eyes in any of the photographs. In each one she seemed guarded and suspicious in a way Sarah couldn't understand.

She stuffed the photos back into the shoebox, held it to her chest as if it were full of silver and carried it past her father, asleep in his La-Z-Boy, an empty bottle of Scotch and a paint roller in a tray of wet paint on the coffee table beside him. He'd painted one wall of the living room a gaudy orange shade. The reek of paint saturated the air.

She set the box of old pictures on the kitchen table, where her mother used to play solitaire, opened the harvest-gold freezer and groaned at the sight of at least twenty Swanson TV dinners. Her mother habitually kept a stash of frozen dinners, the same way she stockpiled cereal, in case she was stuck in her house for weeks or the grocery store ran out of food. For years, Sarah complained to her mother about the glut of frozen dinners, even suggested Sara Lee cakes would be preferable, but her mother either didn't care or didn't listen, because she continued to stockpile unappetizing Salisbury steak dinners until the day she died.

When she heard a crash in the living room, she rushed to see if her father was all right. He was still in his chair, but the coffee table lay on the gold shag carpet, along with the unbroken Scotch bottle, wet roller and tray, with paint seeping onto the floor.

"What happened?"

"No idea." He glanced at the carpet. "Must have knocked the table over."

"You should go to bed." She picked up the roller and tray, darted into the kitchen and returned with a dishtowel, which she used to blot the paint.

He peered at his watch. "Nine fifteen. Too early to fall asleep."

"You were just passed out. I bet you'll be asleep in seconds."

He gripped the arms of the chair and looked up at his daughter. "I'm dreading the idea of going back to work, living without your mother."

His quavering voice made her eyes blur with tears. Sarah clutched the dishtowel with shaky hands. "Me too. I'm not ready."

"Nobody's ever ready." Her father clambered to his feet and went into the kitchen.

Sarah was right behind him.

"My mother died when I was twenty-nine," her father said. "She was sixty-five and lived a good long life, and I still didn't want to say goodbye." He opened the refrigerator, took out a jug of milk and filled a tall glass almost to the brim.

"I remember," Sarah said gently. "Granny wore glasses on a chain around her neck and smelled like caramel."

"Good memory. She had a thing for caramels, always had a bunch in her purse, and whenever she visited, you'd hold your hand out for one." He drank his milk in one long gulp.

"Oh, that's awful. I was so greedy."

"You were a perfectly normal child." He chuckled and set his empty glass on the counter.

"You're biased."

"A little." He gave her a half smile and took a photo from the Kinney Shoes box. "Where'd you find these?"

"Mom's dresser. Have you seen them before?"

He held the photo at arm's length and squinted. "Once. A long time ago. Mom got upset when she caught me looking at them and put them away."

"Why did she keep old photos if she didn't want to talk about them?"

He raised his eyes. "The past seemed to trigger bad memories. I learned, early on, to focus on the present and future when it came to your mother, never the past."

"I wish I knew why," Sarah mused. She poured herself a glass of water, guzzled it and poured another glassful. She ran her finger around the rim. "I went to Grandma's yesterday."

He started. "How was it?"

"Good. Until I asked about my grandfather. Then she practically kicked me out." She took a sip of water and put the glass on the kitchen table.

Her father heaved a sigh. "I'm sorry. Maybe you should wait awhile before seeing her again."

"I can take it, Dad. My boss is a pompous ass who lashes out at me when he's having a bad day. I think I can handle Grandma."

"He is? Whenever I ask about work, you say it's fine."

"What's the point? You can't fix it. I didn't want to worry you and Mom. You know what she's like." Sarah closed her eyes and drew in a long breath. "What she was like."

His eyes grew misty. He turned and made his way to his bedroom down the hall.

Sarah nabbed a bag of Oreos from the pantry and carried the box of photos to her room, across from her father's. She closed her door, took an Oreo apart and licked the icing, then retrieved one of the photos of her mother, from her high school graduation. She propped it up against the lamp on her bedside table and devoured three more cookies, a secret indulgence since childhood; if she had her druthers, she'd take Oreos over the most extravagant dessert in the fanciest of restaurants.

She brushed her teeth and changed into her flannel nightgown, got into bed and turned off the light. She tossed and turned, riddled with curiosity. Prying into her mother's life was like a crutch, enabling Sarah to keep thinking about her in the present tense. She wasn't ready to let go of the mysterious woman whose blood she shared yet whom she barely knew.

9

RIGA, JUNE 1941

Y OU CAN'T FORCE ME."

Ilana's petulant voice rose from the kitchen where Gutte was giving her porridge before school.

"It's cool this morning," Gutte told Ilana in her staunch, commanding voice. "Put your coat on."

"I'm not going."

"Yes, you are."

Miriam, in the children's bedroom changing Monya's diaper, rolled her eyes at Ilana's cheekiness. In their sprawling house, her daughter's defiance hadn't been as easy to hear, but in their cramped apartment, Ilana's voice pealed through the air like the telephone's ring.

"I'm going to ask Mama," Ilana said to Gutte.

Miriam's shoulders went stiff with annoyance at the thought of arguing with Ilana so early in the morning. Just one day, she begged Ilana silently. Let me have one day to myself, to enjoy coffee with Helena and forget about curfews and money and my disobedient daughter.

"You are going to do no such thing," Gutte shot back. "Take your satchel and go, or you'll be late."

Thank God for Gutte, with her severe, no-nonsense expression that could stop you like a wall. This was the reason Miriam had hired her seven years earlier—Gutte's need for orderliness and her consistent discipline, qualities Miriam wanted to encourage within her household and, more importantly, in her willful daughter.

Ilana stomped to the door, opened it and slammed it shut. She was a force, like her grandmother. This gave Miriam pause. Her mother had a sharp tongue and used it often, finding fault with everything and everyone. It was difficult to be near her mother without feeling as if she were going to suffocate.

Monya cooed and wiggled his pudgy legs after Miriam wiped his bottom. She scooped him up and held him close. With his soft, sweet skin that smelled of innocence, he was a light in the Soviet bleakness.

HELENA'S FLAT WAS on the third floor of a yellow-and-white art nouveau building on Elizabete iela, with lions' heads carved into the facade and all sorts of flowery embellishments that reminded Miriam of a fancy wedding cake. The inside was nothing like the ornate exterior. It was like opening a beautifully wrapped present and finding a grimy plate, Miriam thought. She breathed in the stink of dirty feet and onions, and spotted fingerprints on the walls, as well as a large photo of Stalin. Radio voices swirled from above, along with heavy footfalls and a child's plaintive cry.

Before the Soviet occupation, these were spacious flats that belonged to wealthy, single families, like Helena's, who'd owned the entire second level. Now, the floors had been crudely severed into tiny, overcrowded apartments filled with multiple families. Helena's family of six were jammed in one room, and they shared a kitchen and bathroom with three other families.

Miriam climbed the circular staircase and knocked on Helena's door.

"Who's there?" the housekeeper asked without opening the door, in a skittish tone that pinched Miriam's nerves.

"It's Miriam Talan. Helena is expecting me."

No response.

"Hello? Are you there?" Miriam called out.

"She's . . . They took them last night."

"Who are you talking about?"

"They're all gone," the housekeeper continued, her voice breaking. "The flat is a mess . . . So much has been taken, and the neighbors . . . say they were woken by a commotion in the middle of the night."

Miriam's knees swayed. "The children?"

"Gone."

The building went silent. Miriam felt as if her head was under water. Everything around her blurred into globs of wet colors and shapes. She walked home in a daze, pulled Monya, sound asleep, from his crib and held him tight, not even letting go when he wet his diaper and smelled liked a toilet and cried to be changed.

"Miriam, he needs a fresh diaper."

Gutte's voice skidded in and out of Miriam's ears like static on the radio.

"In a minute."

"He's soaking wet, Miriam. Give him to me before he gets a chill." Gutte took him from Miriam and laid him on a towel on Ilana's bed that served as a makeshift change table.

"He's mine."

"Of course he's yours. What happened? Were you caught in the thunderstorm?" Gutte unpinned Monya's cloth diaper, slid it out from under him with the ease of a mother with four children and wiped his bum with a wet towel. The joints of her fingers were puffy and age spots peppered her skin, though she couldn't have been more than forty years old.

"Don't take him away," Miriam said.

Gutte stopped, her hand on Monya's stomach to keep him still, and gave Miriam a long, searching look. "What happened at lunch? Is Helena sick?"

They're all gone.

"She's fine," Miriam answered, avoiding Gutte's probing eyes. Miriam couldn't bring herself to confide in Gutte. Just as she'd concealed her twilight delivery, she buried Helena's deportation in the bowels of her soul, where it chafed her nerves and ravaged her conscience. And shaped her future.

10

CHICAGO, DECEMBER 1975

"ELEPHONE, FOR YOU," HER FATHER CALLED OUT FROM the kitchen on Christmas Eve. "Henry."

Sarah jumped. A slight smile brushed against her lips. For the first time since her mother died, she felt something other than grief. She picked up the telephone.

"Sarah?" Henry's warm voice slid into her ear. "Merry Christmas."

Her throat constricted. "You too. And Happy New Year."

Sarah listened to his rhythmic breathing at the other end of the line. She missed his steadiness, how he approached each day with a single-mindedness that fulfilled him, how he knew what he wanted and how to get it.

"How are you holding up?" he asked in a baritone voice with studied precision.

"Numb. It doesn't seem real yet. I keep hoping I'm going to wake up and find out this is just a bad dream."

"I can imagine. Your mom had such a big presence."

"Huge. The house feels so empty now, even when I'm here with my dad."

"If you need company, I can swing by," he said, his voice rising.

"I appreciate the offer—"

"No strings attached, just one friend helping another."

"Right."

"No, really, I mean it," he said earnestly. "Unless you want strings."

"I told you—" she began.

"I know, I know. But I promise, I have no intention of getting in the way of your career."

"That's what Bob said to Heather, and she's already talking about kids, months before their wedding."

"You're not Heather and I'm not Bob."

"Obviously."

"I miss you," he said.

The emotion in his voice tugged at Sarah. She was afraid to open herself up to him. To anyone. Her future was a mystery she wasn't ready to crack. She pressed the phone against her ear until it hurt.

I miss you too, she wanted to say. "I should go," she said quickly. "Thanks for calling. Goodbye, Henry."

11

RIGA, JULY 1941

ONE YEAR AFTER THE SOVIETS CONQUERED LATVIA, German bombers circled Riga, their engines screeching at a volume that shook the floor. This is it, Miriam thought. Germany is going to defeat the Soviet Union and freedom will be restored. Max sat at the table, his ear to the radio, listening for news. Miriam stood bone-straight at the window. The curtains were drawn shut to obscure their apartment's existence from German pilots looking for targets. She peered through a narrow gap at the street below, where droves of people emerged from apartment buildings. They were carrying sleepy children and bags of what Miriam assumed were their belongings. So far, her parents' building had been left alone.

"To the railway station," a Soviet official shouted. "Quickly."

Miriam shuddered. The people on the street were being deported thousands of kilometers to Siberia, in overcrowded wooden train cars without enough food or water. Hundreds of Jews. Like Helena's family. *Like us.* At any moment, the Soviets could knock on their door and send them away. *Siberia.* At any moment, they could be struck by a German bomb, or brutally exiled. All of a sudden, she wondered if Gutte was all right. Gutte hadn't come in days. It wasn't safe to travel across the city. It was the longest she'd gone without seeing Gutte in seven years.

A cracking sound. From the building across the street. Another crack, followed by an explosion. The Soviets were setting buildings on fire all over the city in retaliation against the Germans, who'd boldly quashed their non-aggression pact with Stalin by attacking Soviet-controlled Latvia. Not only do we live daily under a government we can't trust, Miriam fumed, our governments can't even trust one another.

Flames burst through the windows on the other side of the street, smashing glass that plunged to the ground in shards. The gritty taste of smoke wafted through Miriam's closed windows.

"I'm scared, Mama."

Miriam jumped at her daughter's shrill voice. "You shouldn't be seeing this." She drew the curtains tight, eliminating the gap.

"What if our building catches on fire?" Ilana asked.

Miriam froze, struck by the image of Ilana surrounded by flames. *One second.* That's all it would take to destroy her family.

"Mama?" Ilana said. "Mama?"

"Stand back from the window," Miriam ordered Ilana, her voice sharp as a tack. She grabbed Ilana's arm and pulled her into the center of the sitting room.

"Ow, Mama, you're hurting me!"

Miriam saw her nails digging into her daughter's skin and let go. "It's dangerous near the window."

"Quiet," Max said. "I can't hear a thing with the two of you bickering."

Miriam and Ilana pinched their mouths shut. The only sound was static on the radio.

"Air raid," a man's voice crackled through the radio's speaker. "Go to your shelters at once."

Miriam's face leached of color. Her mouth seemed full of paste.

Ilana shrank into the wall. "What if a plane hits us?"

"It won't," Max replied.

"How do you know?"

"I don't. That's why we have to go to the shelter. Now." Max's voice radiated with urgency. "Ilana, fetch your brother. Miriam, fill a basket with food."

"My parents," Miriam said. "I need to get my parents."

"There's a shelter in their building."

Miriam looked at the curtained window, her breath a whip of panic. This would unhinge her mother.

Ilana wrapped herself around Max's waist. "I'm scared. It sounds like a plane is going to fly into the apartment."

Max squeezed her tight. "Go. Get Monya from your room," he said firmly.

Guilt spooled Miriam's bones like thread. They should have left the country when they had the chance. They should have abandoned their house to get Ilana and Monya to safety. She should have listened to Max. Instead, they all lived with a tiring uncertainty. And now, her children would be stuck like prisoners in a damp, murky shelter that stank of smoke from fires set by the retreating Soviets.

Miriam gathered bread, canned herring, peas, tomatoes and beans, and followed Ilana and Max, with Monya in his arms, down the narrow staircase to the basement. Thirteen strangers had already settled uncomfortably on hard wood benches, listening to gunfire blasts and the ominous rumble of stones and bricks as they crumbled. Max sat on the bench across from Miriam, with Ilana's head in his lap. Monya, curled up beside Miriam, drifted in and out of sleep with an alarming lethargy.

The radio was their only link to the chaos outside, and time, without natural light, was measured in candles and canned food. After two cans of herring, three cans of beans, a can of tomatoes and seven candles, Miriam was woozy with exhaustion yet couldn't sleep, her lower back was cramped from being in the same position for so long, and she was at her wits' end with old Mr. Levenstein's snoring.

"RIGA HAS BEEN liberated by the Germans. Fellow citizens, hang Latvian flags and gather by the general post office for a celebration."

A fatigued cheer rose from the people huddled in the basement shelter as this announcement crackled over the radio. The year of terror under the Soviet regime was finally over.

"Well," Max said to Miriam over the din, "what do you think?"

"I want to go home," Miriam replied without hesitation.

"To our flat?" Ilana asked in a sleepy voice.

"No," Miriam retorted. "To our house in Mežaparks."

THE JULY SUN warmed Miriam's skin as she, Max and their children walked to the post office with her parents, gray and stooped after two nights in their shelter. Latvian flags hung limp from windows; there wasn't even a hint of a breeze. Women and children carried bouquets of daisies as they marched. There was a buoyancy Miriam hadn't seen in months, with people chatting and smiling as they strolled along the sidewalk, music pouring from open windows, laughter punctuating the stillness. The constant sense of fear that had presided over Riga had finally lifted.

In the city center, Miriam was dismayed to see one of the oldest and most beautiful buildings in Riga, the House of Blackheads, ruined. Only a few portions of the walls, built in the 1300s, remained. The town hall lay in heaps of rocks and stones. Ashes floated through the air, so thick Miriam could taste them. Her head pounded with the certainty they'd never go back to the way they had been. Their old life had disintegrated like these buildings. The city would rebuild, and life would be better under the cultured Germans, but unless Latvia became independent, it would never be as good as it was before the Soviets.

Miriam hugged Monya to her chest with a ferocity that made him squirm.

A smile spread across Max's face, revealing the gap between his front teeth. "It's Simon." He waved his hand.

Miriam followed his gaze and saw Simon Dubnow, an author and Max's good friend, at the edge of the square. Before the Soviet occupation, they'd often met for coffee and long, heated discussions about history and politics.

Simon, with white hair and whiskers and round, wire-rimmed spectacles, returned Max's wave and approached, hands in his waistcoat pockets, his watch fob dangling from a buttonhole. His nut-brown suit was creased and his tie a little askew, but otherwise he was impeccably dressed.

The two men shook hands vigorously.

"Miriam." Simon nodded cordially at her.

Miriam was flattered and surprised Simon remembered her name; they'd only met a couple of times.

Max pointed out Miriam's parents and Ilana, walking ahead, and suggested Simon join them on the walk to the post office.

"Lead the way." Simon fell in beside Miriam. He took Monya's chubby hand and shook it gently. "And what is your name?"

Monya yanked his hand back and plunged his face into Miriam's chest.

"Monya," Miriam said, rueful. "He is not himself, after the shelter."

Simon's brow creased. "It is atrocious, what children have seen this year."

Automobiles piled with ecstatic Latvians cruised down Kungu iela, past throngs of cheering people.

"Life is bound to improve with the Germans," Max said once the noise receded.

"I don't know," Simon said. "I have heard disturbing rumors."

Miriam's stomach knotted up.

"What kind of rumors?" Max asked.

Simon looked at him. "My daughter wrote to me about the Germans attacking Jews in Poland. She and her children fled to Lithuania."

Motorcycles and trucks carrying German soldiers rumbled past them.

"Jews have never been safe in Poland," Max said.

"That is what I wrote to my daughter," Simon replied. "Now she's planning to go to America."

Miriam's ears perked up. America was so far away, so unfamiliar. Simon's daughter was overreacting, she hoped.

They walked in silence behind Miriam's parents and Ilana until they reached the post office, bustling with a jubilant crowd. Latvian girls in pretty dresses plied German soldiers with bunches of daisies. Women in smocked dresses, with red-and-white kerchiefs on their heads, offered trays with wheels of cheese, logs of bologna, pickled gherkins and smoked herring to the German soldiers. Public loudspeakers began playing "God Bless Latvia," the national anthem, a piece Miriam hadn't heard in a year.

Miriam's stomach somersaulted with apprehension as a few

soldiers from the Wehrmacht, the armed forces of Nazi Germany, appeared on the balcony of the opera house, across from the post office, waving to people on the street below. Max squeezed Miriam's hand and took Monya from her arms. He hoisted Monya onto his shoulders and turned in a circle to take in the gaiety. Ilana jumped up and down. Miriam grew dizzy and hot in the midst of such a large, boisterous crowd. She wanted to be happy, like everyone around her, but something got in the way—something she felt but couldn't see, a bitterness, like the taste of lemon.

"I'd pick you up so you could see better," Miriam's father told Ilana, "but you're too big now."

"It's all right, Zeyde." She beamed up at him. "I can feel the excitement."

Miriam's mother was unusually docile; she hadn't said a word the entire walk to the opera house, and the color had leached from her face. Miriam took her arm and pulled her through the crowd until they reached a clearing at the canal, the former moat that had encircled the city's walls during Riga's medieval days. As soon as they were at the canal's edge, beneath the shade of a leafy chestnut tree, her mother sank onto the grass.

"I don't feel well," she said. Wisps of her hair rose with static.

"Neither do I." Miriam loosened the collar of her blouse to cool her neck, keeping her eyes on the joyous celebration. Before long she noticed others stepping back, like them, as if they weren't sure what to make of the gleeful welcome for the Germans.

"We will join your father and Max in a few minutes." Miriam's mother extended her legs and crossed her feet. She looked awkward, without a chair's formality. "Once I have a few minutes' rest."

"There is no rush. These celebrations will be going on for some time." Miriam sat upright, to quell the blood rushing to her head.

Her mother hesitated. "Yes, I believe they will . . ."

"Maybe we will be allowed to move back to our houses, with the Soviets gone."

"Perhaps."

"And Jewish schools will reopen."

Her mother's shrewd eyes skimmed the canal, pointedly avoiding Miriam's. Trees hugged the water's edge; their silhouettes, along with the cottony clouds above, were reflected on the flat, unmoving surface.

"This reminds me of the day the Soviets arrived," Miriam said, remembering the misplaced excitement by the train station, on their way to the hospital.

Her mother looked down at the grass. "That's what I'm afraid of."

12

CHICAGO, DECEMBER 1975

TOLD YOU TO CALL FIRST."

Sarah propped her forehead against the closed door and listened to her grandmother's miffed voice rise above the radio's hum. "I called. You kept putting me off."

"Then why are you here?"

"I was worried about you, when you didn't come for Christmas dinner. It's been three weeks since I've seen you."

"I don't know why you invited me."

"We're family. I wanted us to be together."

A lighter clicked on the other side of the door.

"I'm sure your father was happy I didn't come."

"That's not true. He wanted you there. You and my mom were the ones with issues, not you and him."

"Well, I have a sensitive stomach. I didn't want you to go to any trouble."

Sarah recalled her grandmother's hearty appetite for meat loaf and stifled a laugh. A middle-aged couple with matching navy-blue scarves wrapped around their faces emerged on the staircase. They nodded in Sarah's direction and continued.

"Grandma, we can't talk through this door forever. Your neighbors can hear us."

The chain rattled. The door creaked open. Her grandmother's yellow-stained fingers curled around the edge of the door.

"Look." Sarah held up a package wrapped in red-and-white paper with a red bow in the center. "I brought you a gift."

"I don't have anything for you. I don't celebrate Christmas."

"I don't want anything. I just want to talk to you."

The door opened wide. A turquoise-and-black quilted robe hung loosely from Miriam's shoulders, though it was four o'clock in the afternoon. The day after Christmas. Her eyes were watery and droopy and her hair looked as though it hadn't been brushed in days. Sarah stepped inside and was taken aback by the smoky haze and tepid air. The ashtray on the kitchen counter overflowed with cigarette butts. Sarah hung her coat and purse on the hook by the door and removed her boots.

"How about tea?" Sarah asked, putting on a cheery voice to hide her concern with the state of the apartment and her grandmother's dishevelled appearance.

Miriam nodded and headed to the kitchen. Her robe brushed against the floor. She filled the kettle and set it on the burner. Sarah reached for the teapot, but her grandmother got to it first. She shook it. Cold tea swished inside. Miriam moved out of the kitchen into her living room, where she watered one plant, then another, with leftover tea.

"I never considered watering plants with tea," said Sarah. "That must be why yours are so healthy."

Her grandmother emptied the pot onto a purple-and-green

plant whose leaves dangled wildly from a macramé hanger. "Your mother liked flowers," she said.

"She did. But she only planted them outside. Roses mostly. We never had any inside."

Her grandmother smacked her lips together. She carried the pot back into the kitchen. The water in the kettle boiled. "Indoor plants bring life to cold, dreary days. It is always spring in a house with greenery."

"I see that. I'm going to buy a couple of plants for my apartment." Miriam went about preparing their tea.

"Aren't you going to put in new tea bags?"

"There are still many cups left in these ones." Miriam tapped the teapot with her finger.

Sarah wondered if she was running out of money. Tea bags were not expensive; there was no reason to conserve them unless you were concerned about money. But then, her mother hoarded frozen dinners as if she was afraid of running out of food.

Sarah grabbed two teacups from the cupboard. A half-finished game of solitaire was on the table. "Mom played a lot of solitaire."

"Who do you think taught her?" Miriam followed with the teapot and a box of oatmeal cookies. "I don't bake anymore." She offered the box to Sarah.

"It's all right. I love any cookies." She took one and set the box and her gift on the table. She bit down. The cookie was hard and stale. She gnawed her way through it to be polite.

"Another?" her grandmother asked.

"Oh, no, I couldn't." Sarah smiled. "Have to watch my weight or I won't fit into my clothes."

"I don't understand young people's obsession with being skinny." Miriam scowled and poured tea in both cups. "A little weight is good. It means you're healthy."

"That's what Mom used to say." Sarah pinched the extra pounds she'd put on her stomach. Since her mother died, almost two months ago, she'd been baking up a storm, sabotaging plans to lose weight. "You and Mom had a lot of the same opinions." She took a sip of tea. "I don't understand why you went so long without talking."

Miriam's brow creased into deep lines.

"Aren't you going to open the present I brought?"

Miriam set down her cup, pulled off the bow and unwrapped the paper, one side at a time, carefully peeling the Scotch tape to keep it from tearing.

"It was Mom's favorite scarf." Sarah's heart beat in her throat as she pictured her mother in the scarf, draped over her shoulders and tied just under her breasts.

Her grandmother's hands shook when she held two corners for a better look at the silk scarf that resembled a Monet painting, with its splash of lilies. "Thank you." She folded it in half and then in half again, and retrieved the second gift, a framed black-and-white picture.

"It's one of the photos I found, of you and Mom . . . I didn't see any pictures of her when I was here before, so I thought you might like to have it," Sarah said tentatively.

Miriam held the frame with both hands. Her face brightened as she gazed at the image of herself and her daughter, at Ilana's high school graduation.

"I remember the day as if it was yesterday," Miriam began in a halting voice. "Your mother didn't want to go. Insisted it would be hot, long and boring, and that she'd done nothing special, finishing high school. I told her it was important to mark special occasions." She paused. "It was the first good thing that happened in a long time. Her father would have been so proud."

"How old was Mom when he died?"

Miriam traced the contours in the photo with her index finger. "In the beginning, when you were born, I agreed it was the right thing to do. Now, I am not so sure."

"What?" Reflexively, Sarah's eyes followed her grandmother's to the photo that had provoked Miriam into the place she'd been avoiding: the past.

"Modify history. Erase what happened to protect you."

"Protect me from what?"

"Your mother made me promise never to say a word. She made your father promise too."

"But why? Why did she want both of you to lie to me? And why won't you tell me what happened to my grandfather?"

Miriam rose and carried the photo to the deep window ledge. She positioned it between two plants. "I think it looks nice here. Don't you?"

Sarah hunched her shoulders, told herself to be patient and joined her grandmother. "I like the way the sun comes over the frame, lighting the picture." Her eyes wandered to the myriad of plants crammed onto the ledge. Something shiny glinted between the leaves. Sarah leaned closer. A silver menorah stood against the window, practically hidden by the rambling plants. Cobalt-blue-and-white wax had melted in and around the candle holes. "A menorah?"

Her grandmother turned on her heel and went to the dining table, where she sat down and resumed her game of solitaire.

"Do you celebrate Hanukkah? Is that why you and Mom were mad at each other, because you're still Jewish and she's not?"

"I told you. I promised your mother." Miriam eyed the card in her hand and placed it, faceup, on the seven of spades.

"Promises don't matter anymore." Sarah watched her grandmother's face, a patchwork of shadows. "Were you angry Mom didn't marry someone Jewish and bring me up as a Jew?"

Miriam laid her cards on the table and lit a cigarette.

Sarah exhaled. She sat down in the chair next to her grandmother. "Do you know, since you told me Mom was born in Riga, I lie in bed at night and wonder what else she didn't tell me, and why."

Miriam looked at Sarah with a despondency that shook Sarah's core and said: "You can't change the past. All you can do is make the future what you want it to be."

"But you can't forget the past. I see it in your face, how you can't let go, and I saw it in my mother, how she was so tightly wound."

Miriam's eyes fluttered. She swept the cards into a messy pile. "I deserve the bad memories that darken my thoughts, but your mother, she deserved better. She had nothing to be sorry about." Miriam looked out her window with a brooding expression and smoked.

Sarah took in Miriam's shoulders, stooped from the weight of silence, and was afraid of the power of genetics, of becoming like her mother and grandmother, closed off and overwhelmed by burdens she could feel yet couldn't articulate.

Miriam rose from the table.

"Can I do anything for you before I go?" Sarah asked. "Make more tea? Get you something to eat?"

"No. I just need to lie down."

Moved by the sudden frailty in Miriam's voice, Sarah yearned to reach out and hug her, but refrained; if Miriam spurned her, the uneasiness between them would deepen. She put on her coat and boots and told her grandmother she'd be back in a few days.

Her grandmother lifted her shoulder in a half shrug. "With more questions?"

Sarah opened her bag and retrieved the two letters she'd found.

"I found these in a box of old photos." She held them out toward Miriam. "Could you translate them for me?"

Miriam blinked at the letters. Tiny droplets appeared in the corners of her eyes, pearls of sadness.

"Please. I need to know what happened."

Miriam reached for the letters with a shaky hand.

Sarah held her breath as she shrugged on her coat and pulled her boots over her feet. She opened the door and stepped into the corridor. She looked back at Miriam to say goodbye.

"What if you don't like what you find?" Miriam asked bluntly, before closing and locking the door.

13

RIGA, JULY 4, 1941

THE HOT JULY AIR TASTED GRITTY AND DAMP AS MIRIAM and Ilana walked down the stairs from their flat on a Friday afternoon, one week after the Germans defeated the Soviets. Gutte had neatened Ilana's self-cut hair into a chin-length bob, which, Miriam had to admit, accentuated her daughter's high cheekbones and made her eyes look bigger and greener. Miriam's hand flew up to her braided bun, irksomely heavy and warm. She wondered how she'd look with shorter hair. Long hair was a bother, really, all the time it took to care for it and the uncomfortable sensation of having a fur on your head in the summer. Short hair would be much more sensible, but it was too drastic a change right now, when nothing in her world was assured.

The sunflowers were all gone from the front of their apartment building, crushed and torn at the roots from the upheaval of the German occupancy. Miriam had a sinking feeling, seeing the bare, craggy soil, that more strife lay ahead.

Ilana skipped beside her mother and hummed with an energy Miriam coveted. A baby's cries spilled through an open window.

Daisies, roses and lilies flourished in window boxes overhead. Misleading signs of ordinary life. Max was in their flat, nursing a strained back after clearing away debris from collapsed buildings. In just over a year, he'd gone from being a successful dentist to a barely paid Soviet dentist to an unpaid wreckage remover.

At the shop, it was difficult to see through the window, opaque with dust. Inside, Miriam was disconcerted by the almost empty shelves, with just a few stacks of tinned food, shrunken old potatoes, dried-out carrots and moldy strawberries. She asked the woman behind the counter for a can of sweetened condensed milk and two cans of herring.

"Herring?" Ilana groaned.

"It's for your father."

She gave Miriam a relieved smile and produced a round tin of Nivea cream. "Can I get it, please, Mama?"

"What do you want with face cream?"

"Lyolya says it gives you a young complexion," Ilana said in a chirpy imitation of a radio advertisement.

The woman behind the counter chuckled.

"For goodness' sake, Ilana. You're far too young to worry about your complexion." Miriam plucked the Nivea from her hand, put it back on the modest pile beside the cash register and paid for her purchases.

Ilana sulked all the way to the bakery on Stabu iela, where the intoxicating smell of fresh bread hung in the warm air. Miriam's mouth watered at the sight of buns and cakes in the window, delicacies Gutte used to bake regularly, before the shortages of flour, butter, sugar and eggs that arrived with the Soviets and remained with the Germans.

"I'm hungry, Mama," Ilana moaned.

"I only have enough money for one loaf of challah for Shabbat."

"You said things would get better when the Germans came."

"That's what your father said, not me."

"What do you think?" She spoke in the solemn voice of a woman. Ilana's childhood had vanished when the Soviets occupied Latvia.

Miriam was trying to come up with an answer that would satisfy Ilana when a man's friendly voice greeted them.

"Shalom." Mr. Goldberg, beside a basket of apricot turnovers, peered at them through oversized spectacles. He had a kind, grandfatherly face, with cheeks that went round when he smiled.

"Shalom," Miriam replied.

Ilana feasted her eyes on the turnovers. Miriam counted her kopecks. If she didn't eat any bread for two suppers, the loaf would last longer and she could afford one turnover.

"I'll take a challah loaf and one turnover," she told Mr. Goldberg.

Ilana's eyes sparkled. "For me?"

"For you."

She skipped to the basket of turnovers and pointed at the biggest one. Mr. Goldberg picked it up with tongs and gave it to Ilana. She bit into the flaky pastry and heaved a joyful sigh. Miriam's mouth curved up, seeing how food lifted Ilana's spirits. Before the Germans, before the Soviets, they'd enjoyed pastry every week, on Shabbat. Now they were thankful for two loaves of bread a week.

Mr. Goldberg rang Miriam's purchases up on the cash register. Miriam was counting out coins when a terrified shriek erupted from outside. Miriam dropped her coins on the floor. Mr. Goldberg rushed to the window and grasped the top of his balding head. "My God!"

"What is it?" Miriam dashed to his side and was hit by a cold rush of fear.

Ilana hovered by Miriam's side, clutching her elbow.

A stocky Latvian man with a green armband around his sleeve was dragging an old Jewish man down the street.

"*Helfn!* Help!" The Jewish man kicked and shouted in Yiddish.

At the corner, another Latvian with a green armband whacked a Jewish man's head with a rubber truncheon until he was semiconscious, and pulled him along the street behind three other Latvians, all with green armbands, hauling Jewish men like chickens. Goose bumps rose on the back of Miriam's neck. It was a horrifying procession of savagery, led by Latvians with unusual armbands.

Latvians?

German soldiers were there too, with brawny shepherd dogs that barked and snarled at people rushing from the scene.

"*Mishegoss*, craziness," Mr. Goldberg cried.

A deep rumbling noise coiled in the pit of Miriam's stomach. A black truck sped past, rattling the shop window. Latvian soldiers were perched in the front seat like sentinels. Miriam squinted for a better view. Her stomach tightened when she saw green armbands, a makeshift uniform of hatred. It came back to her with a thud: the anti-Jewish groups that had ignited such extreme bigotry, they'd been banned by Ulmanis. The Germans' arrival had unleashed the prejudice that had been brewing within former members for years.

"Mama," Ilana whimpered.

Miriam clasped her wrist.

Mr. Goldberg rushed to his cash register and fumbled for his keys. "Go home. Fast as you can." He slammed the drawer of the register.

Miriam pulled Ilana through the door. Mr. Goldberg locked his bakery and hustled down Stabu iela.

"Don't let go of me," Miriam ordered Ilana.

Down the street, an officer hauled a Jewish man out of the coffee shop and threw him to the ground. An old Hasidic Jew scuttled past Miriam and Ilana, head down, his shoes tapping the sidewalk. A group of girls, a little older than Ilana, hurried by, faces stiff with fright. Miriam felt Ilana's clammy hand and was daunted by her daughter's unwavering trust.

"We don't want any Jewish Bolsheviks here," a Latvian officer hollered at a crowd of people, before lunging at Jewish men on the sidewalk.

Jewish Bolsheviks?

Miriam stumbled at the offensive term. She'd never heard it before, but knew it stemmed from the Soviets' decision to change Latvian Jews into Russian Hebrews. The ignorant officer was accusing Jews of conspiring with the Soviets during the reckless deportations and murders under the Soviet occupation.

She moved sideways down Stabu iela, away from the officer, keeping Ilana close. "Stay quiet, like a shadow," Miriam hissed urgently. "Faster, faster." Earsplitting voices and loud car engines punctuated the air. Ilana pressed her shaking body against her mother's.

"No . . . please, stop . . ."

Miriam froze when she heard Mr. Goldberg's rattled voice.

"Mama, look." Ilana pointed at Mr. Goldberg, hanging like a fish between a pair of Latvian officers.

Miriam covered Ilana's mouth with her hand to keep her from screaming at the sight of Mr. Goldberg struggling in vain. Miriam felt like a coward, close enough to see the whites of Mr. Goldberg's eyes yet unable to help. Ilana crushed Miriam's hand in hers as they pushed forward, reminding Miriam of what she stood to lose if she wasn't careful.

Miriam's heart pounded with relief when the synagogue on Stabu iela came into view. Set back from the street and built like a fortress in brick, with narrow, arched windows, it would be the safest and nearest place to hide from the madness. Yet, as she and Ilana got closer, doubts began circling in Miriam's head. Services hadn't taken place in a year, not since the Soviet occupation. While she'd seen Rabbi Kilov coming out of the building a few times over the last couple of weeks, that didn't mean he was there now.

A glimpse of a mass of sleep-flattened curls that looked terribly familiar diverted her attention from the synagogue. Across the street—a whiskered chin she couldn't help but recognize between two Latvian men with green police armbands and pistols. Max? She blinked and thought, No . . . it can't be. My eyes are playing tricks on me. When she and Ilana left the flat, Max was immobile on the sofa, with cold compresses under his spine.

She craned her neck to get a better look and all the commotion around Miriam dissolved into a high-pitched buzz. *Max.* It really was Max. Her knees went weak. She watched, remote, as the policemen, Latvians, hauled her unconscious husband down Stabu iela. Everything around her stopped as her eyes converged on Max's face. His mouth gaped, his broad nose was swollen and bleeding, his eyes were shut. The officers held Max's underarms and heaved him in the direction of the synagogue. Their afternoon shadows stretched long and thin.

Ilana grabbed the folds of Miriam's linen skirt and looked up, eyes glossy with tears, her freckled chin trembling. Miriam pulled her close, swathing her face with her skirt.

"Why are those men hurting Papa?" Ilana cried.

"You can't see this," Miriam said, her voice faltering. She thrust Ilana's face into her hip.

Ilana squirmed and thrashed against Miriam's hands.

The officers hoisted Max into the air, a human trophy. Miriam was revolted by their callousness. She staggered across the street, toward Max and the synagogue, holding Ilana tight, narrowing the distance between them to half a meter. Both officers raised their sweaty palms in unison, blocking Miriam from getting closer.

Miriam halted and riveted her eyes, hot with tears, on Max.

"Stand back," one officer ordered.

"Papa . . ." Ilana stretched her arm out to touch Max. "Wake up, Papa!"

One of the officers kicked at Ilana, barely missing her knee.

Miriam yanked Ilana away from Max and the officers.

From the corner of her eye, she saw Jews being tossed into the synagogue like bags of flour. She curled her hands over Ilana's eyes. She retreated, her heart in her throat, and committed their faces to memory in case the law ever replaced anarchy. She spotted more Jews being shoved into the synagogue and pressed Ilana's face against her abdomen. Her daughter would never again skip with the innocence of the child she'd been when they set out that afternoon.

The officers heaved Max forward, his head listing side to side, and rammed him through the arched door in the middle of the synagogue, the door his family entered for Shabbat services. Miriam was stunned into numbness. She stared at the closed and locked door with a storm brewing in her gut and rising up into her throat. Monya's chubby face burst in her head. He'd been with Max and Gutte in their apartment. Was he safe? Miriam, still holding Ilana, stumbled backward across the street, onto the sidewalk, and kept going until they met the brick wall of an apartment building.

Cries rang out from across the street, where more people were being hauled toward the synagogue. Gunshots peppered the air. The long block swarmed with Latvian and German officers.

"What's going to happen to Papa?" Ilana managed through her tears.

Miriam shook her head and prayed Max was still unconscious.

Her heart thumped so hard she was afraid it would break her ribs. A Latvian officer nabbed a Jewish boy by the scruff of his black collar with one hand and hauled him around the synagogue, pointing at the ground. The officer flung the boy to his knees and set a can on the ground beside him. The boy got to his feet slowly.

Run, Miriam begged him silently. As fast as you can.

The boy stood with his shoulders wilting, resigned. He picked up the can and started pouring something out of it, moving around the building.

Miriam had an awful premonition of what was to come. She spotted a few Latvian officers laughing as they watched the boy. Revulsion stiffened her spine. She nudged Ilana down the stairs of a nearby cellar. Ilana, her face white, dropped to the ground and wrapped her arms around her knees. Miriam raised her head just enough to see the boy drop the can and jump back. Another officer grabbed the boy by his long hair, opened the synagogue door and tossed him inside like an afterthought.

A scuffle broke out three meters from the synagogue. Rabbi Kilov, easy to distinguish with his frizzy ginger beard that flowed almost to his waist, emerged from a cluster of sobbing people watching the fray. The rabbi straightened his thick-waisted body, stroked his beard and began chanting the *Shema* in Hebrew, traditional last words for Jews, in a loud, unwavering voice. He walked into the synagogue. The doors clanged shut behind him.

Ilana wept softly.

An officer adjusted his high-brimmed cap and nodded at another officer, who dropped a lit match onto the ground, igniting a ring of fire around the synagogue.

Screams from inside the synagogue scorched Miriam's eardrums. *I have to be here for Max.* The screaming escalated into a frantic howling. Miriam covered Ilana's ears but knew her hands were not enough to stifle the cries. Two women shouted and threw themselves at the door of the synagogue. Latvian officers kicked them aside.

Images of Max flared before Miriam's eyes—Max waking up in a haze, choking on smoke. She squeezed her eyes shut, drew in a quick breath and prayed Max remained unconscious. The flames rose quickly, engulfing the synagogue where she and Max were married, where they'd celebrated Rosh Hashanah with their children, where they'd mourned the loss of his parents. Where Max would take his last breath.

"*Sh'ma Yisra'eil Adonai Eloheinu Adonai echad,*" Miriam began, chanting the *Shema* for Max. Hear, Israel, the Lord is our God, the Lord is one.

Ilana broke free from Miriam's grasp and stared at the inferno.

"Papa," Ilana whispered.

Miriam hauled Ilana up the stairs and rushed her down the street, away from the stench of deadly flames and wailing voices, now etched in her memory. And Ilana's.

14

CHICAGO, FEBRUARY 1976

Snow began falling late Friday afternoon, sheets of white that turned to gray slush on downtown Chicago's streets and sidewalks, slowing traffic and commuter trains heading out of the city. At one point, Sarah's train stopped for a good five minutes or so, an eternity at the end of a hectic day when you're among strangers, without ventilation. Through the cold window, smudged with her breath, Sarah watched snow land on the roof of a redbrick apartment building opposite the train. She saw a woman, black hair flecked with snow, usher two small children toting backpacks almost as big as they were into the building, and thought, I would be home now if I'd gone to my apartment.

More than four months since her mother's death, and she still spent most weekends with her father. She claimed she didn't want him to be alone, but in truth, she didn't look forward to two days by herself in her small apartment, where independence felt more like loneliness. She wasn't herself. A melancholy feeling had settled into her bones like an extra ten pounds, sapping her spirit. She trudged through her days on automatic pilot, drafting questionnaires, meeting focus groups, going over responses with indifference, eating McDonald's and Burger King from paper bags in front of the television, all the while thinking, Everyone I loved and trusted lied to me.

She was undone by thoughts of what could have been, if her grandmother had been in her life, if her mother hadn't been overwhelmed by the past, if words had been spoken freely. Sarah forgave her father. He hadn't lied; he just didn't say anything. He was a bystander, and while this still troubled her, his heartache made it impossible to be mad at him. She needed her father. He was a constant in her life, alongside Heather, who was consumed by wedding plans, her fiancé and work. Many times, she'd picked up the phone to call Henry but second-guessed herself when she thought about the heartache of losing her mother. Love meant putting your heart in someone else's hands, and she just wasn't ready to take that risk.

The train grunted to a start, and as it rolled forward, picking up speed, Sarah watched the city recede gradually, with high-density buildings replaced by roads clogged with traffic, open spaces, clumps of trees and the roofs of houses, dripping with marshmallow snow. The suburbs. Where people like her parents moved to raise children. Where she came to hide from the present and to excavate the past.

HER FATHER ORDERED deep-dish pizza, a Friday night tradition ever since he and her mother began dating in college. From the corner of her eye, she glimpsed her father's distended stomach and had a pang of guilt. Here she was, encouraging him to eat what was almost certainly the most fattening food on the planet, with two inches of gooey cheese on a crust thick as a bagel. Next week, she'd convince him to order something different. Or at least try. He was a creature of habit, more so since her mother was gone, maintaining routines with an astonishing rigidity in order to hold on to what he had, and even eating the TV dinners her mother had accumulated, two in a row judging from the kitchen trash.

"I saw Grandma again this week," she said when the pizza had been delivered and they were at the kitchen table with generous slices on their plates and a bottle of her mother's favorite California red wine.

He cocked his head. "You know what? I'm glad you're seeing her." He cut a piece of pizza and brought it to his mouth, a stringy heap on his fork.

She stared at him a minute, flabbergasted. "I thought you didn't want me to get too close to Grandma."

He chewed. Swallowed. "Changed my mind. You seem more settled after being with her, like she's giving you what you need right now."

Sarah set down her fork and knife, no longer hungry. "Why didn't Mom let me see her?"

Her father lowered his gaze to his pizza and carefully cut another piece. "It was wrong of Mom to keep you from your grandmother."

"Was it because Miriam stayed Jewish?"

He tugged at the collar of his turtleneck. "A little. Not exactly."

"Now I'm really confused."

"It's a little more complicated than you think."

She nodded for him to go on.

"Let's eat first, before it gets cold," he suggested.

"You're stalling."

"Can't get anything past you," he joked tiredly.

She shook her head and waited for him to continue.

He wiped the corners of his mouth with his napkin and dropped it onto his half-eaten slice. Rolled his sleeves up. "You know my parents were Catholic."

"Right." She heard the strain in his voice.

"The upshot is, they had no idea your mother was Jewish, and they wouldn't have liked it, to be perfectly frank. So, while they were alive, there was no question of you being anything other than Catholic."

"Wait a minute. Your parents didn't like Jews and you were okay with that, even though Mom was Jewish?"

He folded his napkin in half, pressed the crease with his index finger over and over. "I didn't say I was okay with it. I wasn't. My parents were narrow-minded. They lumped people into two groups: Catholics, who believed in the real God, and everyone else. Neither of them knew anything about Jews. I don't think they'd ever met a Jewish person, but they had negative opinions just the same."

Sarah listened intently, astounded by her grandparents' intolerance.

"Anyway, the upshot was, we didn't tell them about your mother's background, to keep the peace."

"What about Mom? Didn't it bother her, having to hide her real self, because of your parents?"

"It wasn't just my parents. A couple of suburbs near here banned Jews from moving in—"

"Even after the war?"

He nodded. "Nobody talked much about what happened in Europe. It was too hard for people like your mom and grandmother. I was pretty young when the war ended, but I don't remember anyone mentioning the Jews killed by Hitler, not even my teachers."

"It doesn't make sense," Sarah said quietly. "Everyone knew millions were killed. And there are photos, I've seen them."

"You're right. Everyone knew, but nobody talked about it."

"It makes no sense," she repeated.

"How many Jewish kids were in your school?"

Sarah pondered this. "None that I can remember, until college."

"I can think of one."

She looked at him, bemused.

"You. You're considered Jewish because your mother was Jewish."

"I am?"

He nodded. "That's why your mother didn't broadcast her faith. She didn't want you facing the bigotry she encountered. She wanted you so far removed from Judaism you would never consider yourself a Jew."

"But I knew Mom was Jewish."

"Yes, but you'd have to know Jewish law to understand it's passed down on the maternal side. Plus, we raised you in the Catholic Church."

"So your parents would accept me," Sarah said.

"That's not the only reason. Your mother had trouble getting a job when her religion came up. She started identifying herself as Catholic and got a position a couple of weeks later."

"But she never saw herself as Catholic, did she?"

"No." Her father shook his head. "She never sang, never took communion or prayed aloud. She came to church to provide a united front, for you, but her mind was elsewhere."

"So she wasn't mad when I didn't want a First Communion?"

"More amused than anything. You dug your heels in, said you wanted nothing to do with it and didn't believe Jesus rose from the dead."

"You weren't upset?"

"A little, at first. I got over it."

"That would've been a good time to tell me I was considered Jewish."

"Your grandmother and I were sworn to secrecy."

"But you know what they went through."

He hesitated. "Have you asked your grandmother?"

"Have you ever gotten a straight answer from her?"

"Good point." He paused. "Your mother told me her family lost their home when the Soviets occupied Latvia, and . . ."

"And?"

He straightened his place mat.

"And?" she prodded him.

He looked at her solemnly. "A year later, the Nazis came and her father was killed in front of her."

His disclosure brought a quick rush of blood to her throat. "How . . . how was he killed? When?"

"Mom wouldn't tell me. If you could have seen how hard it was for her . . . to talk about him, you'd know why she kept those memories locked inside."

"What about Grandma? Was she there too? Did she see Grandpa killed?"

Her father poured himself a glass of wine, up to the brim. "Yes. She did."

Sarah was dumbfounded.

"I wanted your mother to talk to someone, but she was a nurse who healed wounds you could see. She wanted everyone to think she was invincible, but inside she was fragile as glass. I think Grandma is the same, though she'd never admit it."

His voice swayed on the edge of her consciousness as she absorbed the secret her mother had taken to her grave.

What if you don't like what you find? Miriam's question haunted her thoughts. Sarah's eyes fell on the deck of cards in the middle of the table, the cards her mother used for solitaire.

I need to know everything.

ON SUNDAY AFTERNOON, Sarah took the train to Blackstone Library on South Lake Park Avenue. She stamped her feet on the marble floor to get warm, and unwrapped the burgundy scarf her mother had knitted years earlier from around her black coat. People streamed through the doors, crowding the rotunda.

Sarah gazed at the half-circle murals—Labor, Literature, Art and Science—inspired by Greek mythology. These exquisite murals were the reason Blackstone was her favorite branch in the city. She'd spent many Sunday afternoons curled up in a chair reading in the Blackstone, once she'd started working full-time. It was a place that welcomed people who wanted to be alone, and Sarah basked in the serenity she couldn't find anywhere else in the city.

Armed with a notebook, two pens and change for the copier, Sarah took the stairs two at a time. She found a table near the microfiche catalogs, rolled up the sleeves of her cowl-neck sweater and began with the *Chicago Tribune* archives, just as she'd started her search on Chicago suffragettes for a paper in her junior year of college. She smiled wistfully, thinking about how she'd been so caught up in the research, she'd barely had time to write the paper. Research had a way of grabbing Sarah's attention like nothing else, giving her the heady feeling of being a detective, whenever she embraced a new project. It was the part of college she missed most.

Now, she flipped through the *Tribune* index back to 1939, with the keyword "Latvia." Nothing until December 25, 1940, with an article about unemployment and the high cost of food. Nothing specific from 1942 and 1943, just information about Russians "capturing villages and hamlets" as the enemy, Germany, retreated.

Sarah requested an armful of microfiche boxes and settled into a metal chair in front of a microfiche reader. She inserted the film and scrolled through the eye-burning blue screens with white type, stopping at November 1941.

*The three Baltic states, including Latvia, are recovering from
the Soviet invasion with the aid of the German army. The
Germans are doing their best to make friends in Latvia and
Estonia. Both countries have been treated with considera-
tion and respect. German armies have saved thousands of
Baltic citizens who were deported by the Soviets, which has
promoted a growing friendship between Estonians, Latvians
and Germans. There is no danger of either hunger or pesti-
lence in the Baltic states.*

Odd. This information contradicted the horrific experiences in
other parts of Europe controlled by the Germans. She continued
scrolling in earnest, page after page, wading through headlines.
1942 to 1944. Fragments about the war, the Soviets' invasion and
Germany's defeat. This was going nowhere. She chewed on a hang-
nail and inserted the last reel of film: 1945. Blinked to moisten her
dry, strained eyes. Began scrolling. Stopped when she came to April
1945:

*Germans responsible for the deaths of 577,000 people in
Latvian concentration camps. At least 170,000 civilians
"slaughtered" in mass extermination camps near Riga, and
35,000 Jews confined in Riga ghetto. Germans drove Jews
into 4 synagogues which were then locked and set afire,
burning 2,000 Jews.*

Sarah pressed cold hands to her cheeks and reread the paragraph. Her eyes pulsed. With almost 800,000 people killed, it
was a miracle her mother and grandmother survived. The numbers blurred. She stared at the screen until her vision cleared and
thought, *My grandfather was one of these victims.*

This was not what she'd expected. It was worse. The scale. The methods. And it was inconceivable, how she'd never heard of the atrocities in Latvia. Poland and Germany, yes, but she'd had to dig deep for information about her mother's birthplace, and even then it would have been easy to miss, a tiny paragraph written thirty years earlier, a blip amidst the screeching headlines about Auschwitz and the gas chambers.

The attic of her brain swelled with photos she'd seen of emaciated Jews at the end of the war. She was sick at the thought of her own mother and grandmother looking like skeletons covered in skin, and imagined their faces amidst the gaunt survivors who looked more dead than alive. She shivered.

What if you don't like what you find?

"Are you all right, dear?"

Sarah's ears perked. A librarian holding an armful of books peered down at her.

"Yes. Thanks," she managed.

"You will let me know if I can be of assistance, won't you?"

Sarah nodded tightly. Felt a headache coming on.

The librarian moved away, deposited the books she'd been holding onto a rolling cart and disappeared between two rows of shelves. Sarah longed to follow the librarian to the books and lose herself between the lines of a mystery set in Paris or Italy that didn't involve her grandparents and mother. Her eyes slid back to the microfiche screen and the paragraph that said so much and so little. It was like the write-up on book covers, just enough to pull you in yet leave you wanting more.

She massaged her throbbing temple and resumed her search through the archives, working her way through years and decades, coming up with practically nothing about life in Soviet Latvia except for a couple of short articles about Latvians deported to Siberia—

twenty thousand in 1964 alone--and the struggle for exit visas, with some people still waiting since the end of the war. Thirty years later and not allowed to leave. Latvian Jews had even organized a sit-in for the right to emigrate in 1971, just five years earlier, when she was in college and took freedom for granted.

If her mother and Miriam had remained in Latvia, they might be among those waiting for liberty. Her mother wouldn't have met and married her father. *I wouldn't exist.* If they had been killed during the war, along with her grandfather, she wouldn't exist. This revelation seeped through the crevices of her mind like indelible ink. The photo of Miriam and her mother in front of the Statue of Liberty shimmered before her eyes, a symbol of their perilous journey from oppression to freedom.

It had never occurred to her before, the precariousness of being. How a single decision or event can have a domino effect on future generations. She knew, obviously, the randomness of a sperm fertilizing an egg, the biology of survival, but this was different. This was the story of a family that had nothing to do with cells and everything to do with people. The origin of a family. Where it began and the couple who started it all. Stories and traditions linking generations. Names and places. How traumatic events like the war shaped actions and led to casualties such as her grandfather and their faith. Personalities, faces and genetic diseases. What we inherit and what we pass on. Memories, good and bad.

She felt part of something larger than herself as she reflected on her heritage, picturing a long line of women and men who came before her, all of them part of her, just as she would be part of her children and grandchildren one day.

I am who I am because they were who they were.

But . . . who were they?

15

RIGA, AUGUST 1941

T HE STIFLING HUMIDITY SETTLED INTO MIRIAM'S PORES like mud. She got down on her bruised and calloused hands and knees to wash the living room floor of the Arājs Kommando headquarters, where Latvian men wore green armbands and followed Nazi orders like puppets. Cleaning the townhouse that served as the headquarters was her new job, assigned by the Nazis. Except she wasn't paid. And the cruel irony wasn't lost on her: she cleaned for the men who had burned Max and dozens of other Jews alive. One month earlier.

A man's voice charged through the window, an officer barking out orders at the Esplanade park across the street, where Kommando members participated in marching and rifle exercises. Her bones quaked with dread. She thought of the ruthless Latvians who'd mercilessly steered Max to his death, and the lies about Jews being spread like seeds in a field. The reprehensible photo in the morning paper thudded into her mind: a disconcerting image of young Jewish men stooped over corpses from the Soviet occupation, which the Nazis had forced them to dig up. The false headline: THE JEWS

HAVE KILLED LATVIANS AND THEREFORE THE JEWS SHALL BE KILLED. Proof of the Jews' corroboration with the Soviets. Proof Jews were guilty of murdering Latvians.

Proof of the Nazis' flair for propaganda, she thought dourly.

She glared at the bright-yellow six-pointed star on her blouse, and was seized by a wave of nausea. This was the pervasive symbol of Judaism all Riga Jews were now forced to wear, on the front of their clothing as well as on the middle of their back. If they didn't wear it, they could be killed.

What's next?

She heard footfalls on the stairs. She dunked her rag in the metal pail of water and scrubbed, moving her hand in circles over the oak-plank floor. Pain rippled up her arm muscles to her shoulder as she scoured her way to the grand fireplace. She paused to rub her aching shoulder and wet her sweaty face with water.

"Are you sick?" An acidic voice sliced through the steamy air.

A man's shadow descended over Miriam. She held her breath. Hoped it was the kind officer who offered cheese, raspberries and milk for her children and let her go early whenever he was on duty. Her heart sank when an unfamiliar Kommando member appeared. He blocked the light streaming from the front window.

"I'm fine." She squeezed her rag over the pail, the water oozing through her fingers like filthy paste, and scrubbed, making half-circles on the spot in front of her knees. Max's wilted body flickered in her mind, the way it did whenever she was nervous, whenever a German or Latvian predator came near her. It was as if Max were watching over her, warning her to be careful.

Miriam wiped her runny nose with her sleeve. The officer lit a cigarette and grunted. He didn't budge. When she came to his polished boots, she sat on her heels. He stepped back, one foot at a time, without taking his wide-apart eyes off Miriam. Her stomach growled. She glanced sideways at the grandfather clock. Six o'clock in the evening. All she'd eaten since breakfast was a piece of stale bread with butter and some herring from a can, practically the only food she could find in the Jewish store near her building, the only shop she was allowed to frequent.

Fortunately, Gutte snuck food into their flat, risking imprisonment if she was discovered. Gutte wasn't even supposed to set foot in their apartment, yet she came whenever she could to care for Ilana and Monya, a task Miriam's parents, who'd lived with them since Max's death, wanted to do but couldn't. Her mother had been ordered to slave alongside her father, clearing away the city's rubble from the battle between the departing Soviets and the incoming Germans.

Miriam finished washing the floor and arched her stiff back. The officer sauntered past, his dirty boots leaving a trail of footprints across the clean floor. "What a *shtunk*," Miriam said in Yiddish under her breath, calling the officer a vile human. She rewashed the floor and carried the bucket to the kitchen sink, in an adjacent room. Her shoulder cracked as she raised the heavy bucket. The officer emerged in the doorway and blocked her from leaving, his hand resting on the butt of the pistol at his waist, a cigarette dangling from the corner of his mouth.

"Think it's clean enough?" he jeered.

"Yes."

He flicked cigarette ashes onto the floor. "I don't."

Miriam inhaled and imagined herself kicking him in the shins and pouring her dirty water over his head. She set the bucket down and was about to kneel, to rewash the floor, when he grabbed her elbow and hauled her across the floor like a mop.

"Let go! Stop . . ." she sputtered.

"Poor work is unacceptable," he growled.

"But you dropped the ashes." Miriam regretted her words the second they flew out of her mouth.

He glowered at her with stony eyes and picked her up as easily as if she were a bag of feathers. He threw her over his shoulder and carried her downstairs to the dingy basement. The walls echoed with the sound of his heavy footsteps and the air smelled rough and grainy.

"Don't . . . I promise I'll do better tomorrow." Miriam kicked her feet. "I have children. They need me. Please. Give me another chance."

He continued as if he didn't hear her, carrying Miriam through a dark, narrow corridor. The only light came from a half window that abutted the ceiling. She couldn't see where they were going, only where they'd been. She wanted to be unconscious, like Max, instead of awake with horrible endings screeching through her mind. A door scraped open. He pitched Miriam forward. She landed on a cold, hard floor. The door slammed shut and there was no light at all.

MIRIAM'S BLOOD BEAT hot and loud. Contours emerged through the fetid gloom. Squares of lead gray, circles of mucky black and colorless rectangles smeared together then separated, like oil and water. Her fingertips touched the ground—damp, hard and rough. She reached out and touched something soft. Warm. Flesh. Jerked her hand back.

"Who's there?" a woman moaned in a high and reedy voice.

"Miriam. I am Miriam Talan."

The unseen woman moved, making a swishing sound like pieces of wool rubbing together. "My name is Zelma Shepshelovitz."

"How long have you been here?"

A long pause.

"Can't say. There is no way to tell time," the woman answered slowly.

"Today is Wednesday. Do you remember the day you were brought here?"

"Saturday," Zelma said softly.

"Five days."

This disclosure sat between them like a bad smell as they remained in the fetid blackness, Zelma's shallow breath a comfort for Miriam, a reminder she was not alone. Zelma's hand stretched out through the gloom and seized Miriam's arm. Miriam flinched. Zelma's fingers were strong.

"I want you to know what they did to me in case you get out and I don't," Zelma said.

"What? Don't say that."

"Promise you'll speak, if I can't." Zelma gripped Miriam's arm tighter and asked with such conviction that Miriam's scalp prickled.

"I promise," said Miriam.

Zelma released her arm and explained how she'd worked as a maid for German Wehrmacht officers. One of them brought her down to the basement. He said she had to be punished for sloppy work, but she'd cleaned his house from top to bottom until there wasn't a speck of dirt anywhere.

Miriam shuddered.

"There were three other women down here," Zelma continued. "I never saw their faces. We talked a little. One by one, they were taken and didn't come back. My turn came. I was forced upstairs, to an office. It was smoky. I started coughing and my eyes stung from the light after being in the dark for so long." She paused. "And . . . before I knew what was happening, he . . ." Her voice cracked. "He . . ."

"My God." Miriam wrapped her arms around herself and quivered.

"His hands were rough . . ."

"You don't have to—"

"It was Viktors Arājs—"

"Head of the Kommando?" Miriam jerked her head toward Zelma's faint voice.

"Yes."

Miriam's stomach dropped.

"None of the others came back," Zelma was saying. "I don't know why I'm still here."

Miriam's thoughts turned to Ilana and Monya, alone in the apartment all day, unless Gutte managed to get there. Miriam had a gnawing sense of helplessness. If something happened to her children . . . She started breathing quickly, exhaling air in bursts. She became light-headed and couldn't sit up straight. She leaned against the wall and breathed in through her mouth. Her eyelids grew heavy with exhaustion. She fought the urge to give in and sleep, afraid of being pounced upon, unable to fight back. But her fatigue was stronger than her will. She drifted into a restless sleep, accompanied by the lullaby of Zelma's erratic breathing.

THE SCUFFING AT the door echoed within Miriam's head as if it came from far away. A beam of light jerked her awake. Knuckles cracked and gravelly breathing speared the air. Miriam pressed her back into the corner. The door opened wider, letting in the smell of peppery onions. Miriam shaded her eyes with her hands. The light widened to a circle big enough to reveal Zelma huddled against the wall, knees drawn up to her narrow chin. Stringy, long hair hung over her face like tangled rope.

The intruder's croaky breathing blared as he moved into the room. Miriam buried her head under her arms in a failed attempt to hide. Mitt-sized hands jabbed her armpits and yanked her to her feet. Sharp fingernails cut through her blouse, into her skin. She crumpled when the man let go of one of her underarms. He kicked her in the stomach. Knocked the wind out of her. She gasped for air. Poked his eye with her fingers.

"Goddamn Jew!" He grabbed Miriam's hair and jerked her forward, ripping a clump of hair from her scalp. He lugged her through the hall and up the stairs.

Daylight spilled through tall windows. The man hauled Miriam to the third and top floor of the townhouse, to a small room where a boyish-looking officer sat poised behind a desk. A bare light bulb hung over his head like a spotlight. His wide-apart eyes scrutinized Miriam inch by painful inch. She felt like a piece of meat on display at the butcher's. Without a word, the boyish officer got up and stood behind Miriam, then threw her over the desk, yanked her skirt up and ripped her stockings down. A searing pain, as though she was being cut open. Rage charged through her like a bolt of electricity. She bit the grimy finger pressing her shoulder down, heard an angry shout followed by a cracking pain against her scalp, and sank into a merciful darkness.

Miriam woke in an alley behind the Arājs Kommando headquarters, her skirt and blouse torn and stained with blood, her bleeding skin mottled black and blue. Her emotions turned to ice that day. She stopped feeling pain, happiness, fear and remorse. It was the only way she could face her parents and children without falling apart.

16

CHICAGO, FEBRUARY 1976

Y OUR GRANDMOTHER'S IN THE HOSPITAL."

Sarah pressed the phone against her ear when she heard her father's apprehensive voice. "What happened? How is she?"

"Not sure. Her neighbor called the police when she hadn't seen her for a couple of days, found her in the bathtub when the landlord let her in. I just got the call. I'm on my way now."

"I'll meet you there. Which hospital?"

"Evanston."

Sarah hung up the phone, grabbed her coat from the hook on her door and hurtled out of her office, running right into her six-foot-two-inch boss, Craig, knocking the cigarette out of his hand and mussing his feathered black hair. Her shoulder chafed from hitting his arm.

The vein in Craig's long neck pulsed and his chevron mustache flapped.

She touched her shoulder gingerly and felt the hint of a bump beneath her sweater. By dinnertime, it would be a purplish-yellow bruise.

"What the hell?" Craig said. He crushed the cigarette into the carpet with the toe of his shiny black shoe before picking it up.

"Sorry." Of all the people she could have literally run into. Craig. A star quarterback in college, he had a habit of bringing up his full athletic scholarship within minutes of meeting. In Sarah's case, it took approximately seven minutes, after which he launched into a passionate speech about the value of sports and how being on a team helped expedite his career and made him what he was today. He wore his inflated ego like a loud necktie.

"What's the rush?" he asked. His deep Ted Baxter voice boomed through the office.

Sarah grimaced at the volume of his voice, and quietly explained that her grandmother was in the hospital.

"The hospital?" He shook his head gravely. "That's a place you want to avoid like the plague. Do you know how well those nurses sterilize that equipment? Not enough, if you ask me. My wife got so sick after having our twins, I had to take a whole week off to help because she could barely get out of bed to change diapers. The doctor tried to convince me she had a bug before coming to the hospital, but I wasn't born yesterday." He tapped his head twice with his finger.

"How awful, an entire week off work," Sarah said in the dulcet tone she used to flatter Craig when she wanted something, like her raise six months ago.

Craig leaned against the wall and crossed his feet. "It really was. Do you know how much babies cry? All the time. Day and night. And we had two of them, for Christ's sake. Poor Angela. I felt terrible waking her up in the middle of the night to change their diapers, but that was a no-go for me. The smell." He shuddered dramatically. "Hard to believe something so small could make such a big stink."

What a jerk.

"Well, it's wonderful, how you were there for your wife and sons."

He ran his hand down his tie. "I think so."

"I better go," she said.

"Where is it again, you're going?"

She smiled humbly. "The hospital, to see my grandmother."

"Right." He waved her off and sauntered down the corridor, hands clasped behind his back, humming his alma mater's cheer.

AT THE HOSPITAL, she found her father huddled in a corner of the packed emergency waiting room, suffused with children's cries and people's anxious voices and medicinal air. He'd come straight from his office too; his beige wool coat was unbuttoned over his charcoal-gray suit and his tie hung loose around his bulky neck. His eyes sparked with relief when he spotted her coming his way.

"Miriam has pneumonia and they're worried about her heart," he explained after a quick hug. "They've stabilized her and she'll be moving to a room in a while."

"Her heart?" Sarah plucked her gloves from her fingers. "When can I see her?"

"Not until she's moved."

She looked at the nurses' station, her mind jumping to the last day of her mother's life, when she'd arrived too late. A different hospital, but the same reek of disinfectant, the same helpless tension in the waiting room. It was a regret that polluted her thoughts for weeks, not being able to hold her hand, to say goodbye.

"I need to see her now." Sarah gently pushed past her father and headed to the nurses' station in the corner of the room, where two nurses sat behind open windows. One nurse was talking to a woman clutching her toddler with broken blood vessels on his face. Sarah approached the other nurse, a spindly woman with a square jaw, and asked to see Miriam Talan.

The nurse glanced at a clipboard and shook her head. "She'll be in a room soon—"

"I know, I just want to see her for a second, to let her know I'm here. Please," Sarah implored her.

"I'll be happy to pass along your message," the nurse replied with tight lips.

Sarah jiggled her foot and drew in a long breath. "When I broke my arm and my father brought me to the hospital, he was allowed to stay with me the entire time."

"How old were you?"

"Nine."

"You were a child. That's different."

"I don't think so. Older people are just as vulnerable as children, especially if they don't hear or see well," Sarah retorted, though Miriam's senses were all intact.

The nurse straightened. Cleared her throat. "You haven't been ill in the last ten days, have you?" she asked in a leaden voice. "Germs are highly dangerous to older people with pneumonia."

"Haven't been sick in months. I never get sick."

"Keep it short." She gestured for Sarah to follow her through the door beside the nurses' station.

Sarah thanked the nurse. As they walked down an aisle lined with light-blue vinyl curtains on both sides, Sarah heard unnerving groans rumbling through the curtains. *This is what my mother heard every day at work, the sound of pain.* The nurse stopped at a curtain on the right and drew it open. Sarah's breath quickened. This woman with blanched, sagging flesh was not her fastidious grandmother. Could not be. Then, as if she sensed herself being

117

watched, Miriam opened her eyes. They flickered with recognition when they landed on Sarah.

"Grandma." Sarah tiptoed toward her bedside.

"Ilana," her grandmother murmured.

"No, it's Sarah." She laid her hand on her grandmother's shoulder. "I'm here. I'm not going anywhere."

Miriam's cold hand reached out and grabbed Sarah's with surprising force. She beckoned for Sarah to come closer.

Sarah leaned in, her nerves fired up with dread and anticipation.

"Monya, Monya . . ." Miriam whispered in Sarah's ear.

"Who? No, it's me—"

Miriam strained to lift her head. She met Sarah's gaze. "I'm sorry. About Monya."

"Who's Monya?"

Miriam's eyes watered. Her lips curled down. "You searched for him. Your letters . . . I'm sorry . . . I should have helped you . . . I should have given you the money—"

"What money? What did the letters say? I don't understand, Grandma . . . Ilana didn't have a brother. You have . . . *had* one child, a daughter. Ilana. Remember?"

"Yes, yes." Miriam's voice rattled with phlegm. "And a son."

"Monya?"

"Monya. Your younger brother."

"She's getting agitated." The nurse appeared from behind the curtain. "I'm going to have to ask you to leave."

"Mom had a brother named Monya?"

"You can see her after she's moved to a room," the nurse said.

"Just a minute." Sarah waved the nurse away and whispered into her grandmother's ear. "Is Monya here, in America?"

"Excuse me," the nurse said, impatient. "You need to go."

"No." Tears rolled down Miriam's lined cheeks. "I lost him."

"He died, in Riga?"

"No. I left him there." She started coughing, a hacking, wet cough.

The nurse tugged Sarah's forearm.

"You left him in Riga?"

"Of course. How could you forget?"

Sarah stilled, overtaken by a shocking, cold premonition. This was what kept her mother up at night. Her brother. Monya. Lost or left behind.

"So he might still be alive?" Sarah held her breath. "Is that what the letters say? The letters I left with you?"

"You have"—Miriam coughed—"to find him."

THE NEXT DAY, after work, Sarah waited for Heather at Miyako's, a Japanese restaurant on Clark Street. It had, in Sarah's opinion, the best tempura shrimp in the city and a bring-your-own-bottle policy that kept the bill to a reasonable amount without sacrificing the nothing-matters contentment she enjoyed after a couple of glasses of wine. Inside, the restaurant was dimly lit, with red, black and gold Japanese prints on the walls and disposable chopsticks at every place setting. There were cloth napkins and waitresses dressed in kimonos, giving the place an almost authentic atmosphere, but the bulky television at the hostess station ruined the ambience, as far as Sarah was concerned.

She arrived before Heather, as usual. Heather was never on time. She would be late to her own wedding, Sarah thought with a wry smile as she took her menu from the waitress, a pretty young woman with plump cheeks and dimples and ebony hair gathered into a tall bun almost as large as her head. At the next table, men and women spoke rapid Japanese, their voices cutting in and out with indistinguishable, clipped sounds that fascinated Sarah. All her life she'd wanted to speak a foreign language fluently. She'd taken French in junior high and high school, where she'd learned to conjugate verbs and read children's stories, but her verbal skills were limited to ordering from a menu and simple conversations about the weather. Her intention had been to travel to France one day, but when she had the time after college, she didn't have the money. Now, when she had the money and had accrued two weeks' holiday time, she couldn't find anyone to go with her. Not even Heather, who was engaged and saving for a house.

"Sorry I'm late."

They hugged and fell into conversation as if they'd only been separated a day, not a couple of weeks. Looking chic in a pale-pink pantsuit with a wide white belt and a scarf tied jauntily around her neck, Heather glowed with the sureness of love; she craved marriage and a house as adamantly as Sarah craved adventure and travel. They were opposites in every way, probably why their friendship had endured.

"So, tell me the real reason you called," Heather said, once they'd ordered and were cleaning their hands with the warm, damp towels provided by their waitress. "You sounded so keyed up over the phone."

Sarah squeezed her towel, savoring the heat and lemony scent. She poured two generous glasses of white wine. How to begin. Here she was, twenty-four hours after Miriam's shocking admission, and now it seemed too far-fetched to be true. Yet it had to be. Miriam wouldn't make up something so important, she wouldn't conjure up a son for attention, like some sleazy tabloid. Sarah put herself back in the emergency department, beside her grandmother's bed, and began talking, pausing only when the food came.

"Monya," Heather said reflectively, once Sarah finished. "It's unbelievable."

"Do you think Miriam was telling the truth?" Sarah said.

"Of course. Don't you?"

"Yes." Sarah looked down at her untouched plate of food. "I just can't understand how my mother kept such a big secret all these years."

"Maybe she wanted to tell you but didn't know how," Heather suggested.

Sarah finished her glass of wine and poured herself another. "Maybe. Or maybe she found out Monya died and didn't want to tell Miriam."

Heather raised her brow.

"Last night," Sarah continued, "my dad told me Mom used to call out for someone named Monya when she was asleep, but refused to tell him who he was. She got so upset when my dad pushed her, he left it alone. He said her nightmares seemed to go away when she was pregnant with me."

Heather's brow furrowed with concentration.

"Ironic, isn't it, me healing my mother while she was creating me."

Heather crossed her arms over her chest. "A little spooky, if you ask me."

"I can't stop thinking about Monya and how he was left behind. If he's alive. I was up half the night imagining different scenarios: How he got separated from his mother and sister. If he knows he has a mother in America. And a niece." The idea of being someone's niece made her pulse quicken. As the only child of parents who were only children, she'd reluctantly accepted her limited status as daughter and granddaughter long ago. Monya's existence was like opening a door only to find total darkness.

"How is Miriam, anyway?"

"Better. My dad called me at work today and said she needs a pacemaker. They'll operate once her pneumonia is under control. It's a routine surgery, but I'll be relieved once it's over."

"Why do you think she told you, after all this time?"

"She was delirious and afraid she was going to die and wanted someone to know about him. That's my dad's theory. I think it makes sense."

"Me, too. My uncle told my aunt he'd been having an affair for fifteen years, on his deathbed."

"That's awful."

"My aunt wanted to divorce him, but he died. She still grumbles about him getting away with it, as if dying from lung cancer isn't punishment enough."

Sarah winced. She picked at her rice with her chopsticks. "What do you think of Miriam asking me to find Monya?"

"Find him? Even if he is alive, he could be anywhere," Heather replied, incredulous.

"I know, but I want to start with Riga, if it's even possible. I haven't looked into it yet, but I feel obligated to at least try, for Miriam's sake. Can you imagine not knowing what happened to your child?"

"Not really, seeing as I've never been a mother," Heather said flatly. "Neither have you, unless there's something you're not telling me. And there's no way your grandmother actually meant for you to go behind the Iron Curtain. She was out of it when she was talking. She didn't even know it was you."

"You're right," Sarah said, discouraged. She couldn't go to the Soviet Union on a whim, to look for a person who might not even be there.

=

I LOST HIM.

Miriam's distraught voice scudded into Sarah's head like a jet that night, as she tossed and turned. She pictured her grandmother's eyes locking on Monya's for the first time in thirty years, like the happy ending of a movie, with Monya's and Miriam's smiling faces inside a gradually closing circle of light. This was the last thing she remembered before sleep carried her off through the luminous circle just before it closed.

Find him.

17

RIGA, OCTOBER 1941

A HEADLINE ON THE FRONT PAGE OF THE *TĒVIJA* ANNOUNCED Jews had to move to a ghetto in the Moscow suburb of Riga by October 25. It was the most derelict area in the city, a few blocks above the right bank of the Daugava River, inhabited primarily by poor Russians. This would be Miriam's third forced upheaval in just over a year, each location markedly smaller and more crowded than the one before.

"This has to be the last place we'll live before the war ends," she said to her mother, sitting across from her at their small kitchen table. "There's nowhere else to go, no place worse than this ghetto, which sounds more like a prison."

"What do you mean, a prison?" her mother said in the apathetic tone she had adopted over the five months of German occupation.

Miriam looked closely at her mother, sitting across from her at their small round table, a wool shawl wrapped around her spindly neck and shoulders. The last year and a half of Soviet terror followed by German violence had squeezed the feisty temperament out of her mother like a dishrag wrung dry. Her usually abrasive voice had diminished, and her frame had withered to an old woman's shriveled body, beaten down by the hard labor she faced daily. Even her face had aged dramatically, with deep furrows engraved on her brow and cheeks, as well as the emergence of misshapen brown spots, like smudges of dirt.

"The ghetto will be separated from the rest of Riga with a barbed wire fence," Miriam answered, reading from the newspaper article. "And Latvian guards will be stationed around the perimeter of the sixteen-block area."

"I see," her mother said blandly, as if she were talking about someone else's future, not her own.

Miriam attempted to reconcile the shadow of a woman sitting across from her with the sharp-tongued mother who'd raised her, but couldn't. She was surprised by her unexpected feelings, her sense of loss. Her mother's vigor and critical voice had defined her, set her apart from other, more complacent women.

They sat quietly with the silver samovar they'd managed to sneak past the Soviets, two teacups, an ashtray heaped with squished cigarettes and a package of stale biscuits. Miriam wondered if Ilana noticed changes in her the way she had in her mother, whether evidence of her rape was obvious, despite her best efforts to hide the pain in the recesses of her memory. At times, agony charred the back of her throat, coming to a boil on the tip of her tongue before cooling and retreating. She would never relay her pain to Ilana, just as her mother would never discuss her feelings. Giving in to emotions weakened a person's spirit the way water diluted their well-used tea leaves to an insipid brew.

Miriam was eternally one short moment away from being hurled back to that petrifying day and the men who attacked her. Any little thing set her off: The smell of onions. Darkness. The colors yellow and mint green. An officer's uniform. A shiny badge.

The sound of footfalls on the floor. In the middle of the night she'd hear a smarmy voice telling her the floor wasn't clean, or she'd feel a hand clenching her shoulder and wake in a hot sweat.

Worst of all, she feared she was pregnant. Her monthly hadn't come in weeks. Amidst the chaos, she'd lost track of time. Every morning, she woke, desperate to see a crimson stain, and every morning, she was disappointed. It was impossible to keep her mind from leaping to the potential disaster if her monthly didn't arrive.

The more she thought about that day, the more she believed it was her fault—a gesture she'd made, the way she carried herself, the way she smelled. She stopped bathing with the idea that her body odor would deter another assault. And she slept with her kerosene lantern on. Darkness had become as frightening as the guns the Arājs Kommando officers flaunted.

Monya cried out faintly from the room he shared with Ilana and Miriam, jolting Miriam from that ill-fated day. Miriam estimated Monya had been sleeping almost three hours, far longer than normal.

Ilana emerged from the bedroom, told her mother Monya was awake and closed the drapes.

"You don't like the sun?" Miriam asked.

"I don't want people seeing us."

"We're on the third floor," Miriam said. "Birds are the only things passing by our windows. People would have to sprout wings in order to peek into our apartment. Right, Mama?"

Miriam and Ilana looked to the older woman for her reaction, but she didn't blink. She sat at the table with a faraway expression in her eyes. The newspaper was crumpled into a ball in her hands.

There was a click and the apartment door opened. Miriam froze, afraid it would be soldiers, come to take them away. She breathed a sigh of relief when her father entered, carrying a scrunched paper bag. The circles under his eyes had become sacs of fatigue and his whiskers were overgrown and white.

"For you, *zeisele*, little sweetie." He presented the bag to Ilana. She peeked inside. "Mushrooms?"

"There were hundreds along the road. I couldn't resist. Tonight, we'll eat until our stomachs burst."

Miriam gave her father a look of gratitude for his attempt to bring a semblance of normalcy to their otherwise precarious life.

"Thank you, Zeyde," Ilana said formally. Gone was the open affection she'd shown her grandfather before Max's death. Gone was the laughter, the flicker of rebelliousness in her eyes, the never-ending energy that used to wear out both Gutte and Miriam. Ilana brought the bag to the kitchen and set it in the sink. She slipped down the hall to her bedroom, where Monya's cries had ebbed to a whimper.

"Did you read about the ghetto?" Miriam asked her father.

A shadow crossed his face. "Heard about it."

Another feeble cry sounded from the children's room.

"It won't be easy, but we will be all right in the end, provided we stay strong and keep our wits about us." He removed the newspaper ball from Dora's ink-stained hands, then stood behind her, fingers curled around the chair, eyes riveted on his wife.

Miriam went to her son, lying in a wet diaper on the towels that constituted his "bed" on the floor. She unfastened the safety pins of his diaper.

"I never thought it would get this bad," she said to Monya, as if he could understand. "I never thought my children would be forced to live behind barbed wire, like criminals." She wiped his bottom and pinned a fresh diaper on him.

He looked at her with a listless expression that made the hairs on the back of her neck rise. His energy had dropped to a worrisome low. Hardly surprising, given the limited food rations for Jews, half of what Latvians received. They were all starving, but seeing her child waning put everything in perspective. Monya and Ilana wouldn't survive the ghetto. And it was up to her to make sure they never set foot in there.

18

CHICAGO, FEBRUARY 1976

NEED TO GET OUT OF HERE." MIRIAM GRABBED ON TO THE bedside rail to prop herself up. It had been eight days since she was admitted to the hospital, and she looked small and gray in the requisite white gown, like an underdeveloped negative.

"Not until tomorrow, Miriam," said Sarah's father gently. "The doctor wants to make sure your pacemaker is working properly."

Sarah listened to the kindness in her father's voice and was thankful he'd come, despite his reservations about getting too close to Miriam.

"My heart's beating. It's working," Miriam protested, her voice dry and weak.

"Just one more night," Sarah said.

Late afternoon sun poured through the window, bleaching the room with a white light that exposed its barrenness. Sarah sat on the chair next to Miriam, close enough to see the impact of heart surgery and congested lungs in the hollows of her cheeks and the fatigue in her eyes.

Sarah pulled the lightweight blanket over Miriam's shoulders, then picked up a stack of glossy magazines she'd bought at the newsstand. "You complained all the magazines here were old, so I bought some new ones." She cleared the food tray and set the magazines down.

"That's a lot of reading, Miriam," Sarah's father said. "By the time you get through all those, it'll be time to leave."

"Stop talking to me like a child. I'm perfectly capable of taking care of myself, which includes knowing when I'm ready to go home."

"Someone sounds like she's feeling better." Dr. Fine, the curly-haired surgeon who had implanted the pacemaker, strode into the room and beamed at Miriam through smudged wire-framed glasses.

"Well enough to leave. But everyone around here seems determined to keep me in here another night."

"Because you're such good company," Dr. Fine retorted.

Sarah bit her bottom lip to stifle a smile.

The doctor held Miriam's delicate wrist, peered at his watch and took her pulse. "Excellent. The pacemaker is doing an excellent job."

"So I can go home?"

Dr. Fine put the tips of his stethoscope in his ears and placed the round silver diaphragm on Miriam's chest. "You were a pretty sick lady when you arrived. We don't want to release you until we're positive your lungs are clear and the pacemaker is working perfectly." His forehead tightened as he listened to Miriam's lungs. He moved the diaphragm to another spot. "Sounds clear, but I want to do one more X-ray to be certain."

"Another X-ray? You're going to kill me with radiation."

Dr. Fine chuckled. He removed his glasses and polished the lenses on his white lab coat. "Trust me, Miriam. My sole responsibility is to make sure you go home in tip-top shape. Only a tiny amount of radiation is used. There is absolutely no risk of you dying from radiation."

"I'm not taking any chances. My lungs are clear. I can tell when I breathe. I don't need an X-ray to tell me about my own body, thank you very much."

Sarah's father snorted and crossed his arms. Sarah caught a glint of laughter in her father's eyes. It was the first time she'd seen her father's face lighten since her mother's death, and Miriam was the reason.

"How about we compromise, then, Miriam? No X-ray, provided you stay tonight. You can go home first thing tomorrow morning."

"I guess it would be all right," she said glumly. She sank her head down on her pillow.

"Are you sure she doesn't need an X-ray?" Sarah said.

"Positive." Dr. Fine winked at Sarah. "One more night is all she needs."

The corners of Sarah's lips tweaked as her father thanked the doctor.

"I'll be back later, Miriam." The doctor waved at the three of them and stepped out of the room, followed by Sarah's father, who said he had to use the bathroom.

"Can I get you anything?" Sarah asked.

"A new heart," Miriam replied, deadpan.

"I'll add it to my grocery list," Sarah quipped.

A spark of amusement crossed Miriam's face.

Sarah tried to come up with another humorous line, but she wasn't naturally funny. It was a fluke, her comment about adding a new heart to her list, possibly the result of her time with Henry, who had an innate sense of comedic timing that made him the life of the party. It was what drew Sarah to Henry, his ability to read a room and become the main attraction, while she was content to bask in his glow. They'd complemented one another beautifully, his extroverted personality combined with her more introverted nature. When he got carried away, she was there to tone him down, and when she found herself in uncomfortable situations, he gently tugged her out of her reticent self. She was seized by a powerful urge to call Henry, to tell him about Monya, to hear his attentive voice.

"You don't have to stay with me," Miriam was saying.

"I want to be here. With you."

Miriam squinted at her, unconvinced. She shifted backward until she was sitting up, and glanced cursorily at the *Time* magazine on the top of the pile Sarah had brought.

"How can a Man of the Year Award go to American women?" Miriam asked, gesturing at the cover's headline. "Why isn't it a Woman of the Year Award?"

"Probably because the editors have no intention of honoring women of the year again," Sarah said dryly. "Guess we should be glad they're even doing it this year."

Miriam grunted.

Sarah glimpsed the closed door. No sign of her father. He'd most likely stopped at the cafeteria for coffee, which he now drank like water to keep himself going after recurring nights without sleep. She caught Miriam's contemplative gaze and, on impulse, asked if she remembered their conversation in the emergency room the day she was admitted. A deep horizontal line appeared between Miriam's eyebrows; she shook her head and fumbled with her sheet. Sarah listened to the monitor, beeping her grandmother's heart rate with a comforting regularity, and forged ahead.

"Do you remember telling me about Monya," she began, "when you were in emergency?"

Miriam's face blanched. Her shoulders wilted. "Monya," she said with reverence.

"You said he was Mom's brother. You said you left him in Riga."

Miriam rubbed her eyes. She rolled slowly onto her side, away from Sarah.

"Are you all right?"

Miriam lay still.

"We can talk about something else," Sarah offered, contrite. "I promise I won't mention Mo—him again."

"The truth is so hard to bear. Not many are willing to carry it," Miriam rasped.

"What do you mean?"

"I'm tired. You need to leave."

"I'm sorry."

"Sarah, you ready to go?"

Her father's voice burst into the room.

Sarah stumbled backward. Miriam rustled beneath her covers but said nothing. Sarah shifted her gaze from her father back to her grandmother. She feared she'd pushed too hard and would never get Miriam to talk about Monya again. It crushed her, knowing she'd come so close to solving the mystery that had framed her mother's identity, as well as her grandmother's. She reluctantly followed her father out of the hospital room, imbued with a grating sense of urgency. Miriam's health crisis was a jarring reminder that time was finite—the opportunity to build a relationship was shrinking. The chance to find answers could already be gone.

19

RIGA, OCTOBER 1941

GUTTE LET HERSELF INTO THE APARTMENT, SOLEMNLY greeted Miriam and her mother and set a basket of eggs on the counter. She filled a pot with water to boil the eggs, which Miriam couldn't buy anymore because she wasn't allowed to shop in Gentile stores, stocked with food she hadn't seen in Jewish shops in months: fresh bread, butter, eggs, milk, sour cream, oats, cakes and pastries, coffee and chocolate. Miriam, ashamed she couldn't repay Gutte, couldn't even give her tram fare, lowered her eyes and moved quietly down the hall.

The room Miriam shared with her children had become a cage for Ilana and Monya, who weren't allowed to play in the park or go to school because they were Jewish. Ilana lay in the bed, reading the newspaper (the only reading material available, without books), and Monya was sprawled on the floor with stones his grandfather had gathered, piling them up and watching them fall. There wouldn't be enough room in any ghetto apartment for him to spread out and play. Space was going to be tight. The family would likely end up with one room for all five of them, a situation Miriam couldn't fathom.

"Gutte brought eggs," Miriam told Ilana. "They'll be ready soon."

"All right," Ilana answered listlessly, without looking up from the paper.

Miriam watched her daughter gnaw on her thumbnail as though it were dripping with honey, and felt small and inadequate. Perhaps it was a mistake, not talking about Max. Perhaps Ilana needed to be heard.

"Do you want to talk?" she asked her daughter.

"About what?" Ilana mumbled.

Miriam sat at the edge of the bed, not sure what to say next. Comforting words had been Max's domain.

"Anything," Miriam said slowly, considering each word before it emerged from her lips. "Bubbe, Zayde, your brother." She took a deep breath. "Your father."

Ilana's head dropped. Tears hung from the tips of her long eyelashes like dew on leaves. "I can't," she said, her voice faltering.

Miriam pressed her lips together and stood, relieved. Ilana was right; it was too hard to talk about Max's last moments, to dredge up the past, to try to make sense of the illogical.

She retrieved her satchel, on the floor beside the bed, and pulled out a silk drawstring bag. Inside, a small box contained the pearl bracelet Max had given her as a name day gift a few years earlier, smuggled out of their house in a pair of shoes. Miriam had intended to save it for Ilana, as a wedding gift, but knew Max would approve of her change of heart.

Back in the kitchen, Gutte spooned hard-boiled eggs into a bowl and poured milk into two glasses for the children. Miriam put the box with the pearl bracelet in Gutte's calloused palm and closed her fingers over it.

"What is this?" Gutte asked, without opening her fingers.

"A small token of my gratitude," Miriam replied.

Gutte opened the box and gasped. "I can't accept this."

"Of course you can," Miriam assured her.

"But this . . ." Her brows snapped together. "It is special, from Max?"

"Yes. But I will not be able to keep it in the ghetto. I want you to have it. Max . . . Max would want that too."

"I will hold it for you until this lunacy ends."

"If it ends. And it's a gift, to thank you for all you've done for my family."

Tears shimmered in Gutte's steely eyes. "I come because it's atrocious, the way you're being treated."

Miriam was humbled by her goodness. If she were in Gutte's situation, she didn't know if she could be as brave. She didn't know if she had it in her, the courage to risk her own safety in order to help others. She met Gutte's benevolent eyes and an idea, a way to save her children, began to form in Miriam's mind.

20

CHICAGO, FEBRUARY 1976

Two days after Miriam was released from the hospital, Sarah called to see how she was doing. No answer. She called a few minutes later, but again no answer. At the end of the day, she hurried out of her office to the "L," facing a blustery wind that blew her skirt up to her waist. At her grandmother's apartment, she knocked on her door once, twice, three times before opening it with the key her father had had made, in case of an emergency.

Sarah was greeted by the mustiness of an apartment that hadn't been aired out for a while and the customary smoky haze that defined her grandmother. The toilet flushed. Water streamed in the bathroom sink. The bathroom door opened, revealing a frail, stooped Miriam, who still managed to look as if she were going to a fancy restaurant, in a shiny avocado-green dress, black stockings with a seam running up the back of her legs, slingback pumps that matched her dress and an unbuttoned brown cardigan. A tissue was stuffed in the left sleeve of her cardigan.

"You have the patience of a bear with a jar of honey," Miriam said when she emerged from the bathroom and noticed Sarah at the door.

Sarah could tell, from the upward lilt of her voice, that Miriam was not disappointed to see her. She apologized for barging in, stamped the snow from her knee-high boots and set them on a plastic mat next to Miriam's clunky, more practical winter boots. The apartment was hot. Sarah hung her coat on a hook and followed Miriam into the kitchen.

"Don't you have telephones in your office?" Miriam asked. She filled the kettle with water.

"Of course. I tried calling but kept getting a busy signal, so I was worried." She breathed in Miriam's soapy Nivea aroma and sensed her mother's presence.

"I've been here all day."

"Maybe you were asleep and didn't hear the phone?"

"My heart may be slowing down, but there's nothing wrong with my ears. I can hear Mrs. Levi's alarm clock go off twice a day, reminding her to take her medication, and there's a ceiling between us."

"Strange. Did you accidentally knock your phone off the hook? My friend Heather does it all the time, charges past and hits the phone with her purse or coat, and nobody can reach her until she figures it out."

Miriam gave her a *we'll see* look and stepped out from the kitchen. Sarah listened to the clunk of her heels on the floor, the sound of the telephone receiver being picked up and set in place. A moment later, a flushed Miriam returned, mumbling about medication that made her drowsy and less alert. Sarah tucked her chin to hide her smile; her mother would have reacted in much the same way as Miriam, embarrassed by her own mistake, unable to admit fault.

"Your father was here for hours yesterday," her grandmother went on. "The two of you are wearing me out. I had more rest at the hospital."

"I'm sure Dr. Fine would love to see you," Sarah teased.

"Oh." Her grandmother's arms flapped with annoyance. "That insufferable man with all his charts and medical gibberish." She dumped two tea bags in her pot.

"I thought he was charming."

"You weren't the one lying there helpless, at his mercy."

"I'm sorry, Grandma, but there's nothing helpless about you. I think Dr. Fine met his match with you."

Satisfaction passed briefly across her grandmother's face. "You don't have to babysit me. I can manage perfectly well on my own."

"I know. I want to be here. And I ordered Chinese food for dinner before I left for the train."

"Dinner? I just had lunch. How can I possibly think about dinner?"

"It won't be delivered for half an hour. Maybe you'll be hungry by then."

"I doubt it. I rarely get hungry."

The newspaper article she'd read on microfiche, about Jews in ghettos, flickered in Sarah's mind. Her gut cramped, as if a belt were cinched too tightly around her waist, thinking about her grandmother and mother, who might have gone days without eating during the war. Suddenly, she was racked with guilt for every time she'd complained to her mother about starving. Or being cold. Or not having the "right" clothes.

Steam curled from the kettle's spout. Her grandmother turned off the burner and poured boiling water into the teapot. The polish on her thumbnails and a few of her fingernails was chipped, and the nail on her right ring finger had broken off at the base. Sarah grabbed cups and brought them to the dining table. A well-worn spiral notebook lay open, her grandmother's meticulous cursive filling the lined pages.

"That's private." Miriam snatched the notebook from the table and stuffed it in a kitchen drawer.

"I didn't read anything."

Miriam gave her a cagey look and sat down. Sarah's heart thumped as she rummaged through her brain for a delicate way to steer the conversation toward Monya.

"I really like this tea."

"You haven't even taken a sip yet."

"It's the same kind I had last time."

"I know why you're here."

"To see you, and make sure you're okay."

"That's just a ploy, like Dr. Fine's threat of an X-ray to get me to stay without complaining."

"You knew?"

"What do you take me for?" Her grandmother sipped her tea and inspected her fire-engine-red polished fingernails. "He was so proud of himself, thinking he'd deceived me. I didn't have the heart to let him down. He wasn't a terrible doctor. I've had worse."

Sarah smiled and wiped a bead of sweat from her brow with a napkin. "You don't miss anything, do you?"

"Can't afford to, at my age."

"You're not old."

"Buttering me up isn't going to help your case."

"What case?"

"You want to know about Monya."

Sarah nodded and leaned in closer. "Have you had a chance to read the letters I found? Were they about Monya?"

"I thought I was going to die when I told you about him."

"You only want me to know about him when you're dying?"

"I never should have opened my mouth."

"But you did. And I deserve to know what happened to him,

and why he didn't come here with you. He's my uncle, the only uncle I have."

"We don't always get what we deserve." A shadow darkened her grandmother's stolid face.

Miriam grabbed the spoon from the sugar dish and stirred her tea, though she drank it black. Her eyes flitted around the apartment, settling on a plant with green stripes on one side of the leaves and cranberry-purple undersides, perched in the macramé hanger in front of the window. She rose from her seat and shuffled over to the striped plant and pinched the long, vining tendrils with the nails of her thumb and forefinger. "Do you know what this plant is called?"

"No. Like I said, my mom didn't have any indoor plants."

"It's a wandering Jew."

"Really?" Sarah got up and joined Miriam at the window.

"They don't need much attention." Miriam poked her finger into the container, pulled it out and examined the specks of dirt on her skin. "You can spray it with mist about once a week, but if you forget, it will live for a while."

Sarah was perplexed by her grandmother's tenderness toward a plant.

"This one won't last much longer. They don't age well, wandering Jews."

"Why is it called a wandering Jew?"

Miriam shuffled back to the table and wrapped her hands around her teacup.

A knock at the door.

Her grandmother's forehead creased into folds. "I'm not expecting anyone."

Sarah glanced at her watch. "Must be the Chinese food. Early."

"Who?"

141

"Our dinner." Sarah hurried to the door. "Remember, I told you?" She opened the door and was inundated by the mouthwatering fragrance of sweet and sour chicken balls.

"Delivery for Sarah Byrne?" A square-jawed Chinese teenager held out a large brown paper bag with the receipt stapled to the top.

"That's me." She paid him and carried the bag into the kitchen.

Her grandmother raised her nose and sniffed the air.

"It smells good, doesn't it?" Sarah said brightly. "Rice and egg rolls and chicken balls and—"

"Too spicy for me," her grandmother interjected.

"You don't have to use any of the sauces."

"I'm not hungry. You eat."

"I can make you some soup and toast," Sarah offered.

"I have no appetite." Miriam returned to the table and poured herself a cup of tea.

"I don't want to eat in front of you."

"Then don't." Her grandmother watered the plants on the table with the leftover tea in the pot. One plant overflowed with murky water, which dribbled onto the lace tablecloth.

Sarah opened the paper bag, pulled out the white cardboard containers and set them on the table.

"Who did you think you were feeding, everyone in the building?"

Sarah put a heap of egg foo yong on her plate. "I always order too much." She took an egg roll and some rice. "You can have whatever's left tomorrow. Chinese food is even better the next day."

"What is that?" Miriam pointed at the egg foo yong.

"It's eggs, mushrooms and gravy." Sarah dug her fork into her mound of egg foo yong. "My favorite."

Her grandmother tapped her fingers on the table. Turned her head. Her gaze lingered on Sarah's plate. "Maybe I'll try some. Don't want it to go to waste."

"Terrific." Sarah gave her grandmother a generous portion of egg foo yong.

"Oh, no," she protested. "I could never eat all this."

"Eat what you can."

Her grandmother poked her egg foo yong before taking a small bite.

"Well? What do you think?"

"It's eggs." Miriam lowered her eyes and cleared her plate.

Sarah smiled and cut her egg roll in half with her fork. "I guess you like Chinese food."

"It's all right," Miriam acknowledged, moving her fork around on her plate to scoop up the last bits of fried rice. "I need to pay you for my dinner."

"Not necessary. It's my treat."

"I can pay for my own meal. I may not be rich, but I can afford to feed myself."

"Really. I wanted to do this for you."

"How much did it cost?"

"Grandma, please. I don't need your money. I have a good job." Miriam dabbed the corners of her mouth with her napkin. "How much?"

"I'd take the letters translated in place of the money."

"How much?"

"You're incorrigible, Grandma, you know that?"

"I've been called worse. Tell me what I owe."

"The bill was thirteen dollars, but—"

"Thirteen dollars? For one meal?"

"I don't order Chinese a lot, just for special occasions, like dinner with you."

"I should hope not." Her grandmother stood and slowly made her way to the desk beside the closet. She opened the right drawer and retrieved a worn black leather handbag the size of a briefcase. She extracted her wallet and counted six crisp one-dollar bills and two quarters.

"I can't take your money." Sarah got up to clear the dishes.

"Take it," Miriam insisted. "You can't hold your head high with your hand out."

Sarah leaned against the doorframe between the kitchen and the dining table. "Mom used to . . . say things like that. Proverbs. To make a point."

A glimmer of approval brightened her grandmother's eyes. She pressed the money into Sarah's hand.

"I'll hold on to it, but I won't spend it." Sarah took the bills, folded them and stuck them in her pants pocket. "It's not a charity, treating you to dinner. We're family. It's what families do—eat together, and treat one another."

Her grandmother tilted her head as if she was considering Sarah's words. She took a glass from the kitchen cupboard and filled it with lukewarm tap water. She grabbed a pair of scissors from a drawer and bustled over to her wandering Jew, where she cut several shoots and put them in the glass.

"They'll root in water." She handed the glass to Sarah. "Keep this in a sunny window and add water when the level drops."

Sarah peered through the glass at the veiny plum-colored stems and hoped she'd manage to keep them alive. "Thanks. I will."

"Back home, in Riga, women used to share cuttings. Plants would travel from house to house, from city to city."

"So that's why—"

"I'm exhausted."

"Oh," Sarah said, deflated. "How about I make some more tea?"

"I'll be up all night in the toilet," she said frankly.

"That would be terrible," Sarah said, reminded of her mother, who spoke with the same directness as Miriam and limited herself to one cup of tea after dinner, for the same reason. "Let me put the leftovers in your refrigerator."

"It's too much food!" Miriam protested.

"Eat what you can."

Miriam turned on the television and lowered herself onto the sofa. She lit a cigarette, crossed one leg over the other and sat perfectly serene as she smoked and watched the news.

Sarah set the glass of vines on the coffee table. She brought all the white cardboard food containers from the table into the kitchen, and folded the tops to close them. The refrigerator was jammed with plastic containers of sour cream and cottage cheese, two cartons of eggs, a drawerful of tangerines, a carton of milk, another drawer with cream, butter, cheese and a couple of grapefruits. It was almost exactly like her mother's refrigerator, every square inch filled.

Sarah juggled containers around to make space for the Chinese food, then peeked in the cupboards. Just as she thought—enough cereal, cans of soup, tuna and sardines (gross), crackers and unopened jars of jam to feed three people for a year. Just like her mother.

"Why didn't you and Mom get along?" Sarah asked as she retrieved her jar of wandering Jew roots from the coffee table. "Was it because she was so young when she got married? Did you want her to wait?"

"Your mother was an old soul," Miriam said, reflective. "She'd seen more at nineteen than most people see their entire lives." She paused. "I was happy the day she married your father. He was good for her."

"Then what was the problem?" Sarah pressed.

Miriam leaned forward and tapped her cigarette against the ashtray, releasing a spear of ashes. "You are strong, like Ilana, and stubborn," she replied, evading Sarah's question. "But you are more thoughtful. Ilana was impetuous."

Impetuous? Not once had Sarah seen even a trace of this in her prudent mother, who scheduled every appointment weeks in advance and became visibly flustered at last-minute changes. And she'd berated Sarah for being reckless in high school, occasionally arriving home after curfew, tipsy from a few drinks. Miriam's depiction of her mother didn't fit the person who had raised her. Was Miriam seeing what she wanted to see, or was she recalling her mother as a spirited, carefree child, before the war?

Sarah felt her mother's liminal presence. She was struck by the paradox of war, which destroyed her mother's family and forever limited the woman she might have become. Yet her own existence was a direct consequence of the war. Shivers ran up and down her spine, though it had to be eighty degrees in Miriam's apartment.

"I haven't spoken about Monya in years," her grandmother said abruptly, in a hollow voice.

Sarah's fingers tightened around the glass jar.

"He wasn't even two, the last time I held him."

Sarah listened, afraid to disrupt Miriam's unexpected stream of memories.

"He loved to build things with blocks. He was a happy boy." Miriam gazed out the window as if she were watching a film. "Always with an impish smile on his face. He was too young to know the danger around us. Ilana was nine and had already seen too much." She paused and crushed her cigarette in the ashtray. "Ilana had stopped smiling. I didn't want that for Monya, so our housekeeper, Gutte Meija, took them in, before we were forced to the ghetto." Her voice thickened. "Your mother cried and begged me not to make her go, but it was the only way I knew to keep them safe."

Sarah's hands shook. Her stomach churned. She'd been so

anxious for the truth and now that it dangled in front of her, she wanted it to be different.

"I can't do this." Miriam rose and plodded into the bathroom. She shut the door.

Sarah listened for the toilet flushing. The swish of running water. The silence was deafening.

"Grandma, are you all right?" Sarah asked, dry-mouthed. She tiptoed to the bathroom and pressed her ear against the door.

"I'm fine, just . . ."

"Just what?"

"Go. Please."

"Are you sure? I can stay."

"Just go."

Sarah kept her ear to the door for a few seconds before telling her grandmother to call if she needed anything or wanted to talk, then let herself out of the apartment. In the corridor, she grabbed hold of the handrail and bent over, seized by nausea. Her hairline was wet with perspiration. When the nausea passed, Sarah staggered out of the building, hunched over, clutching her stomach. Unable to fathom the image of her grandmother walking away from her children, not knowing if she'd ever see them again.

Find him.

She had to know if Monya was alive. She had to go to Riga.

21

RIGA, OCTOBER 1941

M IRIAM SCRUBBED MONYA UNTIL HIS SKIN TURNED PINK and dressed him in his finest clothes: long black stockings, black H-bar shorts with suspenders, and a long-sleeved brown shirt. Ilana bathed herself and washed her chopped hair, which dried in ringlets at the base of her scalp. Gutte packed their meager belongings, sobs escaping her lips as she bustled around the apartment. She and her husband had agreed to take Ilana and Monya into their home, posing as their orphaned niece and nephew. As Lutherans, they were in no danger of being persecuted by the Nazis, which meant Miriam's children would be safe there— as long as nobody discovered the ruse. If the truth were exposed, Gutte's entire family, along with Ilana and Monya, would be killed. It was a sacrifice that showed Miriam, beyond a doubt, Gutte's devotion to her children.

Miriam's parents, visiting their closest friends in Mežaparks, would be furious. That was why she waited until Gutte, the children and she were alone, to avoid confrontation. She was afraid her mother would wear her down until she changed her mind. It wouldn't have taken much persuasion. Every five minutes, Miriam wavered, coming up with ways to justify bringing her children to the ghetto, and every time, she had to admit she was thinking more of herself than of them. The best room she and her father had been able to find was a loft in a rickety house on Sadovņikova iela, just inside the main gate. When her mother laid eyes on it, not to mention the ghetto itself, she'd understand why Miriam couldn't let her children waste away in those conditions.

"You're going somewhere special," Miriam told Ilana while she buttoned Monya's shirt and tried to ignore the spasm in her chest.

Ilana's eyes sparked with interest. Miriam immediately regretted her choice of words.

Monya grinned and reached for Miriam's braid and twirled it with his stubby fingers. His joyful innocence made Miriam feel like a failure for not getting him out of harm's way when they had the chance. Her children would still have a father if they'd left Riga the way Max wanted. Now, it was too late. It was a regret that made her doubt her competence as a mother. It was a regret that made her doubt her ability to be loved.

"What about Zeyde and Bubbe?" Ilana asked. "And you? Aren't you coming with us?"

"Not right now," Miriam responded tersely. "Go put on your black dress."

"What's wrong?" Ilana stopped brushing her hair and looked at Miriam. "You look sad."

"Nothing," Miriam replied, unable to look Ilana in the eye. "I told you to put on your dress."

"Why? We can't go anywhere nice."

"Just put it on."

"I don't think it fits anymore."

"It will be fine," Miriam said through clenched teeth. "Wear it over your white blouse, and make sure you choose clean white socks."

"Where are we going?"

"Get dressed." Miriam couldn't keep the edge out of her voice.

Ilana bowed her head and slunk down the hall. Monya toddled over to Miriam and tugged at her hem. She picked him up and planted a kiss on his warm cheek and set him down, afraid that if she held him for too long, she wouldn't be able to let go. War meant unspeakable sacrifices.

Ilana reappeared in her black dress, which was, indeed, too small, falling above her knees. And the sleeves of her white blouse were a good ten centimeters from her slender wrists. Miriam looked at her daughter, saw how hunger had chiseled her face down to her bones, and thought, This is what's best for my children. She held out Ilana's black coat and Monya's red sweater. "Time to go."

Ilana examined her coat, inside and out. "Where are the yellow stars?" She took Monya's sweater and looked at it. "There're no stars on his sweater either."

"Stop with the questions," Miriam snapped.

"We don't have to wear stars anymore? Can we go back to school?"

"Did you hear me?"

Miriam set Monya on a chair and wrestled him into the sweater. His little arms flailed as she tried to poke them into the sleeves.

"Tell me where we're going," Ilana demanded.

Gutte appeared with a bundle of their clothes tied in paper and string, like laundry. "You're coming to live with me and my husband," she said quietly. "Just until the war ends."

Ilana's mouth gaped. She looked from her mother to Gutte then threw herself at Miriam and sobbed into her bosom. "Don't send me away. Please, Mama. I want to stay with you."

Monya's bottom lip quivered. He stared at his sister. Tears pooled in his eyes. He began whimpering.

Miriam swallowed the doubts engorging her throat like a fist and dried her eyes on her sleeve. She had to show Ilana how to tuck her sadness away, to be strong for her brother. She clamped her hands on Ilana's shoulders and said, with resolve: "You are upsetting your brother. Stop crying. Tears are a sign of weakness, and you are not weak. You are strong and brave. You will go with Gutte and help her with Monya and do what she says to stay safe. Do you understand?"

Ilana stared at her mother with red-rimmed eyes, sniffed and nodded.

Miriam caught Gutte's grief-stricken expression and pressed on. "There is more."

"What?" Ilana said through her tears.

"You cannot be Jewish when you are with Gutte and her family."

Ilana cocked her head.

"No Yiddish," Miriam explained. "Speak only Russian and Latvian."

Ilana held her mother's gaze. "That's why Papa was killed, isn't it? Because he was Jewish."

Miriam's breath stuck in her throat. "Yes."

Ilana lowered her eyes, then raised them to meet her mother's. "Papa always told me to be proud I was Jewish."

Miriam's neck stiffened. The Germans not only killed Max, they took away her children's dignity. "Not anymore. It is not safe." She paused to give Ilana time to digest this unsettling information. "There's one more thing. From now on, you will be called Inga, and Monya is Andris. Inga and Andris Kalnina."

"What?" Ilana said, startled.

"It is the only way to keep you safe," Gutte interjected. "Your names would give you away as Jews."

"I don't want to forget my name," Ilana said. "I don't want to be anyone but me."

Miriam took her daughter's face in her hands. "You will always be Ilana in your heart, but outside, you must be Inga." She squeezed Ilana's jaw tighter. "Do you understand?"

Ilana's lips quivered. She gave a slight nod.

"And you must promise me you will take care of your brother. Watch out for him."

"I promise," she said, her voice barely a whisper.

Miriam let go of Ilana and nodded at Gutte. It was time. Her children would not be safe until they made it to Gutte's house in the suburb of Ķīpsala, on the other side of the Daugava River, a journey fraught with danger. She and Gutte had planned this departure to coincide with the busiest part of the day, when soldiers and police were less likely to ask for identity papers. Gutte's husband had arranged for false baptism papers for Ilana and Monya, showing they were Gutte's niece and nephew, orphaned when the Soviets had deported their parents. But Ilana needed more time to get used to her new identity before facing a barrage of questions.

Miriam draped Ilana's coat over her narrow shoulders. When the coat was new, Ilana had filled it out nicely. Children were supposed to grow bigger, not smaller. Parents were supposed to keep their children healthy and safe. Miriam's children were wasting away before her eyes. It broke her heart, not being able to give them what they needed, and this quelled any reservations she had about giving her children away.

Ilana gave Miriam a final, teary hug. Miriam kissed Monya's forehead softly, breathed in his baby scent of powder and soap, and turned her back to the door when they left. She couldn't bear the sight of them walking out, not knowing when, or if, she'd see them again.

22

CHICAGO, FEBRUARY 1976

THE ABSURDITY OF HER DECISION HIT SARAH AT AROUND two in the morning, after she'd tossed and turned for hours. The odds of finding Monya were slim to none, there was a real danger in traveling to the Soviet Union as an American, plus her father, not to mention Miriam, would be dead set against her going. For good reason. It was a crazy idea, totally out of character for Sarah.

She was not a risk-taker. Probably why her relationships never lasted more than three or four months; she was terminally afraid of jumping in with both feet, afraid of surrendering herself to another person, afraid of having her heart broken. This was the reason she'd broken up with Henry, though he was different from the others. More serious. More committed. She'd fallen for him with a deepness that terrified her. The harder she fell, the harder it would be to recover if he let her go.

Frustrated and exhausted, she lay on her back and went through the routine her mother had taught her years earlier, to find sleep. She wiggled her toes and let them go limp. On to her feet and legs. Upward, limb by limb, muscle by muscle, counting to ten slowly, the way her mother showed her to divert her attention from her galloping thoughts. This worked well when Sarah was a child and fretted about simpler things, like an overdue library book, or if a friend would like the birthday present she'd chosen. Traveling to Riga, part of the Soviet Union, was an entirely different matter. It might even be impossible. Which could be for the best. But if that weren't the case . . . Thoughts of Riga wormed their way into her head, undoing the interlude of stillness, winding her up with excitement and apprehension.

He wasn't even two, the last time I saw him.

Miriam's words pealed in Sarah's ears like an alarm clock, telling her it was time to go.

THE FOLLOWING MORNING, Sarah found it difficult to concentrate on a focus group questionnaire for the Kenwood Chef stand mixer, her attention still divided by plans and qualms about traveling to Latvia. After setting and reaching a goal of a dozen focus group questions, she wrote the Soviet embassy in Washington asking for an address, a phone number, anything about Monya Talan in Latvia, his last known location.

At lunch, she dropped the letter in her agency's mail slot and took the elevator to the ground-level travel agency, a small office with two desks and alluring posters of beaches and mountains on ivory walls. There was a distinct chemical rose smell in the office, the kind of aroma that came from a can of air freshener. She waited for a petite woman with a Dorothy Hamill bob to finish a telephone conversation. They were the only people in the office.

The woman cupped her hand over the phone and mouthed, "One minute." She gestured for Sarah to take the chair in front of her desk, lined with mugs from Pan Am, TWA, Northwest Airlines,

Continental Air and Holiday Inn. Typical marketing giveaways, Sarah knew from working at the agency. She had a few in her office, nothing spectacular—a mug with the Pillsbury logo, a poster of an orange Ford Pinto, L'eggs nylons, and a case of Comet cleanser too bulky to carry onto the "L."

The travel agent hung up the phone, apologized for keeping her waiting and introduced herself as Melanie. Sarah gave her name and said she was interested in booking a trip to Riga.

"Where?" Melanie's face went blank.

"Riga. Latvia. In the Baltics."

"The Baltics?"

Sarah forced a smile. She had expected a travel agent to know about Riga, or at least Latvia. "Well, technically, Latvia's part of the Soviet Union."

Melanie looked at her, flabbergasted. "You want to go to the Soviet Union?"

"My mother is from Riga. I may have family there."

"I must admit, this is a first for me, Riga. Usually, at this time of year, people are booking hot destinations like Florida and the Caribbean." Melanie laughed self-consciously and grabbed a thick book from the shelf beside her desk. "I remember my colleague booking a client to Moscow with a company called . . ." Melanie rifled through the pages in her book. "Aha!" She brought her French-manicured finger to the top of a page. "Intourist. The Soviet travel agency." She ran her finger across the page. "Looks like I have to call their agency in New York for more specific information." She reached for the telephone. "You have time for me to call now?"

Sarah glanced at her watch: forty minutes until she had to be back. "Sure." Her heart fluttered. This was it, the moment she'd discover if Americans could actually visit Riga.

Melanie dialed the long-distance number and told the person

on the other end she was looking for information about booking a customer to Riga through Intourist.

Sarah took in the large poster of a beach on the wall to her left while Melanie was on the phone, jotting down information. The turquoise water seemed to melt into the clear sky and the foamy waves curled onto white, velvety sand. It would be so much easier if she wanted a vacation in Florida or the Bahamas. Melanie would actually know how to book the trip and Sarah wouldn't have to lie about it. Maybe this was an ominous sign, not being able to tell the truth. She was as bad as her mother and Miriam, plotting a secret trip to Riga. She wondered if her mother ever regretted lying to her, if she'd ever come close to telling Sarah about being separated from her mother during the war. About Monya. If she cried about him when she was alone.

When Melanie got off the phone, Sarah could tell from the way she exhaled noisily that this wasn't going to be easy. Melanie explained that summer visits were available, but Sarah had to obtain a passport and visa, which would then be sent to Intourist for inspection. Intourist would conduct a background check, and once Sarah was approved as a tourist, Melanie would book her on a summer tour.

"You mean I *can* go to the Soviet Union, to Riga?" Sarah said, tripping over her words.

"Once you have a passport, visa and background check."

"A background check? What are they looking for? Should I be worried?"

"Not at all. Just Soviet bureaucracy, you know, to make sure you're not a threat," Melanie replied casually.

"I'm just a lowly market researcher."

"Then you'll pass with flying colors." Melanie straightened a stack of papers and said there were a couple more issues Sarah needed to consider before making a final decision.

"Like what?"

Melanie folded her hands together and said family visits had to be organized through the embassy.

"So I could visit my uncle, if I can find him?" Sarah asked eagerly.

Melanie scanned her notes. "As long as you have a separate visa and an invitation from your uncle that is approved by the embassy."

"Oh." Sarah's face fell.

"Do you want the special visa form that you'd need to see your uncle?" asked Melanie. "You have to fill it out with your uncle's contact information and get it signed by the Soviet embassy before leaving the United States."

You have to find him.

"Do you?" Melanie repeated.

She thought about the darkness her mother had carried from Monya's absence. A darkness her grandmother still carried. A darkness that was tangible as mud, heaps of trauma folded into a sludge that blocked the light from getting in.

"Yes," Sarah said firmly. "I do."

"Okay." Melanie opened the top-right drawer of her desk and thumbed through her files. She handed Sarah passport and visa application forms, and told her she'd have to get a passport photo and two references to verify she was actually Sarah Byrne. They couldn't be family members and had to be professionals who'd known her for at least five years— a dentist, a doctor, a teacher. Once the applications were completed, Sarah was to bring them back to Melanie.

Sarah studied the documents, a daunting number of pages strewn with blank lines. She itched to get started on them, to be on a plane, her first flight ever, to explore the "Paris of the Baltics," the city where a branch of her family tree was rooted and broken. "Do you think I can be ready to go in July?"

Melanie glanced at a calendar on the wall. "Shouldn't be a

problem, if you get your applications in soon. My colleague said it takes about three months for everything to be approved, but there are no guarantees. It all depends on how fast the wheels of American and Soviet bureaucracy turn."

Over the next couple of weeks, Sarah approached her trip like a project with an unbreakable deadline, crossing items off a to-do list each day, giving her doctor and dentist the same story she'd told her father, Miriam and Heather: she was going to London, England. Not exactly a lie, as she would change planes in London before going on to Riga.

The planning lifted her spirits during endless days of running focus groups and reviewing transcripts, and helped keep her mind off regrets about Henry. He had told her he loved her on their fourth date, an admission that made her anxious and euphoric. It wasn't the first time a man had used the word "love," but it was the first time it hadn't felt like a ploy to get her into bed. It was real, and for a couple of months Sarah envisioned herself staying with Henry, marrying him. Until the habitual feeling of suffocation settled over her, the way it did whenever someone got too close, when she worried their lives were too intertwined, when she couldn't extract herself from their entity as a couple. She broke it off, and only then did it occur to her that she'd never said she loved him too. Even though she did.

THE DAY FINALLY came to bring in the documents required by Intourist. Sarah laid them on Melanie's desk with a triumphant grin, as if they were winning lottery tickets. Then Melanie asked if she'd had any luck in her search for Monya, and Sarah's victory felt hollow somehow.

23

RIGA, OCTOBER 25, 1941

M IRIAM UNFOLDED ILANA'S TEA-COLORED SWEATER AND buried her face in the scratchy wool. Her mother had just finished knitting it a few days before Gutte took her children, and Miriam had forgotten to send it with them. It was too big for Ilana. Miriam's mother intentionally made sweaters and dresses and shirts too big, "so all my hard work won't be for nothing if they outgrow it in a week." Miriam held the sweater up to her chest. The sleeves came to just past her elbows. She inserted her arms in the sleeves and buttoned the front over her woolen dress. Ilana's sweater was tight, especially over her chest, where the buttonholes stretched, but it fit well enough for her to wear until she had her daughter back. It connected her to Ilana.

Miriam pictured Monya sitting forlorn in Gutte's house, wondering where she'd gone, his eyes wet with tears, believing his mother had abandoned him. Her blood ran cold. She bristled. Packed the image away, next to her memory of the officers' attack, next to the image of Max in the burning synagogue, next to her horrible twilight sleep, secrets festering like germs.

Knowing the hovel that awaited them, they'd put off the move to the ghetto as long as they could. Today marked the deadline to go. Miriam's father loaded a pushcart with their scant belongings: a rucksack filled with canned food, two plates, bowls and cups, a shoebox of family photos removed from their frames, tooth- and hairbrushes, and two books Miriam had wrapped in sheets to smuggle out of her house—Tolstoy's *Anna Karenina*, for Ilana when she was a bit older, and the tenth volume of Simon Dubnow's *The History of the Jewish People*. Miriam felt Max's presence whenever she held his book.

On the way out of the apartment, Miriam's mother snipped a tendril from the green-and-magenta spiderwort plant in the kitchen window. "Your grandmother used to say a house is not a home without greenery."

"I remember," Miriam said wistfully. "She had so many plants, her apartment was like an indoor garden."

Her mother set the shoot carefully on top of a blanket and moved the potted plant sideways to catch the light. Long shoots dangled over the edge of the windowsill. Miriam poked her finger into the dry soil, couldn't remember the last time she'd watered it. Spiderworts lasted so long without water, they were often called wandering Jews, an allusion to Moses and the Israelites, wandering the Sinai desert for forty years.

"I grew this from a shoot I cut from my plant in Mežaparks. It reminds me of home," her mother explained.

Miriam stroked the zebra-patterned leaves and recalled the thriving plants in her parents' house; her former life seemed so distant, so unfathomable, so unreal. Conjuring up the past made Miriam homesick. She yearned for Max and her children, for what they'd lost. Instinctively, she reached for her mother, who flinched at her touch. Miriam shut her eyes and choked back her unrequited feelings.

Her mother picked up a bundle of food and walked out of the apartment. Miriam set Max's radio on the kitchen counter, beside the plant, and took in their apartment for the last time, the eerie atmosphere of the place that once abounded with the sounds of her children and husband, now empty and quiet. The last place she and Max lived together. She closed the door and twisted her gold wedding band, her sole bond to Max, the one thing she would keep no matter what.

It had stormed in the night and clouds swelled in the pewter-gray sky, threatening more rain. Miriam had a suitcase in each arm, with clothing for the three of them. Her mother toted a basket filled with butter, eggs wrapped in a cloth, a jar of pickled beets and two loaves of bread Gutte had left for them. Once the ghetto was closed to the rest of the city, they'd only be able to buy food from the ghetto store. After seeing bare shelves in Jewish shops for months, Miriam's expectations were low.

"If Ilana were here, she could carry another suitcase," her mother said brusquely as they joined the exodus of Jews along the street's gutter (they were not allowed on the sidewalk), carting their meager belongings to the ghetto. "We wouldn't have had to leave so much behind."

Miriam welcomed her mother's incensed tone, largely absent during the long months in their apartment as restrictions against Jews had increased. It seemed as if her mother had given up, but now, on their way to the ghetto, where every ounce of fortitude would be necessary for survival, her mother's gumption was returning.

"We would also need more if Ilana and Monya were with us," Miriam pointed out. "And who would carry Monya? I'd only be able to take one suitcase. We'd have two more people and no more suitcases."

"At least your children would be with us." Her mother gestured right, at a family trudging single file down the gutter. "Look—the Rozins kept their children. They didn't throw them away like rotten apples."

"Enough, Dora," Miriam's father said from behind them as he limped along with the pushcart.

"I didn't throw anyone away, Mama."

"And for goodness' sake, Miriam," her mother went on, "when was the last time you bathed? I can barely stand the smell of you." She scrunched her nose and shot Miriam a disdainful glare.

Heat rose up Miriam's neck. She couldn't tell her mother why stinking was a conscious choice.

"Look," her mother declared, "there are the Feinmanns, with all *six* of their children."

"Stop, Dora," Miriam's father huffed. "What's done is done."

"How can you say that?" her mother said, indignant. "Miriam could go get them back. Today."

"So they can live in a shack behind a fence?" Miriam said.

"Children can get used to anything."

"Then they'll get used to staying with Gutte, where there's a decent roof over their heads and enough food to fill their stomachs, and they don't have to wear yellow stars."

"They'll forget who they are and where they come from. Is that what you want?"

"Of course not. I had no choice."

"Ech! You did have a choice. To keep your own flesh and blood with you—"

"Both of you, quiet!" Miriam's father, his face red from the strain of pushing the heavy cart through muddy streets, glared at them.

Dora shot Miriam a look of annoyance that plainly said she wasn't finished. Miriam wanted to march ahead, desperate for a little breathing space, but the road was thronged with wagons on the way to the ghetto, while the other side was mobbed with Russians moving in the opposite direction, away from the ghetto, making way for Jews to claim their homes.

We're like fish swimming upstream and downstream at the same time, Miriam thought with despair.

A screech ricocheted through the air. Miriam turned toward the sound and caught sight of a row of Arājs Kommando members stealing pushcarts and beating Jews with truncheons. She broke into a sweat, watching people treated worse than animals. Dehumanized. For being Jewish.

Directly in front of Miriam, a white-haired woman using a cane stumbled and fell.

"*Steigā*, hurry, get up," an Arājs Kommando officer shouted at the old woman.

Miriam tried to stop, to help the woman to her feet, but the river of people thrust her forward. The officer struck the woman with a whip. Her head contorted and dropped. He seized her arm and dragged her off. No one seemed to notice, and the crowd shuffled on.

IT WAS RAINING and there was a palpable tang of mud and feces when Miriam and her parents streamed past leering Arājs Kommando members, through the gate with hundreds of other Jews, like water through a gap in a dam. Barbed wire divided the ghetto from the rest of Riga, jagged, finite squares that smacked of hopelessness. Above the gate, a sign stated: *Jews provided for a fee. This includes Wehrmacht jobs.* There it was in black and white, Miriam thought, proof they were considered slaves. She gaped at the words and mourned the loss of her dignity.

Miriam glanced sideways at her father, whose hair had gone

from salt-and-pepper to gray in a matter of weeks. His eyes puddled with tears. Her mother's cheeks were hollow from malnutrition, but her face was freshly scrubbed, and she'd tied a lavender scarf around her neck as if she were going somewhere special.

She expected more, Miriam realized with a twinge of sadness. Her mother actually believed, or had convinced herself, that the ghetto was just another place to live.

"This can't be . . ." her mother cried, her voice faltering, when they stopped outside the shoddy old house that Miriam and her father had chosen.

Miriam's feet sank into the muddy ground and her hair, drenched through, made her feel top-heavy. The rain drummed against the sagging wood roof, the shutter was missing from the window beside the door, the joints were blackened, and the rancid stench of urine saturated the air. She peered down the street, crawling with displaced families, and saw nothing better than what they had.

Her father let go of the pushcart. "I never imagined it'd come to this," he mumbled. "I never thought they'd get away with it, locking us up in a cage . . ."

Her mother started down the mucky street with wild eyes. Miriam dropped her suitcases and turned to go after her.

"Don't." Her father stuck his arm out, blocking Miriam's way. "She'll cause a scene if you try to stop her."

Miriam saw her zigzagging down the street in a frenzy, and was overcome by her mother's agitation. This, the ghetto, had pushed her mother over the edge. Miriam watched her return with the stiffness of an old woman and, for the first time, feared her mother wasn't strong enough to survive whatever lay ahead.

"This is temporary, Dora," Miriam's father assured her. "At least we have a roof over our heads and each other."

"Papa's right," Miriam echoed with conviction, though she didn't believe it was true.

Her mother looked at them with blank, glossy eyes, like shards of glass. She'd gone from irate to placid as if she'd been anesthetized.

Miriam followed her father inside, where rain gushed through holes in the roof and people were squabbling about the space on the ground floor. Nine children. Two fathers and two mothers. Thirteen people would be sleeping, cooking and eating in a room about the size of the sitting room in Miriam's apartment on Avotu iela, where the family had been cramped with just a few pieces of furniture.

Miriam and her parents stood at the door for a moment, unnoticed, watching the chaos unfold in front of them like a scene from Pushkin's *Boris Godunov*.

"This must be a mistake," a woman retorted.

"No mistake," a man snapped. "We're all supposed to be here."

"We can't possibly fit enough mattresses for all of us. And what are we supposed to do during the day, trample on each other's beds like chickens?"

"Why are you looking at me? How am I supposed to know?"

A baby squealed, piercing the stale, briny air.

"What is that smell? Did you bring fish in here?"

"Herring. It was too good to leave behind."

"You better eat it soon, or it's gone."

"Are you threatening me?"

"I'm hungry," a child whined.

"Maybe I'll save the fish for another day."

A ripping sound. Heads turned. A little girl with an upturned nose had ripped a section of newspaper from the wall and torn it into pieces. One of the mothers marched over and smacked her hand. The little girl cried out.

"You're crazy, the whole lot of you," one of the men growled.

The suitcase in Miriam's hand slipped onto the wood-plank floor with a resounding thud. Thirteen pairs of eyes targeted her like guns, sending goose bumps up and down her back.

Miriam's father stepped forward and spoke in an amiable voice. "Excuse us. I am Alexander Abramovich. This is my wife, Dora, and our daughter, Miriam. We're upstairs. In the loft."

"My name is Rosen." A man with big front teeth and pencil-straight eyebrows stepped forward and extended his hand. "And here are my wife and children." He gestured with his shoulder at a woman holding a whimpering baby with one arm and the hand of a small boy, a bit older than Monya, with the other. Two older girls clung to her flint-gray shawl. An older boy who looked to be sixteen or seventeen years old, a replica of his father, stood off to the side.

Five children. Miriam couldn't begin to understand how such a large family had coped during the year of the Soviets, or how they'd manage in the ghetto.

Mrs. Rosen's chocolate-brown eyes swept over them with contempt, as if they'd intruded. Miriam's father shook Mr. Rosen's hand vigorously.

Mr. Rosen had crow's-feet around heavily lidded eyes and nostrils that flared when he breathed. His eyes flicked between his wife and four children, avoiding Miriam and her parents. Clearly, the Rosens had been hoping they wouldn't show up to claim the attic. This didn't surprise Miriam. She would have been pleased as well, had there been fewer people living in the house.

Her father stepped toward the other man and offered his hand. "Alexander Abramovich."

"Dr. Blatt." He clumsily shook her father's hand.

The doctor's petite wife cowered behind him, burping a baby

boy over her shoulder. With her smooth, glossy skin, she looked much younger than her husband. A boy, around ten or eleven years old, hovered near his mother. The oldest, a girl of fifteen or so, wore spectacles and had a lustrous mane of sable-black hair. A boy, who looked to be a year or so younger, had freckles across his nose and cheeks and a cluster of spots on his chin.

"We were in the middle of a discussion about this room," Mr. Rosen explained.

"A discussion?" Dr. Blatt snorted and crossed his arms. "More like you telling us what to do."

"Stop kvetching," Mr. Rosen said to Dr. Blatt. "You wouldn't say what you wanted. Someone had to—"

"You didn't give me a chance. I'd hardly walked through the door and you started telling me what I could and couldn't do."

"What?" Mr. Rosen said, indignant. "Is your mind slipping?"

Dr. Blatt's eyes blistered at Mr. Rosen. "Are you accusing me of being crazy?"

"Let's go upstairs," Miriam's father said quietly. He took the basket from Dora's hand and led her up the crudely made pine stairs.

The ceiling of the loft was no higher than one and a half meters and swelled perilously with rainwater. Miriam's father couldn't stand upright. There was no door, and their kerosene lantern would provide the only light. A wood-framed bed with a lumpy mattress sat beneath a drafty window, and the stairs opened directly to the loft, making it impossible to ignore the heated voices of their new neighbors jabbering at one another, along with babies crying, children talking and chairs scraping across the wood floor. Privacy did not exist in the ghetto.

Her father pushed the bed into the middle of the room, where it would be warmer. Her mother dropped onto the bed, drew her knees up and curled into a ball on her side. The flimsy mattress sank with her weight and gave off a dank, mildewed odor. A queasiness burrowed its way into Miriam's abdomen as she created a makeshift bed on the floor using a blanket as a mattress and her coat as a pillow.

"At least we have our own private room," Miriam said. "I'd go mad if we were stuck downstairs with all those people, wouldn't you, Mama?"

Her mother lay still. Said nothing. Part of her mother died the minute they arrived, when she fully comprehended their tenuous circumstances. Miriam felt an instinctive longing for her mother's former critical, willful self.

A CRACKING SOUND, like a horse being whipped, woke Miriam in the sooty darkness.

"What was that?" she said groggily.

Another noise, a popping sound. And another. Followed by a man shouting.

"Gunshots." Her father exhaled, got out of bed and padded over to the window.

Dora was in a deep sleep, thanks to a tablet from Dr. Blatt. He'd brought an impressive supply of medicine to the ghetto, and guarded it like the Czar's jewels, but Miriam's father had coaxed him into parting with a couple of sleeping tablets in return for one of their blankets.

"Dr. Blatt got the better deal," Miriam had complained, "since the blanket will last as long as we're in the ghetto, but the tablets will be gone in two nights."

"Time isn't the same in here as it was out there," her father replied. "We can't think about months and years, only hours and days. We can only hope the sun rises tomorrow, yet live as if the world might end today."

Miriam had shuddered at her father's inference that there was no guarantee of life in the ghetto. Nobody knew the Nazis' plans.

Now, Miriam joined her father at the window and peered outside. Stars glittered in the indigo darkness.

"Papa, you've never said a word about me giving Ilana and Monya to Gutte."

His gaze softened. "I think you're the bravest person I know."

She smiled wanly. "Thank you."

A trio of gunshots rang out from the courtyard.

"I think it's the guards," her father said, his voice choppy. "Someone must be too close to the fence."

A long pause followed by one shot.

"So much has changed," Miriam said. "It's hard to get up in the morning and keep going."

"I know. But you must focus on what you have, Miriam, not on what you've lost."

Miriam nodded and returned to her blanket. She lay awake for hours thinking about her children and listening to her mother's steady breathing, punctuated by the staccato noise of gunshots.

24

CHICAGO, APRIL 1976

EMBASSY OF THE UNION OF SOVIET SOCIALIST REPUBLICS
2650 WISCONSIN AVENUE, WASHINGTON, DC 20007

Dear Ms. Byrne,

Thank you for your query about Monya Talan. Unfortunately, very little information from Latvia can be obtained stateside. However, because the person you are seeking is Jewish, you might want to contact the Hebrew Immigrant Aid Society (HIAS) in America, which has been conducting searches for Jewish survivors since the end of the war. The HIAS will send your request to the International Red Cross, which carries out searches in the Soviet Union, though it could take months before they get any results.

The only way to get specific details about people in Latvia would be to visit the Latvian Records Bureau, located in the National Archives in Riga, where adoption/birth/death/marriage records are kept for the entire country. Here

*is the address if you would like to contact this agency dir-
ectly, though I must advise you the records will be written
in Latvian or Russian and you cannot access them without
permission from the Soviet authorities:*

*Šķūņu iela 11, LV-1050
Riga, Latvia*

The letter was rumpled, with a Lake Michigan–shaped coffee
stain in the bottom corner. Sarah had lost track of how many times
she'd read it since it arrived the previous day. Enough to recite
it almost word for word. Enough to accept it would be virtually
impossible to investigate Monya's whereabouts in Riga, or receive
information from the Hebrew Immigrant Aid Society before
August. And unless she learned Latvian or Russian in the next
couple of months, and miraculously received permission to search
the archives, the records bureau would be about as illuminating as
a flashlight without batteries.

Sarah considered waiting until the following year to go to Riga,
once she'd heard back from the Red Cross and perhaps learned a
few Russian words. But what if something happened to Miriam?
Her grandmother's sallow face in the hospital came to mind. She
straightened and put the letter in the top drawer of her dresser,
where her black and gray socks were folded and tidily arranged in
rows. Her mind was made up.

It had been two months since she'd submitted her passport and
visa to Melanie, with no word about the status of her background
check. Paranoia drove her to the windows at night, though she
lived on the eighteenth floor, in no danger of being watched from
outside. Melanie assured her she had nothing to fear. Nevertheless,
Sarah wasn't encouraged. What did Melanie know? This was

the first time she'd booked anyone for travel to the Soviet Union.

But there was no time to dwell on things that might or might not happen. Not today. She was throwing Heather's bridal shower, and the decorations in her apartment were awful. Pink balloons dangled limply from the curtain rod and pink crepe paper streamers were strung from the ceiling light to the ivory walls, a paltry attempt to make it feel like a carousel.

She was racked with guilt for not putting more time into her best friend's shower. It wasn't like her to be so unprepared; she was the queen of organization. She'd been excited to plan the shower, yet here she was, six hours before guests were due to arrive, with nothing but tacky decorations, sandwiches and fruit in the refrigerator, and a cake waiting to be picked up.

She grabbed her notepad and made a list—pink roses, Hershey's Kisses, bulletin board, pink champagne, pink candies, pink tulle, pick up cake—then grabbed her purse and was off, determined to give Heather the elegant shower she deserved.

THE SCENT OF fresh roses clung to the air after the guests, except for Heather, had gone. Carole King's *Tapestry* played softly in the background. The cake had hardly been touched, save for a handful of macaroons at the bottom, while the jars of Hershey's Kisses were empty. Sarah, in a butter-yellow dress with long sleeves, and Heather, in a cap-sleeved green dress dusted with pink flowers, were sprawled on the white sofa among reams of bows, wrapping paper, and ribbons.

"I don't get it," Sarah said to Heather.

"What?" Heather yawned and stretched her arms over her head.

"Why everyone ate the Kisses, which you can buy anywhere, and ignored the cake I had specially made."

"It's too pretty. Nobody wanted to be the first to spoil it."

Sarah slipped off her pumps and dug her swollen bare feet into her white shag area rug. "That's ridiculous. It's a cake, not a trophy."

"It's okay. Bob and I will eat it, every last crumb."

"Good." Sarah took a sip of pink champagne and made a face. Too warm and flat as tap water.

"You worry too much," Heather said laconically. "It was perfect. Everything—the cake, the roses, the table, the music, your apartment, the champagne."

Sarah flushed with pleasure.

Heather raised her glass. "To my generous friend who put on a shower worthy of *Better Homes and Gardens*."

Sarah's forehead puckered with skepticism.

Heather took a sip of champagne. "Really." She nodded at the table, covered in soft pink tulle, with a tall vase bursting with pink roses, a macaroon cake and small pink candles at every place setting. "It's gorgeous, all of it."

"It was a bit dicey at times, but I guess it worked out in the end."

"Worked out?" Heather rolled her eyes and chuckled. "It's okay to pat yourself on the back once in a while."

Sarah's shoulders relaxed. "I can't help it."

"You're a perfectionist, like your mom."

Sarah took in a sharp breath. She'd spent her entire life trying to be nothing like her mother, only to be singled out as a carbon copy. Was it a sign of what was to come? She considered Miriam and her mother, and was unnerved by their conspicuous similarities. *I am destined to become my mother. It's fate.*

"What's wrong? You look like you're a million miles away," Heather said.

Sarah released her hair from its ponytail and shook her head. "Do you ever worry about turning into your mother?"

"Is that a rhetorical question?"

"No."

Heather shrugged. "At the rate I'm going, I'll be my mother by the time I get married."

"No, you won't," Sarah replied stubbornly.

Heather gave a lopsided grin. "Is this about me calling you a perfectionist?"

"I don't know. Maybe."

"Oh my God, Sarah. Stop worrying about every little thing. You'll drive yourself crazy."

Stop worrying? she thought. As if.

"Let's talk about something else," Heather said brightly.

Sarah exhaled. "Good idea."

"Tell me about your trip to London."

Sarah groaned silently. "Today is supposed to be about you," she demurred. "I want to hear the latest about your honeymoon. California, right?"

"What is going on with you?"

"Meaning?"

"I know you. There's something you're not telling me."

Sarah hesitated. The words expanded in her mouth like steam: "I'm not going to London."

"What? You canceled your trip?"

"No. I was never going to London, other than to change planes." She paused. "I'm going to look for my uncle on a tour of Riga."

Heather's mouth fell open. "You can't visit the Soviet Union. People don't go there voluntarily."

"Actually, you're wrong. Fifteen million people visited the Soviet Union over the last five years," Sarah countered, repeating Melanie's words almost verbatim.

"You're kidding, right?"

"That's what the travel agent told me."

"Where did she get her information, the Soviet Union?"

"It wasn't the Soviet Union directly. It was the tourist agency run by the Soviet Union."

"That makes a big difference. It must be accurate, then," Heather scoffed.

"All right, the number may be a bit inflated—"

"You think?"

"But there wouldn't even be a Soviet travel agency in New York if people couldn't go there safely."

"I don't care how many travel agencies there are, or if fifteen million people want to risk their lives going to the Soviet Union. I care about you, Sarah. It's not a good idea."

Sarah shrugged. "Well, I may not be going anywhere. I'm still waiting for my background check to go through. If it doesn't, I won't be going."

"If someone contacts me, I'll say you're a reporter for *60 Minutes*, working on an exposé about the Soviet Union," Heather said dryly.

Sarah started. "You wouldn't."

"I'd rather have you mad at me than rotting away in a Soviet prison because you were caught looking for your uncle."

Sarah's mouth set in a hard line at the logic of Heather's argument.

"What does your dad say?"

Her expression closed up.

"He thinks you're going to London."

"I can't tell him the truth. He'd worry too much."

"He just lost your mom. You can't risk everything to go to the Soviet Union to search for a man you didn't even know existed until a few months ago, who may not even be alive now. It makes no sense."

"I know it sounds insane. But I can't stop thinking about my mother seeing her father killed. Can you imagine? No wonder she couldn't talk about him."

"It's awful, I agree, but it was your mom's trauma, not yours."

"Maybe." Sarah couldn't bring herself to admit she got a numbing emptiness in the pit of her stomach whenever she thought about her grandfather and Monya. A despondency had rooted in her core like weeds. "It was also Miriam's trauma. And she's had to live with that and the grief of not knowing what happened to her son."

"This isn't a trip to Disney World. And what if you don't find Monya? Things will still be the same here. Your mom will still be gone."

Sarah went stiff at the thought of failure. "I want to be able to look Miriam in the eye and tell her I tried. My mother died without knowing. Miriam deserves the truth, if I can find it. If not, at least I'll see where my mother was raised and I won't have to live with regret for not trying."

Heather gave Sarah a long hard look. From the strain etched on Heather's face, Sarah saw that her decision would come between them, yet she couldn't back down. This trip had become a lifeline of sorts, a reason to get up in the morning, a purpose.

MELANIE CALLED SARAH at work two days after Heather's shower. Her background check was complete. Dumbfounded, Sarah asked her to repeat what she'd said, not sure she'd heard correctly. Melanie laughed and told her again she'd been approved to travel to the Soviet Union. Sarah clutched the phone to her chest and let out a silent scream for joy.

I'm going to Riga.

25

RIGA, NOVEMBER 1941

A REVERBERATING GLOOM FELL UPON MIRIAM WHEN SHE saw two children huddled on the icy curb just inside the ghetto, their bones wrapped in skin. They were too far gone to speak, too shrunken for an observer to guess their ages or even their genders. And they were dire reminders of her children, who would be in similar circumstances had she not sent them with Gutte.

It was one month since she'd moved to the ghetto, and the store's offerings were meager—potatoes (most half-rotten), carrots, beets, cabbage and bruised apples. Food had become so scarce, people risked their lives to bring it into the ghetto, where you would be shot by one of the Latvian guards for hiding a potato in your coat sleeve. Miriam had nothing to give these children, not even a crumb, after working twelve hours in the uniform factory without pay. She stiffened when two Arājs Kommando officers crossed her path, tapping the ground with their truncheons, ignoring two more children about to die. Death had become an unremarkable part of the ghetto's landscape.

Miriam glanced sideways at the young, clean-shaven Kommando

officers, who looked like innocent university students on the outside but inside were so prejudiced against Jews, they'd lost their moral compasses. She bent down stiffly and plucked a few newspaper pages off the ground, to keep the fire going in the house, then tugged her shawl tighter around her shoulders and neck, but it was useless against the severe temperature, which had gone down with the sun. She moved slowly, though she was anxious to get inside. Her knees kept locking. The arctic air had settled into her bones like moss. She craved warmth, the soothing taste of hot tea, the floating sensation of plunging onto a deep feather mattress at the end of the day. The touch of her children's fingers curled around hers.

She crumpled her yearnings and shoved them into the shadows of her past as she opened the door and stepped into the rickety house. It was astonishingly quiet, considering all sixteen residents were present. The Blatt and Rosen children bunched together lethargically, the two oldest girls minding the sleeping babies. It was obvious, from the way the children in both families intermingled, they'd become attached to one another. Miriam never mentioned her children, and did her best to avoid learning the names of the ones in her house, referring to them as one homogeneous group—the children. This was partially because their presence made her long for Ilana and Monya, and partially because she was afraid to get too close to the children in the house. It was easier to lose strangers than people you know and love.

Miriam's father sat by the small fire, rubbing his hands together. Blood trickled at the edges of his palms, sores that never healed because of the daily friction from shoveling debris off the streets. Her mother and the other two women sat on the floor, cutting a handful of small carrots and dividing them among twelve people; the babies, asleep in baskets near the fire, were too young to chew carrots. The three mothers had become friendly over the last four weeks, as they stood in long lines for food, commiserating about hardships since the Russian and German occupations. Mrs. Rosen had lost a sister, a brother and three cousins, and Mrs. Blatt lost her mother.

Miriam set the newspaper pages she'd scavenged beside the stove in the center of the room, the sole warm place in the house, and sat down beside her father. They'd run out of wood. The residents had been burning what they could find, including newspaper and furniture. Now, the dismantled table was in the stove. Miriam spotted one of the legs poking out of the opening, flames licking the wood, with mesmerizing sparks, into twigs.

Her scalp itched from lice. No matter how hard she dug her fingernails into her skin, it was never enough to make the itchiness go away. Lice were a widespread infestation, along with rats dashing across floors seeking crumbs. Almost everyone she worked with had one or the other, or both. Their entire house was infested with lice, not rats, which Dr. Blatt said was a good thing. He also said lice were virtually impossible to eliminate because they thrived on all of them living in such tight quarters, the lice laying eggs and jumping from dirty head to head like grasshoppers.

Dora handed Miriam and her father plates with three carrots, three beet slices and a bruised apple each. Miriam's mother waited hours in line for a few measly vegetables and hadn't been able to get bread in over a week. Miriam tasted meat in her dreams.

"What do you think about the roll call tomorrow, Papa?" Miriam asked, referring to the order for all men in the ghetto to gather before dawn. She licked a beet to make it last, savoring the gritty bitterness on her tongue.

"New jobs, I hope." Her father stretched his right leg out and grimaced. A few days earlier, a wooden beam had fallen on his knee while he was hauling away the remains of the Choral Synagogue, which Arājs Kommando members set on fire with Jews inside the same day as the synagogue where Max had been killed.

"That's not what I heard," Mr. Rosen interjected, chomping on a carrot. He dropped down beside Miriam and pulled his listless young daughter into his lap. "I overheard guards at the gate saying they're planning to get rid of old and sick men who can't work." He gave a piece of carrot to his daughter, who ravenously slapped it into her mouth.

Dr. Blatt and his wife, sitting to the right of Miriam's father, exchanged worried expressions. He was scrawny, half the width of his sturdy wife, with chronic asthma. At night, Miriam fell asleep to the erratic rhythm of his wheezy breath.

"What is this roll call?" Miriam's mother asked.

Miriam nibbled her apple slice as one of the Rosen daughters described the notice from the German police, ordering men to come to Sadovņikova Street at nine o'clock the next morning. The girl hesitated. She went on to say one of the supervisors at her factory believed the men were going to be taken out of Riga to work somewhere else.

The men launched into an animated discussion about the possibility of being removed from the ghetto, with Dr. Blatt wondering where they might be taken. Mr. Rosen mentioned the mounds of debris on the streets, plus the scores of buildings in need of repair, and questioned why the men would be taken away when so much back-breaking work remained.

Miriam's gaze swept from her father's bad leg to his face. He jerked his eyes from hers. He crunched on his carrot and bent his injured leg. His knee cracked. Miriam had the stuffy feeling of imminent doom.

"What about women?" a teenaged Blatt girl asked. She had a serious air about her, with thick-lensed spectacles and hair pulled severely back in a tight braid. "Do you think they'll have a roll call for us?"

"I certainly hope not," Mrs. Rosen said.

"You don't even know what it means, a roll call," one of her sons pointed out. "It could be good—a job, a paid job."

"Or it could be a death sentence," Mr. Rosen lamented.

"Don't talk like that in front of the children," Mrs. Rosen admonished her husband.

Mr. Rosen gave her an incredulous look. "Even if I said nothing, our children can see what's going on for themselves every time they step out the door."

"Mama hasn't let us outside for three days," said a Rosen boy with a severe cowlick.

Mr. Rosen looked from his son to his wife in disbelief. "Keeping them inside won't change the situation. We can't hide the truth from our children."

The smallest Blatt boy shoved a wad of newspaper into his mouth. His lips were stained with ink from eating newspaper off the walls. Miriam had to look away from the hunger he wore like a bleeding scab. She was so angry, she wanted to scream. Except it would have been a waste of valuable energy. Feelings were silent, scrunched away like the paper thrown into the fire.

Mrs. Blatt knelt down to her small boy's level, spat into her hands and tried to rub away the ink on his mouth. He was so still and pale, it almost looked as if she were cleaning a doll's face. She and her husband exchanged glances of unspoken urgency. Dr. Blatt rubbed his puffy eyes and said they had to protect the children, keep them from harm, not frighten them with words about what could happen.

Voices bristled. A stricken expression came over Miriam's mother's face. Her father sat up tall and said he didn't think they were in danger as long as they followed the rules. "Every time a new law has been imposed, we've managed to live through it. When we weren't allowed to walk on the sidewalks, we walked in the gutters. When we were given a curfew, we obeyed it. When we were told to wear Jewish stars, we wore them."

Mr. Rosen waved his hand for Miriam's father to stop talking and called him a "blind optimist." He shook his head tersely and said he'd seen a couple of Jewish girls shot earlier, for smoking in front of the SS headquarters. And when he had returned to the ghetto after his job at the munitions factory that very evening, he watched as a man was beaten with clubs for smuggling a few pieces of bread into the ghetto. "We are starving and they attack us for eating scraps of bread."

The smallest children started to whimper. Miriam's mother turned as white and still as a marble column. Miriam went numb.

Mrs. Blatt held her crying son to her chest and begged Mr. Rosen to stop frightening the children. Dr. Blatt's face went gray and clammy. He looked as if he was going to be sick.

Mr. Rosen got to his feet. He removed his spectacles, blew on the lenses and cleaned them with his sleeve. "It's not just the Nazis who want to get rid of all the Jews, the Latvians do too. And there are no punishments for shooting Jews. Laws to protect us are kaput."

Miriam's mind raced back to the Latvian officers who'd killed Max and countless other Jews, to the Latvians who'd raped her and Zelma. She saw their faces as easily as if they were right in front of her, smelled their malice like the stink of the outhouse, and knew Mr. Rosen was doing what nobody else was willing to do—face the truth.

Her father struggled to his feet, favoring his bad leg, and disagreed, saying there were good officers and good Latvians, who would stop the bad ones from going too far. Miriam wanted to shake the misplaced confidence from him. He was hoping for a miracle.

"It's already gone too far." Mr. Rosen spat out his words. "Yesterday, I took a scarf from a man who'd starved to death on the street. I stole from a corpse so my children wouldn't freeze to death. How much more can we take?"

The house became eerily quiet. Even the babies stopped crying. Nobody spoke. Nobody knew the answer. Looking back later, Miriam understood that the question they should have asked was how far the Latvian and German officers would go.

That night, Miriam watched the street from the loft window, coated with ice. Wind thrashed the paper-thin walls and icicles hung precariously from the ceiling. She'd taken to sleeping in her coat, but the extra layer did little to ease the chill. She tied a kerchief around her head to keep her ears warm, put on leather gloves and wrapped a woolen shawl over her mother, breathing shallowly on the mattress on the floor, with chattering teeth; the bed frame had been taken apart and used as firewood.

Beside her mother's head, the spiderwort, hardy under severe conditions, withered in its glass jar. Still, her mother carried the jar wherever she went, convinced it would eventually come back to life. It reminded Miriam of Ilana's attachment to a doll when she was four or five, except Ilana knew her doll wasn't alive. Her mother's irrationality frightened Miriam more than her frailty.

Miriam lay down alongside her mother, closed her eyes and listened for her heartbeat. She longed to hear her sharp voice. Strange, she thought, how we begin to miss even the worst traits when someone we love is wasting away.

═══

It was dark as coal when men's voices began streaming through the window, waking Miriam from a restless sleep. In a torpor, she got to her feet and watched the men from the ghetto, including her father, standing in rows beneath the glowing streetlights, waiting for the mandatory roll call ordered by the Germans.

"Papa is still standing in the same place," Miriam said.

"How long has it been?" her mother asked in a feeble voice.

"More than an hour."

"What is going on? Why haven't they moved?"

"Maybe they are—"

A piercing scream from the room below cut Miriam off. She ran downstairs. Mrs. Rosen held a lantern above the Blatt family, sprawled across two mattresses. Her hand shook. Light jiggled upon the motionless family like sun dappling on top of fallen autumn leaves. They were dead.

"Mama?" One of Mrs. Rosen's daughters toddled to her mother.

"No!" Mrs. Rosen pushed her girl back. "Don't come any closer."

The little girl fell to the floor in tears.

"Clara, pick up your sister and keep her back," Mrs. Rosen ordered one of her older daughters.

Miriam, her pulse racing, drew nearer to the Blatts. Two of the children lay on their backs, heads hanging at unnatural angles, mouths wide open, chests horribly still. Mrs. Blatt lay on her side, her face an ethereal bluish white. The baby, curled in Mrs. Blatt's arms, was on his stomach. Motionless. Dr. Blatt, also on his side, had his back toward the rest of his family, as if he hadn't wanted to see their final moments.

"Why the children?" Miriam stammered. "The baby."

Mrs. Rosen brought the lantern to her face, casting an oblique glow across her cheeks, her brow and the tip of her nose. "They gave their lives to preserve their souls," she said with reverence. "Blessed is the true judge."

"Miriam, what's taking you so long?" her mother called out thinly.

"You think killing their own children is better than renouncing their faith?" Miriam said, aghast.

"Of course," Mrs. Rosen answered, indignant. "Their faith was stronger than their will to survive."

"But their children didn't have a choice. And I don't recall anyone telling them, or any of us, to give up our Judaism."

"Miriam," her mother cried.

"You can't possibly understand, Miriam," Mrs. Rosen chided her. "You don't have children."

Miriam's stomach clenched in anger. Mrs. Rosen didn't know the first thing about her. But then, whose fault was that?

"The Soviets took away our schools and synagogues," Mrs. Rosen continued. "The Nazis force us to bear stars to publicly condemn us, to make our children feel ashamed of who they are."

"So you think giving up, taking children's lives, is the answer?"

"I don't want my children to go on without being the people they were meant to be." Mrs. Rosen knelt down, set the lantern on the floor and caressed two of her children's heads.

Miriam studied the gaunt, hollow-eyed children, with bedbug sores on their necks and hands. Ilana and Monya were living lies as Lutherans. It was entirely possible they would lose their Jewish souls during their time with Gutte and her family. And if she didn't survive, they might feel empty inside for the rest of their lives, as though they'd lost something they couldn't define.

I may have saved their lives only to destroy their spirits, she realized. I am a terrible Jew—a good mother but a terrible Jew, choosing their lives over their souls. She envied her parents and

Mrs. Rosen, having a faith so pure not even murder could shake it from them. Her convictions were like hinges, moving both ways depending on the pressure. She was not proud of her volatility but knew, if she had it to do over again, she'd make the same choice.

Mrs. Rosen wrung her hands together and sniffled. "You should consider it a blessing you don't have children yet. The more children you have, the more hearts you carry."

Miriam felt a hot, black rush of guilt for lying by omission. She was a fraud in her own life. "You need to get an officer to take the Blatts away," she said in a clipped voice.

Miriam told her mother the Blatts were ill and had been taken to the ghetto hospital. She was afraid the truth would be the end of her.

AFTER STANDING OUTSIDE for more than an hour, waiting for a roll call that never actually took place, the men in the ghetto, including Miriam's father and Mr. Rosen, were allowed to return home. It was still dark when they entered the house, frozen to the bone, their fingers too stiff to crumple paper into balls to kindle the stove. The two families huddled around the fire, diminished to thin wisps of smoke.

Before the sun appeared on the horizon, soldiers banged on the door and announced that all men were being moved to a newly created small ghetto. The rest of the Jews were going to be moved out in two hours. No destination was given.

26

RIGA, JULY 1976

ONE WEEK AFTER THE UNITED STATES CELEBRATED ITS bicentennial, Sarah, aboard an Aeroflot plane, landed in Riga with a tremendous bump. Her ears were blocked and she longed for a shower to wash off the stale, oily air. Muted voices droned around her, like the discordant sounds of adults on *Charlie Brown* specials. Her neck was stiff and she couldn't understand why she was so tired when she'd done nothing but stare out a window for nine hours. She stood on wobbly knees and thought, with a start, I'm here.

Adrenaline flooded her senses as she waited to get out of the uncomfortable seat with its broken arm, away from the body odor that had clogged her nostrils for the entire flight from London. She bent down to peer out the window. Her thigh muscles tightened when she saw armed soldiers on the tarmac. She pressed her elbows into her sides and curled her spine to make herself small and felt completely alone, though she was surrounded by people.

"Quite the welcome," the man behind Sarah remarked in a British accent.

Sarah glanced over her shoulder. A pasty man in his mid-sixties, who'd combed a tuft of silver hair over his shiny scalp, smiled blithely at her. He had floppy ears and twinkly honey-brown eyes, reminding her of a teddy bear. Sarah liked him instantly.

A woman's head popped up beside him. His wife, Sarah deduced, seeing her plump chin brush against the man's shoulder. She appeared to be about the same age, with short, curly gray hair and pink cheeks scored with lines.

"Shhh, George," the woman hushed him. "Remember what the travel agent said?"

"Keep my mouth shut in public, except to eat." He winked at Sarah.

A corner of Sarah's mouth lifted.

The line began to shuffle forward. Her throat closed when she reached the door: two soldiers armed with machine guns were positioned at the foot of the stairs. Sarah was struck by a burning sense of terror.

The passengers in front of Sarah gave their documents to the stone-faced soldiers, who scrutinized passports and visas as if determined to find problems. When Sarah's turn came, the soldier examining her documents gave her a once-over that made her feel slimy before returning her visa and passport.

The sky was watery gray and a cool breeze prickled Sarah's skin. A middle-aged woman with a sleek cap of brown hair and light-blue eyeshadow directed passengers to a red-and-white Intourist tour bus, comparable, on the inside, to the school bus she'd taken to junior high. Sarah's heart skipped a beat at the woman's English shaded with Russian, which reminded her of her mother's and grandmother's voices. A shiny black blazer and skirt hugged the woman's generous curves, and she wore a red scarf around her neck, much like the cranky stewardesses on the plane.

Sarah was pleased the British man and woman took seats behind her on the bus; the man had a cheery air that was comforting, so far away from home. And they were old enough to be her grandparents, which made her feel a tad more optimistic. Elderly, vulnerable people would never have ventured into the Soviet Union if they were worried about their safety. She cast an eye over the rest of the passengers and was surprised to find most were mature couples around her parents' age, with a handful of younger couples. She appeared to be the only solo traveler.

It seemed the bus had finished taking on passengers when a tall man in his early thirties jumped aboard. He strolled down the aisle with the rakish manner of a young Jimmy Stewart, parking himself in the only empty seat, beside Sarah. He wore his flaxen hair in a ponytail, smelled of cigarettes and aftershave, and boasted a pair of shamelessly patriotic red-white-and-blue-striped jeans. He reminded Sarah of the cheeky all-American models her agency had used in a bicentennial ad campaign for Wrangler jeans.

He extended a hand to Sarah. His tanned arm was lean and dusted with blond hairs, and his index finger was stained yellow from smoking. "Roger Munro." He had an infectious smile, with big front teeth and electric-blue eyes that bore into hers with a startling intensity.

"Sarah," she replied, shaking his proffered hand. She shifted closer to the window, to widen the space between herself and Roger, but he spilled onto her side, his knee jutting against hers, a bony elbow poking her ribs. His unshaven chin jutted out prominently over his long neck, and wispy hairs emerged from the collar of his white T-shirt.

"Sorry. They never make seats big enough for tall, clumsy people like me," he said with perfect diction that clashed with his eccentric persona. "My knees were jammed against the seat in front of me the entire flight. I think my bones are going to crack for a week."

She gave him a quick smile and touched her lips, afraid she had crumbs stuck in the corners. None, thank goodness.

He grabbed the seat back in front of him and hoisted himself up. "Looks like we're going to be sitting here awhile." He dropped back down. "We're on Soviet time now. Every *t* has to be crossed, every *i* dotted before we can leave."

"Oh." She glanced down at her lap only to look up at his profile, and tucked her hair behind her ears. "You've been here before?"

"Moscow. Not Riga. It's all the same, though, the rules and procedures."

She couldn't think of what to say next to such a well-traveled man. Her head grew heavy on her neck. She yawned and clapped her hand over her mouth.

"Didn't sleep on the plane?"

"Not one minute." She paused, considered telling him it was her first flight, but didn't want him to know she was an inexperienced traveler.

"What brings you to Riga, alone?"

She flinched at his bluntness. Don't tell anyone you have family there, Melanie had cautioned her. Buses, cars, trains, hotels and restaurants could be bugged. "It sounded interesting, the Soviet Union in general. Riga just happened to be on the tour this summer."

"Do you have a last name, Sarah?" He peered at her as if he knew there was more to her story.

Melanie's voice broke through the fog in her head: *Avoid giving personal information.* "What about you, why Riga?" she asked.

"I go to a different city in the Soviet Union every summer, for work. I'm a professor of Russian architecture at Syracuse University."

"Really?" He seemed young to be a professor. She angled her body toward him. "Do you speak Russian?"

"I do." He thrust out his chest. "It's one of the reasons I come so often, to practice with native speakers—and, of course, to take in the architecture."

"Of course."

"Nice camera," he said, his eyes falling on the Canon slung around her neck.

She rotated the lens back and forth and said it was a college graduation present from her parents.

"Do you know the rules for taking photos here?"

"What rules?"

He extracted a pamphlet from a pocket in the seat back and pointed at a page with black- and-white photos, all covered with Xs. "You can't take photos of any of these things. None of the peasants lining up for food, or workers, none of the crumbling houses in the city. No soldiers, bridges or military equipment."

"Really?"

"See for yourself." He handed her the pamphlet, his fingers grazing hers.

His touch made her pulse quicken.

"Essentially, the government wants you to bring back photos of an ideal Soviet Union," he went on, his voice notched up to derision. "Monuments of Lenin and Stalin, and impressive Byzantine-style buildings. Sometimes, KGB agents pose as foreigners in these tours, just to make sure people obey the rules."

She slanted her head. "What does KGB stand for, anyway? I hear the name in the news, but have no idea what it means."

"The Committee for State Security, and trust me, you don't want to be on their radar."

"That, I know. But what happens if you unintentionally take a photo of something off-limits?"

"Your film, and possibly your camera, could be confiscated and destroyed. And you could even be arrested."

"Now I'm afraid to take any photos. What if I make a mistake?"

"Just take shots of whatever our guide shows us."

"Pardon me." A polite British voice rose over Sarah's seat. "I couldn't help but overhear you talking about photographs," said the man from the plane, "and wondered if I could intrude on your conversation." His round head bobbed over the seat with an eager smile.

Roger swiveled around, planting his sneaker-clad feet in the aisle, and introduced himself and Sarah. The British man extended a shaky hand over the top of the seat and said he was George Cullen, and his wife was Doris.

"Lovely to meet such a fine young couple," Doris added, without showing her face.

Sarah turned crimson. Roger shrugged as if to say it wasn't his fault they'd drawn that conclusion.

"We're not a—"

"Isn't this exciting," Doris interrupted Sarah, "being in the Soviet Union?"

"Yes, but—"

"I must admit, I was hesitant when George proposed the idea." Doris's rosy face emerged in the space between Sarah's and Roger's seats. "But the more he talked about visiting the land of the czars, and seeing what it's really like behind the Iron Curtain, the more exciting it sounded."

"Excuse me, dear," George said. "Weren't you the one who told me, not five minutes ago, to be quiet in public?"

"That was on the airplane, dear. We're not in public anymore. We're with people on our tour now."

"I see. Thank you for clearing that up for me," George said good-naturedly.

Sarah and Roger exchanged amused smiles.

"Getting back to taking photos," George continued, "what's off-limits, Roger? We don't seem to have any information in either seat pocket."

"What you need to avoid are any shots portraying the Soviet Union in a negative light. You know, poor people, long lines—"

"Good afternoon. Welcome to Riga. I am your tour guide, Nina."

A clipped female voice interrupted their conversation. The woman with the light-blue eyeshadow stood ruler-straight at the front of the bus. "When we arrive at the hotel, you must give your passport and visa to the desk clerk to collect your room key. All of your documents will be locked in the hotel's safe."

"What?"

"Why can't we keep them in our room?"

"How do we know they'll be safe?"

Sarah listened to the concerns of her fellow travelers and was glad Melanie had warned her that Intourist would take control of her documents once she arrived.

Nina answered questions with a brusqueness implying she really didn't appreciate their concerns.

When everyone on the bus was satisfied their documents would be safe, Roger's hand flew up. Sarah had a feeling he'd been one of the annoying kids at school who always wanted to show off to the teacher.

Nina nodded impassively at him.

"My name is Roger. I'm a Russian architecture professor," he said, half standing under the bus's low ceiling. "I'm fluent in Russian if anyone needs help."

"*Spaseeba*, thank you," Nina said. Her carefully made-up face looked as if it was frozen.

"*Pazhalsta*. It means 'you're welcome.'" Roger looked down at his fellow passengers as if expecting applause.

Twenty-nine jet-lagged faces gave him curious glances. Sarah couldn't decide if he meant to sound superior or if he was oblivious to how he appeared to other people. Still, she couldn't help but think her trip would be a lot more interesting with Roger.

"How long is the drive to the hotel?" asked a man near the front of the bus.

"It is approximately eighteen miles," Nina responded. "Half an hour at the most."

Thirty minutes and she would be in the city her mother had tried to forget, the city that had haunted her grandmother for decades, the city where her uncle might live. A place where she could get into big trouble just by looking for him. The uncertainty ahead rattled Sarah's insides. It was a sharp, but not unpleasant, transition from the numbness that had been dogging her since her mother's death.

A woman in a wide-brimmed hat with a twangy Southern accent asked about the plan for the rest of the day. Nina explained they would be embarking on a tour of Riga one hour after checking into the hotel, and suggested they get something to eat in the hotel restaurant. She paused and, in a solemn tone, added: "Only those fluent in Russian may request to briefly leave the tour. Otherwise, you are not permitted to separate for any reason."

Monya.

Sarah glanced at Roger. Her mind was piqued. He spoke Russian. He was allowed to disappear. She envisioned him helping her search for Monya, and her mind jumped to the blank visa application in her purse, which she was supposed to have stamped by the embassy in order to visit her uncle. She'd brought it on a whim. For good luck.

Roger turned his head and looked askance at her.

She flushed. She felt as if she'd been caught with her hands on his wallet. She gave him a plastic smile and reminded herself she was in Riga to see where her mother was born, to walk the streets Miriam, her grandfather and her mother had walked, to get a sense of the city and history that had shaped her mother. Finding Monya was a fantasy. And yet . . .

She sighed and looked out the window. Identical leaden slabs stood in rows for miles, like soldiers standing at attention. Gray apartment buildings that looked more like prisons. She thought: Monya could be living in one of those buildings. I could be passing his apartment right now yet never meet him.

A tap on her shoulder. Roger.

"You know, you never did tell me your last name." His eyes locked on hers.

"I didn't?" She feigned confusion.

"I think I would remember."

Her forehead puckered. She realized it was silly, keeping her surname from him. He could easily find out at the hotel when rooms were assigned, but it was a slippery slope, talking about herself. Once she let her guard down, it would be harder to keep him at arm's length.

"Do you think you'll go off by yourself?" she asked him.

"What?"

"You speak Russian, so you can leave the tour, right?"

His mouth twisted. "You know, you have a habit of answering a question with a question."

"A habit? We met less than an hour ago and you think you know my habits?"

He gave a lopsided grin and bent his head down until it was just six inches from hers and whispered into her ear: "Are you a spy?"

Her ear tickled from his warm breath. She laughed self-consciously. "I'm definitely not a spy. Are you?"

He chuckled.

They regarded each other, and the look between them steeped the air with a jumpy excitement that struck Sarah to the core.

They turned off the highway onto a cobblestone road, the old bus bouncing over the bumps with a stomach-turning force. Sarah clutched her purse to her chest and pinned her gaze out the window as they roared past a group of girls wearing matching coffee-brown dresses and white aprons with red scarves tied around their necks. Even their tidy braids were identical. The absence of personal expression brought home the undeniable extent of Soviet oppression.

"Attention, comrades," Nina announced flatly, as if she were reading from a script. "We're driving beside the Daugava River, also called the River of Destiny. The people of many countries have traveled on this water—Swedes, Poles and Lithuanians. Today, Soviet citizens come to this river to cry. Like a mother, it washes our tears."

Sarah peered at the turquoise water spooling alongside the road like a silk ribbon. A communal murmur of appreciation drifted among the passengers as she stared at the river her grandmother had compared to the Seine in Paris, the river her mother, her grandparents and Monya must have strolled beside years ago, the river that witnessed the mass slaughter of people killed because they were Jews.

The bus scudded over a huge bump and came to a stop outside their hotel, a pewter-gray tower with rows of identical windows, like graph paper, every second square filled in with ink.

Another line to get off the bus. It was like an endless school field trip. She followed Roger down the steps and inhaled the cool, fresh morning air. At last, she'd made it to Riga. After all the months of planning and waiting, she was finally in her mother's birthplace. She threw her head back to take in the sweeping, leaden sky. It seemed higher than the sky above Chicago, where endless skyscrapers towered over streets like walls, cluttering the atmosphere.

She followed Nina and the rest of the group, passing half a dozen young people with streaks of purple and blue and red in their hair, piercings in their noses and mouths, and chains hanging from their clothes. They looked somewhat like the rebellious teens Sarah had seen loitering near Union Station in Chicago, a familiar scene that put her oddly at ease. Then she noticed the barrel-chested soldier at the hotel door, scrutinizing every passport before letting people enter, and her ease flipped to angst.

Inside, the lobby had an intentional, featureless aura with dull gray walls, wafer-thin moss-green carpet, and a vinyl sofa and chairs (same hue as the carpet) arranged in a semicircle in the middle of the room. Sarah couldn't imagine anyone actually wanting to sit there, on a sofa that looked as comfortable as concrete, in plain sight of the stern-faced receptionists checking guests into rooms.

The female elevator operator, who smelled as if she'd slept in mothballs, inspected them with flinty eyes as they crowded into the one car serving the entire hotel. It inched its way upward, stopping at every floor with an alarming ka-chunk. By the time Sarah got off at the seventh floor, with Roger and the Cullens, and discovered another old woman with penetrating eyes sitting beside the elevator, her chest was tight with nerves.

Welcome to Riga, Sarah told herself as she trudged down the narrow corridor to her room. Where Big Brother is watching you.

27

RIGA, NOVEMBER 1941

T HE STINK OF THE CHAMBER POT LEACHED INTO THE FRI-
gid air, combined with the whiff of dirty skin and hair and
charred wood. Moonlight glowed through the frozen window, a misty beam delineating the cramped loft. One floor below,
the Rosens spoke in disheartened voices. The babies were too
weak to cry.

Miriam's mother, wilted on the mattress, folded clothes with a
mindless precision.

"Sh'ma yisrael, Adonai Eloheinu . . ." Miriam's father bowed
his head east, toward their window, and began chanting the Shema
in Hebrew. A shaft of moonlight set off the severe contours of his
stooped, devout figure.

"How can you pray now, after everything we've been through?"
Miriam asked, her voice jagged with disdain.

He turned. Half his face was lit. "There is no better time to
pray—"

"But you've prayed every day for months and nothing has
improved. We don't need more prayers. We need powerful, brave

people to stand up to the Nazis and Latvians. That's what we really need."

"Prayer gives me hope," he said with conviction. He resumed chanting the *Shema*.

Miriam watched him, unmoved. She didn't see the point. Nobody was listening. Mired in depression, she packed her rucksack with Ilana's tattered sweater, three pieces of bread she'd smuggled in from the factory, a pair of ribbed socks, her documents, and photos of Ilana, Monya, Max and her parents; and, in an effort to lighten the weight, she chose *Anna Karenina* over Simon Dubnow's book. The sack would have been lighter without any book, but it was the only thing, apart from the photos, left from her former, civilized life. And unlike the photos, which brought Miriam to tears, the book carried her out of the ghetto to a fantasy world of exquisite clothes and beautiful music.

Her parents spoke in low voices as they packed, exchanging subtle looks of endearment, her father's hand often stroking her mother's back. Their love for one another, concealed behind closed doors before the war, was now as obvious as the frost on the window, which heartened Miriam. But it was a satisfaction so like disappointment, she drooped her head.

SHOTS FIRED INTO the clear, black night. Dogs barked. A woman cried for help. Miriam's mother placed the lifeless spiderwort vine in her valise. They waited. Miriam crouched on the floor and wrapped herself in a scratchy wool blanket. Her father looked sideways through the window. Her mother shrank back against the newspaper-covered wall, eyes pasted on Miriam's father.

"*Celies!* Wake up!" a man bellowed from the street in Latvian.

It was one o'clock in the morning.

More screams. More gunshots. Miriam's cheeks went stiff when her father declared the shots were coming from Jēkabpils Street, only a couple of blocks away. Horses trotted up and down the street below, their jarring neighs divulging their anxiety within the madness. Glass shattered. Shrieks punctured the air.

The door of their house burst open. "Everybody get out!" a man shouted in Yiddish, demonstrating his traitorous clout as a member of the Judenrat, the Jewish council, established by the Nazis to police the ghetto.

The Judenrat member ascended the stairs to the loft, each rung creaking under his step. Miriam and her mother clung to her father like wet pages of a book. The man's head appeared. He climbed into the loft, wielding a baton, and gave them five minutes to pack.

Miriam's father looked the man in the eye, pushed his baton down and said, "I don't know how you live with yourself, choosing power over your own people," in a cool voice.

His nerve made Miriam proud to be his daughter.

"It's a matter of survival," the man retorted.

Miriam's father crinkled his nose. "I'd rather die than survive at the expense of my family and friends."

The man started. He clutched his baton in front of his body and looked at the floor.

Miriam's father led them past the officer, down the stairs and out the door, where people trundled silently along the street, too weak from hunger to resist. Miriam stayed close to him the way she did when she was little, grateful her children were with Gutte; their lives weren't going to end brutally and unfinished.

A shot rang out, shattering the quiet.

The thump of a body falling to the ground.

A raucous shout.

Another piercing shot.

Another thump.

A body crumpled on the ground, blood around the head like a crown.

A woman's cry.

Another shot.

Another thump.

Another body.

Miriam's mother started mumbling to herself. Her legs slowed then faltered. Miriam's father inserted his shoulder under his wife's arm to hold her steady, but he sagged under her weight. Dora slid out from under him and fell to the ground. Miriam's father swayed like a flag in a gentle wind, arms out to keep his balance. Miriam lifted her mother back to her feet. Dora teetered as people pushed past.

Her father reached out to catch his wife. A Kommando officer stepped toward them, shot Dora in the head, then ordered them to keep moving. Miriam's father fell to his knees. He clutched his wife and wept. The officer raised his rifle to Miriam's father's head and shot him. It all happened so fast it didn't seem real, until Miriam saw blood oozing from her father's head. She froze. Couldn't make sense of what had happened.

People kept marching past, some moving around Miriam's parents, some walking on top of them as if they were stains on the road. Miriam felt herself swept up by the crowd as if she were dust in a broom. She despised herself for leaving her parents in the street but had to keep moving unless she wanted to be next.

In a daze, she walked, passing dozens of bodies abandoned in the streets. Puddles of icy blood. The crack of gunshots. She took it all in, detached. As if her mind were outside herself, a spectator, looking on without being part of the horror.

After they'd been marching for what seemed like hours, Latvian guards ordered them to form columns in a school courtyard on Sadovņiknova iela and stand still. Two Latvian policemen with machine guns stood guard. They were forced to stand in silence in the courtyard until dawn. There were no clouds in the sky and the sun took the edge off the arctic-cold morning.

Two German police officers appeared and, in an oddly congenial tone, one officer explained that it was a long walk to their new camp. They'd requisitioned a blue public bus to take those who preferred to ride. Many of the old and lame stepped forward and were told to follow a Latvian Kommando officer. One row over, she saw Simon Dubnow, Max's writer friend. He was withered by starvation and his suit was ripped, with a patina of dirt. He lifted his chin. He stayed put.

"There is still room in the camp for men able to work," another officer announced in a hauntingly familiar voice that caught Miriam's attention. "If you're interested, come with me."

Miriam tracked the voice to the Kommando officer who'd dragged Max to his death and set the synagogue on fire. She stared at him. Her powerlessness in the face of inhumanity left her with a rank sense of doom. There was nothing she could do, no way to get revenge or, more importantly, stop him from killing more innocent people. Justice was a myth. Like God.

A handful of young men nodded goodbye to their mothers and wives and left the courtyard with the Kommando officer. A majority, including Mr. Rosen, stayed with their families, gambling on the unknown as the safer decision. It seemed to Miriam they were all pawns in a game of chess, trying to outsmart their opponents by anticipating their next moves.

A Kommando officer announced that people remaining in the courtyard were going to return to the ghetto. Miriam shuffled out of the courtyard and down the street. The snow glittered in the sun. Discarded bundles and satchels, from people shoved along in the darkness, were strewn on both sides of the street. There was an uneasy silence as they passed splotches of blood in the snow.

Miriam tried not to look. She tried not to think, tried to block her memory, but the quiet provoked her like an open door. Were her parents still lying in the street? Reflexively, she recited the mourner's Kaddish, then realized that if she didn't survive, nobody would say the prayer for her. Ilana and Monya would be raised as Gentiles, with no connection to Judaism. Though she'd lost her faith in God, her children, all Jewish children, deserved the chance to know their own religion. Judaism could not end with her generation. The Nazis could not win.

28

RIGA, JULY 1976

S ARAH LUGGED HER SUITCASE INTO A SMALL ROOM AND recoiled in disappointment. A narrow bed was covered in a faded red-and-white-striped bedspread, there was no dresser or closet for her clothes (only hooks on the wall), the red carpet was torn at the foot of the bed, and there was no bathroom, only a sink. She skimmed the room information posted above the light switch and found she would have to share the toilet and shower, down the hall, with three other guests. Privacy is clearly an uncommon luxury, she thought as she rummaged through her suitcase for her toiletries, clean underwear and a change of clothes. She hurried to the bathroom, hoping to get there before anyone else from her group, only to find it occupied and another woman waiting.

She leaned her shoulder against the wall, resigned to the choice of either showering or eating—there wasn't time for both. She lowered her nose to smell her underarms. A tinge of body odor. *Unacceptable,* her mother would have said. *You don't want others noticing you because you smell bad.* Sarah smiled to herself, recalling her mother leaving a bag filled with aerosol deodorants on her bed when she was around eleven and just entering puberty, a not so subtle hint to spray her armpits every day. She wondered what her mother would think of her daughter being in the city whose memory she'd tried so hard to repress.

Nine minutes before she had to meet her group in the lobby, Sarah was slightly revived after a lukewarm shower, with clean hair and clothes—black jeans and a cap-sleeved ivory blouse. She reapplied her CoverGirl eyeliner and mascara and caught her tired reflection in the oval mirror above the sink. In the ashen early afternoon light peeking through the tiny window, she saw her mother's hazel eyes looking back at her, and was moved to tears. Her mother should have been here, in her place.

NINA POINTED OUT the hammer-and-sickle iron railing along the edge of the Daugava River and said: "Before the Great War, the hammer represented the working class, and the sickle was for the peasants, laboring on farms. Combined, they stood proudly for socialism. After 1918, they symbolized peaceful labor in the Soviet Union. The Latvian Socialist Republic began in 1939 with the Hitler–Stalin Non-Aggression Pact. The People's Parliament was elected the same year, and the creation of the Latvian Socialist Republic was declared."

Sarah stepped back from the group to get photos of the railing, a long shot then a close-up of the hammer and sickle, hard to look at yet harder to ignore. She faced the railing head-on and snapped a photo of the Daugava River. A bridge spanned the river, connecting their side to what appeared to be an older, more ornate part of the city, with intricate spires rising over red roofs and masses of greenery. She peered into her camera, used the zoom feature to get a close-up, and was struck by the glaring contrast between the elaborate buildings across the river and the bland Soviet boxes on her side. It seemed as though the bridge straddled the past and the present.

"What happened in Riga during World War II?"

Mr. Cullen's distinctive voice startled Sarah back to the tour.

"Didn't the Nazis overpower the Soviets?"

"Here we go," Roger moaned softly.

What? Sarah thought.

"Go where?" Doris said.

Nina shaded her eyes with one hand and looked fixedly at Mr. Cullen. "The Nazis tried to gain permanent control during the Great Patriotic War," she said with reproach, "but the Soviet Union conquered Latvia again in 1944 and it has been the Latvian Socialist Republic since then."

A couple of people raised their hands, but Nina spun around on the heel of her bulky shoe, said there was no more time for questions if they were going to keep to their schedule, and announced they would be heading across the October Bridge to Red Riflemen Square.

"Why is World War II off-limits?" Sarah asked Roger when Nina was out of earshot. "And why does Nina call it the Great Patriotic War?"

He gave her a long, searching look and asked in a genial tone: "Are you a journalist?"

"No." She shook her head vehemently and noticed the rest of the group had already reached the bridge. "I'm a market researcher at an ad agency, and can give you more information than you'd ever want to know about Star-Kist tuna or Frosted Flakes."

He smiled and gestured for her to start moving. They walked quickly toward the bridge.

"You don't like reporters?" Sarah said.

"They're all right, as long as they're honest about who they are. Intourist doesn't let journalists on these tours, so sometimes people lie. They caught one last summer, on my tour to Moscow. I couldn't believe the guy had the nerve to enter the Soviet Union as an impostor."

His face blurred and the sounds of cars driving over the bridge muted and she thought: He's just described me. I'm here under false pretences.

"It ruined half the day," Roger continued. "The police searched our bags and interviewed all of us to make sure nobody else was hiding anything. The guy was a royal pain in the ass."

"We should catch up to the group," Sarah said, increasing the length of her strides.

Roger moved alongside her. "You wanted to know why Nina didn't want to talk about the war, right?"

"Yes."

"The short answer is the Soviet government wants citizens focused on their history, Lenin and Stalin. That's why it's called the Great Patriotic War, to remind people to be loyal to their country. Books are censored or banned, so children grow up with a skewed version of history. Citizens are even put in prison for having foreign currency, like American dollars, and they aren't allowed in stores for tourists. The government is bent on keeping its people from knowing what they're missing."

Sarah's throat constricted at the idea of Monya never knowing freedom. She and Roger joined the group at an imposing red statue of three men, their angular faces blocks of severity.

"This is the Red Riflemen Monument," Nina began. "It is made of red granite and was built in 1970 to commemorate Lenin's private bodyguards."

Sarah took a few photos of the forbidding expressions on the granite men.

"I wouldn't want to run into one of these fellows by myself," Mr. Cullen said to Roger.

"You wouldn't want to run into them with a hundred people behind you," Roger quipped.

Nina called out for everyone to follow closely so as to keep to her schedule. Sarah, Roger and the Cullens lagged behind the group as they walked along a road hugging the river, coming to a large building with red roofs and two copper-green towers. Nina explained it was Pioneer Castle, founded in 1330 and completely rebuilt by 1515.

"Today, it is home to the Young Pioneer Organization, which is the reason for its name. This is a voluntary group every child joins at the age of six . . ."

Roger chortled. "That's the Soviet Union in a nutshell," he said to Sarah and the Cullens. "A voluntary group that is mandatory."

Mr. Cullen grinned at his wife. Sarah smiled vaguely, her mind on Monya and whether he had been a Young Pioneer. If he was, in fact, living in Riga. Why he was left behind. Her mother's silence made her mourn what had been lost. Miriam's silence made her want to dig deeper, to understand the people and events that had traumatized both women.

They turned onto Valdemāra iela, a fairly wide street congested with automobiles and pedestrians. An old man shuffled past; his down-turned mouth and droopy eyes smacked of despair. Sarah was not a car person, but she couldn't help but notice how small they were, and rusty, compared with the shiny sedans and station wagons in Chicago.

Nina led them down Elizabetes iela, a narrow road with a large park of overgrown flower beds and potholed paths. A scruffily dressed woman lay on her side on a grungy bench, her head on a plastic bag. Sarah's heart lurched the same as it did in Chicago whenever she came across a homeless person.

Nina hustled them past the woman as if she weren't there, and stopped at a redbrick church with a domed tower. "This is the Dome Church," she began, "the largest medieval church in Latvia. The foundation stone was laid in 1211."

Sarah looked up at the tower and spotted the clock. Twenty-five minutes after three. Before she knew it, they would be back at the hotel for dinner then out to the ballet for the evening. She got antsy, thinking about how the first of only four nights in Riga would soon be over.

Nina cupped her mouth with her hands to speak. "We are now going to the Swedish Gate, comrades. It was built in 1698 to give access to barracks located outside the walls of the city."

Sarah, preoccupied with thoughts of Monya, stepped forward to follow the group, and bumped into Roger. Her forehead hit his bony shoulder. She brought her hand to her head and looked up, stunned. She met his knowing, friendly eyes and decided to take a chance. She tugged Roger's elbow and motioned, with her sore head, for him to move back, away from the group.

"I need to ask you something," she said, her voice low and urgent.

29

RIGA, DECEMBER 1941

"MIRIAM, IS THAT YOU?"

Miriam was roaming the ghetto in search of wood and paper for the dwindling fire, after returning from her job sewing sleeves on Nazi uniforms. She recognized the tinny voice immediately. She reeled sideways. Beneath the streetlight's glow, she saw a narrow face, concave cheeks tinged peach from the cold. "Zelma?"

"I can't believe you're here," Zelma said, her breath rising into the clear evening sky in smoky tendrils.

The cobblestone streets were almost deserted, except for the Jewish police and a handful of people foraging for supplies.

"How did you get out of the Arājs building?" Miriam asked.

"You won't believe it."

"Tell me."

"The man I worked for, Lieutenant Henkemann, arranged for my escape."

"Impossible."

"I knew you wouldn't believe me."

"After the way they—"

"He is one good soul in a sea of enemies." She drew the collar of her flimsy coat against her neck.

"My father used to believe good people would stop the murderers. Then he was shot for holding my mother, who'd just been killed because she fainted."

"I'm sorry."

"I'm afraid my sea is full of sharks."

"Or your good soul hasn't appeared yet."

Zelma's fervent voice did not sway Miriam. She'd been lucky. That was all.

"Do you know what happened to the people who got in the blue bus the other night?" Miriam asked.

"I don't think they're coming back."

"What about the people who volunteered to go to the other camp?"

"I've asked around. Nobody knows. There's been no word from them or from the people who took the bus. Only rumors."

Miriam heard her father's voice in her ear, denouncing rumors. "If there are any decent people," she said, "why aren't they speaking up, letting the world know about the violence here, before we become extinct?"

"The truth will surface. I will bear witness to make sure the men who attacked me are punished," Zelma declared with a startling doggedness.

Miriam nodded, unmoved. She returned to her house. She sat by the fire and was nearly overcome with confusion. It was hard to imagine an officer helping Zelma, an enemy who was also a good person. But Zelma had no reason to lie. Perhaps there were people out there willing to help. If only she could find just one.

———

THEY'D BURNED ALMOST everything in sight. It had been one week since Miriam's parents were murdered, and she'd taken to sleeping by the fire, with the Rosens, to keep from freezing. And to stave off the loneliness. The children, whose names she was beginning to learn in spite of her intention to remain aloof, were lethargic from hunger. They ate the pigeons and sparrows Mr. Rosen managed to kill with a slingshot, but there was never enough. They were always famished.

Miriam's stomach was too weak to growl when Mr. Rosen arrived home with three pigeons dangling from his hand. Mrs. Rosen took the birds from her husband and began plucking their feathers. Miriam sat on a filthy mattress near the fire, mending a pair of trousers with fingers cracking with stiffness. She wore Ilana's sweater, which now hung loosely from her skeletal frame. The children slumped on another mattress, all with vacant expressions and ink-stained lips from eating newspaper.

Boots crunched in the snow outside the door. Miriam's ears perked up.

"Out of your house now," a scathing voice bellowed in Latvian. "Bring nothing."

Hope died with those two menacing words.

"Can't we hide in here?" Mrs. Rosen begged her husband. She dropped the pigeon and shrank against the wall, her children pressed against her. "Surely they won't check every house."

The words had just left her mouth when a furious knock sounded at the door. The two oldest children jumped to their feet and clutched their father's arm. Mr. Rosen dropped the cigarette he'd rolled from newspaper and squished it with the toe of his frayed leather boots.

"Outside," the officer repeated.

Miriam tasted the bile of her stomach.

Mr. Rosen swung his gaze from the door to his wife.

"We have to go," Clara, the oldest daughter, said urgently.

"Let's hurry." Ilya, the oldest boy, struggled to keep his jaw from trembling. He was sixteen years old, but his haggard expression aged him by at least ten years.

Miriam rushed up to the loft, grabbed photos of Max, her children and her parents, and stuffed them down her sweater.

"We have orders to shoot if you don't cooperate," the officer shouted through the door as Miriam descended the stairs.

Mr. Rosen's smallest daughter reached up for him to carry her. She was so skinny, she looked barely alive. And her hair had begun to fall out, leaving bald spots on her scalp. He picked her up and set her on his shoulders.

The door flung open and Mrs. Rosen stood face-to-face with an Arājs Kommando officer. He aimed his rifle and shot Mrs. Rosen in the neck in one swift movement.

"Hanna!" Mr. Rosen shouted.

Mrs. Rosen's eyes rolled back.

The children screamed.

Mrs. Rosen collapsed.

Miriam covered her ears to cut the deafening sound of grief, but it shook her insides.

Mr. Rosen's youngest children threw themselves at him, their hysterical cries rising above their father's. Clara and Ilya stumbled backward, against Miriam.

The officer shoved past Mrs. Rosen. "*Ārpus*. Outside. *Tagad*. Now, or I'll shoot you all!"

Miriam grabbed Ilya's and Clara's hands and hurried out the door, where they joined a herd of shrunken Jews. Children groaned softly, too hungry to make much noise. Babies whimpered.

"Please, I need food for my children," a woman cried.

"Some milk for my baby," another woman said. "She's had nothing for two days."

Miriam felt as if her heart was going to fall out of her chest. If not for Gutte, she would be one of these poor women, begging for scraps to feed her children. She looked at the skeletal faces around her, with sunken eyes and unnaturally white skin. It occurred to her that she looked the same, as if she were hovering between death and barely living, and she was relieved her children couldn't see her this way. She was glad they'd remember her mostly as the woman she was before the Nazis, in case she never made it back to them. Then she wondered if they'd remember her at all if she didn't survive.

A shot pealed through the air. A man killed for straying from the crowd. Another shot. This time a woman who was too weak to stand. Another shot. Ilya and Clara pressed themselves closer to Miriam. Their teeth were chattering. Strident male voices rose above the din, ordering people to be calm and fall into columns.

Snow fell gently from the dark sky. White tears. Miriam, Ilya and Clara hunched together to stay warm, waiting for the rest of the Rosen family to appear. Police continued rousing people from their homes, yelling, *"Arpus."* Men, women and children, young and old, streamed from houses, quickly filling the street. Miriam thought she saw Zelma in the crowd ahead, but it was impossible to be sure amidst the lost souls of Riga.

"Where's Papa?" Ilya asked.

"They should be out by now." Clara stood on tiptoes to see over the heads of people gathered in clumps.

Miriam caught a glimpse of their closed front door and was seized by dread. Mr. Rosen and his remaining children would not be coming.

"It's so crowded, they could be just a few meters away and we wouldn't see them," she said. She pivoted in a circle to avoid

Clara's panicked eyes, saw a patch of white hair not quite one meter away, directly below a streetlight—Simon Dubnow, feverish, with bright-red cheeks. The skin on his neck sagged. His spectacles hung crooked on his face and his bloodshot eyes were dilated. He pitched from side to side as if he didn't have the strength to stand. He started to fall to the ground. An officer grabbed his arm and yanked him aside. Miriam bent in fright. The scene with her parents played out in her mind. She stepped back, physically and mentally disconnecting from the inevitable.

Simon called out in Yiddish, his voice surprisingly strong: "*Yiden, shraybt un farshraybt.*" Jews, write and record.

The officer shot Simon in the head.

Ilya and Clara exchanged looks of terror. They threw their arms around Miriam. An image of Monya and Ilana in their places flashed in front of Miriam's eyes. She squeezed them against her and silently thanked Gutte for saving her children.

"Help us!"

"Please, stop!"

"*Sh'ma yisrael . . .*"

Someone shoved Miriam into a tall man. Her face met his scrawny ribs. A woman shrieked and received a shot in the back. Miriam held Clara and Ilya tight and pressed through the growing crowd, to put distance between them and the officer shooting as if he were at target practice.

"*Doties tālāk.* Move on," an officer shouted from behind.

They were swept along in columns, five abreast, through the slushy streets. Snow fell fast and hard as tacks. The temperature plummeted below zero, a wintry chill that burned exposed skin. For at least an hour, the group traipsed along Ludzas iela onto Līksnas iela, finally stopping at a three-story building where they were packed in so tight, nobody could move or even sit down. The bodily smells of shit and urine and sweat and dirty feet and fear blended into one indescribable stench, inhabiting Miriam's nostrils like mucus. She hugged Clara and Ilya tight. She needed them as much as they needed her. Maybe more.

All night, the remaining ghetto residents stood still as gravestones in the confined space, moaning and weeping. Clara passed out, wedged between Miriam and Ilya, who fought to stay awake, his eyes occasionally drooping shut, his head falling forward. Miriam held them close, afraid to let go. They were allowed to return to the ghetto in the morning, but when Miriam discovered half the residents were missing, she knew her time was running out.

30

RIGA, JULY 1976

SARAH PERUSED THE LAMINATED MENU THAT CLEARLY hadn't changed in years, with its yellowed, brittle edges. She, Roger and the Cullens sat at a square table in the middle of the hotel restaurant waiting for the waitress to notice them. They'd been waiting twenty minutes already and couldn't seem to get her attention as she inched from table to table with the speed of a slug. Not ideal when they had to leave for the ballet in ninety minutes, though Sarah couldn't bring herself to be excited about the performance, not with Roger's warnings about the difficulties she was up against clanging in her head.

"You have to get special permission to see relatives here," he'd said through clenched teeth when she'd given him an abbreviated version of her story and asked for his help. "Didn't your travel agent tell you?"

"Yes, of course." She'd taken the blank visa form out of her purse. Her hand trembled as she gave it to him. "If I find my uncle, I'm supposed to fill this out."

Roger appraised the document and handed it back to Sarah. "This is useless without an embassy stamp."

"I know, but I thought it might help. I thought it was better than nothing." Sarah saw herself through his shrewd eyes and was embarrassed by her naïveté. "It was stupid. I'm sorry."

"Shit!" Roger looked at Sarah. "Why didn't you put off coming until you knew more about your uncle?"

Sarah swallowed. "My grandmother's been in the hospital. She's all right, but I don't know how much time she has left."

Roger nodded tightly. His eyes shifted from her to his watch to her again.

She flinched under his unwavering gaze. "I don't want my grandmother to die without knowing what happened to her son," she began quietly. "But now that I'm here, I see it would be too risky to find him. I just didn't want to go home without trying."

He stopped in front of her, planted his feet, looked her in the eye and told her not to give up so quickly, that he might be able to find out if Monya was in Riga. He had a professor friend who'd know the ins and outs of government bureaucracy. He'd call him and, if possible, set up a meeting, but that was as far as he was willing to go.

AMIDST THE COLLECTION of drab, utilitarian Soviet buildings, the ballet theater stood out like a diamond, with its marble pillars and opulent facade, a sculpture of a boy holding a man's head beside a lion crowning the top of the building.

"Extraordinary, isn't it?" Roger said in awe. He looked thin yet sturdy in a sky-blue leisure suit over a crisp collared shirt as white as his eyelashes.

"Stunning," Sarah agreed.

"That's Apollo on top." He pointed at the boy with the lion

and said Apollo was holding the mask of life's experiences through theater.

"I remember Apollo from a Greek mythology class in college," Sarah murmured. "He was one of the most revered gods, who cleansed people's guilt."

"I'm impressed."

"There's a library in Chicago, the Blackstone." She shrugged. "It's nothing like this, but there are four beautiful half-circle murals in the rotunda—"

"Art, Labor, Science and Literature, from Greek mythology. I know it well. One of my favorite places in the Windy City."

"Me too," she said, heart in her throat. She twisted her necklace and watched the way his face became animated and his hands gestured fervently as he described a triangular section of the facade, catching the interest of others in their tour.

"Apollo, god of art, is in the center, and next to the swimming dolphin is Dionysus, the opposite of Apollo, representing tragedy," he explained. "And the six Ionic columns symbolize the rhythm of the facade. The point of the sculpture is to show how everything— the ocean, sky, music, comedy and tragedy—is interconnected."

Beads of perspiration rolled down his forehead. Sarah resisted the urge to reach up and dry his skin with her fingers. She wanted him to keep talking, to keep telling her new things, rousing her mind, practically dormant since college.

"The ballet waits for nobody," Nina called out tersely from the entrance. One hand was on her waist, and her eyes were small and glowering. "Come."

"Who would have thought," Doris said, "Riga having such a beautiful theater."

"Between you and me," George said, patting Roger on the back, "I think you'd make a first-class tour guide."

"Thanks, but I think I'll stick to teaching." His sharp eyes fell on Sarah.

She flushed.

"Sorry." He opened his palms. "You probably think I'm a know-it-all blabbermouth."

"Not at all. I think your students are lucky to have you."

He moved closer until their shoulders almost touched and she inhaled his cologne, a rich blend of cedarwood and mint.

"I got carried away but I knew Nina wouldn't talk about the building," he said.

"Why not?"

"Because it's not a Soviet achievement. The Latvians built the theater."

"But it's a tour of Latvia."

"A Soviet tour of Latvia."

"Right."

He held out his arm. She didn't hesitate in linking her arm through his, though she told herself he was merely being a gentleman. It meant nothing, she was sure, and it wasn't as if she and Henry were still together.

They filed into the theater. At first glance, it was lush with red velvet seats and gold floors and railings, but as they sat down, Sarah noticed the velvet was faded and torn in spots, and the gold paint was chipped. There was a distinct sense of disrepair. A pity—it would have been magnificent during its heyday.

She settled into her seat, beside Roger's, and felt a tremor of excitement as the lights dimmed. The theater grew dark. The stage appeared, lit up, then the orchestra sounded with the clash of cymbals and the curtains drew open with a pageantry that took Sarah's breath away. She leaned forward when a lone dancer floated across the stage, eager to soak it all in.

"We're meeting my friend tomorrow."

Sarah jumped at Roger's voice in her ear.

"I'm telling you here because the hotel rooms are bugged," Roger continued.

"When?"

"You'll find out tomorrow." He leaned closer, his lips almost brushing Sarah's ear. "And I need twenty-five dollars for Nina."

"What for?"

"Nothing is free here, not even walking on your own." He sat upright in his seat and focused on the stage.

Sarah's hands shook with anticipation and nerves. It all seemed too easy, too convenient, how Roger had been able to set up a meeting so quickly. Then again, how hard should it be, to arrange a meeting with an old friend? She chastised herself for being paranoid, and focused on the dancers. She tried to concentrate, but the story played out incoherently, like a French film without subtitles.

31

RIGA, DECEMBER 1941

DAYLIGHT HAD NOT YET APPEARED WHEN ARĀJS
Kommando officers announced residents had to move out of
the ghetto, one week after they'd been forced to stand all night
in the ice-cold building. One week after the ghetto population was
halved. They were going to work in a fish cannery. Miriam had a
feeling the fish cannery was a ruse. Still, she desperately hoped it
was true, just as she hoped rumors were true that Jews from the
ghetto who'd vanished one week ago were alive, in a camp elsewhere. Outside, the snow had stopped, but the roads were sheets of
ice. Miriam clutched Ilya and Clara with the little strength she had
remaining, and made a vow: if they fell, she'd go down with them.
She couldn't let children die alone. *She* didn't want to die alone.

In columns led by a Nazi, surrounded by Arājs Kommando
members on foot and on horseback, they wound through the dark,
narrow Zhidu alley to Moscow Boulevard, at the eastern edge of
Riga. Mournful cries broke the steady refrain of footsteps chinking
the icy snow. Officers prodded Jews forward with truncheons, as if
they were pigs being led to slaughter. A middle-aged woman lost

her balance and crashed to the ground. An Arājs Kommando officer shot her and kept walking, barely missing a step.

Miriam bowed her head. From the corner of her eye, she saw a child lying at the side of the road. Dead. She stumbled. A whip lashed centimeters over her scalp, emitting a gust of wind. She reeled and saw the bloated face of a Latvian officer.

"Faster," the officer barked. He raised his arm and snapped his whip again, skinning her head.

She tottered from the blistering pain. Felt herself plunging backward. Hands gripped her waist. Clara's and Ilya's hands. They kept her from falling over. They yanked her onward. She moved as if she were unconscious, her legs numb, her mind withdrawn. She didn't even flinch as she passed two more dead people, lying facedown in the snow at the edge of the road, as she saw children, unable to keep the swift pace, shot and abandoned in the street. It was too horrid to be real.

They continued, a river of people, past the sprawling central market where German supplies were now stored in the Zeppelin hangars. Past the rubber factory, Quadrat, smoke pouring from cylinders on the roof, giving off a burning odor that turned Miriam's dry, empty stomach. Past the Delka textile factory. Past the VEF factory, which made Max's beloved radio and the Minox camera that had captured so many special moments, long gone.

Daylight slunk over the horizon, a yellow-and-orange glow that provoked Miriam's mind and taunted her with the possibility of an ordinary day for other people, not her. Shriveled faces became all too visible. Bruises, cuts and sickly gray skin emerged in the soft light, along with blood seeping from lifeless bodies at the side of the road.

Any expectations of leaving on a train were squashed when they continued marching past the small redbrick Šķirotava railway station, past a clump of pine trees and up a hill to Rumbula, a wide-open, grassy area. They stopped at Crow Forest, thirty meters from Rumbula. Gunshots punctured the air nearby. Over and over. Clara and Ilya shook quietly, without letting go of Miriam. This is the end, Miriam thought, too malnourished to fight or cry or feel.

Miriam feebly searched for a place, a hole in the crowd to escape through, but she, Ilya and Clara were jammed with hundreds of others, a knot of people minutes from death. She closed her eyes, but the shooting sounds were more ominous in the dark. Clara and Ilya gripped her hands when Arājs Kommando officers funneled them into narrower columns. Miriam felt noticeably useless.

"Valuables go here," a Kommando officer ordered in a callous voice that tugged at Miriam's memory.

She looked up. It was the man who'd shot her parents. Instead of surviving to raise her children and take vengeance on the monsters who'd slaughtered thousands of innocent people, she would be murdered by the brute who'd killed her parents. Miriam was revolted by this quirk of fate.

"Here," the officer grunted, pointing with a rubber truncheon to a wooden box filled to the brim with gold, diamonds and silver that people had smuggled into the ghetto.

Miriam wanted to call him a murderer and a thief, but Clara yanked her hand. In her shock at seeing him, Miriam had forgotten about her unspoken vow to stay with Clara and Ilya to the end. If she aggravated him, he'd shoot her on the spot, in front of the two children, and they'd be left to face their deaths on their own.

"Rings too." The officer struck Miriam's right hand with his truncheon.

A sob stuck in Miriam's throat. She caressed her gold wedding band. It had been Max's mother's ring. Part of his family for two generations.

"Hurry up."

She pulled the ring from her finger and set it in the box. Giving it up was like cutting a final cord between herself and Max. She longed for the unshakable faith of her parents and Max, a faith that comforted them as they faced death. But she felt nothing inside. Her spirit had wilted like flowers after an early frost.

Up ahead, where the forest began, gunshots grew louder, stronger, like a dozen thunderbolts at once. An officer ordered people to take their coats off and throw them in a pile; his voice was hazy, as though he were far away. Ilya and Clara removed their coats with subdued compliance and threw them in the pile, almost two meters high. Miriam fumbled with the buttons on her coat with clumsy, frozen fingers.

The officer, in a belted overcoat with boots to his knees, gloves and a fur hat, pointed at another large pile and ordered them to remove the rest of their clothes. Miriam looked around. She saw Jews undressing with a startling meekness. They'd given up. She understood. There was no cannery. The people who'd disappeared a week earlier were dead. It seemed useless to fight the inevitable. In a daze, Miriam pulled her dress over her head. Clara cowered in her underwear. Miriam avoided looking at Ilya.

"But I'm a dressmaker. I can be useful to you."

Miriam spun around when she heard Frida Frid's unmistakable, assertive voice. Frida owned the shop where Miriam had bought her dresses, a lifetime ago. Frida's auburn hair sat like a nest on her head, dull, frizzy tufts sticking out in every direction.

"Read." Frida held a stack of papers up to a Latvian officer.

"Get undressed." The officer slapped the papers from her hand.

The papers fluttered to the snowy ground. An officer taking photos of people undressing stepped on some of the papers, leaving a wet footprint that made the ink run. He continued taking photos, ignoring the documents that defined Frida's life.

"Go." The Latvian officer shoved Frida out of his way.

Frida stumbled and fell. She sat on the ground and looked as if she wanted to stay there, but another officer barked at her to get up. Miriam caught her eye as she stood. Frida blinked at Miriam with such determination, Miriam wouldn't have been surprised if she was already thinking up another scheme to escape.

Clara, Ilya and Miriam were whisked from their column and shoved through a gauntlet of Arājs Kommando members into a clearing. A deep pit stretched out in front of them. A squad of Nazi soldiers was positioned on all sides, with machine guns. Fifty Jews in their underwear, including a mother holding her baby, staggered down into the pit on a ramp carved into the earth. Arājs Kommando officers stood on the ramp, prodding people to descend faster, into the pit stacked with dead bodies. Like herring in a can. Like a cannery, she seethed. Like a sick joke.

It was quiet enough to hear Jews descending into the pit chanting the *Shema*: "Hear, O Israel, Adonai is our God, Adonai is One."

A Nazi soldier filmed the pit. Others took photos, documenting their cruelty. Did they plan to watch the slaughter later, as if it were a Joan Crawford film? Several officers, clutching bottles of *degvīns*, vodka, stumbled at the edge of the pit. The acid from Miriam's stomach rose to her throat. She vomited phlegm and bile, the only things in her stomach.

Viktors Arājs himself staggered on the edge of the pit with a gun, his words slurred from alcohol. Miriam stiffened. The sight of him brought on a fury that rose in her throat like venom. He and his men ordered the Jews, stunned into obedience, to lie facedown on top of dead bodies like sardines. Then, Arājs and his officers moved away from the pit. Nazi soldiers raised their guns in unison and fired one shot apiece at the backs of heads. A second later, a couple of Kommando officers with pistols ventured into the pit, finishing off people who somehow weren't killed by the Nazis. Clara and Ilya clung to Miriam as the next group of Jews marched down the ramp to the pit.

"I'm sorry," Miriam whispered to Ilya and Clara. If she'd known what they were going to face, she would have left them to die in the house with the rest of their family.

Shots fired. Miriam's shoulders hunched. Clara trembled.

"You're both very brave," Miriam said. "I'm proud to know you."

Clara looked at Miriam with sad eyes.

"Let's go," Viktors Arājs ordered the next fifty people—which included Miriam, Ilya and Clara.

Miriam unflinchingly met his stare. She wanted him to remember her in his nightmares. They moved with the rest of their doomed group. Miriam shivered. She felt Max's presence and spontaneously began to chant the *Shema*: "*Sh'ma yisrael, Adonai . . .*" Clara joined in. Then Ilya. And the hunched-over man in front of Miriam. And the two women behind her. Miriam saw how they were forever linked by the deep-rooted words of their culture. Hearing her own voice among others', people on the cusp of death, chanting identical words imprinted on their souls, in unison, made Miriam feel she belonged to something bigger than herself. Faith made her spirits soar.

Miriam recalled her father saying prayer gave him hope. Until her voice blended with the voices of strangers who shared her faith, she'd been certain she could give up her Judaism, which incited such hatred. Until that moment, she didn't know what she was fighting for.

One of the men yelled for them to get down into the pit and lie still on the dead bodies. Miriam caught a glimpse of writhing people on her right, and steered her gaze to a pair of tall black boots perched on the edge of the pit above. She got to her knees and pulled the children down with her.

"I can't," Clara cried. "The blood . . ."

On Miriam's other side, Ilya sobbed.

"Close your eyes," Miriam told Clara. "Close your eyes and keep holding my hand."

The body underneath Miriam was lukewarm, and something sharp, a knee, poked against her hip. Clara shook and sobbed. Ilya lay still. Miriam heard the order to shoot and was overcome by the metallic taste of blood.

32

RIGA, JULY 1976

SARAH LIKED THE HOTEL BREAKFAST: KASHA (BUCKWHEAT with a nutty taste), bread with butter, and fried eggs. It had a reassuring familiarity that appealed to her first thing in the morning. No sign of Roger or the Cullens, so she sat alone at a table for four, sipping black coffee and dragging her bread across her plate to get every last drop of runny egg yolk.

Her pulse quickened when Roger appeared.

He slid into the chair beside her, caught the waitress's eye and pointed to his empty coffee cup, then lit a cigarette in one swift, orchestrated motion. The waitress sidled over and poured coffee. He asked for eggs and bread with jam, drank his coffee in one loud gulp, sat back and puffed on his cigarette with a satisfied smile.

The caustic whiff of smoke reminded Sarah of Miriam. She pictured her grandmother, alone in her apartment, only the television and radio to keep her company, filling her lungs with tar and nicotine, shortening her life with every puff.

"Sorry. I should have asked if it bothered you." Roger scrunched his cigarette in the ashtray and waved his hands to disperse the smoke.

"It's fine," she lied.

"I can tell from the look on your face it's not," he countered.

"You're right," she admitted. "I don't like it."

The waitress set Roger's food on the table. He nodded thanks and lathered his bread with strawberry jam.

"It's a terrible habit," he said. "I wish I'd never started, but I did and I've tried to quit but can't." He took a bite of his bread.

"My dad quit cold turkey." She sipped her coffee. Bitter. She made a face and set it down. "He was tired of waking up with a mouth tasting like sandpaper, so he flushed his cigarettes down the toilet and never smoked again."

Roger paused, keeping his eyes on her. "He must be really solid, to kick the habit."

"He is. But he's been struggling since my mom died, eating when he craves a cigarette."

"That's tough." He doused his eggs with salt. "Any sisters or brothers?"

"Just me. What about you?"

"Same."

"Where are you from?" she asked.

He glanced at his watch, expensive-looking, with three small dials set within the main face. "George and Doris better hurry up if they want to eat before we head out of here."

"You didn't answer my question," she pressed.

"Because I don't have a good answer. I'm an army brat. We moved every couple of years. I'm from everywhere and nowhere."

She heard resentment in his voice. "That would be tough, so many new schools."

He scooped eggs onto his fork and looked at her with inscrutable eyes. "You have to leave your camera in the hotel today."

"Why?"

He bent sideways and said quietly, "Latvians don't own American cameras. If you walk around with one dangling around your neck when we go meet my friend, we could draw unwanted attention. And don't smile—your white teeth will give you away. Don't talk, either. You may as well have a target on your back if you're heard speaking English."

Sarah clamped her lips shut. Roger made walking down the street sound underhanded. Sarah slipped twenty-five dollars into Roger's open palm. She felt as if she were at the edge of a high diving board and could either go down the safe way, on the stairs, or take her chances and plunge headfirst into the water.

SARAH TOOK IN the lofty statue of Vladimir Lenin, leader of the Soviet Union before Stalin, his chin as high as the columns of trees behind it, right arm raised like a consummate politician's. Nina announced it was built in 1950 and Lenin was facing east, toward Moscow.

"Under Lenin," Nina continued, her voice ringing with pride, "the Soviet Union became a one-party Communist state. We admire Lenin because he removed capitalism from the Soviet Union by giving working-class citizens education and leadership skills. He established a Bolshevik supremacy called Leninism that Stalin combined with his Marxist policies to create the state ideology we have today."

Sarah listened to Nina talk about the Soviet Union as if it was a model other nations coveted, and thought, She really believes what she's saying. At this moment Sarah understood, for the first time, just how buffered Soviet citizens were from the rest of the world.

"It's time," Roger said quietly to Sarah.

The hair on her arms rose.

Roger told the befuddled Cullens that Nina had approved his request to leave the tour for a while, with Sarah, and then they merged into the crowd on the sidewalk. Different-colored Ladas drove both ways down the street, small, boxy cars that were strikingly identical.

Subdued Russian voices poked the clammy air. Sarah balked at the despair carved in people's faces and postures—the downturned lips, the listless eyes, the sagging shoulders. And the grayness. She saw clunky black shoes, women's dresses in varying shades of gray and black, and men in somber dark trousers and shirts. It was almost like being contained within a black-and-white photo, except for the scarves, in vibrant floral prints, tied around women's heads or necks, allowing a hint of individuality. And some of the younger women, Sarah's age, wore vivid miniskirts with white knee socks, revealing a desire to escape the bland Soviet fashion mold. Yet Sarah couldn't shake the gloominess she felt, seeing the worn-out expressions on people's faces.

Roger took her elbow to guide her in the right direction. Her heart raced at his touch, at the nearness of him, at the risk he was taking to help her—someone he had no reason to help. She trusted him. He was a good person. He nudged her right at the corner, and they continued in silence, the city's canal on their right, the water calm and glittering beneath the hot sun. There was not a speck of wind to cool the rising temperature. This surprised Sarah, the stifling heat; she'd assumed Latvia would be cold even in the summer, but then Chicago was called the Windy City and she'd never found it that gusty.

"This is where we're going," Roger said. "University of Latvia." He stopped in front of a salmon-stone building with a striking curved wood door in the center and two smaller arched windows on each side. Three larger windows, about the same size as the door, were on the second level. Roger gestured to the stone steps flanking the door.

She followed him into a poorly lit vestibule where a young woman, with braided hair that fell to her waist, sat reading a magazine. Gray metal filing cabinets lined the wall behind the woman, and smoke rose in wisps from a lit cigarette balanced on the edge of a glass ashtray.

"*Dobroye utro,*" Roger said genially to the woman.

She flipped a page. Didn't look up.

"*Dobroye utro,*" Roger repeated.

The woman plucked her cigarette from the ashtray and glowered, as if Sarah and Roger were in her way.

Roger identified himself as Professor Munro, from Syracuse University, and Sarah as his wife, Svetlana.

The dour woman gave them the once-over and went back to her magazine.

"Why isn't she—" Sarah whispered.

Roger squeezed her hand until it throbbed.

Sarah nodded, chagrined.

He pulled her back and whispered into her ear: "We're on her time, not ours. She'll let us in when she's good and ready. That's the way it is here. Everyone has jobs, but it doesn't mean they actually work. They get paid no matter what."

Sarah gave him an incredulous look.

The receptionist read a couple of pages, moving her index finger slowly along the text. She lifted her lashes to see if they were still there, drew her lips back in a snarl and heaved her podgy torso out of the chair. She moved at possum speed to the far end of the barricade, reminding Sarah of their waitress the previous night, and unlocked the door. Roger placed his hand against the small of Sarah's back and prodded her through. The receptionist locked the door again, turned and unlocked another door, leading into the university.

"*Spaseebo*," Roger said before the woman locked the door behind them.

She grunted.

Sarah gritted her teeth to keep from saying what she thought about the lazy woman, who'd cost them ten valuable minutes. They had to be back at the hotel when their group returned at five o'clock. Roger said the babushkas knew exactly how many guests were staying on each floor and would report them as missing if they didn't show.

He strode purposefully through the marble-floored hall, leading them up a flight of stairs and through a set of heavy wood doors into a long wing with doors on both sides. The light was harsh and there was a disconcerting odor of mildew and sour milk. Sarah stuck close behind him, thankful for his confident air. Roger stopped at door number 203 and knocked. A diminutive man with round wire-framed glasses opened the door.

"Professor Kulda?" Roger asked.

"*Nyet,*" the man replied. He spoke in Russian to Roger.

"*Tak.*" Roger gave him a quick wave and steered Sarah down the hall.

They went through another set of double doors, ascended a different staircase and walked down a second corridor lined with more office doors. At room 347, Roger tapped lightly. Dr. Kulda, like Roger, seemed far too young to be a professor, with his boyish, smooth face and crewcut. His teeth were small and off-white, and he wore steel-framed glasses that were too large for his face. Dr. Kulda gave Sarah a cursory glance and turned his attention to Roger.

The two men lit cigarettes and launched into a spirited conversation in Russian, Roger's hands moving as he spoke, Dr. Kulda's voice rising and falling in waves, his stoic expression betraying nothing. Sarah stood uncomfortably in front of the window and peered at the busy street below. She turned and took in the formality of the office, the floor-to-ceiling bookshelves against the wall opposite the oak desk. Cyrillic letters embossed in gold adorned many of the spines, pristine books that looked as if they'd never been opened. Dr. Kulda's desktop seemed almost too neat and empty, with a clean black leather blotter and a jar of identical pens. There were no photos anywhere, no clues about the professor's personal life, unlike the offices in her agency, where people filled every blank space with photos, awards, funny mugs or clippings to stamp their identity on otherwise impersonal spaces.

"Okay, Sarah," Roger said. "Ludvigs is up to speed and he's agreed to help."

She caught her breath at the sound of his voice telling her what she thought she wanted to hear. Deep down, she had hoped Dr. Kulda would refuse, giving her a valid excuse to abandon her dangerous search.

Dr. Kulda propped himself against the edge of his desk. "I need a bit more information," he said in surprisingly good English. "Roger says your uncle's name was Monya Talan but you have no idea what happened to him."

"Right."

"Do you know the name of the woman who looked after your mother and uncle during the war?"

"Gutte Meija. She was their housekeeper before the war."

"What about your uncle's birthdate?"

"He was born in 1940, but I don't know the day or month."

Dr. Kulda adjusted his glasses. "Before we go any further, I must warn you, contacting your uncle could put his entire family in jeopardy. He could lose his position or be imprisoned for planning to defect. If he's married, his wife could lose her job."

She was torn between her precarious yearning to find her uncle, for Miriam's sake (and for herself), and leaving him alone, forever in the dark about his mother and niece, oblivious to the truth. She attempted to put herself in Monya's shoes, but how could she possibly understand what his life was like? He might have no idea about his roots. He could be perfectly happy. Who was she to come along and shake up his world?

Her thoughts strayed to the moment she'd heard of Monya's existence. The range of emotions she'd experienced: confusion, betrayal, anger, curiosity, exhilaration. Most of all, an overwhelming need to find the truth. Her grandmother's cryptic words, about truth being a burden few wanted to bear, suddenly made complete sense.

"I understand. But I believe Monya deserves to know the truth."

"Are you sure?" Roger asked.

She thought about the guilt that had whittled Miriam's consciousness down to slivers of shame, diminishing her life.

"Positive," she said, her voice tremulous.

"Very well." Dr. Kulda's nostrils flared. He flashed Roger a tight-lipped smile. "I'll be in touch."

"Thank you, Ludvigs." Roger extended his hand.

Dr. Kulda gave a dismissive wave.

"You have no idea how much this will mean to my grandmother," Sarah added. "If I can tell her what happened, good or bad, at least she'll have some closure."

"Be that as it may," Dr. Kulda said, before shutting the door.

OUTSIDE, THE SKY had clouded over and there was the earthy scent of rain. Sarah, confused by Dr. Kulda's parting words, let

Roger steer her back over the canal and down Lenin Street toward the October Bridge. Dr. Kulda clearly didn't approve of her decision to locate Monya, yet he was willing to help. Which meant he didn't totally disagree. She was about to ask Roger what he thought when a police officer crossed their path and stopped to wait for a green light. Sarah blanched, intimidated by the force of his blue-gray uniform, tall black boots and black-brimmed cap. She looked up at Roger. The muscles in his jaw clenched. His arm stiffened around her waist as they approached the traffic light.

The officer's eyes swept over Roger and lingered on Sarah. He thrust his chest out and spoke brusquely to Roger. Sarah had never felt so vulnerable, facing a Soviet officer with no idea of what was being said. The officer's dark eyes, like smears of ink, probed her from head to toe. *If he asks me a question, I'm finished.* A flapping commotion overhead diverted the officer's glare. Sarah looked up as a flock of birds soared through the clouds in a V-formation, following the curve of the river.

The light changed to green. The officer said something to Roger, a long-winded sentence that made her fear the worst. Roger reached into his pocket, took an American fifty-dollar bill from his wallet and handed it to the officer. The officer sucked in his cheeks, nodded curtly and proceeded across the street. Sarah didn't realize she'd been holding her breath until she was on the other side of the street. She was dizzy. Her knees folded. Roger grabbed her elbows and told her to keep moving.

"Walk faster," he said with a sobering harshness as they stepped onto the bridge straddling the Daugava River. "We're sitting ducks here. No way out if another officer sees us and decides to ask questions."

Sarah increased her pace on legs that buzzed with pins and needles. They passed a group of schoolchildren in identical white tops, blue neck scarves and the omnipresent bulky black shoes that seemed to be the only footwear option in Riga.

At the end of the bridge, Roger prodded her right, onto the road leading to the hotel.

"We've got about an hour to kill before the tour gets back," he said, his voice still abrasive, his posture wooden. "I need a drink, but you can't be seen in the hotel bar."

She swallowed. "You go. It's fine."

"No, it's not." He raked his hand through his hair. "Do you know how close we came to getting caught back there?"

"What did he say?"

"For starters, he knew we were tourists."

"You speak Russian. You're allowed to go off from the tour."

"True. But you don't."

"How could he tell? I didn't open my mouth."

"Exactly. You looked scared. You didn't say a word. And maybe your shoes gave you away. I don't know."

"My shoes?"

"People here buy American sneakers through the black market, but they're usually second-hand, dirty, not brand spanking new."

She looked at the clean white Converses she'd bought especially for the trip, and wilted. "I had no idea."

"It's just a hunch. I don't know for sure. Just be glad it only took fifty dollars to get him to look the other way. It's all I had."

"I'll pay you back." She paled. "I shouldn't have asked you to help. I would never forgive myself if you got in trouble because of me."

He gave her a long hard stare. "Don't worry about me. You're the one who stands to lose the most if the KGB gets wind of your plan."

Roger wandered off toward the tour's bus, pulling in front of the hotel.

Sarah felt something shift between them, a subtle hint that they were no longer on the same side. She had to watch her back. As she observed her fellow tourists disembark, she stepped backward, toward the shrubs lining the walkway, dug the toes of her sneakers into the soil and rubbed them with dirt until they looked old and worn. And as she showed her room key to the guard at the hotel door, an inexplicable longing for Henry tightened her throat.

33

RIGA, DECEMBER 1941

H ER SPINE BOWED FROM A CRUSHING PRESSURE. MIRIAM
opened her eyes to a smoky darkness, certain she was dead,
that her spirit was floating over the ditch of corpses.

"Mama," a child wailed.

A shot rang out and the child stopped crying.

The steamy, sulfuric gunpowder odor invaded Miriam's icy
nostrils. German and Latvian voices brayed above her. Where
were Clara and Ilya? A gut-wrenching moan ricocheted through
the air. Something heavy squashed Miriam's head, moved to her
back, then her legs. Feet. Officers were walking over the bodies as if
they formed a boulevard, shooting survivors. Miriam's cheeks grew
taut. She was buried alive in a trench of dead people.

"One more," a man's intoxicated voice said in Latvian.

He sounded terribly close.

Another shot cracked like a whip through the night.

Someone moaned.

The crunch of footsteps nearby.

The blast of a gunshot.

Silence.

How long have I been lying here?

Cold soaked through Miriam's underwear. Her skin tingled. Her eyelashes were frozen. She had a pins-and-needles sensation in her feet and hands. Her breaths were short and labored. It was like breathing mud.

The scrape of shovels digging.

A smattering of German.

A sneeze pushed against the inside of Miriam's nose and mouth. She clamped her jaw tight but couldn't stop it from coming. She turned her head until her face was down, against someone's ice-cold feet.

She sneezed quietly. She tensed her muscles. A sneeze wasn't going to be her undoing. Somehow she'd been spared for Ilana and Monya. She had to survive.

"Mama, Mama," a child whimpered.

A shot ricocheted above her head, blasting her eardrums. All she could hear was an ethereal buzz. She felt a heavy thud between her shoulders. Someone was walking over her.

Is it almost over?

The erratic boom of gunshots kept Miriam from drifting to unconsciousness. She tried to count, to stay alert, but her mind was too fuzzy to get past one hundred.

Above the pit, Latvian and German voices slithered away. A car engine rumbled and faded. Another car engine started and receded. Miriam didn't move until a hush had fallen over the woods.

Miriam set her palms on the feet at her head. Someone, a man from the size, had walked on these feet just hours ago. A man with dreams, hope, love and family. Now, she was using them as leverage to save herself. Revulsion mounted in her chest like fire, sucking all the oxygen from the air. The bodies on top of Miriam

crushed against her with an enormous heft. Using her entire forearms, she pushed down and raised her shoulders and head. She felt
the weight disburse slightly. Not nearly enough.

I can't.

She felt the icy, hard skin of the feet at her head, and adrenaline
torched her muscles. She thrust her shoulders against the corpses
with an astonishing ferocity. Her head emerged from the bodies. She
took a quick breath of the frigid air through her mouth. Her nostrils
were frozen. She opened her eyes. The full moon suffused the night
with a white glow that illuminated the dead. Miriam wept sound-
lessly. She grabbed hold of someone's head and wrenched herself
from the mound. She crawled across dead bodies, her joints searing
as she inched her way to the edge of the pit. She was naked except
for her undergarments, flecked with other people's blood, skin and
bits of organs. And she was exhausted and confused and frightened.

Why did I survive?

Miriam pivoted slowly, her eyes raking the area for guards. She
saw no one under the hazy moonlight, but managed to locate the
clearing where she'd entered between the gauntlet of Arājs members. With Clara and Ilya. Her heart welled up. Her existence felt
like a betrayal.

Why were children killed?

She listened for the sound of footfalls, voices, the click of a gun,
but heard only her own slow and shallow breaths. She swallowed
the knot of revulsion in her throat. She stood on the body closest to the top of the pit, lifted her arms over the rim and clamped
her forearms on the ground, bumpy with hoarfrost. Pressing down
with her hands, she hoisted herself up, catching the surface with
one foot. She heard the crack of her bare foot on the icy ground and
went stiff. Her left leg dangled over the edge. Not a sound.

She scrambled out of the pit and crouched low. Empty liquor

bottles, dusted with snow, were strewn along the edge of the pit. She moved stealthily toward the clearing, thirty meters away. Her bare feet pricked from the icy snow. On impulse, she went to twist her wedding ring around her finger, but it was gone. She looked at her hand and was overcome by grief when she saw her bare ring finger.

Miriam caught the sheen of limbs under the moonlight, and knew she had to keep going. Clumsily, she skulked forward. In the distance, dogs barked. She halted, afraid they were coming closer, afraid they were the Nazis' shepherds, with razor-sharp teeth that could rip skin like paper. The barking ebbed and she carried on. Footsteps cracked the snow on the other side of the pit. *A guard?* Miriam sank to the ground and slithered left, to a clump of trees. She lay still, in the trees' shadows, her nerves like blades under her skin. The footsteps marched around the perimeter, getting louder as the person neared her, then fading as he moved farther and farther. This was her chance.

She crept away from the trees and continued until she came to stacks of discarded clothing and shoes. Miriam rummaged through the piles, steeling herself against the fact that everything came from murdered Jews. She pulled trousers over her legs, then rolled thick socks onto her feet. Next, she pulled the yellow stars from two wool sweaters and a coat and layered them over her shivering body. Finally, a wool hat that covered her ears, and a pair of mitts.

She turned to another, more disorganized pile of mementos, family photos strewn across the ground like irrelevant scraps of paper. Her gut churned with rage as she rummaged through thousands of photos, thousands of faces, thousands of families whose fate would be unknown forever. *They will be remembered*, she vowed. *I will speak for these people when this heinous war is over.* She stuffed her coat pockets with photos, to keep until the end of the war, then crept through the trees, careful to stay in the shadows.

Minutes later, she came to the Šķirotava railway station. She paused. It would be busy and unsafe in the morning, but the tracks would lead her out of Riga. She continued, flinching at the sound of her feet crunching through the snow; her feet chafed in the boots, a size too big, and her hands and face were seared from the cold. The light from the moon and stars guided her along the railway tracks; she kept to the side, where the light didn't get in.

As night gave way to a pallid morning, Miriam came to a gate leading to a farmhouse on a hill. A well-kept barn stood about six meters in front of her. The lane beyond the gate curved left, around a stand of pine trees, up the hill. She pressed her ear against the barn door and heard the soft baying of goats. She slipped inside. It was dark and smelled of hay and manure. She held her hands out to the goats. Their breaths warmed her skin. She crumpled. Exhausted, she covered herself with hay, only planning to rest for a few minutes.

"*Ko jūs darāt?* What are you doing?"

An indignant voice bolted into Miriam's ears.

"*Kas tu esi?* Who are you?" the voice asked in Latvian.

"Papa, they're shooting at me," she mumbled.

"Papa? *Par ko tu runā?* What are you talking about?"

A rough hand shook Miriam's shoulder. The officers! She cowered and opened her eyes. A bull-necked man with ginger hair looked at her with a stricken expression.

"Don't hit me! Please," she cried, her voice practically inaudible after her long night in the cold.

He threw his arms back. "I'm not going to touch you."

She caught sight of his bewilderment and realized he was not a Latvian officer. "I had . . . nowhere else to go."

"What happened to you? Where did you come from?"

She looked down at the ill-fitting coat, so filthy it was impossible to make out the original color, the trousers stiff with dirt, her long hair, matted with blood and lice. For a moment, she was back in the pit, in a mound of human flesh. She couldn't imagine how her face looked; it had been months since she'd seen herself in a mirror. She was afraid she looked as scraggy as the children she'd seen in the ghetto.

"The forest. Rumbula," she said quietly.

"Why were you in the forest?"

She wavered. What if he hated Jews like the men who'd pulled their triggers and callously aimed at the pit? His appearance gave nothing away, just as the Latvian men who'd joined forces with the Germans looked perfectly ordinary out of uniform.

"I will leave now. You will never be bothered by me again." She struggled to her feet.

"Don't go," he countered, holding his hands out, palms facing Miriam. "You are safe here."

Miriam hesitated, then sank down into the hay. She wasn't sure whether to trust the farmer but dreaded the thought of going back outside. She knew she could only endure the cold for a short while and had no idea if she'd find another barn in time.

"You must be hungry," the farmer said.

Miriam gave a faint nod.

"I will be back with some food." He hurried from the barn, still shaking his head in disbelief as he closed the door.

She was drifting off when the farmer returned with thick slices of bread covered with butter, a jug of milk and a gray wool blanket.

"Eat," he said with a tenderness that reminded Miriam of her father. He set the food on the ground. "My wife will make sandwiches for your supper." His round cheeks flushed. "She apologizes for not coming to meet you. She thinks it is better if only I see you."

Miriam heard the words he didn't say, how his wife was afraid of her, afraid of keeping her; if his wife never laid eyes on her, she didn't exist. Miriam nibbled at a piece of bread, afraid of eating too much too fast. It had been so long since she'd had an entire piece of bread, and even longer since she'd tasted butter or milk.

"You are welcome to stay a couple of days," the farmer went on, "but you cannot leave the barn."

"Thank you." Miriam held his gaze for a moment. Then he was gone.

Despite her efforts to eat slowly, Miriam's stomach had shrunk too much for the bread and milk. She threw up, her shoulders convulsing as she vomited. She was worn out after her stomach was purged, and instantly fell into a restless sleep.

She heard a child cry for his mother. She saw Clara's and Ilya's terrified faces. Felt their fingers curled around hers. She woke sweating, her heart racing. She was back in the pit with the dead. But she couldn't cry. All she could do was remember.

Miriam curled her knees to her chest and pined for her children. It had only been two months since she'd seen them, yet she was already starting to forget the feel of Ilana's hand in hers, the softness of Monya's curls in her fingers, the sounds of their voices. The tension in the base of her neck increased. She forced their images from her head. Dwelling on the past made her weak. She couldn't let her guard down. She couldn't make any mistakes.

"There's a new law," the farmer explained sadly a few days later. "Landowners are responsible for all people found on their land. I have a family to consider."

His words landed like a blow. Miriam wondered how long she'd last if she couldn't find another barn. As if he could read her mind, the farmer told her to keep the blanket. Then he held up a sack with a loaf of bread, still warm, six boiled eggs and a jar of milk.

"Thank you for what you have done," she said.

"I wish I could do more."

"You have done more than anyone since this war began. You and your wife are good souls," she added, thinking ruefully of Zelma's optimism.

He smiled faintly.

Miriam set off with enough food for a week if she rationed it properly, one blanket to protect her from the wintry Russian air, and a sliver of hope.

34

RIGA, JULY 1976

SARAH WOKE WITH A MUSTY SENSE OF DEFEAT. SHE HAD reached a dead end. Without Roger's help navigating language and cultural barriers, it would not only be impossible to search for Monya, it would be reckless. I'm an idiot, she thought, expecting to find Monya, as if I could simply look him up in a telephone directory and pay him a visit.

She retrieved the envelope of photos of her mother and Miriam she'd brought from home, images she'd intended to give Monya, and was overwhelmed by a sad exhaustion. Monya's life would continue to be a mystery. Miriam would most likely die without knowing her son's fate.

She wanted to go home. Tears pressed against the back of her eyes when she thought about how she'd lied to her father and Miriam. She heard footfalls in the corridor, a door slamming shut, and felt separate from the other travelers, adrift, with her ulterior motives for being in Riga. Early morning light spilled into the room. She wept in despair.

THE DAUGAVA RIVER glittered beneath the cloudless sky as the bus rumbled over the bridge from their hotel in Ķīpsala to the old city, the second morning in Riga. Sarah's hands clutched her camera, in her lap. She was careful to press her arms against her sides, to avoid touching Roger. Things had been awkward between them since their excursion to see Dr. Kulda. Breakfast had been an ordeal, with Roger barely speaking and looking through her as if she weren't there. He didn't even react when George teased Doris about the Laima chocolates she'd bought for her grandchildren only to break open the box and sample one of each kind.

Doris brought her hands to her pink-smudged face and Sarah caught a glimpse of the cunning young girl still there, with shrewd eyes that missed nothing and full lips twitching with laughter.

"Dreadful, aren't I," Doris joked about the chocolates.

"I wouldn't be able to resist either," Sarah said.

Roger's face dulled.

"Your own grandchildren," George said with an exaggerated sigh.

An awkward silence fell over the table until the waitress arrived with their food.

"Well, now you have a good excuse to buy more chocolate," Sarah offered once their meals had been served.

George said yes, of course, they would buy more, but he'd keep it in his luggage so Doris wouldn't be tempted.

"Sounds like a good idea, right, Roger?" Sarah pressed.

A long pause.

"Children won't miss what they didn't expect," he said, his voice tight, the cords in his neck throbbing.

Doris and George exchanged anxious glances.

"Is everything all right?" Doris asked gingerly, her gaze flitting from Sarah to Roger.

They still think Roger and I are a couple, Sarah realized. She glanced sideways at Roger. He dunked his knife in the jam jar, pointedly avoiding the question.

George clamped his hand over Doris's and squeezed affectionately. "Traveling together can be a—"

"We're not together," Sarah interjected. "Roger and I. We met on the bus at the airport."

"Oh, my," Doris said, flustered.

"Is that so," George said.

Roger nodded and took a bite of bread, unmoved by the shift in the conversation.

"I don't mean to interfere—" Doris began.

"Then don't," George said. "It's none of our business."

"I know, dear, but we were all having such fun together . . ." Her voice trailed off wistfully.

"Yes, we were," Sarah agreed.

"I do hope we can continue enjoying the tour together," Doris added.

Sarah stared at Roger. He sat rigid, poker-faced.

"So do I," Sarah said to Doris, her eyes lingering on Roger.

THE BOLD ORANGE hue of a woman's headscarf caught Sarah's eye as the bus turned right off the bridge. On the next block she noticed more women, all in dark clothes except for their brightly colored scarves. The burst of vibrant colors made Sarah think of her mother Ilana's nail polish collection. Perhaps her love of bright hues stemmed from the dinginess of Riga during the war. Perhaps her mother's need for privacy, for the permanently drawn curtains and blinds, pointed to her fear of being discovered, when she hid with Gutte. Perhaps Ilana's father's murder caused her loss of faith. Or not.

In Riga, she'd begun to appreciate how difficult it would be to get an authentic sense of the city and events that had shaped her mother and Miriam. While the history was undeniable, she would never understand the impact of the war and its aftermath on her mother and Miriam. The only thing she knew for sure was that she couldn't create a narrative based solely on facts. There were gaping holes in her maternal history—family stories, memories, habits and traditions—that would never be filled. This untold heritage would have given texture to her identity, a vividness that couldn't be found in old photos or statistics or newspaper articles.

"On your right, you will see the Central Kolkhoz Market." Nina's dogmatic voice crackled with static over the microphone.

Sarah pressed her forehead against the window. Five massive arched pavilions stood in a row.

"Every day, fifty to seventy thousand customers visit this market," Nina continued.

Roger leaned over Sarah to look, his chin hovering over her shoulder. "They're old German Zeppelin hangars," he said. "The pavilions. The market was built in the early 1900s, well before the Soviets came."

Her whole body thrummed at his nearness. She looked at him, puzzled. "You're talking to me now?"

He turned crimson. "About that . . ."

Her gaze drifted from his eyes to his lips

"I feel so guilty."

"For what?"

"Our run-in with the officer."

"That was my fault. It was my sneakers. You said so."

"I should have noticed. I feel responsible."

"Even if you did, what could you have done differently?"

"Tell you to put on the sandals you wore on the bus the first day."

She turned sideways. "You noticed my sandals?"

"And your red toenails. Very nice."

Her mouth fell open.

"Anyway," he went on, "it would be my fault if something happened to you."

"That's not true."

"I'm the one who agreed to help you."

"I'm the one who asked you to help."

She held his gaze and saw her feelings mirrored in his eyes.

The bus shuddered to a stop, pitching her forward against the seat in front of her. He grasped her shoulder, and her chest caught and filled at his touch.

SARAH STEPPED OFF the bus and heard Roger, behind her, apologizing to the Cullens for his bad mood at breakfast.

"I had a headache," he said, polishing the truth.

Roger's words, and the ease with which they were spoken, rankled Sarah, but she knew his lie was necessary, to keep Doris and George in the dark.

"What a shame," Doris said.

"You're better now?" George asked.

"Headache's gone," he said brightly.

"Good to hear." George emerged from the bus, patted Roger on the back and followed Doris, bustling toward another older couple they'd befriended.

Roger lit a cigarette and glanced at Sarah's freshly soiled sneakers. "I like what you've done with your shoes."

She grinned, lifted her right foot and pointed at her toe. "I call it Vintage Soviet," she joked.

He chuckled aloud. He unfolded his map, holding it out for

Sarah to look. With his finger, Roger showed where they were standing in relation to the first stop of the day, the Academy of Sciences building, one block north.

"Hmmm . . ." he mumbled, and turned so his back was toward the bus.

"What?" She pivoted on the heels of her sneakers, following his gaze.

"That's the ghetto." He pointed down the street.

"You mean the Riga ghetto, where Jews were forced to live," she said breathlessly.

"Exactly."

Her feet carried her onward as if they had a mind of their own, oblivious to Nina calling out for the group to gather, oblivious to the bus driver, at the side of the road, smoking and shaking his head at her.

"What are you doing?"

Roger's incensed voice swooshed into her ears. Sarah kept going, jittery with adrenaline. This was the only section of Riga where she knew, without a doubt, Miriam had lived. She stopped at the fence rising at least two feet above her head, overlaying the ghetto like a screen. It was still hazardous, with sharp strands of twisted wire every few inches. The narrow cobblestone street was lined with derelict wooden shacks, shutters missing or hanging at odd angles, most with windows boarded up and several covered in graffiti, undecipherable Cyrillic characters in bubble script. Foot-high weeds sprouted from the sidewalk's cracks, grassy green spears in an otherwise monotonous landscape, and the gutter was strewn with empty cans, newspapers, broken glass and sticks.

"Sarah, you can't just take off." Roger came up behind her. "Didn't yesterday's near disaster teach you anything?"

"I have to see this."

The air was rough and skunky. Two ragged-looking men sucked on joints beyond the fence. The nearby road buzzed with traffic. Birds chirped overhead, their cheery noise a startling contradiction to the bleakness of the ghetto. Sarah was overcome by a crippling grief like a fever, seeing the ghetto she'd read about on a microfiche screen, where innocent people had been kept like animals, where the blood of thousands had spilled, where her grandfather may have been murdered.

Her heart swelled with compassion for her grandmother, forced to make an unimaginable decision that left a permanent scar in their family, a wound that had spread through generations like eye, skin and hair color, personality traits, genetic diseases and Jewish blood.

"Would people . . . I mean, because I'm only half-Jewish, would I have been put in the ghetto too?" she asked, tripping on her words.

"One Jewish grandparent was enough to get you sent to the ghetto or the gas chamber," Roger answered solemnly.

"I have two." It came to her the way she uncovered a nugget of valuable information buried in a pile of facts: I am defined, in part, by anti-Semitism. This was hard to wrap her head around. This was undeniable. This gave her a stronger sense of self. With the ghetto unfurled before her, she felt part of a bigger life, of a history where she was deeply connected to generations who came before and those yet to be born.

"Looks like hardly anything has changed here since the end of the war," Roger commented.

She nodded vaguely, her mind on the gravity of her mother's decision to cut all ties with her past, erasing her Jewish heritage. Now, looking into the ghetto, Sarah was conflicted. She understood her mother's rationale a little more yet was frustrated by her secrecy. She felt rooted in the past but didn't know enough to carry on the traditions that had shaped her mother and Miriam. It was like transplanting the roots of a wandering Jew to a jar without water.

Roger peered down the street. Their group was still gathered around Nina. "We should get back—"

"What do you think happened to the people killed in the ghetto?" she blurted.

"No idea," he answered quietly.

She drew in her breath. "I'd like to think they're in graves with personalized headstones, like my mother, but thousands were killed all at once, so I know it's impossible."

"Did your grandmother tell you what happened in the ghetto?"

She shook her head. "I found a small newspaper article on microfiche at the library, a piece in the *Tribune* about what sounded like a massacre."

"I'm not surprised. Hardly anything about the war has been made public in Soviet countries. The government just wants to brush it under the rug."

"But what about people like my grandfather, who were killed here? There must be a cemetery for family to visit."

"What family?" he snorted. "There are hardly any Jews left in Riga, and they aren't allowed to be religious. All religions are banned in the Soviet Union. Believe it or not, atheism is a mandatory subject in school. People revere Brezhnev, not God."

She turned to him. "You mean even if my uncle was raised by a Jewish family, he wouldn't know anything about the religion?"

"That's right." He tilted back on his heels and scrutinized at the people in their tour, walking in the opposite direction, widening the space between them. "We have to go now."

She removed the lens cap from her camera and feverishly began taking photos of the ghetto.

"You can't . . ." Roger reached for her camera. "Stop—before someone sees you."

Sarah angled away from him and kept shooting, determined to return home with something that would show her future children what their ancestors had endured.

"Come on, Sarah," he said nervously. "Didn't yesterday's scare affect you at all?"

"This is part of my history. If I can't search for Monya, I should at least be allowed to take a few photos."

"Under most governments, yes, you should. But not here."

She snapped one last photo of the street and put the lens cap back on. "I have no family stories, no names other than my uncle's, no precious heirlooms to remind me of special relatives. Photographs are the only things I can hold on to, to remember the past."

"Why can't you let go, when you're back home? Why can't you make peace with the past, now that you've been here?"

Sarah contemplated his question. "I don't want it to die with me."

35

RIGA, FEBRUARY 1942

THE TERRIFYING SOUNDS OF GUNS FIRING AND THE PUTRID smell of death haunted Miriam with every step on the crusty snow, in every snap of branches in the wind. She wound her way through a patch of birch trees rising to the leaden sky like white pillars. A train thundered along the tracks on the other side of the forest. She dropped to the ground until the train disappeared. She continued but couldn't stop looking over her shoulder, convinced a Nazi or Arājs Kommando officer was following her trail.

Snow began falling and the wind picked up, scouring her face as she trudged forward across an open field, to a mass of towering pine trees. The prickly green needles shielded Miriam from the wind and snow and camouflaged her from cars on the road. She leaned against a bumpy tree trunk and closed her eyes. She wanted to sleep, but every time she drifted into unconsciousness, her eyes popped open and she struggled for air and she was back in the pit, trapped under dead bodies.

Daylight was beginning to fade. Miriam couldn't feel her toes. Her eyelashes were frozen. She had to keep moving, to find someplace warm for the night. Her feet were like stones attached to her legs, awkward and heavy, as she plodded through the forest. She hit a patch of ice and slid into a tree, her shoulder colliding with the trunk. She stumbled to her feet and kept moving though her shoulder ached. It wasn't safe, standing still. The spaces between the trees started to grow larger and larger. The setting sun painted the horizon with vivid strokes of gold and red and the trees gave way to flat, open land. She was a recluse in a desert of snow. It was beautiful and terrifying all at once.

She zigzagged across the cottony white field and came to an old farmhouse and barn. Stacks of hay lined the ground, and horses grazed in the snowy pasture behind the barn. Square windows in the house were lit up. For all she knew, the residents could be related to a member of the Arājs Kommando. Or they could be as kind as the farmer who'd given her blankets, food and refuge. She watched the house for a long time, torn between knocking on the door and sneaking into the barn. She needed a hot bath, a hot meal, a warm bed, four walls and a roof. Stirred by the prospect of compassion, Miriam approached the house.

A top-heavy middle-aged woman opened the door. The pupils in her bulging eyes flared at Miriam. The woman stood tall, as if she was trying to intimidate Miriam with her height. The intoxicating aroma of fresh bread swirled through the door, the scent of Shabbat. Family. Normalcy.

"*Ludzu*, please," Miriam said in Latvian. "Could you spare a piece of bread, and perhaps some warm water to clean myself?"

"*Nē.*" The woman started to shut the door.

"Please." Miriam stuck her foot between the door jamb and the door. "Just a warm cloth and a corner of your barn. I won't make a sound and I'll leave first thing in the morning."

The woman's ink-blue eyes skidded over Miriam with apprehension. Miriam looked down and saw herself through the woman's lens—a woman in tattered men's clothes.

"This isn't me," she began. "I mean, I don't usually look so bad, but—"

"Where are you from?" the woman demanded.

Miriam wasn't sure how to answer. Did the woman hate Jews? She couldn't afford to take the chance. "The Soviets sent my family to Siberia and stole my apartment," she said, recalling her friend Helena's exile, "and I haven't managed to get back on my feet."

The woman studied Miriam's face and shook her head. "I cannot take the chance of hiding you on my property."

"Just one night?"

She slammed the door. Miriam's heart plummeted. She wouldn't last much longer, with no refuge from the cold. As she turned to leave, the door opened again and the woman presented her with a paper sack.

"A beef sandwich. It is all I can give you. You must go now, before someone sees you and reports us."

"Thank you, but I've been walking for hours and it will be dark soon—"

The door shut. The lock clicked. Miriam wanted to scream at her. She wanted to tell her what she'd lost, what she'd endured while this woman went on with her life in a warm house and with more than enough food to fill her stomach. Miriam retraced her steps to the road, her fury rousing a new-found fortitude to survive.

FOR THE NEXT few weeks, haystacks protected Miriam during the day, shielding her from the unforgiving wind and below-zero temperatures. She hid in the shadows and moved as little as possible to conserve her strength. Sometimes she climbed trees for relief from the frozen ground, but she couldn't escape the persistent frost inhabiting her bones like a fungus.

At night, she crept into barns and scrounged for leftover animal feed scattered on the ground. If she was really lucky, there would be sunflower seeds, corn grains or drops of molasses poured over a coarse feed for cows, horses and pigs. The animals never gave her away. Their mooing and clucking sounds made Miriam feel safe and often lulled her to sleep. In the mornings, she stuffed her clothes with hay for extra insulation and left before the farmers arrived to feed their animals.

One particularly cold and blustery afternoon, she approached a house in Salaspils, a small town eighteen kilometers southeast of Riga, that looked welcoming with its butter-yellow exterior, white trim and shutters. The steep-roofed home had been built on a high stone foundation next to rows of spindly birch trees draped with ice. The white-and-bloodred Latvian flag flew proudly from a staff attached to the roof.

A round-shouldered woman with chapped lips opened the door halfway. Her small nose twitched when Miriam said she was looking for work in return for room and board. Miriam braced herself for the inevitable door slamming shut, but the woman opened the door wider and clutched her plum-colored shawl tight around her short neck. In a fretful voice, she asked what kind of work Miriam could do. Miriam said she cooked, sewed, cleaned and cleared snow.

The woman fiddled with the silver cross on her necklace and peered anxiously over Miriam's shoulder. Her eyes and mouth were smooshed into her face, giving her a perpetually anxious expression. "We have been talking about getting help." She shivered and twisted the plain silver wedding band around her finger. "A blizzard is coming. You may as well come in until my husband gets home."

Miriam's nerves trilled with hope. She gave the woman her name.

"I'm Mrs. Vanag," the woman replied as she ushered Miriam inside and shut and bolted the door. She smelled faintly of carbolic soap and her gray hair was braided and coiled around her head.

Snow dripped from Miriam's felt boots and coat, puddling on the wooden floor of the large room that made up the entire main level of the house. A brick oven, cookstove and round pine table furnished the back corner, where copper kettles hung on the wall. To the right of the door, a large cross hung on the wall above the sofa, and there were two oak chairs facing the sofa.

A clock on the wall ticked the seconds away. Almost three o'clock in the afternoon. Miriam noticed photos hanging on the wall, portraits of children who bore a striking resemblance to Mrs. Vanag.

"Your children are very handsome," Miriam said, her voice catching in her throat. She pointed at two photos of young boys in sailor suits, much like the one Monya had worn the day Gutte took him home.

"They are my nephews," Mrs. Vanag replied briskly. "My husband and I were not blessed with children."

"I'm sorry. I didn't mean to—"

"Come. You must be hungry."

Miriam removed her boots and followed Mrs. Vanag to the kitchen area. Mrs. Vanag gestured for Miriam to sit at the round pine table in the corner. White tapered candles had been planted in tin holders, with dried clumps of wax along the sides of the candles and the tin. Miriam's heart warmed at the familiar sight of a samovar boiling gently on the wood countertop beside the enamel sink. Through the window above the table, a carpet of snow stretched to the horizon, with stands of birch and oak trees rising like frozen skeletons.

Mrs. Vanag tied on an apron and began cutting a head of cabbage into small chunks.

"Can I help?"

"You can cut the potatoes." Mrs. Vanag lifted her elbow toward a basket of potatoes on the floor near the back door.

Miriam washed her hands, stiff and chapped from the cold, in the sink's basin. She dried her hands on a towel and began scraping dirt from a potato with a sharp knife. Her knuckles stung and her fingers moved clumsily. She had difficulty gripping the knife in her right hand. It slipped and gouged a finger of her left hand, which was holding a potato, drawing blood immediately. A bright cherry-red blotch. The all too familiar scent of wet coins that had choked her nostrils in the pit. Miriam nearly fainted.

"For goodness' sake," Mrs. Vanag said, her plump face strained with derision, "you look as if you'd cut your finger off. It's just a scratch. Run some water over it and wrap it with this." She tore a muslin strip from a rag and handed it to Miriam.

Miriam took the rag without a word; fright had temporarily snatched her voice and her spirit. She turned on the tap at the basin and held her bleeding hand beneath cold water, unable to take her eyes off the blood spilling onto the white enamel, going from deep red to pale pink as it swirled toward the drain. With quivering fingers, she wound the muslin strip around the wound. It took two attempts to get it tight enough; it was as if her strength had been watered down with the blood.

Mrs. Vanag impatiently motioned to the knife and half-sliced potato. Miriam looked at Mrs. Vanag, meticulously chopping the cabbage, and saw Gutte preparing a meal in her Mežaparks kitchen with a similar diligence. There was a profound comfort in relying on such a durable woman. Miriam resumed her task of slicing potatoes, working slowly, careful to keep the knife's blade from her skin.

Mrs. Vanag poured water into an enamel pot, threw in cabbage, added Miriam's potatoes, carrots, a few garlic cloves and sausage, and turned on the burner. She stirred the stew with a wooden spoon. The sausage floated on top, giving off a briny aroma that made Miriam's mouth water. Sausage, or any kind of pork, was forbidden for Jews, but she'd long since abandoned those archaic laws. Surely God would understand her choosing food, any food, over starving. Or not.

I am a lapsed Jew.

The sun dipped over the horizon, casting long, thin shadows from the trees over the snow. Mrs. Vanag poured two cups of strong black tea from the samovar. They sat down at the table. Miriam pined for her children amidst the rare calmness and felt herself sinking into a black hole of depression. The necessary absence of news caused her thoughts to spiral in catastrophic directions; she was deflated by the unknown. Were her children safe and healthy? Or had they been discovered and reported? The possibility was too awful to consider, yet too awful to ignore.

Time crawled in the awkward silence. Miriam sipped the black tea. Hot and bitter, just the way she liked it. Just the way her mother used to make it. A lump of guilt lodged in her throat. The gruesome image of her mother's body in the street loomed in her head. *I should have been able to protect her. I should have tried harder to keep her moving.* If her mother hadn't been shot, her father wouldn't have stopped. He wouldn't have been killed. It was a mantra that ravaged her thoughts, with the sound of the gunshots and the image of her parents lying in the street playing over and over in her head when she was awake and when she was asleep. She recalled the way people stepped over and around her parents' bodies. She felt helpless, afraid, as if she should have been killed as well. She despised herself for surviving.

The front door was flung open and a man entered. Mrs. Vanag's husband. He stomped his feet to get the snow off his boots and gestured with a stubby thumb at Miriam. "Who's she?"

Miriam squirmed in her chair beneath the heat of his disapproving eyes.

Mrs. Vanag sprang to her feet. "She came to the door, offering work for room and food." Her apologetic voice trailed off. Her eyes flitted from Miriam to her husband. "She has nowhere else to go. She's a Jew."

Miriam tensed.

He looked at Miriam with a deliberate grimace that made her heart shrivel. He grunted, took off his coat and beaver fur hat, revealing brown overalls over a long-sleeved white shirt. He plodded toward the women and set the paper bag he was carrying on a wood counter beside the sink. Close up, Miriam noticed his lower jaw stuck out and he had a chip in his front tooth. Mrs. Vanag took a tin of mustard, some chicory, a box of matches and a packet of candles out of the bag.

"I'm Miriam," she said as he pulled out a chair across from her.

"What can she do?" He turned to his wife as if Miriam wasn't there.

Mrs. Vanag placed a basket of rye bread in the center of the table, and a bowl of stew, heat rising from the food in tendrils of smoke, in front of her husband. "Says she sews and cleans." She put a bowl down for Miriam and sat with her own bowl.

They bowed their heads over the table and Mr. Vanag recited a prayer: "Bless us O Lord and these thy gifts, which we are about to receive, through thy bounty, through Christ, our Lord . . . Amen."

Miriam lifted her spoon to her bowl. Mr. Vanag eyed her expectantly.

"Amen?"

He grunted and dug his spoon into his stew.

It struck Miriam that her children were probably reciting the same prayer, or something similar, by now. Ilana for certain. Monya was still too young to memorize so many words. Thank goodness. Perhaps he would never be forced to learn the Gentiles' prayers if the war ended soon. Perhaps it might even be possible to salvage Ilana's Jewish soul. Miriam longed for the ordinary, the rituals that had framed their days, the weekly Shabbat prayers and food that centered their family and obliged them to think about what mattered. She felt unrooted, as though she didn't belong anywhere, and feared she'd be wandering, with no direction or purpose, for the rest of her life.

Miriam ate her stew slowly. It was the first time she'd sat at a table for a hot meal in more than five months. She prayed her stomach wouldn't rebel the way it had that first night in the barn. She had a feeling Mr. Vanag would toss her out if she vomited in his house.

"You must stay in the attic during the day," Mr. Vanag said in an accusatory tone, as if Miriam had already done something wrong. "No exceptions. Understand?"

"I do." Miriam stared at her bowl. His presence made her uneasy.

"At any time, a policeman could show up at the door, and if he sees you—"

Mrs. Vanag dropped her spoon on the table. Mr. Vanag fixed his eyes on Miriam, shoveled a forkful of stew in his mouth and chewed loudly. Bits of food spewed from his wide-open lips.

As soon as Miriam emptied her bowl, Mrs. Vanag rose, took a kerosene lantern from a shelf and gestured for her to follow. Mr. Vanag dropped heavily onto the sofa, the floral pattern faded to spots of color, practically the only brightness in the sepia-toned house. He smoked a cigarette rolled from newspaper and opened the Bible. His lips moved as he silently recited the words. Miriam followed Mrs. Vanag up the creaky stairs and past their bedroom, directly above the kitchen, a spartan room with a window above the bed and chest of drawers. The staircase narrowed and it grew dramatically colder as they climbed to the attic.

Miriam would be staying directly under the steep-pitched roof that made the space feel smaller than it was. There were no windows to let in light, and cold air streamed through cracks in the walls. A chamber pot had been placed on the plywood floor near the stairs and blankets lay in a heap against one of the slanted walls, as if the Vanags knew Miriam was coming.

"It's good. It's a good room," Miriam said.

"I'll bring the lantern up in the morning, with your breakfast, along with some mending for you."

You're leaving me in total darkness? "Thank you."

Mrs. Vanag paused. It seemed that she had something else to say. But no. She turned to go down the stairs, holding the lantern at shoulder height.

"Why did you agree to take me in?" Miriam blurted.

Mrs. Vanag touched the cross around her neck. The lantern smoldered under her chin, casting her face in an unearthly glow. "It is God's will you survive. If I did not help you, I would be committing a sin that could never be atoned."

Miriam was taken aback by her honesty and morality. She had seen crosses around the necks of the Latvians and Germans who'd tortured and murdered innocent people in Riga. Faith was not a guarantee of decency.

Mrs. Vanag continued down the stairs with the lantern, leaving Miriam alone in the frigid blackness. She curled up under the blankets, closed her eyes and was plunged back to the basement where she'd met Zelma. Her chest rose and fell with quick breaths. She longed to forget that terrible day, but it was embedded in her soul. She didn't feel safe in the dark anymore. She didn't trust men, especially those in uniform who flaunted their power like medals. And strange men who weren't in uniform. Like Mr. Vanag.

36

RIGA, JULY 1976

A RAPPING NOISE WORMED ITS WAY INTO HER SLEEP. Sarah rolled over to escape the sound. Tap, tap, tap. Was it real or in her head? She propped herself up on her elbows. Her mind was fuzzy, her eyes were bleary. The room was bathed in a bizarre pinkish glow. *Maybe I'm dreaming.* Taptaptap. The knocks came faster, more insistent. She threw off the covers and stumbled to her door.

"Hello?" she whispered.

"Don't make a sound." Roger's urgent voice seeped through the door. "Get dressed. We're going to meet Dr. Kulda."

She stood without moving as his words sank into her consciousness. "I thought we'd stopped—"

"Shhhh! No talking," he hissed.

She remembered her room could be bugged, and shivered. She put on the clothes she'd worn that day, jolts of excitement running up and down her spine like electricity. Roger, in jeans and a Led Zeppelin T-shirt, his hair loose, led her down a back staircase. She held her breath, afraid of running into a formidable babushka.

Outside, a nightingale sang a shrill chirruping melody and the sky was an incandescent pink and blue.

"The sky . . . I've never seen anything like it," she said, entranced.

"It's a white night," Roger whispered. "From around April to the end of August, the sky never gets darker than twilight because the sun is so close to the Arctic Circle."

"I wish I'd brought my camera," she said, her gaze fixed on the pastel sky.

"I would have made you put it back in your room," he upbraided her. "Imagine what Dr. Kulda would think if he saw a camera around your neck."

"Right."

They continued in silence through the warm, softly lit evening, leaves rustling gently when puffs of air broke the stillness. Sarah glanced sideways at Roger. The pinkish sheen cast an ethereal glimmer over his profile, drawing attention to his prominent cheekbones and high brow. His pin-straight hair, ashy under the white light, fell to his shoulders like silk and smelled lemony. Her gaze drifted between his eyes and lips and she had a sudden urge to stroke his hair, to trail her fingers across the nape of his neck.

Her breath hitched. "Why are we doing this? You said it was too dangerous."

"It is." He stopped dead in his tracks and stared at her with winsome eyes that made her tremble with angst and desire. "When I told Dr. Kulda not to bother," Roger continued, "he said he already had information that might interest you."

"He did?"

Roger turned and resumed his quick pace. Sarah increased her stride to keep up, her hands clenched with impatience.

"*Eto ty, Roger?*" A barely audible Russian voice limped toward them. Dr. Kulda's voice.

"*Da. Ya zdes's Sarah,*" Roger answered.

The shine of Dr. Kulda's glasses converged on Sarah.

"Your uncle is alive," Dr. Kulda declared in a brittle tone.

"Oh my God!" A sob escaped her throat. "I knew it! I just knew he was alive."

Roger smiled and wrapped his arm around her shoulders and squeezed tight.

"His name has been changed," Dr. Kulda went on.

"So he's not Monya Talan anymore?"

Roger let go of Sarah. He lit two cigarettes and gave one to Dr. Kulda.

"He was adopted at three years of age. His name is Andris Jansons."

"Andris Jansons?" Sarah listened to the sound of his name roll awkwardly off her tongue. She took a sharp breath. "Are you sure? What if files were mixed up and you found the wrong person? How can you be positive it's Monya Talan?"

"Soviet documents don't lie," Dr. Kulda snapped. "We also know he is married and has four children—"

"Four! I have four cousins?"

"This is all the time I have for now." Dr. Kulda stepped back.

"But his address . . . You haven't given me his address."

Roger cleared his throat and said it wasn't the way things worked. She needed to come up with five hundred American if she wanted her uncle's address.

"Five hundred dollars?"

"And five hundred more to meet him," Dr. Kulda added, as if he were telling her the price of beef.

"A thousand dollars? Who do you think I am, Patty Hearst?"

Both men eyed her blankly.

"You know, granddaughter of the newspaper billionaire William Hearst, kidnapped a couple of years ago?"

"Oh, right." Roger snapped his fingers and nodded. "Patty Hearst."

Dr. Kulda coughed, a dry, hacking smoker's cough. He blinked, looked at Sarah with a vacant expression. She felt indifference radiate from his body and wondered if ice ran through his veins instead of blood.

"My father's an accountant. We've lived in the same small bungalow in a Chicago suburb for twenty years. I don't have that kind of money. This trip has drained my savings."

"Listen, Sarah," Roger said. "I have some cash—"

"I can't ask you to lend me money. And I can't go home to my grandmother without talking to Monya." She turned to Dr. Kulda. "Don't you understand? His mother, my grandmother, lost him during the war and hasn't seen him since he was a baby. All I want to do is talk to him for a few minutes and take a couple of photos. You can't ransom a meeting—"

"Enough," Dr. Kulda said, resolute.

"No. It's not fair. He's my uncle. He deserves to know his mother has never forgotten him and that he has family in America. My cousins deserve to know about us."

"In the Soviet army, it takes more courage to retreat than to advance," Dr. Kulda said.

"What?" Sarah gasped. "I'm not in the Soviet army and I don't care if you think I'm a coward. All I'm asking—"

"It is for the best," Dr. Kulda said. "What good would it do, meeting when it is unlikely you will ever see each other again? It would be like putting candy in front of a child and not letting him eat it."

"No . . . It wouldn't be like that at all. I'd be able to get a photo of him for my grandmother, I'd be able to let him know his mother never forgot him. Please, just give me the address." Roger grasped her waist. She yanked his arms away. "Wait, Dr. Kulda."

"I must go now." He turned his back to her.

"No, please," Sarah begged him. "Roger, can't you convince him to do the right thing? Even if I wanted to pay him, we're taking the train to Moscow the day after tomorrow. How am I supposed to get that much money and see Monya before we leave?"

Dr. Kulda silently vanished into the white night like a firefly that has lost its glow.

"Don't go," she called out.

"It won't do any good, Sarah. This is the way things get done here. How do you think we were able to get out of the hotel tonight?"

"We snuck out the back."

"You don't think the babushka heard us?"

"You mean . . ."

"A few American bucks and she didn't hear a thing."

The Soviet way of doing business left her with a sour taste in her mouth.

Roger kicked the ground. "I can't believe he didn't keep his word. Especially since he owed me a favor."

"I came so close." Tears of defeat pressed against the back of Sarah's eyes.

Roger drew her into his arms. "Listen, I know I said we shouldn't take any more chances," he began, "but I have an idea that just might work, if we're willing to go out on our own one more time."

Sarah lifted her head from his shoulder and looked up at him.

"There are telephone booths all over Riga. At least some will have directories. We have Monya's new name. It's worth a shot, don't you think?"

"What if we run into another officer?"

He dropped his arms and kneaded his jawline. The heat from his skin lingered on her shoulders like dew.

"You don't have to do this," she offered. "I won't be upset if you decide not to. It may even be for the best, like Dr. Kulda said."

"No. You're here, probably for the first and last time." His face softened. "This is your only chance to meet your uncle, unless the Soviet Union miraculously becomes a democracy one day."

A warm glow spread in Sarah's heart. He cared. He wanted her to find Monya. And she wanted him to keep looking.

"As for running into an officer, I may have a plan," Roger said.

"What kind of plan?" His nearness was unbearable.

"You'll find out."

The coyness in his tone emboldened her spirit. She reached for his hand. "Stay with me tonight."

He bent forward and pressed his lips on hers. She kissed him hungrily. The trees and sky faded and she felt as though they were the only two people on earth. They ran out of air and pulled away.

He lifted her chin with his free hand. "You sure?"

No, she thought. *But I'll never see you again after this trip, which means no promises. No messy feelings.* "Positive," she said. She threaded her arm through Roger's and led him up to her room, her heart pulsing in her ear so loud, she was sure he could hear it.

EARLY MORNING LIGHT and the relentless cries of seagulls over the river drizzled through the hotel window. She lay in the crook of Roger's arm and listened to his steady breathing. What had gotten into her? It wasn't like her to invite a man she'd only known a few days into her bed. And she had a nagging sense of being unfaithful to Henry, even though she was the one who'd ended their relationship.

Roger opened his eyes halfway and kissed her nose. He rolled on top of her and ran the back of his thumb along her cheekbone. She smiled, but inside, a tiny part of herself admitted she'd slept with him for all the wrong reasons. She felt like a horrible person. She felt like an impostor in her own life.

37

SALASPILS, MARCH 1942

M IRIAM'S DAYS IN THE ATTIC WERE LONG AND TEDIOUS, each one like the next. Mrs. Vanag brought her morning meal, which never varied: chicory, a roll and a cup of tea, along with whatever she wanted Miriam to stitch by dim kerosene light, straining her eyes until they scorched and watered. A hole in Mr. Vanag's shirt needed a patch. The hem of her floral dress was torn. The pocket of Mr. Vanag's jacket needed mending. An endless number of wool socks and stockings with holes in the toes or heels. The ripped lapel on Mr. Vanag's suit jacket he wore to church. A seam in Mrs. Vanag's linen skirt needed letting out. Miriam tried to keep track of the days, cutting pieces of thread every morning, but lost track after twenty or so, when Mrs. Vanag rushed in, late for church, creating a breeze as she moved, scattering the threads.

At night, Miriam covered herself with two blankets and plugged her ears with her fingers to keep out the sounds of Mr. Vanag shouting at his wife. There was nothing too small to set him off. His complaints were endless. Dinner was cold. Too much salt on the beef. His boots were wet. Whenever he exploded, Miriam strained to hear Mrs. Vanag's voice, to make sure she was all right.

Miriam was flummoxed by the change in Mrs. Vanag in her husband's presence, how she diminished, lost her backbone, the strong parts of herself. I shouldn't be so quick to judge someone's temperament, she chastised herself, the way she'd scolded Ilana for criticizing her teachers.

A troublesome thought crossed her mind. She'd never met Gutte's husband. What if he was as mean as Mrs. Vanag's husband? For all she knew, Gutte was like Mrs. Vanag, with a crusty exterior easily ripped apart by her husband, a lump of clay in her husband's domineering hands. For all she knew, Ilana and Monya saw dreadful fights in Gutte's house.

Miriam felt a shiver of panic. She pictured her children hiding to get away from Gutte's husband. Then she recalled Gutte's firm attentiveness toward Ilana and Monya, and Gutte's ability to get Ilana to cooperate without raising her voice. There would have been signs, Miriam deduced with a hopeful uncertainty. I would have noticed something. And Gutte would never have agreed to take Ilana and Monya if things were bad with her husband.

Miriam kept her eyes on the attic opening whenever Mr. Vanag was home, afraid he'd decide to take out his rage on her instead of his wife. She hadn't seen him since her first night, at dinner, and would have been quite content if she never saw him again.

"You must really like pork," Miriam ventured one evening, when Mrs. Vanag appeared with her dinner. Pork chops and boiled potatoes, practically the same dinner every night, except carrots often replaced the potatoes.

Mrs. Vanag shrugged. "We are pork farmers."

Miriam nearly choked on her pork chop. The irony of a Jew being hidden by people who raised animals Jews were forbidden to eat was clearly lost on Mrs. Vanag. Miriam wondered if the Vanags knew anything about Jews.

"How long have I been here?" Miriam asked. She wanted to prolong Mrs. Vanag's time with her; she needed the bustle of people, the hum of voices, for energy.

"A month," Mrs. Vanag replied.

"Oh," Miriam said, dejected. It felt longer. Time seemed infinite without the visible cycles of the sun and moon, without the freedom to come and go.

Heavy footsteps thudded up the stairs. Mrs. Vanag cowered and picked at her shawl. The hairs on the back of Miriam's neck rose when Mr. Vanag appeared. He smelled of onions and hops, and stood with his legs straight, arms folded across his chest. Mrs. Vanag hurried down the stairs as if she couldn't wait to get out of the attic.

"Didn't want you to think I'd forgotten you," he slurred.

His smug condescension reminded Miriam of the officer standing over her while she washed the floors. She brimmed with apprehension. Mr. Vanag's eyes fell on Miriam with a lusty glint. Miriam took a deep breath, leveled her shoulders and asked him for news about the war to divert his attention.

He belched and said, "The British have launched balloons full of hydrogen into Germany to damage power lines and start fires."

"Balloons? Where did you get this information?" she asked skeptically.

His eyes flickered with annoyance. "Heard it on the radio."

"How much harm can balloons cause?" she said.

"Guess we'll find out." He stumbled forward, toward Miriam. "Don't think you'll be leaving us any time soon, though."

She extended her arm and pushed him back. "You never know."

"Right. You never know what will happen," he said with a menacing wink.

He retreated, but his ominous words left Miriam with a sense of dread she couldn't shake long after he'd gone. There was nothing to stop him from coming into the attic at night. Nobody except Mrs. Vanag would hear Miriam's cries for help, yet she wasn't strong enough to oppose her beast of a husband. Miriam needed another place to hide, but it was still winter for another month or so. Another month of hiding in barns before she could sleep outside, in stacks of hay. At least a month . . . Still, it was better than having another despicable man's hands on her body.

That night, she crept to the stairs and listened to the Vanags eating dinner in an uneasy silence. Mrs. Vanag washed the dishes. The radio broadcast the news, too quietly for Miriam to make out words. Mr. Vanag grumbled about Mrs. Vanag going through salt too fast, "spending money as if it fell out of the sky." The floor below creaked as they got ready for bed.

She waited until she heard the erratic rhythm of Mr. Vanag's snoring, counted to five hundred and tiptoed down the stairs, her rucksack pressed against her chest. The floorboard at the foot of the stairs squeaked when she stepped on it. She froze.

"Who's there?" Mr. Vanag called out.

Blankets rustled from the bedroom.

Miriam's heart pounded against her ribs.

"What the devil is going on?" he muttered. The mattress sighed. His bare feet padded across the floor.

A strand of moonlight spooled through the front window, barely enough to make out the furniture by shape. Miriam rifled through the coats on the hooks but couldn't find hers. She grabbed a wool coat that felt like Mrs. Vanag's, from the sleeves' length, and put it on. Her boots were not with the Vanags', on the mat by the door. She took Mrs. Vanag's and tried to get them on while standing but started to wobble as she pulled one over her right foot. It was tight and squished her toes.

"Where are you going?"

Mr. Vanag's intoxicated voice fired into the darkness.

Miriam fell.

He lunged toward her, eclipsing her shadow with his. He planted his hands on her shoulders and sloppily pushed her head to the ground. Miriam recoiled from his rotten breath. She spat in his face and kneed him in the groin. He moaned, clutched his groin and rolled off her easily, like water over a stone.

Miriam spotted the second boot near his leg. She scrambled for the boot, but he kicked it away from her grasp. Miriam noticed his bare feet.

"Thief," he snarled. "Those aren't your boots."

Emboldened, she stood and raised her chin. "Fine. I'll go in mine. Where are they?"

"I burned them, along with your coat. They weren't fit for a *pakala*, an ass."

Miriam's eyes flared. "Actually, they belonged to dead people."

"What?" He stumbled to his feet.

Miriam heard the shock in his voice and her lips curled with satisfaction. "Don't you know? I came from a pit of dead people."

He stepped back. "Nonsense."

She extended her foot toward the boot, her gaze fixed to his shadowy face. "You haven't heard about it on the radio?"

"Of course not. The radio gives real news, not made-up stories."

She caught the boot and slid it closer. "Go. See for yourself. Rumbula forest. Thousands of dead bodies in a pile."

"Lying lips are an abomination to the Lord."

She thrust her foot into the boot and slunk to the door. "Lying is also frowned upon in my religion." She fumbled for the doorknob, wrapped her fingers around it. "My husband used to say God loathes people who say one thing with their mouth and another with their heart." She turned the knob, opened the door and charged into the icy night.

"Where . . . going?" Mr. Vanag shouted, his ornery voice ruptured by the wind. "You'll freeze . . . death . . . out . . ."

STARS DOTTED THE charcoal sky, providing just enough light to guide Miriam along the snowy road. Her tired vision smeared into hazy blobs. She slogged forward, feet dragging with every step. She felt exposed on the flat, white, open field with nowhere to hide.

She pushed herself along the road for what seemed like hours, her feet chafing in Mrs. Vanag's boots, until the heady scent of pine needles wafted through the air. She crept toward the scent and walked right into a scratchy pine tree. The pointy needles grazed her cheeks and hands. She picked her way through a cluster of massive, craggy trunks, and heaved a sigh of relief when soaring pines encircled her like walls.

SHE SAW THE wolf as the night melded into day, the sun rising over the horizon imbuing the sky with a soft yellow glow. The whites of its eyes flickered with danger. Miriam crouched beneath a pine tree and looked left then right, to see if there were more than one. Wolves hunted in packs. This one was alone, thank God. She stayed motionless and silent until the wolf backed up and ran into the forest. Her knees gave way and she dropped to the ground. She clambered to her feet and proceeded on her journey with no destination, following the river's edge, one eye out for wolves, the other for soldiers who hunted Jews.

38

RIGA, JULY 1976

THE CONTRAST BETWEEN SOVIET RIGA AND THE MEDIEVAL core was most apparent above the canal, on Alberta iela, the first stop on Sarah's last full day in the city. Low-lying clouds had settled over Riga, throwing a foggy shadow over the streets, and the air was oppressively humid. It was the kind of summer day that made Sarah appreciate the air-conditioning at work. The so-called air-conditioning at the hotel was useless at best, blowing stale, tepid air into the already thick, heavy atmosphere.

Nina, in front of a sumptuous blue-and-white house, began speaking: "One-third of the buildings in Riga were designed in the art nouveau style, a combination of rationality and orna-ment. This house was designed by a Soviet architect who built three additional houses on the street." She strode past the ornate blue-and-white house and gestured at another, with a lion's head crowning the top, as well as intricately carved faces, flowers and wreaths in the columns.

Sarah instinctively reached for her camera and panicked when it wasn't hanging over her shoulder. Then she remembered she'd had to leave it at the hotel because she and Roger would be on their own again. Roger . . .

His head turned as if he knew she was thinking about him.

"Mikhail Eisenstein designed this house in 1903," he said to Sarah and the Cullens. "He was the architect for a number of buildings in Riga but had to hide the fact he was Jewish to get the work."

Inside, Sarah had a growing sense of rage. For Jews, it seemed, hiding their faith was essential to succeed. Suddenly, a vast, inexplicable part of her mother's secretive persona made sense.

"Horrible," Doris murmured, waving her map like a fan in front of her glistening face. "Just horrible."

George looked somberly at the building, his comb-over pasted in sweat to his bald head.

Sarah looked left and right, taking in the row of elegant houses, unable to reconcile the scene with the ghetto in the same city, just a few miles east. She felt guilty for pressing Miriam to dredge up an unthinkable past. Still, letting this chapter of history go forgotten or ignored would be tantamount to the way the Soviets approached the war's aftermath, revising facts to fit their preferred narrative.

"My goodness, we're falling behind again," Doris exclaimed.

The rest of their group was rounding the corner.

"Indeed we are," George added. "We better get moving."

"Actually," Roger began, "Sarah and I have to leave again for a couple of hours."

Sarah straightened.

Doris's eyes darted from Sarah to Roger. "Must you? I worry about the two of you on your own."

"I'm afraid I agree," George said. "You made out fine last time. Why chance fate again?"

"We're just going on a walk," Roger said. "I want to see more than the Soviet version of Riga."

"And Nina gave us permission," Sarah added.

George and Doris exchanged looks of apprehension but, to Sarah's relief, asked no further questions.

"Please don't be too long," Mrs. Cullen implored them.

"We'll be back before you know it," Roger assured her.

Sarah waved goodbye and watched the couple join the tour, Mr. Cullen holding his wife's elbow protectively.

"That's what I want," she said.

Roger followed her gaze and grinned. "Bad knees and age spots?"

"Yes. Bad knees and age spots," she agreed, surprised by her own admission.

He took her hand.

"What are we going to do if we run into another officer?" she asked nervously.

"You have to cough and sniffle whenever we're walking. Officers will be less inclined to question you, or even be near you, to avoid getting sick."

"You really think it will work?" she said, unconvinced.

"No idea." He shrugged. "But it's the best I could come up with."

She started coughing.

THE SOUND OF footsteps marching made Sarah's nerves screech. She and Roger were in a phone booth on Elizabetes iela. Soldiers in beige trench coats with gray belts, collars and caps marched past, their legs rising to forty-five-degree angles, in unison, like wind-up toys—only they were real, with actual rifles slung across their backs, moving down the street like a tidal wave.

"Don't stare," Roger scolded her.

Sweat pooled in her underarms. She looked down until the sound of their marching feet was a distant murmur.

"No telephone directory." Roger sighed. "Let's find another booth."

It was the third booth they'd checked and hope was dwindling in Sarah. Arm in arm, they veered down a side street, past old wood houses that looked as if they'd fall apart in a gust of wind. Shops made of brick were defiled with graffiti. A gold hammer and sickle had been spray-painted onto a wall. Lenin's face covered the entire side of a six-story building.

Her mother and grandmother had endured propaganda for years, from two brutal occupations established on lies and misinformation. No wonder they both had an air of suspicion, Sarah thought. They'd been targets, prey, for Stalin and Hitler. Sarah's gut cramped when she pictured Nazis rounding up Jews like cattle, gunshots ringing through the air, her grandmother, mother and Monya publicly identified as Jews, with yellow stars on their clothing. Not just for days, or weeks, or months, but years.

How many families had been ripped apart like her mother's? How many people were descended from Jews but had no idea because the past had been buried? These questions festered in her mind like an itch she couldn't scratch. Her mother's family was just one of thousands of Jewish families in Riga before the war, all with their own stories and tragedies. And this was just one city in one country. She couldn't fathom the enormous impact, the domino effect, of multiple futures lost.

She swallowed a scratchy lump of grief in her throat and caught sight of a letter box attached to a building with *Pasts* engraved in the stone above the door. "A post office," she said under her breath. "They'll have a phone directory."

"Too risky," said Roger, "going into a government building."

"I know." She paused. "But we're running out of time and phone booths."

He looked down at her. "It's hard to say no to you."

She smiled up at him.

"Let's go," he said.

Inside the post office, Sarah followed Roger to a telephone directory on a table across from a young woman selling stamps and envelopes. Roger opened it to the Js and scanned the names with his finger.

Sarah smelled the decadent aroma of fresh bread. She looked through the window at a line of women across the street, waiting to get into the bakery. A woman holding a basket with one hand and a small boy with the other joined the line. Sarah couldn't tell if the woman was the mother or grandmother. The little boy wore a tan cap that slipped over his eyes. His shirt was too large for his wafer-thin body. The sleeves of his shirt were ripped and dirty at the cuffs and hung past his fingers. Seeing him waiting for bread that might or might not be there when he reached the front of the line brought a rush of anger to Sarah. How could any developed country not be able to produce enough bread?

Roger wrote something on the back of one of his business cards. He squeezed Sarah's hand and drew her out of the post office. "You're not going to believe this," he whispered.

"What? Is it bad?"

He looked left and right. Sarah followed his gaze. No officers in sight.

"Monya's on Nometņu iela, in Ķīpsala, close to our hotel," he said.

"You mean I've been near him the whole time we've been in Riga?"

"Practically neighbors."

Roger said they were going to calmly walk down the street at a normal pace, so as not to attract unwanted attention.

Sarah nodded. She was going to burst.

He nudged her along Elizabetes iela, past large townhomes once lavish with intricate architectural details, now rundown with peeling paint and broken windows. She held her messenger bag tight, barely noticing the homes or the thickening humidity setting in the air like gel. This was it, the reason she'd come to Riga. But what if her uncle didn't want to see her? What if he'd never been told he was adopted? Finding out he had a birth mother in Chicago could bring enormous grief and shock. It could change everything he thought he knew about himself, just as discovering her mother's turbulent past had forever altered her world. Her intrusion might pose a fundamental threat to his identity. She yearned to talk to Henry, to get his thoughtful opinion.

Sarah glanced up at Roger, saw the determination in his brow and considered how vital he'd been in her search for Monya. Without him, she'd still be with the rest of her group, no closer to finding her uncle than she'd been before coming to Riga. It seemed almost too good to be true, meeting Roger and getting Monya's new name. Or it was fate.

They turned left onto Valdemāra Street and passed the Museum of Art, a beauty salon, an Orthodox church, a newspaper kiosk and a café. The small bridge over the canal led them to the park they'd seen their first day, with its broken benches and weed-covered flower beds, and on to the October Bridge crossing the river at Lenin Street.

A Soviet officer, sporting an impressive array of medals on the chest of his uniform, strutted toward them when they were almost halfway across the bridge. They were suspended over the River of Destiny. A wave of trepidation rose through her as she remembered Nina's story from their first day.

"Start coughing," Roger hissed from the side of his mouth.

She gathered phlegm at the back of her throat and coughed it out, a wet, hacking sound. She covered her mouth with her hand and folded over, eyes on the ground.

Roger planted his arm over her shoulders and held her close.

"*Dobryy den,*" Roger said affably to the officer. "Good afternoon."

The officer halted in front of them. Sarah lifted her head. He had eyes like brake lights. She choked on his glare.

They exchanged heated words while she coughed. She was skittish with fear, convinced they were in deep. Roger withdrew two American fifty-dollar bills from his wallet. The officer tucked the bills in the pocket of his jacket and tipped the brim of his cap, as if they'd just exchanged pleasantries about the weather.

"*Priyti*, come," Roger said to Sarah. They sidled gingerly past the officer. "Don't look back," Roger warned her when they'd gone thirty feet.

Sarah resisted the urge to glance over her shoulder to see if the soldier was still there. A mint-green Lada sputtered past, its muffler totally useless, leaving a trail of throat-gagging exhaust in its wake. Sarah coughed for real. Her eyes watered. She waved her hand, a futile attempt to clear the air.

"He demanded to see our identification," Roger said when their feet touched down on the other side of the bridge, in Ķīpsala, the Riga suburb where their hotel was located. "I told him I was an American professor and you were my wife, but he didn't believe me, so I had to give him Dr. Kulda's name as a reference and a hundred bucks."

"A hundred?"

"He was a lot more intense than the other officer we met."

"Do you trust Dr. Kulda?"

"No. But I didn't have a choice. Let's just hope we're long gone by the time he checks."

Sarah stopped. "We should forget about Monya. It's too dangerous."

Roger shook his head vehemently. "As long as we're quick, it will be okay. The hotel is five minutes from Monya's place."

"If you say so."

Sarah trailed Roger onto Raņķa Dambis, which ran parallel to the river. A couple of minutes later they went left again, onto Nometņu iela, her uncle's street, and found his shabby five-story apartment building. Balconies, once white, hung like dirty gray boxes from the facade, reminding Sarah of public housing in Chicago.

If her grandmother had not taken her mother out of Latvia, they might have lived in a similar building, under the Communist regime, enduring lives without color or freedom.

"Maybe we should have called first," Sarah said, her voice faltering.

"You tell me how to explain the situation in a few words, over the phone," Roger shot back. "Not to mention their line's probably bugged." He moved onto the slab of concrete in front of the black door. Swirls of black graffiti decorated the building's puke-colored foundation.

"What do I say? How do I begin?" Panic raced through Sarah.

"Tell him the truth about his mother and sister."

She glimpsed Roger's inscrutable eyes and had a fleeting urge to run. How much did she really know about Roger or his motives? She recalled their passionate night together, the gentle way his hands moved over her skin. A flush crept up her face. He couldn't have faked his passion, she thought. Or could he?

Roger opened the door and lowered his arm like a crossing guard, beckoning her to walk inside.

She looked at him. She thought about how he'd put himself in danger to help her find Monya. She thought about how he'd led her, safely, to this point. She stepped forward.

39

SALASPILS, AUGUST 1942

A BLACK CAR PUTTERED ALONG THE ROAD. MIRIAM HELD her breath, hoped she'd be mistaken for a peasant. It passed without slowing down, the engine grumbling noisily and expelling clouds of smoke. She didn't exhale until the car was a speck on the road ahead. She cupped her hand over her eyes to shield them from the bright sun and turned in a circle. Not a forest in sight. She walked faster, straining to see what lay ahead, listening for the rumble of another car coming up behind her.

The sun was over her head when she came to a strawberry field. She was dazzled by rows and rows of bright-green leaves with plump strawberries trailing on the ground. Her lips were parched. She could have drunk a river dry. Miriam climbed over a half-meter-high log-and-wire fence, knelt down and bit a ripe strawberry from its stem. It tasted like summer. She kept low to the ground, plucking berries with both hands, stuffing them into her mouth as fast as she could swallow. When her abdomen bloated, she gathered more and put them in her rucksack for later.

Finally satiated, she looked around for a safe place to rest and spied a long row of bushes at the edge of the field, in front of a fence dividing the farm from the adjacent property. She crawled toward the bushes but halted when she spotted a cluster of narrow buildings behind them, on the other side of the fence.

The one-story buildings were long, the length of three houses in Riga, and there had to be at least seven or eight. Heaps of chopped wood lay scattered around the property and telephone poles lined the empty dirt road leading to the buildings.

The door of the largest building opened. Miriam crouched lower. Men in German uniforms strolled toward a row of smaller buildings. Nazi eagles garnished their sleeves and the brims of their caps. Miriam stumbled back, tripped over her own feet. A second door opened and more men appeared, in shabby clothes with prominent yellow stars. Jewish prisoners.

The Jews formed a row facing the officers. Names were called out in German. Just like the roll call in the ghetto. Miriam dropped to the ground, curled her neck and tucked her head into her chest until the wooziness passed. The click of a hinge. She jumped and peered through the trees. Two German soldiers carried the body of a small boy in her direction, toward the fence. A gate opened about fifteen meters from Miriam. They tossed the boy into a ditch as if he were a slashed tire and shut the gate.

Miriam gasped and dropped her head to the ground.

The soldiers lit cigarettes and sauntered back to the largest building.

Miriam began to crawl backward, toward the woods.

"*Hör auf, wo du bist.* Stop where you are," a German voice bellowed from the other side of the fence.

Miriam fumbled, looked sideways and met cagey blue eyes not two meters away. "I am on my way home," she said unconvincingly in Latvian.

The German officer tugged the bottom of his double chin. His belly hung over his belt like a pillow cinched in the middle.

"*Kriechen?* Crawling?" he said, skeptical.

Miriam got to her feet and brushed dry mud from her dress. She hoped he didn't smell the months of grime on her skin and clothes. "I was . . . looking for my . . . my key," she stuttered.

His eyes raked over her coat, in her arms, as if he knew there should have been a yellow star. He brandished his rifle, hanging from his belt on his right side, and ordered her to come closer.

She couldn't take her eyes off his rifle. She stumbled to the fence.

"*Bist du ein Jude?*" he asked.

"*Nein,*" Miriam answered quickly. "I am Latvian."

"*Lass mich deine Papiere sehen.*"

Miriam opened her bag and rummaged through it as if she had the Latvian baptism papers he'd demanded. She opened her eyes wide, pretending to be surprised they weren't there.

"*Zuhause.* At home." She feigned a contrite smile. She clutched her rucksack to her side. Her knees trembled.

He grabbed her sleeve and yanked her to the fence. He snatched the strap of her rucksack and turned it upside down. A pained expression crossed Miriam's face as the photos she'd taken from the pit fell to the ground. Still gripping her sleeve, he bent down and snatched a studio portrait of a young family. He squinted at the image then looked at another, of a little boy, and another, of an elderly couple. With the man's long gray whiskers and the couple's dark, conservative clothing, their Jewishness screamed.

He lifted his foot and trampled every one, stomping down hard with his heel until the images were smears of black and white. Remnants of people's lives scattered on the ground like dirt. Miriam kicked him in the groin with the heel of her boot. He cried out. He let go of her and clutched himself. She sprinted toward a birch forest a hundred meters ahead, at the other end of the field.

A gun discharged. A bullet whooshed over Miriam's head. Faster, faster, she pushed herself, digging deep into her reserves for a burst of energy. Another shot fired. The pop of a bullet hitting something to her right. She reached the forest, dove through the trees and rolled onto the ground. She crept on all fours as shots flew overhead.

A wrenching spasm twisted her side. She pressed her fingers against the cramp to ease the pain. In the distance, she heard the soldier's feet tramping over the strawberries and dandelions. She plunged ahead, her hand gripping her side, but the shooting pain was too intense to run through. Another shot pealed through the trees.

Miriam glanced up at the canopy of branches, festooned with golden-yellow leaves, and caught site of a substantial branch that would hold her weight. She grabbed hold of the branch and hoisted herself up, clenching her teeth from the pain in her side. She reached for a higher branch, swung her legs up and missed. She persisted and made it on the second go. Up she went, climbing the tree as shots continued, until she saw nothing but leaves below.

The soldier's footfalls drew near. He paused a few short meters from the tree that camouflaged her. She tensed. He moved furtively across the ground, too close for comfort. Miriam was afraid her rancid stink would give her away. Her cramp worsened. From the sound of his feet, she could tell he was looping around the trees, traveling in one direction before returning and proceeding in the other.

The branch she was holding with her left hand broke from the tree with a loud snap. Her hand slipped, knocking her off-balance. She managed to swing her arm around the trunk and went still. Didn't dare look below for fear of making a sound. His footsteps came dangerously close to the tree she clung to. He stopped. She pinched her eyes shut and chanted the *Shema* in her head, convinced death was one shot away.

The officer fired into the air, scattering birds and squirrels. Miriam hugged the tree and waited for the pain. Nothing. She opened her eyes and found herself still alive, suspended in the birch tree. The footsteps below moved away. Miriam didn't make a sound. It could be a trick to get her to come down. She waited until her cramp had subsided and the sun dipped low, speckling through the leaves, before venturing to the ground and winding her way through the forest, following the setting sun.

40

RIGA, JULY 1976

SARAH AND ROGER SLIPPED INTO A DANK, NARROW STAIR-
well reeking of cabbage, onions and dirty socks. Their footsteps echoed as they climbed concrete stairs leading to her
uncle's apartment. Roger knocked three times and stepped back.
Sarah hovered behind him. A bolt clicked and a woman with a
sallow complexion, wearing a white kerchief on her head, opened
the door a crack. She and Roger exchanged a few words in Russian
before she closed the door. Sarah shot Roger a questioning look. He
put his finger over his lips.

The door opened again, this time wider. The woman, with an
apron over a boxy, lead-gray dress, silently ushered them into a
sitting area with a low ceiling and a tiny kitchen in one corner. It
was plain and unremarkable but for the piano pushed up against
a wall lined with shelves of books. The woman gestured for them
to take a seat on the brown-and-turquoise sofa with rounded
wood arms. She drew the beige curtains shut and turned the old-
fashioned wooden radio to a station with a Russian man speaking.

"The radio deflects our conversation," Roger murmured in Sarah's ear. "In case someone is listening."

Sarah's knees went weak. It was bad enough having to watch for officers on the street, knowing the hotel could very well be bugged, but a private home . . . The absolute lack of privacy people endured was reprehensible. The woman wrung her hands with a nervousness that reminded Sarah of Edith Bunker. She said something inaudible, moved to the kitchen, an alcove off the main room, and filled a kettle with water.

A skinny man in navy trousers and a beige collared shirt, with a tuft of curly brown hair, gray at the temples, emerged through a door across from the piano.

Monya.

His resemblance to Sarah's mother and Miriam was uncanny, with identical half-moon sacs under his eyes, the same thin lips, the same high forehead. Monya.

Immediately, she had the sense of returning to a familiar place after being gone a long time, the feeling they'd met before. It was nostalgia without memory.

Life in the Soviet Union had prematurely aged Monya, Sarah thought as she viewed the deep creases in his face and the folds in his neck. He was only thirty-six years old, yet seemed fragile, as if he might break if pushed too hard. Monya took the wooden armchair across from the sofa and rubbed his hands over his knees. His head swiveled from side to side, taking in the unexpected visitors, eyes wide with paranoia. Sarah's stomach heaved.

Roger began talking in Russian. Everything Sarah wanted to say, everything she'd been thinking for months, rose from her chest to her throat like motion sickness. The language barrier was an obstacle too big to overcome. She couldn't talk directly to her uncle. With Roger speaking for both of them, so much would be lost in translation. Sarah felt inadequate, sitting idly beside Roger.

"*Ya. Andris a takzhe moya zhena,*" Monya said, pointing at the woman bustling around in the kitchen.

"He is Andris and she is called Gundega," Roger said to Sarah.

"Oh." Sarah squeezed her bag's strap. She could not think of him as Andris, only Monya.

Gundega, like Monya, looked older than her years, with eyes set deep within pale sockets and curved lines from the corners of her lips to her chin, reminding Sarah of a wooden marionette. Gundega began opening and closing cupboard doors, occasionally looking over at the door as if she expected it to burst open at any minute.

Roger continued in Russian.

"*Nyet.*" Monya shook his head at something Roger said. The color drained from his face. He went limp in his chair.

Gundega paled and dropped a teacup and saucer. They smashed into pieces on the linoleum floor. She got to her knees and brushed the fragments into a pile with her hands, lips moving silently as if she was praying.

Roger tossed Sarah an anxious glance.

She started. "What did you say?"

Monya knelt down with a whisk broom, elbowed his wife away from the broken china and swept the shards onto a piece of cardboard. He dumped them in a metal garbage can beneath the sink, and paced the floor in front of the window.

"I told Monya his father was murdered at the beginning of the war because he was Jewish," Roger said, in answer to Sarah's question. "And his mother entrusted him and your mother to Gutte so they wouldn't be put in the Jewish ghetto. Then I told him his birth parents named him Monya Talan."

Monya began speaking with a nervous energy, eyes sliding from Roger to Sarah. Gundega resumed her frenetic pace in the kitchen, setting four cups and saucers on a wood tray and arranging oblong-shaped biscuits on a plate.

Sarah tried not to think the worst—that Monya was furious she'd turned his world upside down and wanted nothing to do with her or her grandmother. When Monya finished talking, he poured two shots from a syrup-brown bottle and offered one to Roger. They raised their glasses and swallowed the shots in one gulp.

Roger set his glass down and twisted his watch around his wrist. "He only found out he was adopted after his mother died six years ago, when he found the papers."

Sarah bristled. She couldn't believe Monya's parents went their entire lives without telling him he'd been adopted.

"Andris says he wasn't completely surprised," Roger went on, "because he didn't look like his mother or father, and he had such a different personality."

"It must have been hard, feeling like he didn't fit," Sarah said.

"Probably." Roger shrugged. "But I can tell he loved his parents, from the way he talks about them."

"I'm glad. And my grandmother will be relieved he was happy."

Gundega brought in the tray of refreshments and glanced at Monya as if she wanted his approval. He eyeballed the wooden chair beside him. She set the tray on a three-legged coffee table with a triangular surface and perched at the edge of the chair, fleshy hands folded in her lap, her round face pale and taut.

"There's more, but you're not going to like it," Roger said grimly.

She braced herself. "Just tell me."

"Your grandmother must have arranged for fake baptism records, because Andris still has his. He insists he's not Jewish, says his parents were not friendly with *those* people." Roger lowered his voice. "His father was a Latvian officer during the war. He would have been ashamed to have a Jew for a son."

"Monya's adoptive father could have killed my grandfather," she said, dismayed.

"Don't go there." Roger hesitated. He averted his eyes from Sarah and continued in a low voice. "Monya doesn't believe he is related to you because Gutte was named as his mother on the adoption papers, and her religion was not Jewish. It was Lutheran."

"No. That doesn't make sense," she said in a stricken voice. "Gutte would not have forged legal documents. My grandmother entrusted her children's lives to her. Gutte knew my grandmother would come back for them at the end of the war."

"There must have been a reason. Maybe you don't have all the facts." Roger paused. *Find him.*

Sarah recalled Miriam's sallow, desperate face in the hospital.

"It is the truth," Sarah insisted. "There has to be a way to get Monya to understand those documents are phony, for my grandmother's sake, and his."

"I don't know how to convince him," Roger said.

Gundega poured a cup of tea for Sarah and offered her a biscuit. Monya sat with his arms crossed over his chest, his foot tapping the floor nervously. The announcer's voice on the radio droned on in the background like a stream.

"*Spaseebo,*" Sarah said. Thank you—one of the few Russian expressions she'd picked up.

Gundega nodded politely and hovered awkwardly over Sarah, as if she wasn't sure what to do next. Sarah bit a corner of her biscuit and gagged on the unexpectedly strong taste of rum.

"Not like the arrowroot you expected, right?" Roger quipped.

Sarah glimpsed Monya and Gundega watching her and pasted on a smile. She took another bite, tasted raisins and apricots as well as the rum. "Delicious."

Roger shot her an amused look and said something to Monya and Gundega, coaxing guarded smiles.

As Sarah chewed, she noticed a framed black-and-white portrait of four children on a shelf of the wall unit. She stood and moved to the photo. She estimated the oldest was around fifteen and the youngest about ten. "Yours?" She pointed at the image and looked at Gundega.

"*Da.*"

Sarah studied the portrait, taken in front of the apartment's curtain, the children all with freshly scrubbed faces, two girls with shoulder-length brown hair in braids tied with red ribbons, two boys with floppy ears protruding from jet-black short hair parted severely on the side. Not one smile among the four children, who wore matching expressions of boredom.

Sarah turned on her heel and asked where they were. Roger posed the question to the couple. Gundega answered.

"The two youngest are at Pioneer Camp and the two oldest are working on a farm for the summer."

Sarah returned her gaze to the photo of her first cousins, the only cousins she had, and was struck by a twinge of sadness. They were strangers to her. She and Miriam would never meet them. They would never know they were half-Jewish. Their existence would be rooted in lies—unless she planted a seed in Monya's head. She rummaged through her bag for the envelope of photos she'd carried all the way from Chicago.

"If Monya sees pictures of my mother and grandmother, if he sees the resemblance, I think he'll believe me." She plucked out a yellowed shot of her grandmother, taken soon after they'd arrived in Chicago. "Can you tell Monya it's a picture of his mother, Miriam?" she asked Roger.

"I don't think it'll do much good, but okay." He cleared his throat, handed the photo to Monya and repeated Sarah's words in Russian.

Monya brought the picture closer to his face. His brow furrowed in bewilderment. Gundega stared at the photo and then at her husband. They conversed in serious voices.

"Gundega says she sees a slight resemblance between Andris and your grandmother," Roger translated, "but an old photo proves nothing."

"Tell him this is Miriam, a few months ago." She handed the photo to Monya.

Roger identified Miriam. Monya blinked repeatedly, avoiding Sarah's vigilant eyes, and shook his head. Her hands trembled as she rummaged through photos, searching for one that would jog his memory. She stopped when she came to the close-up of her mother at the Statue of Liberty, taken right after she arrived in America. She pressed the photo into Monya's hands and said: "This is your sister. Her name was Ilana."

Monya gave it a long, appraising look. Gundega tried to sneak a glimpse over his shoulder, but he turned his back to her, his fingers gripping the photo so tight the tips were white.

"Lana," he whispered to the photo. "Lana."

Sarah's breath caught in her throat.

Gundega wrung her hands together and looked askance at Sarah.

"He remembers her face," Roger began, translating. "She used to read books to him. He says it is what he remembers most, sitting in her lap while she read books with colorful pages."

"My mom," Sarah said, breathless. "Tell him he's talking about his sister, when they were little. Tell him his sister became my mother."

Roger relayed the information to Monya.

Monya hunched his shoulders and tugged at his shaggy eyebrow. He looked sideways at Gundega and spoke to her. Gundega nodded but said nothing.

Roger's face fell as Monya talked.

"What is it?" Sarah asked Roger.

"He doesn't trust you."

"Why not?"

He let out a big sigh. "Why should he?"

"What do you mean?"

"Think about it. You show up out of the blue, claiming to be his American Jewish niece."

"But the photos—"

"He vaguely remembers Ilana reading to him. He doesn't remember her as his sister."

"How old was he when he was adopted?"

Roger asked Monya, who showed Sarah three fingers.

Sarah's spirits deflated. "Why would I have photos of someone he admits he knew?" she said. "It doesn't make sense."

"People here don't trust their own government, they don't trust one another, so why should they trust you, an American stranger?"

Sarah was bruised by Monya's rejection. She tried to see the situation from his point of view, the way she put herself in a buyer's state of mind when she had to compose questions for consumers. But how do you step into the shoes of someone who doesn't understand what it's like to live with the freedom to make your own decisions?

"We're related by blood, but our cultures and family made us who we are," Sarah said, resigned. "I may see my mother and

Miriam in Monya, but similar features don't add up to an identity. I can say he's Miriam's Jewish son. I can say he's my mother's younger brother. And I can say he's my uncle. But if he disagrees, if he doesn't see himself this way, then I guess he's not the person we want him to be—he is Andris, son of a Latvian officer."

Monya and Gundega looked at her with blank expressions.

Roger tapped his watch with his index finger. Time was running out.

Sarah's eyes welled with tears. "Before we go," she said to Roger, her voice breaking, "please tell him he was, he is, wanted. His mother cried out for him in her sleep and asked me to find him. Tell him Ilana, my mother, died last year but his mother is still alive and living in Chicago, near me."

Monya listened, his face tight with concentration, while Roger conveyed Sarah's message. Gundega, huddled on her chair, dabbed her eyes with a frayed handkerchief. When Roger finished, Monya closed his eyes for a moment. Sarah noticed a red splotch on his right eyelid. A birthmark.

Monya opened his eyes and mumbled, his voice papery thin. Roger leaned over the coffee table to listen. Sarah looked at Monya to get a sense of his reaction, but he didn't make eye contact. A bad sign. To leave without Monya acknowledging his rightful heritage was synonymous with failure.

"He says he's sorry, but he just doesn't believe he is Miriam's son," Roger explained. He grasped his knees and rose from the sofa.

Disappointment rattled her bones. With a shaky hand, Sarah extracted a photo of her mother and Miriam with her address written on the back, and asked Roger to give it to Monya, and to point out her address in case he ever changed his mind. Monya blinked at the photo then raised his eyes to meet Sarah's. Her skin prickled when she saw her grandmother's willful face looking back at her.

At the door, while Monya and Roger were shaking hands, Gundega thrust something into the palm of Sarah's hand. She looked down: a recent black-and-white headshot of Monya, much like yearbook photos of teachers. On the back, Gundega had written their address.

"Monya," Gundega whispered, and wrapped her fingers around Sarah's wrist.

Sarah felt a swell of appreciation. She embraced Gundega.

"We have to go," Roger said.

Reluctantly, Sarah pulled away from Gundega and clasped Monya's hand in hers. She caught his eyes poring over her, as if he didn't want to forget her. She kissed his cheek and followed Roger out of the apartment without looking back, remembering one of her mother's many superstitions: if you look back when you say goodbye, you will never see the person again.

They descended the stairs. At the entrance to the street, Roger opened the door and then staggered backward into Sarah as two black cars screeched to a stop in front of them. Four Soviet officers hopped out, guns pointed at Sarah and Roger. Sarah grabbed hold of Roger and held on tight, her heart racing with panic.

41

OUTSKIRTS OF RIGA, NOVEMBER 1943

WINTER ARRIVED OVERNIGHT, WITH SEVERAL CENTIME-
ters of snow and a Siberian wind that thrashed Miriam's
bones. It was her second winter without a permanent roof
over her head, her second winter of foraging for shelter and food
like a wild fox, creeping into barns while owners slept, sneaking out
before daybreak, relying on goats, cows, pigs or horses, whatever
animals were housed in the barn, to wake her with their morning
cries to be fed.

"Who are you?"

A shrill voice tumbled into her head like coins falling into a
jar. Miriam, in a bed of hay, breathed in the pungent manure smell
and twitched her nose. She pried her frozen eyelids open to find a
cow with brown spots looking back at her with suspicion. Miriam
turned her head and saw a little girl with messy braids at the barn
door, three meters away, ogling her with large, blinking eyes.

Miriam gaped at the girl, about the same age as Ilana would
be now.

The girl gripped a tin pail with white knuckles. Her arms protruded from her coat sleeves like sticks. She set the metal bucket on the ground, inched forward and asked: "What's your name?"

"Miriam," she croaked, surprised by the flimsy sound of her voice. It had been ages since she'd spoken to anyone.

"Who are Ilana and Monya?" the girl asked. "You said their names in your sleep."

"May I have some water?"

"You are Jewish, aren't you?" the girl replied, ignoring Miriam's request.

"What business is it of yours?" Miriam retorted.

The girl glanced back at the barn door. "You're lucky my father didn't find you."

"He doesn't like Jews?"

"He likes them as much as anyone else, but says it's dangerous to mix with them . . . right now."

They looked at each other.

The cow sank its enormous teeth into the straw near Miriam's foot and chomped noisily.

Miriam watched the cow. What a pity she couldn't survive on hay. She padded her coat and boots with straw, summoned her last morsels of strength and lowered her feet to the ground. Her legs went limp when she put weight on them. She collapsed.

"What are you doing?" The girl inched closer.

"I have to go."

"You can't. You look sick."

"Lower your voice," Miriam hissed.

The girl cupped her hands around her mouth and whispered, "You'll be safe here. My father has a broken leg and can't walk in the snow. It's my job to milk the cows."

A broken leg? Her father's injury was a stroke of luck for Miriam. "What about your mother?"

"She just had my baby brother a few days ago, so she'll be staying inside for a few weeks, until he's stronger."

It all seemed too perfect, both parents temporarily confined to the house. And it was inconceivable, the girl's father entrusting difficult chores to a young girl for weeks on end. Most certainly, he was searching for help. Still, it wouldn't hurt to rest a couple more days before returning outside into the perils of winter. Miriam sank gratefully back into the hay.

"I'll stay a few more days, until I regain my strength, as long as you promise not to tell your parents."

The girl nodded somberly. Miriam caught a glimpse of the beauty she would be one day, with her high cheekbones, up-slanted blue eyes and porcelain skin. There was a regal air about her even as she sat on a rudimentary wood stool and grabbed the cow's teats.

"You may as well tell me your name, since you know mine," Miriam said.

The girl glanced sideways at Miriam and said, "I'm called Jolanta, which means flower in Latvian. My father chose the name once I was born, because he said I was as beautiful as any flower he'd seen." Jolanta tossed Miriam a droll smile far beyond her years. "But I've helped my mother birth other women's babies and I know they are ugly at first, wrinkled and covered in blood."

The corner of Miriam's mouth tugged.

"I think he gave me the name hoping I'd get better-looking," Jolanta said.

Miriam chuckled at her innocent logic. She could have listened to her talk for hours. Jolanta's naive voice was like a glass of warm tea after months of icy solitude with only the forest's refrain for company—birds twittering, branches cracking under the weight of snow, twigs crunching underfoot and animals scampering.

Jolanta deftly began milking the cow. Miriam watched, struck by the fact that her survival was now in the hands of a child.

"MY FATHER IS coming! You must hide."

It had been fifty-six days (fifty-six pieces of hay) since Miriam's first conversation with Jolanta when the child ran into the barn one afternoon, red in the face. Her warm breath coiled in the glacial air that ponged with shit, the sweetness of hay and Miriam's everlasting body odor.

Miriam darted behind a two-meter-high stack of hay. The barn door flung open.

"Jolanta, you're supposed to be helping Māte," her father said in a clipped voice.

"I just wanted to see the cow, Papai," Jolanta replied.

"Why?" he demanded. "The cow is the same as she was yesterday and the day before."

"I mean . . . I was going to milk the cow."

Miriam grimaced at Jolanta's implausible lie.

A long silence.

"Strange. I must have imagined the milk you brought in this morning," her father replied, sarcastic.

"Oh."

"What's the matter? You look like you're afraid I'm going to bite your head off."

Hay crunched beneath steady footsteps that were moving toward Miriam as if there was an *X* on the stack of hay in front of her. *Why didn't I leave when I had the chance?*

"Māte is calling us," Jolanta said. "We better go."

The footsteps stopped.

"I don't hear anything," her father replied, his voice closer, louder.

"She needs me—us," Jolanta said, insistent.

"I don't think so."

"But Papai—"

"I think you're up to something in here."

"No, I'm not."

"Are you going to tell me or am I going to have to figure it out myself?"

"There's nothing to tell, Papai," Jolanta cried.

"You're lying. It's as plain as the nose on your face," he said sternly.

Jolanta sniffled loudly.

"What are you hiding, Jolanta?"

"Nothing. Don't. Papai, please."

The shuffle of feet. The crackle of hay.

A man's astonished face appeared at the top of the haystack. Miriam shrank back, feeling like a mouse cornered by a cat.

RIGA, JULY 1976

S ARAH COULDN'T PEEL HER EYES FROM THE BARREL OF the Soviet officer's gun. Her mouth went dry with terror. The officer grabbed Sarah by the elbow. He mumbled in Russian and hauled her toward him. She felt numb, as though she were watching a scene unfold from a distance. He tore her camera bag and purse from her shoulders.

"Wait! You can't just take my things." She didn't recognize the high pitch in her voice.

"Stop talking," Roger snapped.

His abrasiveness shook her up.

A woman across the street pushed a baby in a wicker buggy, eyes straight ahead as if she didn't see or hear the commotion.

The officer threw her in the back seat. He plunked himself beside Sarah and the car shot forward. The seat was cold and the new-leather smell turned her stomach. The officer lit a cigarette and exhaled smoke in Sarah's direction. She choked on the fumes and fumbled for the lever to open the window. It didn't budge. She pressed herself into the corner of the seat and stared out the window, shivering and perspiring. Riga flew by like a silent movie. Blocks of utilitarian Soviet apartment buildings. The polished turquoise river under the airy light-blue sky. Local women, identifiable by their garish headscarves and ugly shoes. Opulent rows of houses. Tourists in brightly colored shorts and skirts, cameras around their necks, huddled around a guide.

The car jolted up and down as they drove along the old cobblestone road. Sarah turned to look out the rear window, to see if Roger was behind her, but a tram blocked her view. The jolting stopped when they turned onto a wide boulevard with stately buildings on both sides of the street. Sarah sucked quick gulps of air when the driver entered through an imposing iron gate into a courtyard and turned off the engine at a black steel garage door. The officer grabbed Sarah's upper arm and lugged her from the back seat, through the door, into a gray stone room. The doors clanged shut with a menacing echo. The air smelled caustic.

A KGB officer sat behind an oak desk. He and the arresting officer exchanged a few brusque words. Sarah tried to free her arm, but the officer clamped his fingers tighter, cutting off her circulation. He set her purse and camera on the desk. The officer behind the desk opened her purse and withdrew her wallet and photos, including the one from Gundega. He peered at her driver's license and looked skeptically at Sarah, as if he wasn't sure she was the person in the photo. He retrieved a form from his top drawer and scrawled on the lines, his head turning from her license to the form and back again. Sarah chomped on her thumbnail. Her legs trembled.

In stilted English, the officer commanded her to give him the names of the people in her family. He ran his fingers down his tie then held his pen over a blank space on the document. Sarah gave him her father's name. The officer looked up from the form and narrowed his eyes with impatience.

"My mother died last year. I'm an only child."

He dropped his pen and drummed his fingers on the desk. Said she would only make things worse by lying.

Sarah took a deep breath. "Miriam Talan, my grandmother, is the only other family I have."

The officer adjusted his metal-framed glasses. "That is not true, is it?"

Sarah gritted her teeth and balled her hands into fists.

He interlaced his ropy fingers and leaned forward.

"I don't know what you're talking about," she said through clenched teeth.

The officer lifted his eyes to the ceiling. "Americans." He sighed dramatically. "You talk too much about your plans to strangers."

Dr. Kulda. Of course. There was no point in trying to keep Monya out of it; the officers already knew the answer to their question. She reluctantly admitted Monya was her uncle, then begged the officer to leave him alone.

"I searched for Monya. His only fault was opening the door and letting me in. He had nothing to do with me coming here. He didn't even know I existed until I showed up. He didn't know he had family in America and had—has—no plans to leave Riga. All I wanted to do was see him so I could tell Miriam, his mother, he's alive."

The officer planted his burly forearms on the desk and leaned forward, close enough for Sarah to smell his sour breath. "Your uncle is not called Monya, and if you know what is good for you, you will tell me his real name."

Her gut tightened with anger. "His name was changed to Andris Jansons when he was adopted."

The officer gave her a long, searching look. He resumed filling out the form and muttered something in Russian under his breath.

Sarah asked again if Monya and his family would be left alone.

Neither officer responded. Neither one acted as if they heard her. She was about to ask again when the arresting officer suddenly let go of her and took a small camera from the pocket of his jacket. He pointed to the center of the room, under the bare light bulb dangling from the ceiling. Sarah moved to the spot and looked him in the eyes. He took a photo of her face, as well as two profile shots, and returned the camera to his jacket.

The officer behind the desk put Sarah's purse and camera in separate clear plastic bags. He slipped her wallet and photos into a manila envelope, opened a file cabinet and stuck it in a folder.

"Wait! You can't take my things. Give them back, please," Sarah said in a tremulous voice.

He penned a few words in Cyrillic on a pad of paper, ripped off the page and gave it to Sarah. "Your receipt." He gestured with his thumb for her to be brought through double doors.

"No. There's been a misunderstanding. I shouldn't be here. Please, let me go." She squirmed, but the officer's hand was like an iron vise on her arm.

He dragged her through the doors into a narrow, claustrophobic hall lined with rusty, barred cells giving off the metallic stench of blood. In one cell, a man lay in a heap on the floor, a puddle of blood at his feet. Sarah quailed. Spotted a room at the end of the corridor with a steel door and had a sinking feeling it was her destination. Sure enough, the officer heaved her into the windowless room with a distinct mildew-and-urine scent and peeling seafoam-green walls. Dry blood flecks clogged a sewer grate in the corner.

The officer shut the door and planted his feet shoulder width apart on the concrete floor. He ordered her to remove her clothing.

Sarah hugged herself and shook her head. "No. I haven't done anything wrong. I'm an American tourist. I want a lawyer. I want to call my embassy."

The officer's face hardened. He told her to remove her clothes or he would remove them for her. Sarah stepped back and hit her head against the wall. The officer plunged forward, arm raised.

"No. I'll do it myself." She glanced at the door. "Isn't there a woman who could—"

"No woman. Only me."

Sarah bent down to remove her sandals, her fingers clumsy with fear. She raised her head to keep her eyes on the officer and unzipped her jeans. The officer extracted a long knife from a pouch on his belt, stabbed one sandal and dragged it toward him, then stabbed the other. Told her to go faster.

She pulled down her jeans. Tears poured from her eyes. She couldn't believe this was real, having to take off her clothes in front of a police officer as if she were a criminal. Goose bumps covered every inch of her skin. She focused on the doorknob and pulled her T-shirt over her head. Her teeth chattered when she stood naked in front of the officer, arms over her breasts.

He ran the knife's blade over his palm and stepped toward Sarah. She crossed her legs and crouched down to conceal herself. He poked the top of her head with the tip of the blade. Growled at her to stand.

Sarah rose with the blade jabbing into her scalp. He removed the blade and walked around her, ogling her as if she were a *Playboy* centerfold. She breathed in his putrid breath and realized why her mother had walked her to school until she was practically grown: because the streets she'd known as a child were lethal. Sarah started hyperventilating.

"Please, don't hurt me," she begged him.

He laughed mirthlessly. Ran the tip of the knife along the side of her leg, up to her waist and over her left breast. Moved to her back and roughly parted her buttocks. Sarah grew dizzy. He continued, slowly probing the crevices of her body before going through her clothing. He removed her shoelaces, slashed the button on her jeans and cut out the zipper. Sliced the hook from her bra. Sarah's lips and toes tingled.

"Get dressed," he ordered abruptly. He shoved her clothes toward her with his knife and stared as she swayed on her feet and put on her zipperless jeans, her T-shirt without her now-useless bra, and her sandals.

The officer shut and locked the door. Sarah fell into the corner and buried her face in her hands. Pearls of sweat clung to her temple. She agonized over her situation, couldn't believe she'd been stupid enough to get into such a huge mess. She ogled the closed door, afraid of it opening and afraid of it not opening, and hugged her knees to make herself small.

Where was Roger?

The door scraped open after what seemed like hours; Sarah had no sense of time in the windowless cell. She lifted her head and spotted a cobweb in the corner above the door. Two officers filed in, the burly one who'd brought her to the station and a slimmer, older man with a long face.

"What's going to happen to me?" She was hot and thirsty but afraid to ask for a drink. It could be poisoned. If Soviet officers could arrest her for visiting her uncle, they could poison her water for no reason. "What's going to happen to my uncle?"

The arresting officer stood silently in front of the door, rifle by his side. The gray-haired officer moved closer until he stood over Sarah. He had the manner of someone who could look a rattlesnake in the eyes and not flinch.

"You think we are stupid, yes?" His English pronunciation was harsh. Scathing.

"N—no."

"You think our rules don't apply to you?"

"What? No. I mean—"

"You are impersonating a tourist. You were recruited by a Jewish group to spread Zionist materials to convert your uncle's ideology, and slant him and his family toward hostile actions against the Soviet government."

"What are you talking about?"

His eyes narrowed to slits. "I have no patience for liars."

"I'm not lying. Nobody recruited me. I don't even belong to a synagogue. I'm Jewish by blood—that's all. The only thing I'm guilty of is leaving my tour to look for my uncle, who disappeared after the war. My grandmother, Monya's mother, hasn't stopped thinking about him. She's getting old. I only wanted to meet him. I know he can't leave."

"Why should we believe what you say? Many Americans parade as tourists but are here to remove Soviet citizens or come as spies."

Sarah snorted at the idea of herself as a spy, and covered her mouth.

"You find humor with spies?"

"No, no. I'm sorry. It's just so crazy. I'm not a spy. I'm a market researcher at an advertising agency in Chicago, and I came on this tour to see where my mother was born. I didn't really expect to find my uncle, but when I did, I just wanted to see him, to tell my grandmother he's all right."

The gray-haired officer pursed his lips and said something to the arresting officer, who turned with the precision of a robot, opened the door and marched from the room.

"I need to talk to someone in the American embassy," Sarah said, her voice shrill. "This can all be cleared up with a quick phone call to the embassy. I have the number in my purse if you'd just give it back . . ."

The gray-haired officer fastened his hostile eyes on Sarah. "Aren't you going to contact the embassy?"

He stood unnervingly still. Said nothing.

The door opened and the other officer returned with Sarah's passport and visa.

"Wait a second," Sarah said, pointing at her passport and visa. "Those were in the hotel's safe. How did you get them?"

The officer smiled haughtily. "We can get anything we want."

Sarah grimaced.

The gray-haired officer pored over her passport. "You have been arrested for conspiring to help Soviet citizens leave the country," he said finally.

"That's not true. All I did was visit my uncle for a few minutes, to tell him about his mother and sister. We talked about our families and showed each other photos."

He suggested she take some time to think about her answer. He pivoted on the ball of his foot and followed the other officer out of the cell.

The door closed with an ominous thud. She darted to the door and banged on it with her fists. "I'm telling the truth! Please let me out. I have to go to the bathroom. Please. Let me call the embassy. I want to go home."

She clobbered the door until her fists were bruised to the bone. Nobody came. She leaned against the wall and slid down to the floor. Crossed her legs. Her bladder swelled against her abdomen. She squeezed her thighs together to keep from peeing. She massaged her achy head. Urine dribbled onto her panties. She closed her thighs and tensed her muscles, but it was no use. The dam broke. Urine gushed through her panties and down the legs of her jeans.

Now I know what it feels like to be alive.

43

OUTSKIRTS OF RIGA, DECEMBER 1943

W<small>E HAVE TO GO OR WE'LL BE LATE," J</small>OLANTA'S FATHER said in a terse voice that belied his soft heart. He had short reddish hair, a clean-shaven, ruddy complexion, and the same clear and kind eyes as his daughter. Though he'd been angry with Jolanta for not telling him about Miriam, for risking his family's safety, he'd also insisted Miriam stay until he could find a safer place for her to hide.

Now he gestured to his gray truck with its oblong grille and black fenders. Miriam stole one last appreciative look at the brave girl who had taken her in and cared for her as if she were family, and followed Jolanta's father, still limping from his not quite healed broken leg. She wasn't sure whether or not to believe he was telling the truth about his friend who'd agreed to hide her. It was hard to accept there were people willing to risk their own lives to help perfect strangers—Jews, no less.

Jolanta's father supported Miriam's elbow as she climbed into the cargo hold, where she would ride alone, hidden underneath a canvas shell. It smelled of wood and tobacco and was burning cold.

"You're sure about this?" Miriam said. She looked back at the house, where his wife and son were asleep, blissfully unaware of the gamble he was about to take. His wife still had no idea Miriam even existed.

He nodded and fastened the canvas in place, leaving Miriam lying on her back in total darkness, unable to sit up. Miriam's stomach lurched as the truck grinded into gear and rolled forward, skidding over dirt roads slippery with ice. For a few minutes they hummed over flat country roads. She could tell they'd entered Riga when the truck started bouncing over cobblestones. Miriam bumped up and down, landing hard on her tailbone, her shoulders, her spine, the back of her head. Vomit rose in her throat. She gagged.

Vomit ejected through her lips spontaneously, too powerful to ignore, like a contraction. She choked. Spat out what she could. The noxious smell brought on a wave of nausea. The truck swerved sharply and Jolanta's father cut the engine.

His door opened. He walked to the back of the truck. He unfastened the canvas, and all at once Miriam was looking up at the moonlit sky, her face smeared with vomit. He looked down on her impassively. Disappeared.

She was afraid he was getting his gun. To shoot her.

He came back. He gave her a handkerchief.

Miriam sat up and wiped her face.

"Sorry about the rough drive," he said, rueful. "I should have gone slower."

Miriam stopped. His sincerity cracked a hole in her facade. Her eyes began to tear up.

"Did I say something wrong?" His breath made spiral mists in the cold air.

Tears dribbled down her cheeks. She thought, I can't remember the last time I cried.

"Are you all right?"

Miriam's lashes were freezing from her tears, but she didn't wipe them away. "You made me feel human," she began, her voice dry and brittle from neglect. "Nobody's apologized to me since the day before my husband was killed."

His eyes flickered with sympathy.

"Your daughter was the first person who's been kind to me in a long time," she continued.

His face twisted with modest pride.

She planted her hands on the edges of the box to hoist herself up.

He clamped his hand over hers. "I'm sorry. You have to stay there until he comes. If anyone else were to see you . . ."

"I understand." She lowered her head again and held her nose to keep out the vomit smell.

He gave her a quiet smile. "I'm not one for long goodbyes."

"Thank you," Miriam said, her voice breaking. "For everything."

"Stay safe." He returned to the driver's seat and shut his door.

MIRIAM WAS GROWING convinced that the man who'd promised to take her had backed out when she heard footfalls approach the truck. She tensed. It could easily be a Nazi.

A man with a broad nose and bleary eyes appeared over the edge of the truck.

"Come, Miriam. We don't have much time," he said in an unflappable tone, immediately setting her at ease.

She struggled to get out of the cargo hold, her bones stiff, her mind numb.

"My name's Janis." He extended his hand and helped her step down. A mariner's cap sat crookedly on his head and his ears jutted out prominently.

Jolanta's father started up his truck and drove off as soon as her feet touched the ground. Miriam peered at the dwindling taillights, then jumped at a street-shaking blast overhead.

"We're near German antiaircraft guns," Janis whispered. He led her down a narrow alley that diverged from the street.

Another blast shattered a window somewhere in the vicinity. Miriam froze.

"We're almost there," Janis said. "Keep going."

He prodded her gently. They proceeded down the alley onto another street lined with shop windows, most boarded up. Janis stopped at a nondescript wall and, to Miriam's surprise, removed a section of bricks, just enough for one person to pass through. Janis ducked, motioned for Miriam to follow and entered the gap he'd cleared. Miriam crouched and shuffled along the passage for a couple of minutes. It opened to a cellar. A paraffin lantern blinded her temporarily. When her eyes adjusted to the light, she saw Janis's wiry face more clearly. He had lines like commas around the corners of his lips and comforting eyes.

She took in the cellar, impressed by three tidy levels of sleeping shelves, guns hanging on one wall, and cans and boxes of food stacked on a makeshift table. People who appeared to have been there for a long time, judging from their translucent skin, nodded at her as they listened intently to a radio broadcast in Russian.

Janis shook hands with a couple of the men and introduced Miriam. He stuffed his hands in his pockets and turned to a young, bearded man. "Semyon can show you around. I have to go."

"I . . . I don't know how to repay you," Miriam began.

"You don't owe me a thing. You're not responsible for the madness out there." Janis tipped his hat at Miriam and vanished down the passageway.

"Don't worry," Semyon said in Yiddish. "He'll be back."

Miriam nodded stiffly. She wasn't about to let her guard down. Even in this underground haven, surrounded by Jews, the only person she trusted was herself.

Semyon introduced Miriam to the other cellar occupants, ten men, one woman and her young daughter. Twelve Jews who, like Miriam, would not see the sky or breathe fresh air until the Soviets liberated Latvia ten months later, in October 1944.

44

RIGA, JULY 1976

SARAH PLUGGED HER NOSE AND BREATHED THROUGH HER mouth to keep out the acidic reek of urine. The crotch of her jeans was cold and damp. She sat cross-legged, to let air dry the denim. She'd lost track of time, and hunger pangs had been replaced by cramps that spread to her muscles like spilled paint. Frightening visions of a knife dragging across her skin, guns pointed at her head, ran through her mind on a loop. Her entire body stung with exhaustion, but she was afraid to fall asleep. She clutched her head and cried dry, silent tears.

The door squeaked open. She curled into a ball and peeked at the expanding crack of light.

"Sarah?" Roger's anxious voice trickled through the opening.

"Roger?"

The door shut. The corridor light evaporated. Sarah stumbled to her feet. She leaned against the wall. Caught the whites of his eyes.

"Are you okay?" he asked.

"Okay? I've been strip-searched, interrogated and locked up like a criminal. And I want to wring Dr. Kulda's neck."

"Get in line," Roger said.

"I never imagined Dr. Kulda turning us in. I thought he was your friend."

"So did I. But when money speaks, the truth is silent."

"You mean he was paid for turning us in?"

"Now you're thinking like a Soviet."

Sarah groaned. She grasped the nearness of Roger. Something wasn't right. "Why did they let you in here, without a guard?"

Roger stepped forward, under the dim light. The overhead bulb fuzzily revealed the sharp planes of his face, giving him an imposing air. "Do you remember the day we met, when I said KGB agents sometimes pose as tourists?"

She staggered backward, numb with disbelief and shock. A KGB agent. Of course. Her mind reeled with things that had seemed odd about him, clues that should have given him away: His eerie knowledge of Riga's streets. His over-the-top patriotic clothes that screamed "trying too hard to fit in." Not knowing about Patty Hearst. In hindsight, it seemed so obvious, but at the time, she'd ignored the pesky voice in her head telling her he was a little too obliging. Disgust flooded through her. She slid down the wall and clasped her head in her hands. She imagined her gullibility was as clear as the stench of urine.

Roger was never her friend. She'd been completely honest with him about her uncle and her motives for coming to Riga, yet he'd hidden the most important part of himself. Her heart stiffened at his outright betrayal.

"Why did you help me find my uncle?" she asked. "Were you on my tour to set me up?"

He shook his head vehemently. "Absolutely not. I didn't know anything about you or Monya. I sat beside you because that was the only empty seat on the bus."

"But you broke the law to help me. A KGB agent would never do that."

He crouched down to her level. Rolled his shoulders forward. "You're right. I shouldn't have gotten involved."

"If you knew it was wrong, why did you?"

He held her gaze and said, "I wanted to keep you from getting into trouble. I figured as long as I knew what you were doing, and kept you from going too far, you'd be safe."

"I suppose the night we spent together was just part of the job."

His steely blue eyes bored into hers. "I never meant for it to happen. I should have stopped myself."

As his words sank in, she thought about how she'd been deceived by a cold-blooded spy. He'd been pretending to be someone he wasn't from the moment he sat down beside her on the airport bus to the moment she was arrested. He'd helped her find Monya, but he'd also led her straight into the KGB's callous hands. Her life might be completely ruined because of Roger.

"But you didn't," she said. "You didn't stop yourself."

"If things were different . . ."

"But they aren't. You lied. My mother lied. My grandmother lied. I've had it with people lying to me." Her voice notched up to rage.

"Shhh." He pressed his clammy hand over her mouth, lifted his eyes to the ceiling. "I've convinced them to let you go home. Today. But they could change their minds if you say something wrong. Until you're on the plane and it's taxiing down the runway, there's no guarantee you'll be on your way home. Understand?"

Sarah looked at him, incredulous. There was no way he'd talked the KGB into releasing her; they were letting her go because she'd done nothing wrong. He wanted her to see him as a hero. After all they'd been through, he'd rather lie to impress her than be honest.

Roger removed his hand, told her to be quiet and listen carefully. An officer was going to drive her to the airport, where her purse and identification, along with her luggage from the hotel, would be returned. She'd be allowed to change into clean clothes before the officer escorted her onto a plane going to Chicago, with a stopover in Frankfurt. The officer would leave once she was on the flight in Frankfurt. She was forbidden to return to the Soviet Union.

"Are Monya and Gundega going to be punished?"

"No. It's a lucky break you didn't meet Monya's children. One of the KGB's biggest fears is Americans tempting Soviet youth with the allure of the Western way of life. Officers entered Monya's apartment right after we were caught, so they know you only spoke to Monya and Gundega. Their apartment was searched and the two of them were interrogated for a couple of hours, with the KGB focusing on Monya's dedication to the Soviet Union and his religious identity. When the search turned up zero Jewish books or papers, and Monya made it clear he didn't accept you as his niece and had no intention of leaving, the KGB seized the photos you left and gave them a stern warning not to open their door to strangers again."

Sarah realized that Monya's rejection of her, Miriam and his faith was necessary under the circumstances, yet couldn't help but feel disappointed.

"Unfortunately," Roger continued, "the KGB also confiscated the film in your camera, and the photo of Monya that Gundega gave you."

Sarah balled her shaky hands into fists and brought them to her mouth. She'd ruined everything. Her grandmother would never know what her son looked like as an adult.

Roger leaned closer. "Don't be too hard on yourself. Because of you, your grandmother will know Monya is alive, and that she has four other grandchildren."

He had a point, but it wasn't enough for Sarah. She wanted the impossible. She wanted Miriam to get her son back.

The door squeaked open. She shielded her eyes from the blinding light behind the silhouette of an officer.

Roger jolted, his shoulders hunched as if he were trying to make himself small. His breaths grew quick and shallow. His left arm crossed his body and grabbed his right elbow. He was in trouble. Because of her. She'd used him to get what she wanted, just as he'd used her for reasons she'd never really understand.

"I'm sorry," she said, "for getting you involved."

He looked at her. "You didn't force me to do anything I didn't want to do."

"But if I hadn't told you about Monya—"

"You and your grandmother might never know what happened to him."

Sarah caught an unfamiliar tremor in his voice and was struck by the enigma of Roger. He was complicated, indefinable, impossible to know, impossible to trust. He was exciting and dangerous. And he'd acted from a sense of doing what was right, not what was expected of him. He had a shred of integrity. That was something.

The officer hovering in the doorway spoke to Roger in Russian.

Roger cleared his throat. He told Sarah the officer was going to take her to the airport.

"What about you?" she asked Roger.

"It's just another normal day at the office for me," he said, his voice tremoring with false bravado.

Sarah's stomach knotted. "Really?"

He averted his eyes from hers. "I'll be fine. As long as you're on the plane today."

She clutched the waist of her zipperless jeans to keep them from falling and moved toward the light. "I didn't get to say goodbye to the Cullens."

"I'll tell them you went home sick. I'll say goodbye for you."

"No. Don't say goodbye. Tell them I said . . . so long."

"Oh. Okay." He hesitated. Cleared his throat. "Then . . . so long."

Sarah lifted her eyes for one last look at Roger. But all she saw were white spots from the light.

45

RIGA, OCTOBER 1944

THE DAY LATVIA WAS LIBERATED BY THE SOVIETS, MIRIAM emerged from her underground cocoon and felt woozy from the detritus—bodies strewn about the cobblestones like flies on a windowsill, crimson blood spattered on the dead, the ground, the walls of buildings and the wreckage that now delineated Riga. The regal city she loved, where her roots ran deep, was unrecognizable. For a cold second she wanted to retreat to her nest below, to the black-and-white shades of darkness that had comforted her with their reliability. Now, the only certainty was uncertainty, she realized, as she waded through the vestiges of Riga surrounded by Soviet soldiers who had, ironically, saved Latvia from the Nazis, three years after the Nazis had rescued Latvians from the Soviets.

ONE DAY LATER, after sleeping in an actual bedroom in a house owned by members of a Lutheran church, after her first normal meal, bath and clean clothes in three years (all donated by the church), Miriam received a written summons from the KGB. Her stomach dropped at the unexpected order and the motive behind it. At first, she presumed she was being called as a witness to the murders carried out by the Nazis and Latvians. Then she remembered the Soviets hauling people from their homes and deporting them to Siberia, and knew she couldn't assume anything. She also knew it wasn't safe to fetch her children until after her meeting with the Soviets.

Just before seven o'clock the next evening, Miriam approached the KGB headquarters. She tasted the bile in her stomach at the sight of the gloomy six-story corner building on Raiņa bulvāris.

The door opened and a tall man wearing a newsboy cap and a yellow Star of David on his coat emerged through the fissure of light. Miriam couldn't see his face in the shadows, only his sharp contours.

"Why haven't you ripped off the Star of David?" she blurted.

He covered the patch with his hand. "Can't get it off. My wife sewed it too . . ." His voice broke.

Miriam's chin trembled. She heard the words he couldn't say. "Were you summoned?"

"Me and my brother."

"Why? What do they want?" she asked.

"An explanation."

"What?"

He stared at her. "Just tell the truth." His voice dropped to a hush. He was off, down the street.

"About what?" she called after him. "Tell the truth about what?"

He vanished in the October darkness.

Miriam felt her fingers digging into her palm. She'd crushed the summons in her hand. She pried her fist open and smoothed the paper. A familiar sense of powerlessness coursed through her. *I have to get out of Latvia.* She inhaled, entered the headquarters and presented her summons to the male registering clerk. He led her to a tiny, windowless room with off-white, dirty walls. A commandant sat behind a small desk, illuminated by a dim light bulb hanging from a wire. The low ceiling made Miriam feel trapped.

She felt a chill pass through her and was back in the Arājs Kommando building, with the monsters who'd attacked her. Sweat dampened the underarms of her borrowed wool sweater. She tensed her shaky knees.

The commandant gestured for her to sit in the chair across from him. He had short copper hair and pleasant jade eyes that eased her nerves slightly.

She perched at the edge of the chair.

He nodded and folded his hands together. "Tell me," he said in a scratchy voice that sounded as if he hadn't slept in days, "why did you survive when most of the others were shot?"

A thorn lodged in her throat. She didn't know if she had it in her to reach back and unravel the past she'd spooled deep in her core.

"Well?" he prodded.

Her neck stiffened.

Just tell the truth.

She grasped the seat of her chair with both hands and started to recount the night the Arājs Kommando marched ghetto residents to the pit.

"Stop." The commandant interrupted her as she was telling him about walking through the Kommando's gauntlet.

She tilted her head sideways.

"You can't possibly expect me to believe Latvians were responsible for killing Jews," he said.

She winced at his bullying timbre, then found her voice. "They raped women and shot people in the ghetto for no reason. They shot my parents, and hundreds of other Jews, for not walking fast enough. They led us to the Rumbula forest, where the Nazis shot us with machine guns."

The commandant waved his hands for her to be quiet. "Nothing you say coincides with the facts."

"Are you calling me a liar?" she said, stunned.

He gave her an insinuating smile. "Did you conspire with the Germans?"

"What?" she gasped.

"Did you conspire—"

"I heard you. I just can't believe you would ask such a ludicrous question."

The corners of his lips twitched. "We have found just one hundred and fifty Jews alive in Riga, which begs the question, how did you survive?"

"Because of a few kind people who gave me food and a corner in their barn to sleep," she replied, her voice strong and urgent. "Because I somehow managed to evade the Nazis and Latvians hunting for Jews. *They* collaborated to get rid of us. *That's* the truth."

The commandant squared his shoulders at her. His eyes had hardened to shards of stone. "You are dismissed," he said curtly.

"You don't believe me?"

"You are dismissed," he repeated.

Miriam's jaw went slack. She was outraged. She stumbled to her feet and left the KGB headquarters feeling like a fool. Nothing had changed. The Soviets weren't seeking the truth. They had no intention of punishing those responsible for murder. They wanted to rewrite history by accusing Jews of working with the people who'd murdered them. The same way the Nazis blamed Jews for killing Latvians that the Soviets had executed.

Just tell the truth.

The man's illogical advice roiled in her mind as she tossed and turned that night. Truth was an illusion as far as the Soviets were concerned. The Latvians weren't going to be held accountable for their heinous actions.

I saved myself only to discover there will be no justice for me and my parents. There will be no justice for the people murdered in the Rumbula forest and in the ghetto.

MIRIAM'S HEAD POUNDED like heavy footsteps after her sleepless night. She drank two cups of black tea and ate a piece of dry toast before setting off for her children. The streets teemed with Soviet soldiers, red lines and angles in Miriam's bleary eyes. She felt like a piece of thread about to break. She saw herself holding Monya and Ilana, and quickened her pace; she had to focus on the future, not the past, if she had any hope of being the mother they deserved.

Crossing the Daugava River was not easy with all the bridges destroyed. Miriam had to beg a ride aboard a fisherman's small boat, which took time since she was one of at least fifty trying to get to the other side. Gutte's house was a short walk from the riverbank, along a dirt road running alongside the river, followed by a smaller road that veered sharp left, like a finger, with one-story wood houses and fences on one side and oak trees with bare branches on the other.

Gutte and her family lived in a square wood house with a stone foundation abutting the road. Four windows overlooked the street and the entrance was at the side. Miriam's heart fluttered when she neared the door. She raised her pale hand, knuckles swollen with arthritis from years of inexorable cold and dampness, to knock, then stopped, overcome by doubt. What if Ilana didn't recognize her? What if she and Monya had forgotten her?

Miriam hadn't seen her own face in ages. She lifted both hands to her face. Her skin was as rough as bark, her cheekbones were like spikes, her lips scabbed. Miriam dropped her hand. Opened and closed her rigid fingers. Knocked.

A slight man in his late fifties, his face blotchy red and purple, opened the door and gave Miriam a blank look. Pjotrs, Gutte's husband. It was the first time they had laid eyes on one another. There was so much she wanted to say, but first she needed to see her children.

"I'm Miriam," she said.

He blanched. Stared at Miriam as though she were a ghost. Her eyes followed his, to her wrinkled dress, two sizes too big, her hair chopped short to get rid of the lice.

Pjotrs cleared his throat and said, "We didn't expect you to . . ."

"Survive?"

He glanced over his shoulder and looked back at her, desperation written across his face. His discomfort was sobering. Miriam was afraid her appearance would shock her children and Gutte. Instinctively, Miriam rambled on about Janis and the cellar, the only portion of her time in hiding she would ever discuss. Even in the cellar, she told no one about the ghetto and Rumbula to keep the unthinkable memories buried in the nadir of her mind, and to keep from reliving the pain.

Pjotrs opened the door wider as Miriam was explaining how Janis appeared once a week with supplies and the latest news of the war efforts.

"Come in," he said, sounding as if the last thing he wanted was for her to enter.

Miriam stepped into a small, dimly lit vestibule that smelled of paraffin, an odor she'd never forget after ten months of living in the underground bunker. Pjotrs gestured for her to follow him through a door on the left, into a sitting room with a drab beige sofa and a birch coffee table littered with *Laikmets* magazines. He said Gutte and Ilana would be back soon; they'd gone to the market.

"What about Monya? Is he with them?"

Pjotrs lowered his eyes and sidled down the hall without another word.

Miriam felt the ceiling slip. The walls closed in. Her breath caught in her throat. Dread rippled through her chest. She didn't have the strength for more bad news. Fear infested her thoughts like lice burrowing in her scalp, ruthless pests she could feel but couldn't see.

The door opened and a wisp of a girl, with a bone-gray complexion, appeared. Her sea-green eyes were the only recognizable part of her, though they'd lost their luster. A wave of relief broke over Miriam, so intense she had to shut her eyes. When she opened them, her daughter was standing in front of her.

"Ilana." Miriam rose from the sofa.

Ilana's eyes flashed with recognition. She stiffened at Miriam's approach. Tottered. Fell against the door jamb.

Miriam's rubbery legs gave way. She dropped back onto the sofa. A layer of ice enveloped Miriam's heart. *My daughter is afraid of me.*

Gutte, entering on Ilana's heels, jolted upright. Her pale eyelashes melted into her haggard face. She'd lost weight. Her hair was silvery white. Her face was mottled with age spots. "You're . . . alive," she stammered.

Ilana pressed against Gutte the way she used to press against Miriam when she was little and scared. Miriam stared at her daughter, searching for the mischievous gleam in her eye, a hint of the girl she used to be. But Ilana's eyes teemed with a mistrust that made Miriam's throat close in grief.

"You look all grown-up," she said to Ilana.

Ilana looked up at Gutte as if seeking approval, before replying shyly: "I'm thirteen. And I'm Inga."

Miriam cringed at the Latvian identity that had saved her

daughter's life, but didn't want their reunion to become an argument about her name. She tried to reconcile this docile, subdued girl with the stubborn, lively child she'd left behind. Her spirit was gone, like the core of an apple, cut and discarded.

"I thought none of you survived," Gutte said. "How did you—"

"People with good souls, like you," Miriam said, her mind turning to Zelma.

Gutte blinked and touched her throat.

"Where are Zeyde and Bubbe?" Ilana asked her mother.

Her parents' names rose in her throat like a lump. Miriam caught Ilana's eye and held it. The silence between them was transparent and vast. Ilana let out a guttural cry. Gutte clamped her large hands on Ilana's shoulders. Ilana burrowed into Gutte with an ease that made Miriam feel redundant. Watching her daughter seek comfort from Gutte, Miriam was torn between being grateful and jealous. Gutte reached out and touched Miriam's cheek. Her skin tingled. She longed for and dreaded contact.

"I can't imagine how difficult it's been for you," Gutte said.

Her sympathetic voice brought Miriam back to her home in Mežaparks, and the last days of their ordinary lives, when Gutte had been a mainstay in her life. How long ago it seemed, a different life in a world that was now extinct. "Surviving was easy, compared to giving up my children. It was the hardest thing I've done." Miriam dabbed tears from her eyes with the tips of her fingers.

Gutte offered a white handkerchief. Miriam hadn't seen anything so clean or soft in years.

"The children . . ." In her mind's eye, Miriam saw the Blatt children, lying facedown with their parents. She saw Clara and Ilya and broke into a cold sweat. "It was the right decision," she said to Ilana. "You would not be here if I hadn't left you with Gutte."

Ilana shuddered violently.

"You shouldn't say such things to her," Gutte admonished Miriam.

Miriam looked at Ilana and nodded. Gutte was right—it was an awful thing to say. She watched, envious, as Gutte comforted Ilana with a motherly intuitiveness; Miriam hadn't been a mother for three years.

Gutte offered tea and bread with jam, pointing out that Ilana made the jam. "Inga—I mean Ilana—has become a good cook."

Miriam's shoulders tensed at Gutte's slip-up.

"But she refuses to bake, or even eat one of my biscuits. I don't know why." Gutte looked at Ilana. "You used to love my biscuits."

Miriam recalled the day she'd bought Ilana a bun at the bakery three years earlier, the day Ilana's childhood ended. Miriam patted the cushion beside her and looked hopefully at her daughter. Ilana moved slowly to the sofa, perching at the other end, as far away as possible without being off the sofa entirely. Miriam longed to hold her, the way she had when Ilana was young.

"Where's Monya?" Miriam asked uneasily.

The color leached from Ilana's face. She shrank into the corner of the sofa.

Miriam's mind raced with unthinkable possibilities: Monya being dragged from the street like his father. Being caught in a storm of bullets.

"I'll make the tea and cut the bread." Gutte started for the kitchen as if she hadn't heard Miriam.

"Wait. Where's Monya?" Miriam stood unsteadily and fixed her gaze on Gutte's darting eyes.

"After our tea," Gutte said.

"No. Forget the tea. Where is my son?"

Gutte lifted her eyes heavenward. In a faltering voice, she said: "Pjotrs's cousin knocked on our door a year after you left. He'd heard rumors about us hiding Jewish children. I told him he was wrong, we'd taken in my orphaned niece and nephew. The cousin didn't believe me. Insisted on seeing their papers. He knew at once they were phony, and threatened to turn us all in unless we gave him Monya."

Miriam's chest tightened. "You didn't."

Gutte reached for a handkerchief in a pocket of her dress and blew her nose. "I tried to convince Pjotrs's cousin the papers were genuine, but he wouldn't leave. Not even after Ilana kicked him in the shin and said he couldn't take her brother."

Miriam glanced at her daughter, curled in a ball on the sofa as if she wanted no part of the conversation.

"I asked Pjotrs's cousin why he wanted a little boy when his children were almost grown, and he claimed he wasn't asking for himself," Gutte continued. "A colleague who'd lost his infant son to pneumonia offered a great sum of money if he'd find a boy to be adopted. When Pjotrs heard we would receive one-quarter of the proceeds, well, I didn't have a choice."

She spoke with a harsh resignation that stunned Miriam. The only reason she agreed to leave her children with Gutte in the first place was her assurance she'd love and protect them as her own. Yet she'd readily handed Monya over when some oily relative called her bluff.

"What about the pearl bracelet I gave you?" Miriam asked. "Didn't you sell it?"

Gutte hung her head. "Yes, of course, but jewelry isn't worth much during a war. People like us needed food more than pearls. The money we got for the bracelet didn't last long."

Miriam let this sink in. "Even still, I trusted you, believed you'd do anything to keep my children safe."

"I'm not the same person I was before the war." Gutte folded her hands together and brought them to her mouth, as if in prayer.

"My children and yours were starving. My parents' farm was taken by the Soviets, Pjotrs wasn't getting much work and, as you know, I wasn't working at all. We had eight mouths to feed and would have been killed if the identity of your children had been discovered. I did what I had to do to keep us all alive."

"You sold my son like a farm animal."

"You asked me to take your children but gave me nothing to support them."

"Everything we owned was taken from us. You know that. You know I would have given you—"

"It was my fault," Ilana cried out, her voice anguished and raw. "I promised to look after Monya and I failed."

"That's ridiculous," Miriam retorted. "You're just a child. I don't blame you."

Ilana jumped from the sofa and scurried through the door at the end of the room.

Miriam felt utterly helpless, seeing her daughter ridden with unwarranted guilt. She stood, to go after Ilana.

Gutte clasped her arm and said, "Leave her be. She will be fine after some time alone."

"Don't tell me how to manage my own daughter," Miriam snapped.

Gutte recoiled.

Miriam took a deep breath to steady her nerves and asked Gutte for the cousin's name.

"He died a year ago." Gutte paused. "I spoke to his wife at the funeral, but she knew nothing about her husband arranging an adoption, though she did recall a sudden improvement in their finances right around the time Monya was taken."

"There must be documents somewhere. You can't adopt a child legally without signing papers. You must know where he is."

"Would you like a loaf of bread for your journey?" Gutte's nose twitched. She folded her arms. Her eyes darted from Miriam to the magazines on the table.

"No, I don't want bread, I want answers."

Gutte arranged the magazines into a neat pile before fixing her gaze on Miriam. "If I remember correctly, you asked me to care for Ilana and Monya because you knew, above all else, your children's true identity would be safe with me."

"Not just their identity, their lives. I trusted you with their lives."

"His money put food in our stomachs, in your daughter's stomach."

Miriam's heart tightened when she caught the mulish fleck in Gutte's eyes. "Pack Ilana's things and bring her to me at once."

"My name is Inga," Ilana said from the doorway, "and I'm not leaving."

"You are Ilana, named after your father's grandmother. It is the name your father and I chose for you. And you are coming with me because I'm your mother."

Ilana lifted her gaze to Gutte, who set her mouth in a hard line and nodded slightly.

"Why do you want me?" Ilana asked. "Whenever you look at me, you'll remember I didn't keep Monya safe, like I promised."

Her words were like a kick in Miriam's stomach. Miriam combed the dusty recesses of her mind for the right words. "If Zeyde were here, he would know how to make you understand Monya's disappearance is not your fault."

Ilana looked blankly at her mother.

"Zeyde always knew how to soothe me when I was a child, growing up in the eclipse of my domineering mother," Miriam said with a wistful look in her eyes. "Once, I lit the Hannukah candles too close to the curtains, setting them on fire. I poured water over the flames, so just the bottom edges were singed, but I felt so guilty. I had nightmares about burning our house down. My father made me feel better. He said, 'You can't always control what happens. It's how you react that matters.'

"I'm proud of the way you kicked that horrible man and told him to leave your brother alone. There was nothing more you could have done, Ilana."

The tightness in Ilana's face slowly ebbed, but the wariness in her eyes remained. Miriam was afraid Ilana would never forgive herself if they didn't find Monya.

"I'm going to search every inch of Riga for Monya, and I need your help," Miriam said.

"All right," Ilana replied, her lips quivering. "I'll get my things."

She slipped through the door and returned a few minutes later with a satchel containing a change of clothes and the family photos Miriam had packed the day they separated. Miriam bit down hard on her bottom lip to keep from crying; she'd forgotten about these photos, the only images remaining of Max, her parents and Monya.

Ilana and Gutte embraced. Both sobbed quietly. Miriam looked away. In her heart, Miriam knew Gutte had done what she thought was necessary at the time. Still, Miriam could never look at her again without thinking of her own former, self-centered life. Gutte was a stark reminder of her own fallacies, her inability to recognize the soundness of Max's intuition about the danger of staying in Latvia.

46

EN ROUTE TO CHICAGO, JULY 1976

T HE PLANE QUAKED WITH TURBULENCE, THRUSTING
Sarah against the bathroom door. She hit her head, a blow that
shook her fragile composure. Bits and pieces of her time in
Riga surfaced like blisters . . . Monya recoiling in disgust at the news
he was Jewish, his grim apartment and the photos telling the story
of his life apart from his mother and sister. The sour disappointment of his rejection, most likely their first and last meeting. The
Soviet officer's slimy hands and the hot, black rush of terror that
devoured her in the cell. Roger's charade.

Sarah rocked herself. Pressed her hands on the mirror.
Examined her grubby, blotchy skin, red-rimmed eyes, flat, oily hair.
She leaned in closer and got a hint of how she'd look in ten, twenty
years. And she began to comprehend the magnitude of what she'd
inherited, beneath her skin—Miriam's unbelievable courage, her
mother's resilience, her father's empathy. Her half-Jewish blood
she shared with cousins she'd never meet, unless a miracle took
place and the Soviet Union became a free society.

She was disheartened by her visit with Monya, almost wished it hadn't occurred, that she hadn't learned about his adoptive father. Now that she knew, she had to figure out what to do with the truth. If she didn't tell Miriam, she'd be as bad as her parents, keeping rightful information a secret. Would it be enough for Miriam, knowing her son was alive and well, knowing she had four more grandchildren, even though they were imprisoned by Communism, even though they were unaware of their genetic legacy? This overwhelmed Sarah; she was the only descendant who could reclaim her Jewish identity. If she didn't carry on the Jewish faith, it would die with Miriam.

The pilot's voice came over the speakers when she was back in her seat, announcing they'd be landing in thirty minutes. Sarah rooted through her purse for her passport. The Soviet officer had stuffed it in the zippered pocket after she'd shown it in Frankfurt right before she boarded the plane to Chicago.

There was something else in the pocket besides her passport. She didn't remember putting anything there. Sarah pulled out a photo of Monya, the one from Gundega, with their address. Sarah's eyes widened. She ran her finger over the contour of her uncle's face in the photo and was gripped by an acute restlessness. Roger said it had been destroyed. He must have bribed the officer to slip it into her purse. Just as he'd bribed the babushka in their hotel to look the other way. Heat bolted down Sarah's spine when she recalled their night together, a night she would never have contemplated in her ordinary world, a night she would never regret.

Roger. His intentions were murky and their short relationship had been built on lies, but somehow he'd turned her inside out. Somehow he'd shone a light on her consciousness, like the X-rays that showed images of Miriam's lungs. Now, like Roger and like

Monya, she knew who she was and what she wanted. She knew where she had to go and what she had to do. And that was enough.

Sarah's mouth set in a hard line. She wished she could redo her last heated conversation with her mother. How different it would be, now that she had a better understanding of the events that had formed her mother, now that she felt part of a bigger life and family, of a history connected to generations that came before and would come after all of them. Now that she knew the truth about Monya, even if it was not what she'd expected or wanted.

The truth is so hard to bear. Not many people are willing to carry it.

Miriam's solemn voice tunneled through her mind. Sarah was struck by a heady exhilaration for the courage she'd discovered within herself—going to Riga alone, accomplishing her goal of finding Monya—and by a tremor of fear, knowing how close she'd come to losing everything. It was ironic, how she had her own frightening memories of Riga but would stuff them away in her subconscious to keep her father and Miriam from worrying. She was her mother's daughter, all right.

Sarah took a deep breath and felt lighter, somehow, as if she'd emerged from the wormhole that was her search for the past and herself. She exhaled on the window, fogging up the glass, watched the mist evaporate, and thought about Henry. She missed him. Not because she was afraid of being alone, not because she wanted to please her mother, but because he was knowable. And because Henry would have told her the truth about himself, even if it meant she wouldn't have liked it. Henry would rather be honest than impressive. Henry was worth risking her heart for.

As soon as she landed, before catching a cab, Sarah found a pay phone and dialed Henry's number.

"It's me. Sarah," she said when he answered.

Silence.

She swallowed the knot in her throat. She twirled the telephone cord.

"I was hoping you'd call," he said.

47

RIGA, OCTOBER 1944

GUTTE DIDN'T WANT TO GIVE UP MONYA," ILANA TOLD Miriam their first night together, in their modest room in Riga. "She cried for weeks," Ilana added.

"I know." Miriam lay on her side, in the narrow cot, her back to Ilana. Close enough to hear her daughter's shallow breaths and to feel Ilana's scratchy linen nightdress brush against the backs of her legs. It was hard to grasp the changes in Ilana; she'd gone away as a child and was now practically a woman. The time they'd lost divided them the way the Daugava River divided Riga.

"Then why were you so mean to her?" Ilana asked pointedly.

Miriam stiffened. "I wasn't mean."

"Yes, you were."

"Go to sleep. We have a busy day ahead of us."

The sheets rustled as Ilana settled into her side of the cot. Miriam stared at the lace-curtained window directly across from her. Sleep was out of the question. Night, with its murky, silent darkness that gave way to her worst fears, had become a relentless foe. Intermittent periods of restless slumber were the most she could expect.

She didn't know what to say about her years away from Ilana. There were no adequate words to describe the heinous acts she'd witnessed. The truth was, Miriam didn't really want her to know. She didn't want Ilana waking three or four times a night in a hot sweat, seeing corpses and smelling rotten flesh. She didn't want her memory scarred with wide-open eyes that could no longer see. Her ears tainted with the staccato blast of bullets, louder and louder, until she had to hold her ears and curl into a ball and wait out the nightmare.

"What if we don't find him?" Ilana asked softly.

Miriam shivered and hugged her knees to her chest. "Are you giving up already?"

"No. I just don't want to get my hopes up."

"Is that what Gutte said?"

An elongated pause. "Yes," Ilana answered.

"Your father used to say we can always hope for a miracle, we just can't rely on one."

A deep-from-the-chest moan erupted from Ilana's chest. She pressed her face into her pillow and cried without making a sound. Miriam caught her own tears in her throat and swallowed them back down. She had to keep her emotions in check if she wanted to be the mother she needed to be for her children.

OVER THE NEXT few days, Ilana and Miriam moved stealthily through heavily guarded streets, searching for Monya. They had to avoid drunken Soviets who pulled women into alleys and raped them. And the streets themselves were hazardous, littered with glass, stone, bricks and shingles from fallen buildings. As they searched for Monya, an opaque dust clogged the brisk fall air and the metallic stench of blood lingered at every corner. Trees that hadn't been destroyed were bare and spindly. Miriam tried to imagine how Monya would look now, at four; the last time she'd seen him, he was sixteen months old. Did he still have curly hair? An impish grin that could light up a room?

One late afternoon, when the sun was dropping over the Baltic Sea, Miriam spotted a curly-haired boy getting out of an automobile on Marx Street. She and Ilana edged nearer. His hair was a lighter shade than Monya's, and finer. And his eyes were wider apart. The boy's mother glared when she caught Miriam watching her son. She put her hand between his shoulder blades and steered him down the sidewalk.

Ilana's hand slipped around Miriam's. "We've been out here all day," Ilana said. "It's time to go home."

"The flat is not our home," Miriam said.

"I know, I know, Mama. It's just a place to stay until we find Monya."

SEVERAL WEEKS HAD passed since Miriam and Ilana's reunion. Miriam had gained a few necessary pounds thanks to regular meals, and her monthly had finally returned. She still couldn't bear the sight of herself in a mirror, with her rudimentary haircut and unnaturally pale skin, but she felt like a woman again, with her body functioning the way it was supposed to.

The American Jewish Joint Distribution Committee had provided money for displaced Jews, offsetting rent, clothes and food, which nagged at Miriam's conscience. She craved financial stability after years of homelessness, but not through the charity of others. Upon discovering it could take months, possibly a year, to obtain the necessary papers and funding to travel to the United States, Miriam applied to emigrate through the Hebrew Immigrant Aid Society. She emphasized her skill and experience as a bookkeeper, and expressed her determination to learn English and be self-reliant. Surely Monya would be found by the time they received permission and money, Miriam told herself, as she posted her request to the closest HIAS office, located in Munich.

"Look, Māte," said Ilana in Latvian.

Ilana pointed at a small boy bundled in a smart wool coat on the sidewalk across the street from Jacob's Barracks. Curls poked out from under his red cap. He held hands with a petite woman in an expensive sable coat, who walked with quiet dignity. It was the ninth or tenth boy they'd seen who resembled Monya. The disappointment never got easier.

Miriam crossed the street and hurried toward them, Ilana at her heels. Miriam crouched down when she reached the boy, and pulled his cap off. The curls were longer, looser and a shade darker.

"Monya?" Miriam touched his chubby pink cheek.

His amber eyes were wide open, without a flicker of recognition.

The woman drew the boy into the folds of her extravagant coat and plucked his cap from Miriam's hand. "What do you think you're doing, taking my son's cap?"

Miriam was riven with anger and shame. She saw herself through the dignified woman's eyes—in felt boots, ripped at the toes and stuffed with newspaper, a worn gray wool coat, donated by the church, made for a woman twice her weight, hanging from Miriam like a sack. Her shorn hair and gray teeth that made her look unfit to be anyone's mother.

"I'm sorry—" Miriam began.

"He's not your son," Ilana interrupted her mother, eyes blazing. "His name is Monya and he's my brother."

"Preposterous," the woman said, incensed.

"We could be mistaken," Miriam said, regarding Ilana.

"No." Ilana knelt down to the boy's level. "Monya. It's me, Ilana. Your sister. You were Andris when we lived with Gutte, so people wouldn't know we're Jewish."

"That's . . . that's a lie," the woman stammered.

Miriam felt a primal stirring in her womb when she spotted a birthmark on the boy's right eyelid. "Did you adopt him?"

The woman jolted upright. "How dare you." She fiddled with her coat collar and stepped back.

Miriam saw, in the woman's caginess, what she didn't want to admit. Not that it mattered, because even if this boy had been adopted, Miriam had no tangible proof he was Monya, no birth papers, nothing. It would come down to her word against this mother's. And, in her mind, there was no question of who would be believed.

"Your real name is Monya," Ilana continued patiently. "Don't you remember?"

He wrapped his arms around the woman's leg. She clasped him tight, ran her hand over his back and soothed him with a compassion that brought a lump to Miriam's throat. If this was Monya, he'd lived with this woman for two years, several months longer than he'd lived with Miriam and Ilana. They'd been apart almost three years, long enough for him to forget his mother and sister. Long enough to forget his own name. Long enough to forget the day they'd lost everything. Which might not be so bad.

Miriam tugged Ilana's hand and met the woman's petulant gaze. "So sorry. We've made a mistake."

The woman's relief was as clear as the tangerine sun setting over the river.

"No," Ilana cried. "It's Monya. You know it's him, Mama."

The woman clamped her right arm over Monya's shoulder. He fit tidily into the auburn nest of fur.

"Mama, don't let her take him," Ilana begged Miriam.

The woman and Monya started down the street, the boy tucked into the woman's side like an appendage.

"Mama, why did you let her go?"

"He looked a lot like your brother. But we were mistaken."

"No, we weren't. It was Monya."

"We must get back for supper."

"No. We have to go after Monya." Ilana dug her heels into the sidewalk and yanked Miriam's arm so hard, her shoulder almost came out of its socket.

Miriam wrenched her arm from Ilana's strong grip.

Ilana sank to her knees on the sooty cobblestones. "I'm not moving until you say you'll go after Monya."

"Stand up. You're getting your stockings wet."

"Stockings? Is that all you care about?"

"Ask me later, when your knees are cold and wet."

"I don't care about my knees or the cold. I just want my brother back."

"It wasn't Monya."

Ilana squared her shoulders at her mother. "You're sure it wasn't Monya?"

Miriam met her daughter's pleading gaze with a steadfast expression, though her heart raced with qualms. "Positive," Miriam said, with a firmness that almost made her believe it herself.

Ilana's face fell with disappointment. She turned on the ball of her foot and walked in the direction of the art museum and their temporary lodgings.

Miriam followed, dragging her feet. She looked ahead, at Ilana, and felt a wide terrain of friction stretch between them.

48

CHICAGO, AUGUST 1976

M IRIAM POLISHED HER COFFEE TABLE TO KEEP HER MIND
off Sarah, who'd flown across the Atlantic, to London, without so much as a postcard. She couldn't sleep, not knowing
if Sarah was all right. She missed the anticipation of her visits, how
she brightened the apartment with a cheerfulness that reminded
Miriam of Max. What if something happened to Sarah? Miriam's
heart twisted.

Don't go there.

She took a deep breath, then moved her rag in bigger circles,
increasing the pressure on the wood. Her fan rattled as it scattered
Pine-Sol droplets into the humid air, a chemical lemony odor that
caused a pounding headache. She didn't understand how something that cleaned furniture smelled so terrible. She dried her
sweaty face with a tissue and switched off the fan, better at making
noise than cooling her apartment, and turned on the television for
the *CBS Evening News.*

Walter Cronkite's reverent voice sauntered into her living room
with a comforting familiarity, the only newsman worth his salt. He

was a companion who demanded nothing of her. He reminded Miriam of Max, with his steady voice and kind eyes, had Max lived to reach his sixties.

"Gerald Ford has won the Republican presidential primary," Walter announced in the measured tone that had garnered the trust of American viewers for years. "He'll be running against Jimmy Carter for president."

"Ford has no chance against Carter," Miriam told Walter, as if he were sitting beside her on the sofa.

She jumped when there was a knock at her door.

"I'm not home," she snipped.

"Grandma, it's me and Dad," Sarah announced from the corridor.

Her heart skipped a beat at her granddaughter's voice.

"What is this? I don't see you for months and suddenly you show up at my door, expecting to be greeted like royalty?"

"It's been three weeks, not months," Sarah called out. "Remember we went out for deep dish on Dad's birthday? You said it was so doughy and cheesy, it would give you indigestion."

Miriam licked her lips, recalling the piquant tomato sauce and the mozzarella that stretched from her mouth to her pizza like strands of taffy. Of course she remembered. Who could forget pizza heavy enough to be a doorstop? Did Sarah think she was losing her marbles?

"I have a surprise for you," Sarah continued.

"I don't like surprises."

"I guarantee you'll like this one, Grandma."

"Nothing is guaranteed," she mumbled.

Miriam opened her door and was overwhelmed by the flowery English Yardley scent oozing from Sarah. The same perfume she'd bought Ilana after they arrived in America. The first gift Miriam gave Ilana after the war. The first time Ilana smiled. Perfume and bright colors had been bandages on Ilana's deep and silent wounds.

Sarah's face glowed from too much sun. Her hair was tied in a messy ponytail, and errant, wispy strands framed her small red face. She breezed past Miriam in a faded denim skirt (too short) and a peach blouse with wide sleeves that made her arms look too skinny.

"Sorry for barging in on you like this," Paul said, contrite. He sank his freckled hands into his shorts pockets, which puckered at the seams from an extra ten pounds.

"No, you're not," Miriam quipped.

A corner of his mouth lifted. He stopped in front of Miriam's television. "Do you mind if I turn it off?"

"You don't ask if you can come over, why ask about the TV?"

"Talk to your granddaughter." He gestured with his thumb at Sarah, already making herself comfortable on the sofa. "This is all her doing." Paul switched off the television and plunked down beside Sarah. The cushion gasped from his weight.

Miriam frowned, seeing the bottom of his navy shirt lift up over his ever-expanding potbelly. She sat in her tub chair, hands clinging to the edges of the armrests, her nerves like springs.

"I planted the roots of the wandering Jew, the one you gave me, remember? And it's doing really well, even though I forget to water it," Sarah began.

"That's your surprise?" Miriam retorted. "Your plant?"

Sarah crossed her arms into her stomach. "Not exactly." She glanced sideways at her father and took a deep breath. "Actually, I just came back from Riga," she said, the words charging from her lips as if she'd been forced to hold them in.

Miriam stiffened. "Are you joking?" She cocked an eye at Paul, watching his daughter with a steadfast expression.

"No," Sarah answered. "It's not a joke."

"You told me you were going to London."

Sarah twirled loose strands of hair around her finger. "I knew you'd worry if I told you the truth."

"If it makes you feel any better," Paul interjected, "she told me she was going to London, too."

Miriam yanked at her collar, which was suddenly pinching her neck. Her head pulsed and sweat dribbled from her hairline. She grabbed the *TV Guide* and fanned her face and said deliberately: "*Klieg, klieg, klieg. Du bist a nar.*"

"What did you say?" Sarah asked.

Miriam slapped the *TV Guide* on her lap. "It is a Yiddish expression. You are smart, but not so smart."

Sarah's chin shot up. Acknowledgment, or maybe it was remorse, passed briefly across her face.

Miriam turned to Paul. "How could you let her go to Riga?"

"I didn't—"

"You lied to both of us," Miriam snapped at Sarah.

"I'm sorry. I didn't want you to worry."

"You could have been . . ." Miriam's breath caught in her chest. "Do you have any idea how ruthless the Soviets are?"

Sarah flinched and hugged her purse to her abdomen.

"Let's try not to think about what could have happened, and focus on the fact she's home, safe and sound, without a scratch," Paul suggested.

Miriam caught a glimpse of Sarah's evasive eyes and knew Sarah had not returned unscathed, as Paul implied. Deep wounds were not always visible. God, she needed a cigarette.

"I should have told you," Sarah went on, "but I was afraid you'd try to talk me out of going, and I couldn't take a chance. I had to go. I had to see where you and Mom came from."

Miriam's gaze faltered at her granddaughter's curiosity in bloom. "And?"

"And it was beautiful and ugly and sad."

Miriam looked at Sarah for a long moment.

"What does that mean?" Paul asked.

"She means it was beautiful, ugly and sad," Miriam repeated, without taking her eyes off Sarah.

Sarah blinked and blinked.

Paul raised his eyebrow. "If you hadn't lost your photos, I'd know what you two are talking about."

"You lost your photos?" Miriam said to Sarah.

A flush rose up Sarah's neck. "Not exactly. They didn't turn out, for some reason. None of the ones I took of the city, anyway."

"How strange," Miriam remarked.

"Very strange," Sarah said, her eyes darting from the television to the plants in Miriam's window to the dining table.

"But you did manage to get a few—monuments of Stalin and Lenin, no doubt," Miriam added with a tint of sarcasm.

Sarah bit her lip and looked expectantly at her father. He nodded and ran his fingers over his pasty knees.

"No monuments," Sarah began, "but one of Monya."

Monya.

The name evoked the cherubic face of the curly-haired little boy with the red cap she'd seen all those years ago, when his future in Riga looked sound, once the Soviets were defeated. Except, as Ilana used to say in a barbed tone that cut Miriam to the core, the Soviets never left.

"You found Monya?" Miriam whispered.

In answer, Sarah put the photo from Gundega on the coffee table and slid it over to Miriam. "It's the only one I could bring home."

"He's alive?" Miriam whispered.

"Yes." Sarah paused. "It was hard to talk to him, with the language barrier, but through my friend, who translated, I discovered he didn't know he'd been adopted until after his parents died. His name is Andris Jansons."

Miriam's gaze drifted to the photo on the coffee table. The image was blurry. Dust in my eyes, she supposed.

"Did you hear me, Grandma? His name—"

"Were they good people, his parents? Did he have a good life?" Miriam hardly recognized her own voice; it sounded as if she was talking from under a blanket.

"I . . . I think so," Sarah demurred.

Miriam raised her brow. What was Sarah not telling her?

Sarah averted her gaze from Miriam's eyes and directed her attention to Monya's photo. "Monya went to university and is a math teacher. He and his wife, Gundega, have four children—"

"Four children?"

"I didn't meet them. There wasn't enough time."

"It was a mistake, leaving Monya in Riga," Miriam whispered.

"You didn't know where he was, Grandma. It wasn't your fault."

"Sarah's right," Paul added. "You can't beat yourself up for things you can't control."

Miriam choked on the truth. The rupture within the family was, most definitely, all her fault. She was racked with guilt for surviving, for coming to America without Monya, for not reconciling with Ilana.

"You're white as a ghost, Miriam," said Paul. "I'll get you some water." He jumped up and strode to the kitchen.

"One thing I still don't understand," Sarah went on, "is why Gutte gave Monya away."

Miriam pinched her eyes shut. "Gutte loved your mother and Monya as if they were her own." She opened her eyes. "I should have thanked her for everything she did."

"I wish I'd had time to find Gutte," Sarah said.

"For the love of God." Paul groaned. He set a glass of water on the table for Miriam and resumed his seat beside Sarah. "Don't you dare think about going back to Riga."

"Don't worry. I couldn't go back even if I wanted to."

"What? Why?" Paul asked.

"Forget it."

Miriam shivered and perspired at the same time, knowing her granddaughter had suffered. "Moses." She took a sip of water, then brushed her fingers over the photograph.

"Moses?" Sarah straightened. "Don't you mean Monya?"

"His father, your grandfather, named him Moses, but I thought it was too big a name for a baby."

"The name fits, though, when you think about the story of Moses," Paul said.

"Which part?" Miriam deadpanned. "When he's given away to be raised by a Gentile, or when he leads the Jews out of slavery?"

"You never miss a beat, do you, Miriam," Paul joked.

She shrugged and returned her attention to the photograph. "Moses was named after Max's great-uncle Moses, a charismatic man who arrived in Riga with nothing and established a successful timber company. I never met him but saw a photo once." She sighed. "Uncle Moses had the most beautiful curly hair, like Max's."

"And like Monya's." Sarah gestured to the photograph.

"Like Monya's," Miriam agreed, her eyes glued to the photograph.

"Monya's youngest daughter has curls too. I saw her photo."

This shattered Miriam, realizing she'd never meet Monya, his wife and his children.

"What happened to Max's uncle Moses?" Paul asked.

Miriam grimaced. "He was exiled to Siberia in 1917 for being involved in the Revolution. Never heard from him again. Most died on the way."

Sarah gaped at Miriam.

"Not knowing is the worst thing," Paul said.

"Sometimes," Miriam said. "Other times, when you find out what happened, you wish you were still in the dark."

"True," Sarah replied softly.

They sat quietly, considering.

"Am I named after anyone?" Sarah asked Miriam, breaking the silence.

"Your great-grandmother. My mother. A tiny woman with a mighty presence. She had long white hair that hung like straw down her back, and enormous olive-green eyes that could make a strong man wither. Even Max."

"Why would Mom name me after a woman who sounds terrifying?"

"Can I just say I've always liked the name Sarah," Paul said earnestly.

Sarah's gaze shifted to her father and back to Miriam.

"Bubbe had a soft spot for one person—your mother." Miriam chuckled out loud. "Once, when Ilana was five or six years old, she lifted the cover off the challah Bubbe had just baked for Shabbat, and took a huge bite."

"Really?" Sarah said.

"I was furious," Miriam continued. "But Bubbe, she examined the challah and said someone who needed the bread more than us, someone who was truly starving, must have smelled it and snuck into our house."

"A little far-fetched, don't you think?" Paul said.

"Of course, it was a ridiculous explanation. We all knew who the real culprit was. Ilana lived for Bubbe's challah. It was her favorite part of Shabbat."

"If everyone knew, why did Bubbe make up a story to protect Mom?"

Miriam's burnished eyes settled on Sarah. "To show your mother she loved her, no matter what."

"Did Mom ever confess, about eating the challah?"

Miriam shook her head. "Your mother was very good at keeping secrets."

"I know."

"But she never did it again. That was one thing about your mother. She never made the same mistake twice."

"I've never had challah, Grandma. Do you think you could make it for me sometime?"

Miriam's lips parted dryly with approval. "How... how did you find Monya?"

"To be honest, I didn't think it was possible. I'd resigned myself to the idea of not meeting him, but a man on my tour, Roger, who spoke Russian, helped me," she replied, stumbling over her words.

"Roger? You didn't tell me about him." Paul's brows arched.

"He translated for Monya and me at Monya's apartment."

"But who is he, and how on earth did he help you find Monya?" Paul pressed her.

"She doesn't have to give you every detail," Miriam interrupted. "Sarah's a young lady, not a child, for goodness' sake."

Sarah gave Miriam a grateful smile. "Monya seems content with his life and family . . ." she said with a lilt in her voice, as if she wasn't sure of her own observations.

"He doesn't know any better," Miriam said. "He can't travel, or speak his mind, or read news that isn't censored."

"I see where Ilana got her optimism," Paul remarked.

"You make pragmatism sound like a defect," Miriam said.

"I'd rather accept things as they are than hold out hope for the impossible."

"I bet a lot of people didn't think a peanut farmer had a chance of winning the Democratic primary. Carter didn't give up," he pointed out.

Miriam's nose twitched.

Sarah turned the photograph over. "Here's Monya's address, but I'm not sure we can contact him. The Soviets censor mail. They might think he's planning to defect if they see letters from family in America."

Miriam's dewy eyes blurred the Cyrillic script. "Your mother wanted to find Monya," she said. "That's what I discovered in the letters you gave me to translate."

Sarah's face paled. "When . . . when did she—"

"Ten years ago. She sent money to a Soviet agency, a bribe of sorts, to search for Monya."

"You're kidding," Paul said.

"Did they take the money? Did they look for him?" Sarah asked.

"They took the money, but from the letters, it was obvious they didn't look beyond their noses."

"Mom must have been so disappointed."

"God, I wish she'd told me," Paul muttered.

"I wish she were here now," Miriam said, turning to Sarah. "Your mother could not put the past to rest without knowing what happened to Monya. Finding him would have filled the empty space in her soul."

Tears slid down Sarah's cheeks. "What about you, Grandma?"

"What about me?"

"How do you feel?"

Miriam blinked back tears and took the photo of Monya from Sarah's hand. She traced the Cyrillic script with her finger. "What did Monya say when you told him about your mother and me?"

"He said . . ." She paused, looked uncomfortable. "He was confused, because his baptism papers show he is Lutheran, with Gutte as his birth mother."

A helpless fury rose in Miriam's chest like heartburn. "It doesn't matter," she managed to say. "He can't practice religion there anyway."

"At least you know he's all right," Sarah said. "It's better than nothing."

"Knowing he's alive is better than anything," Miriam replied, her voice thickening with resolve. "You grandchildren are my best revenge against the Latvian officers who killed Max and my parents. Seeing Jewish families grow is exactly what those Nazi and Latvian murderers didn't want."

"But Monya didn't marry a Jewish woman," Sarah reminded her. "You're not considered Jewish unless it's on the mother's side. That's what Dad told me."

Miriam peered around the room for a pack of cigarettes, remembered she'd quit—for Sarah.

"Blood is blood. Monya's children are just as Jewish as you are, not that it matters. Monya has no idea what it means to be Jewish."

"Neither do I," Sarah said gently. "But I want you to show me—and my boyfriend, Henry."

Miriam stilled.

A cool gust of air wafted through her open window. Crickets chirped from somewhere nearby, reminding her of all the things she heard but couldn't see. She sensed Max's presence and heard his steady voice in her ear: *Focus on what you have left, not what you have lost.*

A knock sounded at the door. Miriam's shoulders tensed at the intrusion. There was so much more she needed to say.

"Chinese food is here," Paul announced. "I'll get it." He lumbered over to the door.

"I didn't order any food," Miriam said.

"We did. All the things you ate last time," Sarah said.

"I'm not hungry."

Sarah peered at her grandmother. "Something's different. You haven't had one cigarette since we arrived." She sniffed. "No smoky smell, either. Did you quit?"

"I'm trying."

"That's terrific, Grandma. I'm so proud of you."

"It's only been a week."

"You can do it," Sarah said vehemently.

Miriam saw Ilana in the way Sarah's brow furrowed with concentration, in her sea-green eyes, her obstinacy. This consoled Miriam, knowing her daughter lived on through Sarah, knowing she and Max lived on through Monya and his children. Now, in the winter of her heart, she wanted her tapestried life to have meaning. Simon Dubnow's plaintive voice echoed in her ears: "Jews, write and record." She would not take her secrets to the grave. Instead, she would leave her journal to Sarah, who deserved the unvarnished truth. Miriam's words, her silent legacy, were all she had left to give.

ACKNOWLEDGMENTS

T HE FIRST TIME I WALKED THE COBBLESTONE STREETS OF old Riga, saw Jossel Talan's house and took in the mass graves at Rumbula forest, I knew I had to write about the Latvian Holocaust. I had to do it for my family, for the Latvian Jews who didn't live to tell their own stories and for myself, to try to understand the people who came before me. Throughout the years of researching and writing this book, I kept a photo of my grandmother, her father, her sister and her uncle, Jossel Talan, on my desk. Seeing them together, blissfully unaware of Jossel's fate, pushed me through some dark writing days.

This book would not be here without several people who've championed my work. I am forever grateful to Joy Fielding for her encouraging words and for connecting me with my agent, Beverley Slopen; Beverley's editorial suggestions were vital in bringing my manuscript to completion. I feel lucky to have her as my agent.

I am fortunate to have had faithful readers throughout the many versions of this book: Gayle Geary, Michael Lavigne, Rabbi Steven Wise, Amanda and Bethany Greer, Shelley Rosen, Karen Clyde,

Darlene Morden, Penny Headrick, Jennifer Benson, Anne Walls, Mary Philbrook, Joan Taylor and Jean McCharles. Moreover, Dennis Bock's editing prowess helped me see and mend the flaws in my writing.

In Riga, I was fortunate to meet with Ilya Lensky, director of the museum Jews in Latvia, and Dr. Ruvin Ferber, head of the board, Center for Judaic Studies, University of Latvia. They generously answered my questions, giving me a better sense of Jewish Latvia during WWII and the Soviet occupation. As well, one of Dr. Ferber's graduate students, Ronit Kirshner, kindly translated documents for me.

Dr. Ferber also connected me with Riga ghetto survivor George Schwab, professor emeritus, the City College of New York, and recipient of the 2018 Elie Wiesel Award from the United States Holocaust Memorial Museum. Professor Schwab described his experiences during and after the war over tea at his New York City apartment.

I owe heartfelt thanks to HarperCollins, especially editors Patrick Crean and Sara Nelson, for embracing my book, for their thoughtful feedback and for their unbridled enthusiasm. I must also thank the team at HarperCollins who helped bring this book to publication: John Sweet, for his meticulous copyediting, Natalie Meditsky for coordinating the production of this novel, and Alan Jones for his stunning cover design.

Finally, I am most grateful to my parents, Ann and Dick Sanders, for their unwavering support, and to my husband, Steven Greer, who never complained when I was so consumed with writing, I forgot about groceries or dinner. Thank you for your love and understanding.

Insights,
Interviews
& More ...

Author's Note

It started with a photo I discovered in the National Archives in Riga, Latvia, a small black-and-white headshot of my great-grandfather's brother, Jossel Talan, on an identity paper. Until that day, I only knew his name and fate from online resources: murdered in the Rumbula forest, 1941, with his wife and two children. Seeing his face, so much like my Nana's, gave me pause. How did my great-grandfather, Mendel Talan, a prosperous merchant in Riga, end up in Siberia, where my grandmother was born?

The answer came from a conversation with the director of the Museum "Jews in Latvia," Ilya Lensky, born and raised in Latvia, and an expert in Jewish history. This is what he told me: In 1905, Mendel's involvement with the Russian Revolution led to a hasty marriage with my great-grandmother (Sophie) and exile from Riga to Siberia, an event that dramatically altered their future. Jossel, and the rest of the extended family, remained in Latvia, where they ended up in the Riga ghetto and were murdered at Rumbula forest.

That's why my grandmother was born in Siberia. She lived because she was not in Latvia during the war. My mother and I were born because my great-grandparents were exiled.

Nana suppressed her childhood in Novosibirsk, Siberia, her family's escape from an anti-Semitic pogrom, their involvement in the 1917 Russian Revolution and subsequent exile to Shanghai. She was the only grandparent I knew, and I am her namesake, but she died when I was thirteen and more interested in boys than my ancestry. I didn't understand what it meant to be Jewish until a few years ago, when I began exploring Nana's past and reclaimed my faith.

Before delving into my family's history, I'd never heard about the Rumbula forest massacre, where 26,000 Jews were killed over two nights, a tragedy in the manner and on the scale of Ukraine's Babi Yar. I knew practically nothing about Latvia, its Soviet and Nazi occupations, and the fact that the execution of 90 percent of its Jews (including twenty-six of my relatives) was organized by a death squad also employed at Babi Yar, *SS-Einsatzgruppen*.

My search for answers planted the seeds for this novel, rooted in truth. Miriam Talan's character is inspired by Frida Michelson, who survived the Rumbula massacre. For three years, Frida hid in the forest, where she dug holes in the ground to keep warm, hid in barns, and received help from farmers and Seventh-Day Adventists. Her ability to "pass" as Latvian, her seamstress skills, and her proficiency with Lettish helped her endure the relentless terror she faced.

Frida testified at the Nuremberg trials and, in 1979, bore witness against a former Latvian policeman who'd emigrated to Baltimore, stating he "was the green-uniformed Nazi collaborator who had ordered her to remove her clothes and valuables as she was driven to an execution ditch with scores of other Latvian Jews, five abreast."

Salaspils, where Miriam witnesses a dead boy being tossed into a trench, was a concentration camp near the Rumbula forest. Though it was touted as a Police Prison and Work Education Camp, it was a place where children were given poison that made their eyes itch and caused diarrhea, leading to their deaths within a week, and where the blood of Jews was taken for wounded German soldiers. And where at least 632 corpses of children between three and nine years of age were found, along with the remains of thousands of adults.

One of the things I couldn't fathom, at the beginning of my search, was why Jews didn't leave Latvia when they had the chance. One reason had roots dating back almost twenty years prior to World War II, when the former premier of the Soviet Union, Vladimir Lenin, signed a peace treaty recognizing Latvian independence. A second reason originated with Prime Minister Kārlis Ulmanis's takeover, by military force, of the Latvian government in 1934. He established an authoritarian regime that censored all news. Finally, the signed nonaggression pact between Germany and the Soviet Union in 1939, and Ulmanis's ▶

Author's Note *(continued)*

assurances that Latvia was neutral and therefore safe from attack, gave Latvians a false sense of security.

Unbeknownst to Latvians (including Ulmanis), a secret protocol, within the nonaggression pact between Hitler and Stalin, sealed Latvia's fate ten months before the first Soviet tank appeared. The terms of this agreement divided Poland between Germany and the Soviet Union, and Latvia was given to the Soviets. This chain of events meant Latvians were completely unprepared when Soviet tanks rolled through the border.

The lack of blatant anti-Semitism also contributed to the Jews' overconfidence in Latvia. They were treated quite well, with Jews represented in Parliament and frequenting more than one hundred Jewish schools and sixty-five synagogues. In fact, Latvia's tolerance of Jewish culture and religion was renowned throughout Europe, prompting other Jews, such as historian and author Simon Dubnow, to move from Germany to Riga before the war. In 1941, there were 66,000 Jews in Latvia; more than 43,000 lived in Riga, including Jossel Talan, who prospered as a second-class merchant with a house in a well-heeled part of Riga that still stands today.

Yet a furtive tide of anti-Semitism prevailed. Jews were forbidden to attend the University of Latvia, for instance, and only two Jewish professors were admitted to the university during the country's twenty-three years of independence. Anti-Semitism became more visible as a disturbing wave of nationalism swelled, driven by student fraternities in Riga, far-right periodicals, and two extremist nationalist organizations, touting the slogan "Latvia for Latvians." Both groups were banned by 1934, but their attitudes remained, foreshadowing a disastrous future for Latvian Jews.

Days after Latvia was illegally declared a Soviet Socialist Republic, the country's Home Guard was disarmed and Red Army commanders replaced some Latvian officers, while others were deported to Siberia or executed. This was the beginning of the end of a flourishing Jewish population, with Latvians defining Jews as Bolsheviks, falsely implying that Communism was a Jewish conspiracy. These accusations stirred up the underlying hatred among university students and professionals, many of whom would later collaborate with the Germans.

With continued censorship under the Soviets, Latvian Jews were largely unaware of the deepening anti-Semitism throughout the rest of Europe. For this reason (and because Latvians viewed Germans as sophisticated and honorable, compared to the brutal Soviets), crowds of Latvians welcomed the Germans as liberators rather than occupiers when they arrived.

Immediately, Nazis began spreading anti-Semitic propaganda, linking Jews to the Communist Soviets. Newspaper stories blamed Jews for Stalin's atrocities. Jews were "guilty of spilling the blood of Latvians, torturing, and maiming them," the newspapers said. "One must remember it was the Jews who greeted the Red Army in July 1940, and enslaved, tortured, and killed Latvians during Communist rule." Meanwhile, as Andrew Ezergailis points out in *The Holocaust in Latvia*, "It is a matter of historical record that Jews had very little (almost nothing) to do with the Latvian communist movement."

The SD (the security service of the SS), commanded by Franz Walter Stahlecker, played a large and devastating role in the annihilation of Latvian Jews. It began with the announcement that all Jews had to wear a yellow star, not smaller than ten centimeters by ten centimeters, on the middle of their backs and on their chests—two stars instead of one, so that Jews could be easily identified in a crowd. Then, to escalate hatred towards the Jews in Riga, the Nazis apprehended young Jewish men and ordered them to dig up graves of victims murdered by the Soviets. Once the bodies were above ground, photos were taken and printed beneath a phony headline stating that these Jewish men had killed these Latvians.

I was dismayed to find that Jossel Talan's twenty-one-year-old son, Ewsey, was one of the Jews forced to dig up graves. Instead of dying in the Rumbula massacre, as I'd believed, Ewsey was taken to the prison's central courtyard, along with the rest of the Jewish gravediggers, and shot. Nobody knows where they are buried.

Jews were burned to death in synagogues on July 4, 1941, by Latvian collaborators, the Arājs Kommando, a notorious killing unit of volunteers, mostly university students, created by Stahlecker and led by Viktors Arājs, a lawyer. Curiously, many members of *Einsatzgruppe A*, which operated in Latvia, were also academics, with PhDs. Nazi anti-Semitic propaganda was so forceful, it turned intellectuals into murderers.

In October, Jossel and his family, along with 30,000 Jews, were forced to move into the ghetto. I walked the cobblestone streets of the ghetto, ▶

on the same stones that were there in 1941, looking at the same wooden shacks. I toured a ghetto house and saw layers of newspaper stuck to the walls for insulation. I saw how people had tried to make these hovels feel a bit like home, with lace squares draped over bureaus, porcelain jugs, and crystal trinkets from their former lives. Standing there, I couldn't imagine Jossel's anguish, or that of his wife and daughter, but I could believe it.

Their time in the ghetto would be short. Heinrich Himmler, head of the SD, brought Friedrich Jeckeln from the Ukraine, where he had organized the mass murder at Babi Yar, to Riga to plan the Rumbula massacre. Jeckeln devised a chilling strategy to murder the ghetto Jews over two days, under cover of darkness, employing 1,700 men. Six pits were excavated by Russian prisoners of war, and the Jews were ruthlessly killed using Jeckeln's system of "sardine packing": forcing people to lie on top of dead bodies so that time wasn't wasted pushing corpses into the pits.

Jeckeln's methods were monstrous with their cold, calculated rationale—stripping victims of their clothing and valuables; using "neck shot specialists" as executioners; and shooting each person once, to save ammunition, so that Jews not shot were buried alive.

On November 30, 1941, the Arājs Kommando marched half the residents through arctic-cold air, along icy streets, seven miles to the Rumbula forest. Members of the *Einsatzgruppen* shot column after column with Russian machine guns that could be set to fire single shots. The same ordeal took place the following week, on December 8, the day Simon Dubnow, too ill to walk to the forest, said, "Jews, write and record," before he was shot in the ghetto.

Janis Lipke, a dockworker in Riga, did, in fact, save forty Jews, risking his life as well as the lives of his wife and three children. He dug out a bunker in his yard, where a number of people hid during the war. Janis saved more Jews by hiding them in the cellars of trusted friends' homes, as well as another bunker, though several were caught and killed.

My description of the hiding place where Jan takes Miriam comes from one of the people Jan rescued, Semyon Ostrovsky. Janis Lipke was posthumously awarded the title Righteous Among the Nations by Yad Vashem, Israel's Holocaust memorial, for non-Jews who risked their lives to help Jews during the Holocaust.

Ironically, the Soviets invaded Latvia a second time, in 1944, overthrowing the Nazis and reinstalling Communism. Only 5,000 Jews remained in Latvia, mostly in camps and ghettos. The mass graves, the burned synagogues, and the ghetto were not publicly acknowledged for the next forty years. In fact, as survivor Bernhard Press writes in his memoir, *The Murder of the Jews in Latvia,* many Jews who "saved their own lives, were sent to Siberia." People he knew who were deported by the Soviets included a physician, a tailor, a pharmacist, and the wife of a jeweler.

Judaism, along with all religions, was banished. Intourist did bring North Americans to Riga during the 1970s, but tourists were closely monitored and kept away from locals. Exceptions were made for those who spoke Russian.

Sarah's horrifying time in KGB custody was based on information from the KGB building in Riga. Her overall experience in Riga was inspired by a friend's visit, with Intourist, to the Soviet Union in 1977, as well as a Soviet tour I took in Riga.

The end of the war, for Latvians, came on May 4, 1990, when the country adopted its own declaration of independence. In 1991, the Soviets left the country for good, and the atrocities finally came to light.

Viktors Arājs was charged with war crimes in a British court but was inexplicably released in 1948. Though his Kommando collaborated with the Nazis at the Rumbula forest and murdered 22,000 Jews in other actions, Arājs wasn't brought to justice until 1979, in Germany, where he was convicted of murder. He died in 1988.

In 1942, Friedrich Jeckeln was awarded the War Merit Cross First Class with Swords for his ruthless efficiency. He was captured by the Soviets, however, after the war, put on trial for his war crimes, and hanged in Riga in 1946.

I arrived at Rumbula forest in the late afternoon. The sun cast long shadows, like bars, over orange, yellow, and burgundy leaves that crunched underfoot. Rectangular mounds, in concrete frames, denoted mass graves where thousands, including Jossel, his wife, Baschewa, and daughter, Witalia, lay. Nausea rose to my throat, knowing how they were killed. They had no funeral. There is no grave marking their lives. It's as if they never existed. Jossel's branch of my family tree was ▶

forever broken. There are no descendants, no survivors bearing witness at Holocaust memorial events. It's inconceivable, what was lost.

I put a stone on one of the mass graves, a Jewish tradition symbolizing the permanence of memory, and was struck by the sense that my identity was shallow compared to Nana's trauma-filled self. After exploring the city that brought her family wealth and ruin, I'd begun to appreciate her resilience, private grief, and weariness at not knowing the fate of those who disappeared. I'd begun to understand her silence.

After I returned home, I compared the photos of relatives I'd discovered in the archives with faces I hadn't been able to identify in Nana's photos. One young man had piqued my curiosity for years, as he was in many photos with Nana and the rest of her family. Now, there was something familiar about his face. I rummaged through the archive photos and pulled out Jossel's image. The hairs on the back of my neck rose when I realized the young man standing beside Nana was Jossel, about twenty years prior to the photo on his identity paper. This was a bittersweet moment, knowing he mattered to Nana, knowing his fate, knowing he has no descendants. And it was the reason I chose "Talan" as Miriam's surname for my novel, to make sure the people on this broken branch of my family tree are not forgotten. ❧

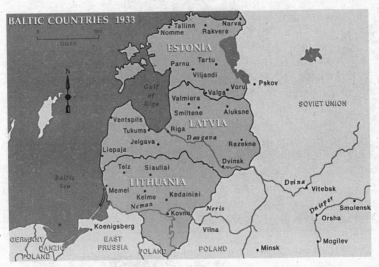

Courtesy of the United States Holocaust Museum

An image of the actual forced march to Rumbula

The memorial at
Rumbula today
(courtesy of the
author)

(*Seated, left to right*) Mendel Talan, Anna
Talan, Jossel Talan; (*standing*) Rachel
(Shelly) Talan, author's grandmother.

Jews in Latvia (Michelson Family Collection/Museum)

Frida Michelson (Michelson Family Collection/
Museum)

Further Reading

Latvian Holocaust

The Holocaust in Latvia, 1941–1944: The Missing Center by Andrew Ezergailis

Extermination of the Jews in Latvia, 1941–1945, a series of lectures edited by Rabbi Menachem Barkahan

The Murder of the Jews in Latvia 1941–1945 by Bernhard Press

Like a Star in the Darkness: Recollections about Janis (Zhan) Lipke by David Silberman

Behind the Barbed Wire by Gwendolyn Chabrier

I Survived Rumbuli by Frida Michelson

Endless Miracles by Jack Ratz

Odyssey of a Child Survivor: From Latvia through the Camps to the United States by George David Schwab

City of Life, City of Death: Memories of Riga by Max Michelson

One Who Came Back: The Diary of a Jewish Survivor by Josef Katz

Churbn Lettland: The Destruction of the Jews of Latvia by Max Kaufmann

Memoirs by Elmar Rivosh

Journey into Terror: Story of the Riga Ghetto by Gertrude Schneider

Life Under Soviet Regime

Soviet Milk by Nora Ikstena

Young Heroes of the Soviet Union: A Memoir and a Reckoning by Alex Halberstadt

A Mountain of Crumbs: A Memoir by Elena Gorokhova

Jewish Memoirs

Suddenly Jewish: Jews Raised as Gentiles Discover Their Jewish Roots by Barbara Kessel

Survivor Café: The Legacy of Trauma and the Labyrinth of Memory by Elizabeth Rosner

On the Creation of Evil

Masters of Death: The SS-Einsatzgruppen and the Invention of the Holocaust by Richard Rhodes

East West Street: On the Origins of "Genocide" and "Crimes Against Humanity" by Philippe Sands ∾

Book Club Questions

1. After reading the Author's Note and finding that this novel is inspired by the author's ancestors, how did your views of the characters and events change? Does the author effectively weave fact and fiction within the narrative? What are some examples that resonated with you?

2. Motherhood is a dominant theme in this novel. Miriam and her mother have a strained relationship, as do Miriam and Ilana, and Ilana and Sarah. How are these tense relations worsened by current events within the different generations? How are they affected by secrets?

3. After Sarah researches Latvian Jewish history at the Blackstone Library and connects these events with her mother and grandmother, she concludes, "I am who I am because they were who they were." Within your own family, who has shaped the person you have become?

4. Although you only see Ilana as an adult through Sarah's eyes, you do get a sense of who she is as a mother and as a wife. What do you think she would say about Sarah diving into her past and traveling to Riga?

5. Throughout the novel, Sarah cannot stop thinking about her last conversation with her mother, when they disagree about marriage. Why do you think her mother is so concerned about Sarah settling down with a husband? Do you think Sarah gains a modicum of peace after her trip to Riga?

6. To pursue the career she desires within a male-dominated industry in the 1970s, Sarah puts her job ahead of her friends and Henry. She must also tolerate a misogynous boss. How have things improved since then for women in the workforce? How have things stagnated?

7. Sarah's mother is determined to keep her Jewish heritage, as well as her struggle to survive the Latvian Holocaust, from Sarah. To ensure Sarah is shielded from the past, she insists Miriam and Sarah's father say nothing. Was this the right thing to do? How did this decision affect Sarah? How would you feel if a secret about your identity was kept from you?

8. What do you think Roger's motives are for helping Sarah? How did you feel about him when you discovered he is a KGB agent? What are some examples about living behind the Iron Curtain that surprised you?

9. Freedom is a recurring motif within this narrative, in both 1940s and 1970s Riga. In fact, Latvia didn't regain its independence until 1991, and since then, people have struggled to adapt to democracy and capitalism. Having read about the lives of some of these citizens within this narrative, what are possible reasons people are finding it so hard to succeed in a newly free country?

10. *The Canadian Journal of Psychiatry* found Holocaust survivors' grandchildren were overrepresented by about 300 percent in psychiatric care referrals in 1988. More recently, Rachel Yehuda, professor of psychiatry and neuroscience at New ▶

Book Club Questions *(continued)*

York's Mount Sinai School of Medicine, has conducted research showing that children of Holocaust survivors with PTSD were born with low cortisol levels, "predisposing them to relive the PTSD symptoms of the previous generation." (Cortisol is a stress hormone that helps bodies return to normal after trauma.) In other words, descendants experience their ancestors' unresolved trauma. This concept of "intergenerational trauma" is prevalent in *Daughters of the Occupation*, as well as in descendants of Holocaust and indigenous residential school survivors. Do you believe it is possible to pass trauma down through generations? Are there examples of this within your family?

11. This novel shows how many local citizens, who lived peacefully among Jews before World War II, collaborated with the Nazis by joining the Arājs Kommando and murdering Jews. How do you think ordinary people become killers? What are some current examples of this type of behavior?

12. By the end of *Daughters of the Occupation*, Miriam gets closure, knowing what happened to Monya, and Sarah has a stronger sense of identity, after discovering her maternal history. Assuming Miriam has a long life, where do you see these characters in five or ten years? Do you think Sarah will reclaim her faith and live as a Jew? Do you think they will try to get Monya and his family out of Latvia? ∼

Discover great authors, exclusive offers, and more at hc.com.